ALSO BY MICHAEL KORYTA

Rise the Dark
Last Words
Those Who Wish Me Dead
The Prophet
The Ridge
The Cypress House
So Cold the River
The Silent Hour
Envy the Night
A Welcome Grave
Sorrow's Anthem
Tonight I Said Goodbye

HOW IT
HAPPENED

MICHAEL
KORYTA

LITTLE, BROWN AND COMPANY

LARGE PRINT EDITION

Copyright © 2018 by Michael Koryta

Little, Brown and Company
Hachette Book Group
1290 Avenue of the Americas, New York, NY 10104
littlebrown.com

First Edition: May 2018

Little, Brown and Company is a division of Hachette Book Group, Inc. The Little, Brown name and logo are trademarks of Hachette Book Group, Inc.

The Hachette Speakers Bureau provides a wide range of authors for speaking events. To find out more, go to hachettespeakersbureau.com or call (866) 376-6591.

Excerpt from "Nobody Wins" (p. 265) by Brian Fallon (2016), used with permission.
Excerpts from "Sparks Fly" (pp. 242–243) by Waxahatchee (2017), used with permission.

ISBN 978-0-316-29393-8 (hc) / 978-0-316-55250-9 (large print)
LCCN 2017957404

10 9 8 7 6 5 4 3 2 1

LSC-C

Printed in the United States of America

For Christine

Part One

ALONG FOR THE RIDE

And it would make a great story
If I ever could remember it right.
— Jason Isbell,
"Super 8"

I

I'd never seen him before the day we killed him.

Now, Jackie, I knew her. I'd known her forever, really. We were never friends or anything, but it's a small town, so all the girls know each other. We were in the same classes, at least until high school. Then she was in the smart classes. She didn't party much either. What I remember most about her is from fifth grade, when her mom died. What made you ask me about that, anyhow? That was a long time ago, and it doesn't have anything to do with this. But up until we killed her, that's probably what I remember best, sure.

Her mom died in a car wreck. I think she slid across the center line in the snow or something. Jackie missed a few days of school, and we all had to make her cards, you know, draw pictures and write notes about how sad we were for her. She came back to school the next week and her dad walked her into the room, and he was holding her hand so tight. Like he just couldn't let her go. I watched that, and I was thinking of the cards we'd all made her, and...this will make me sound bad, but I was kind of pissed off about that. Because,

3

sure, it was sad that her mom was dead, but she still had her dad, right? Well, I was living with my grand-mother, and neither of my parents were dead, but they might as well have been. I mean, my dad never held my hand the way Howard Pelletier held Jackie's hand. Nobody ever did. So I felt bad for her, but . . . nobody was having the whole class write me cards, you know? Nobody gave a shit what was going on in my life. I wasn't one of the girls people cared about, I was al-ways just . . . overlooked.

I can't believe she kept that card. Did she keep them all? Whatever, it doesn't matter. None of it matters. I don't understand why you brought that up, Barrett. It's got nothing to do with anything that happened last summer.

Okay, so the day that does matter was the last really hot day of the summer. It got hotter in the beginning of September than it had been all of August. I think that had something to do with it. I mean, I'm not making excuses, but I keep thinking about how it started and where we went and I just feel, like, positive *we would never have been out that way if it hadn't been for the heat. And for the way the heat made everybody feel, especially Mathias. Am I supposed to say his full name in this one, like we don't all know it? Mathias Burke. You know what's funny? Your eyes get tight at the cor-ners when you hear his full name. That's really weird. Every time I say it, I can see you tighten up. Like you're bracing for a punch. Or want to throw one. Which is it? Hey, you said to tell it in my own words, right? Careful what you wish for, Barrett.*

All right...it was the first weekend that the tourists were gone, or most of them, the ones with kids were all gone and so it was a little quieter, and Mathias had gotten stir-crazy or something. That night—Friday night—he was jacked up, buzzing. He was just waiting to pop off. Like there was something living underneath his skin, looking for a way out. And he kept bitching about the heat. Cass, she was the same way about the heat, but that's because she didn't want to sweat, she had to stay just right. She always looked like a whore when she put on makeup, didn't understand how to do anything subtle, you know? Always a lot where a little would do. I know I'm not supposed to say anything mean about her because she's dead, but it's just the truth.

Oh, let me back up—I was working the day shift at the liquor store. I was off at six, and Cass was walking over to meet me and then we were just going to go into town or whatever. Maybe back to her trailer, just hang out. We didn't really have a plan. If we'd had anywhere to go, we wouldn't have ended up with him that night. But we were free.

Mathias came in at...I want to say it was five thirty? A little before quitting time for me. I've known him for years, but we never dated or anything. We didn't really hang out, even. So I was surprised when he asked what I was doing that night. I never knew Mathias to party much. He was always working, it seemed like. If you saw him drinking, it was in the winter. In the summer, he was, like, twenty-hours-a-day working. I told him Cass and I were supposed to go out to the bars, and he seemed kind of disappointed, and for a moment there, I wondered if he actually was *hitting on me. But then he just shifted gears when Cass showed up.*

He was telling us about this client's house he had access to. Some rich bitch who used the place only two weeks a year or something, but it was a real special spot and he wanted to go out there and drink and swim. I was kind of interested, but then he said he knew he could get a score too, and that put me off because I'd been trying to get clean. But Cass was all about it.

We went out into the parking lot because I'd finished my shift. We drank some booze out there—I think it was like a six-pack of Twisted Tea and a couple forties of beer, and Cass had some vodka. One of the flavored kinds, apple or raspberry or something. We sat on the tailgate of his truck and smoked cigarettes and drank. Oh, this was his work truck. Not the one we were in when we killed them.

Mostly we were talking about the heat. That's why I remember that it seemed to bother him. Because he was looking up at the sun and talking about it like it was personal. As if the sun had come up hot that day looking only for him, like somebody picking a fight.

We chilled for a little while and then he said he had a good place to party and that he'd made a score, and he'd share it if I gave him a ride back to his truck. I was like, You're sitting on your truck, genius. *But he said the truck he wanted was at a client's house, so he needed a ride out there. You know he's a caretaker, so he has all these summerhouses he's always working on.*

Now, I hadn't done much all summer but drink. Maybe a little weed, but that was about it. I mean, I guess a few pills. But nothing serious, because, you know, people kept dying last summer, even before Cass. It was all over the news. There was bad heroin somebody brought up from Washington, DC. A black guy, I think. Or maybe he was Mexican. But I know it was from DC, because people kept calling it that. It was moving around like a fever that summer. People were dying without even OD'ing because of what it was cut with, some chemical thing I never really understood. I just knew it was bad shit and people were dying, more people that single summer than had died in Maine the entire year before from drugs, I think. Maybe that's not a fact, but it's what I heard.

So, like I said, I was trying to get clean, but if Cass and Mathias left together, it would've been just me, right? Just me and a friggin' six-pack of Twisted Tea on a Friday night. Who wants that? So I just...you know how it goes. You give in. You never think anything bad is going to happen. I said I'd go along but I didn't want to do any drugs, and Mathias just kind of winked and said, We'll see.

We left, and I was driving and he was shotgun and Cass should've been in the backseat but she crawled up into the middle, and she was basically sitting on his lap. Annoying, but that was just Cass. Only thing that surprised me was that Mathias seemed to be going along with it. He'd never struck me as the type who'd...how do I say this? He was just a more serious type of dude, right? Always kind of locked into his own thing, so it was strange to see him act like that.

That's when I figured he was riding something more than a beer buzz.

Anyhow, I was driving and focused on his directions, because I didn't want to get pulled over. He was telling us that once we got to his truck, he'd take us down to this summer person's house that he had access to, telling us how great it was, really hyping it. I was picturing something different than where we ended up, something fancier.

His truck was at a house somewhere on the Archer's Mill Road. I honestly don't remember the spot all that well. He just told me to pull into a driveway, and I did. His truck was parked down at the bottom of the driveway, and you couldn't see it from the road. There was a tarp over the hood, and I asked what that was about, and he gave this big grin and was like, Check this shit out, *and pulled the tarp off.*

He'd painted the hood real bright white, and then in the center there was this black cat, a bad drawing of one, like a little kid would do of a Halloween cat, you know? Fur sticking out, back arched, tail up. All these black squiggles.

It was getting dark by then, and he was using his cell phone to light it up for us, and when I got closer, I saw that he'd painted the cat's eyes red. The whole thing was strange, but there was something about the eyes that didn't match the rest. It sounds dumb, but for some reason the eyes bothered me.

I didn't understand why he was proud of that truck. It was just…dumb. This cartoon black cat with red eyes painted in the middle of the friggin' hood against that white paint that was so bright it was kind of hard to look at. The paint job was dumb and the truck was pretty shitty.

He got the drugs out then. First time anyone shot up was down there where he'd left his truck, and it was just him and Cass. I said no, thanks, I was good with beer. I don't know how long we stayed down there. They shot up and drank and I just had a couple cigarettes and a beer or two. Maybe a hit of vodka. I was still sober when Mathias said it was time to go to the pond, and he was going to drive us in that dumb truck.

There was no extended cab, only a bench seat in front.

I usually get stuck in the middle because I'm small, right? But Cass took the middle that night. She wanted to be close to Mathias.

But, hey, before I keep going, I want to make one thing clear, okay?

I was just along for the ride.

You know what the Archer's Mill Road is like, all those curves. Mathias was drunk and messed up and driving too fast, and it seemed like something could go wrong easy. He was playing some sort of bad rock-country music. Not like Nickelback-bad, but still pretty awful. I looked over and saw Cass had her hand on his crotch, and then I wished I hadn't gone along. It's better to be alone than third-wheeling it in a truck with crap like that going on right next to you. But that's how she would get when she was using. When Cass was messed up, she was easy. You don't need to take my word for that; ask around.

When we got out to the camp, though, I felt better. It was just like he'd said—there was a dock and a raft and it was warm and there were a million stars. I remember the stars real well, because after Mathias and Cass got in the water and swam out to the raft, I just lay on my back on the dock so I didn't have to listen to them out there. That was the first time I hit any of the heroin. Only reason I did that was because I didn't want to listen to them doing whatever they did out there, and it was just…it was just so pretty out. All those stars.

I might have passed out for a while. I guess I must have, because I don't remember much between the stars and the sun. Cass and Mathias were out of the water and dressed again. She came down to the dock and had a beer with me—the beers were all warm by then—and I told her I'd like to have a place like that camp someday. It wasn't so much, you know, but it was real pretty and peaceful and I've never felt like I needed all that much. There was a lot of room for my animals. My dogs, Sparky and Bama, they'd have loved a place like that. I think Cass wanted me to ask about her and Mathias, but I wasn't going to. I didn't give a shit what they'd done. I figured I'd find out about it when I took her to the clinic at some point down the road.

Everything was pretty chill but then Mathias was rushing all of a sudden, and he couldn't find his keys. He said he'd lost them when he and Cass swam out to the raft. So he's cussing like crazy and blaming her and splashing around in the water like he's actually going to find his damn keys, and she was shouting back, and I was just trying to get away from it all, so I went to sit in the truck. That was when I saw the keys were still in the ignition.

I thought that was funny, you know? He's losing his mind out in the pond, and the keys are in the friggin' ignition. I told Cass, and I was laughing, but by then her temper was up, and so she got the keys and held them up and shouted at him, telling him what a dumb son of a bitch he was. Then she got in the truck and started it, so I got in too. Mathias came running up, soaked, and that was the first time I saw the knife.

Cass was behind the wheel. She could've just driven off. But he was holding the knife up and punching the truck and saying how he'd kill her, and he—well, this is the thing—I was going to say he scared her. But I'm not positive about that. For whatever part of her he scared, he excited some other part. Because the thing to do would be to get out, but she just slid over and opened the door.

I've thought about that a lot. What if she gets out? What if we both get out?

Instead, she stayed, and she told me not to leave. I didn't know what to do. I just wanted him to keep focused on her, I guess. He opened the door and told us to get out, that we were walking home. Cass told him to go to hell, she wasn't getting out of the truck and neither was I. I never spoke for myself. It was so intense right then...she was almost like a shield, you know? I didn't want to call attention to myself. And I was scared for what he'd do to her if I left them alone. I was scared, period.

So he gets in and says, Fine, you bitches will get what you want. *And right then I'm thinking I've got to get out of the truck with or without her, but he peeled out. After that, there was no getting out.*

We were going way too fast by then.

He came out of the camp and turned right instead of left, and I thought he'd turned in the wrong direction, but I wasn't going to say that to him, not the way he was. He kept punching the dashboard and saying how we'd get what we wanted now. He was driving fast, crazy *fast. We were all over the road. The worse the curves, the faster he took them. I was afraid he was going to lose control. Considering what happened, pretty dumb thought, right? But that memory is crystal to me. What I was afraid of, back then, was that he'd roll the truck.*

Mostly what I remember from that ride is staring at the cat. It started to look a little crazier to me on that ride. The night before it had been dumb, right? But when we were flying down the road that morning, it looked...mean.

There's that orchard on the Archer's Mill Road, and we passed that doing, I don't know, maybe seventy. Felt like a hundred. We passed the orchard and then there's the cemetery. The old one. Nobody goes out there except at Halloween or maybe tourists to take pictures. Cass and Mathias were screaming at each other and all of a sudden he says something like, If you want to die, I'll take you to the right place. *Then he drove right—well, to me, it felt like he drove right off the road. But there's actually this old dirt path that goes through that cemetery, goes all the way down to the water almost. We bounced through the ditch and ended up on that path, and the tombstones were flying right by us. I was sure he was planning on driving us into the biggest one. What do they call those things, the ones that look like forts for ghosts or something? Not museums but a word like that. Museums for the dead. There's a big one in there, about halfway back, up on this little rise with a view of the water. I think he was aiming for that. Crash into it and kill us all, just because he had a bad high and the sun had been too hot for him the day before. There was no reason for anything that was happening.*

The path through there is real rough, rocky. We were bouncing like crazy—my ass was literally in the air half the time, and Mathias was barely in control of the truck, and I was glad he'd turned off the paved road, because there wasn't anybody else to hit. At least whatever happened, it was only going to happen to us.

That was the last thought I had before I saw Jackie.

She was standing in the middle of the path, facing the water. The sun was coming up. Everything was pink and gold. We flew up over the hill and she turned and she was smiling. I remember her face changing, and that seemed slow. You know those blinds where you turn the rod and they shut the light out? It was like that.

I don't think she ever quite…comprehended it. I mean, we didn't belong there, right? I think she was confused the whole time. Like, What is going on?

She moved either too early or too late, depending on how you want to look at it. She tried to avoid us and Mathias tried to avoid her and they both went the same direction. Well...let me stop. I think he *tried to avoid her. I want to believe that. Because otherwise it means that when he swerved...you know, he was trying.*

When he hit her, she popped up in the air and hit the windshield hard enough that it cracked, and then she was gone and Mathias slammed on the brakes and we spun and that's when the back of the truck hit one of the old stones. The one that split right in half, that you all took pictures of and put in the paper and people were saying it was a satanic cult killing or whatever. Really, it was just that the bed of the truck hit that stone when we spun.

There was a moment when it was real still. Real quiet. Nobody was even breathing, it seemed. I was just staring through the windshield at the hood and there was more red on it now, and I knew that was blood but somehow it blended in, almost. Like it was part of the design with the cat. Like it had always belonged there.

I started to get out of the truck to go help her, right? Mathias got out too. Cass stayed in a little longer. I could see where Jackie had landed and then I saw him too. Ian Kelly. Didn't know his name then, of course. He was just a guy. He was coming down the path behind us, but as fast as we'd been going, we must have passed him and missed him. It was easy to do. We were driving so fast and heading right into the sunrise.

He was up above us a little bit. Standing there, staring. Jackie's body was between us. It was like a standoff. Then he started shouting. He was shouting What the hell are you doing? and I had this weird thought that it was a strange question, because it had already happened, you know? It wasn't, like, in progress. Not something we could stop.

He started walking toward us. He wasn't running, just walking. Mathias was moving too, and I saw he had something in his hand. This bar or pipe or something. And they're walking toward each other, Jackie right in the middle, her blood all over the place. Cass was finally out of the truck by then and I was kind of frozen. I didn't want to go near all that blood. The guy kept walking toward us, and he was sort of in shock.

They were almost right beside her body when Mathias hit him with the pipe. He just swung it once, right at the guy's head, and the guy never so much as got a hand up. I remember the sound it made. It was like a fist going through drywall. Wet drywall.

I screamed then. I was still screaming when Mathias turned around and looked at me, and then I stopped real fast. The way he looked at me...I knew he would kill me.

He walked back to us and he looked at us and told

us to help him put them in the truck. Everybody in the world will say, Why did you do that? Why didn't you say no, why didn't you run, why didn't you call the police? *But no one saw the way he was looking at us. It was do what he said or die. That was clear. That was the choice.*

I only half remember picking them up. Mathias got in the truck and backed it up and got these tarps out of the bed. Not tarps, but the clear kind, like they put over broken windows. And then we, um...sorry. I need a second. Sorry.

We...uh, we...kind of...folded them up. Wrapped them up. I was trying not to look. Mathias was yelling at us to hurry before somebody came along. We're in an old cemetery out of sight of the road and it's like six in the morning—who is going to come along? That was the first time I wondered what they had been doing out there. So early too. Then later, it was all over the news, of course. That made me feel even worse, knowing why they'd gone out there. I mean, that was real sweet, you know? That was a real sweet thing. I never dated a guy who'd get up so early to do something like that. Shit, I've never even met a guy like that.

We got them in the bed of the truck, and Mathias told us to get back in. I don't think either Cass or I had said a word. I couldn't stop crying. I was having trouble breathing. I was just going to do everything Mathias told us to do until it was over. I was more scared of him than anything. I hadn't even thought of you guys yet, to be honest. Hadn't thought about anything bigger than that little stretch of road. That was the whole world right then. The world was gone and it was just that road and the truck and Mathias. That's all that was left.

People won't understand that.

Cass asked where he was going, and he said we had to hide them. He drove away like he knew exactly where he wanted to go. He was driving fast but not the same way he had been before. Under control, staying in his lane. He said we were going to dump them and get the hell out of there and clean the truck, bleach it down. Then he said that if either one of us told anybody, he'd kill us. That was the first time he said it, but it didn't really have any impact because we already understood that. At least I did.

He took us back to the camp by the pond. Pulled us all the way down to the water, right where he'd been looking for his keys just a few minutes earlier.

When I found them in the ignition.

We took her first. I couldn't see much of her face. There was too much blood. Mathias used duct tape to wrap some of those pipes he had in the truck bed around her. So she would sink. When I realized we were going to put them in the water, I thought it was a real dumb choice. Because if we'd just walked fifty *yards or so down from where we'd hit her back at the cemetery, we'd have been at the tidal flats. It was high tide too. Wouldn't have had to go far. And then with the current...they'd have been carried right out. All the way to the ocean. Unless somebody pulled them up with a lobster trap or something, nobody ever would have found them. If we'd done that, I could tell you exactly how it went, and you'd still never find them. But instead, Mathias panicked, and we took them away from the ocean and back to a pond. That was pretty stupid, when you think about it. And he put them in the truck. He didn't have to do that either. All we would have had to do was drag them down to the tidal flats and let the current do what it does.*

Instead, we went back to that camp, and that pond. We waded out until it was up to my neck and then he swam a little farther, dragging her out toward the raft. Then he let her go. She sank pretty easily. I remember you could see some blood in the water, but it was gone fast.

Then we went back for the guy.

We had him out of the truck before we realized he was moving. I think I felt it first, but I didn't want to believe it. Then I looked up...I remember that when I looked up at where his head was, the plastic sucked in and moved out and then sucked in again, and I realized he was breathing. Trying to breathe, at least.

Cass said, Oh, shit, *then. That was all, just* Oh, shit.

And Mathias stabbed him. I never even saw him get the knife out. I just saw him lean over and stab him through the plastic, right where his heart had to be.

I started to freak out. Mathias stood up and looked at me and he held the knife out. I kind of jumped back, because I expected him to cut me. Kill me. And he said—his voice was calm; I'll never forget how steady his voice was, like he was explaining the rules to a game—he said, You're both going to do that too. Because we are all in this together now.

He was waiting on me, but Cass took the knife. She…she didn't really hesitate. She just stabbed him. He wasn't moving anymore then. The plastic over his mouth wasn't moving either.

She held the knife out to me. She looked at me and said, Kimmy, we gotta hurry. *Mathias was watching. I didn't take the knife, and he said,* Either you do it or you go into the water with them. Make a choice, Kimmy.

So I…um, I took the knife. I dropped it, because I was shaking so bad. I got down on my hands and knees and picked it up and I…I reached out and jabbed it in there and then I crawled away. Mathias picked the knife back up and said I hadn't done it hard enough. He told me to do it again.

So I did it again.

We took him out into the water. Same way, same place. As far as I can wade up to my neck, and I'm five one, and then Mathias swam him out maybe ten feet farther. They're down there between the raft and the dock. Closer to the raft. You'll find them there. I don't know how deep. They aren't down there very far, though. It's just dark water, and a lonely place.

You'll find them easy.

Mathias drove us back to my car. The whole time he was giving us instructions, what to do with our clothes and how to wash the shower with bleach and use rags with bleach on everything we touched, and also threatening us, promising us he'd kill us if we talked to anyone and telling us how he'd know as soon as we went to the police and he didn't care about going to prison, he'd stay out long enough to kill us first. It was back and forth with that—what we needed to do and what he would do to us if we didn't listen.

The rest of it, I don't know about. What he did after, and what happened to the truck, I don't know. I can't even make guesses about that stuff, no matter how many ways you try to get me to.

But that is how it happened.

Can we stop now?

2

Rob Barrett was the only one in the room with Kimberly Crepeaux, a five-foot-nothing, 102-pound woman who was twenty-two years old but already had five arrests and one child when she confessed to her role in the murders of Jackie Pelletier and Ian Kelly.

Other investigators were watching on a live video feed, and once Kimberly was gone, one of them joined him. Lieutenant Don Johansson of the Maine State Police was ten years older than Barrett and had been around more murder cases—which was to say he'd been around any—but when he walked into the room, his eyes were wide and he said, "Holy *shit*," like he couldn't quite believe what he'd just watched and heard.

They'd been talking to Kimberly for months, and nobody had expected her to confess today.

"You got her," Johansson said, sitting down. "You actually got her."

Barrett only nodded. He was still in his chair, but his heart was pounding with adrenaline and he felt physically drained, as if he were in the locker room after a playoff game. For the past twenty minutes, he'd worked on keeping his face steady and his body still, afraid any disruption might cut Kimberly off in midstride. He'd long been convinced that she both knew the truth and wanted to confess, but even so, he hadn't been entirely ready for what he'd heard.

"It was the card," Johansson said, staring at Barrett with a bit of disbelief. "That's how you got her. How in the hell did you think to go to the card?"

The card was still on the table. Barrett picked it up now, handling it gingerly. It was made of folded construction paper and featured a crudely drawn cross beneath a rainbow. Inside, the message *She was a nice mom and you were lucky to have her and I am sorry she is gone but do not forget that you still have a good dad* was printed in pink Magic Marker and signed in blue by an eleven-year-old Kimberly Crepeaux.

Barrett had found a reference to the old handmade card in a list of possessions put together by the investigators who had searched Jackie Pelletier's home after she disappeared, and he'd asked her father if he could see it. Nobody understood why he wanted it. The card was, as Kimberly had noted, completely irrelevant to any of the horrifying events that had happened more than a decade later.

And yet it was the card that finally got her talking.

"It gave them a relationship," he told Johansson as he looked at that child's drawing of the rainbow over the cross. "Her knowing that Jackie kept that card gave them the type of relationship Kimberly didn't want to admit that they had. I thought if I brought Jackie home like that, if I made Kimberly think of what they shared, then maybe she'd give me something, finally." He let out a long breath and shook his head. "But I sure as hell did not expect her to give me *that*."

Johansson nodded, ran a hand over his jaw, and then looked away when he said, "Do you think it's true?"

"Hell yes, I think it's true." Barrett was almost surprised the question had been asked. Johansson had heard the same words he had; he'd even gotten to watch her face on the video feed as she told the story. Barrett wasn't sure how there could be any doubt.

"I'm just saying, Kimmy's not known for honesty," Johansson said.

"She just confessed to murder, Don. It's not like she gave us a tip about someone else."

"Plenty of people have confessed to murders they didn't actually commit."

"I know that better than anyone. This is what I do. This is what I spent ten years studying and teaching."

"Oh, I'm aware of that."

Barrett felt a flash of anger. He'd been brought in from the Boston division of the FBI precisely because Johansson and his team hadn't been able to make any progress getting Kimberly Crepeaux to talk, despite numerous accounts of her implicating herself to acquaintances. Now that Barrett had gotten the confession, Johansson seemed reluctant to believe it. There had been friction between them ever since Barrett arrived, and he understood that— no local cop liked a fed looking over his shoulder— but still he was stunned that Johansson could offer resistance on this of all days.

"The dive team ought to be able to settle the truth of it," Barrett said, fighting to keep his tone measured. "If she's lying, then that pond will be empty. If she's not, then they're down there. So let's get a search team assembled."

"Right. And I'll need to get Colleen looped in, obviously."

Colleen Davis was the prosecutor.

"And the families," Barrett said, and Johansson seemed to wince a little.

"It's your confession," Johansson said. "You were the one who finally got it, and I'll let you share it with them."

As if that were a privilege and not a burden.

"Thanks," Barrett said, and if Johansson heard

the sarcasm, he didn't show it. He was looking at the chair where Kimberly Crepeaux had sat as if she were still in it, and he shook his head.

"I'm still surprised that it was Mathias," he said. "Kimmy? Sure. Cass Odom too, may her troubled dead soul rest in peace. I've got no problem buying the two of them being involved. But Mathias Burke…what Kimmy described just does not fit the man I know. Or the man anybody around here seems to know." He shook his head once more, and then he got to his feet. "I'll update Colleen and then get the divers together. I guess we'll know by morning, won't we?"

"Yes," Barrett said, the construction-paper card still in his hands. "I guess we will."

Johansson clapped him on the shoulder. "Nice work, Barrett. You just closed one. This is your first, right?"

Was that a question or a reminder?

"It's my first," Barrett acknowledged, and the older cop nodded and congratulated him on his fine work once more before leaving the room to update the prosecutor and assemble the dive team, and then it was just Rob Barrett sitting there with the old sympathy card in his hands, a card written by one eleven-year-old girl to another eleven-year-old girl whose body she would later help wrap in plastic and sink in lonely, dark water.

I've got to tell their parents, he thought, and suddenly he wished Johansson were there, since he wouldn't have minded passing the buck back to him on this one, even if it meant he had to kiss Johansson's ass and praise his superior experience.

The truth was, Barrett had *no* experience. At thirty-four, he wasn't particularly young for an FBI agent, but he'd gotten a late start, spending more than a decade in school before moving into law enforcement. He was in only his ninth month with the Bureau and had worked precisely zero murder cases. That wasn't abnormal; FBI agents didn't tend to work murder cases, with some notable famous exceptions: serial killers and profiling. What the FBI offered to homicide detectives was, technically, *assistance*.

Rob Barrett had volunteered his assistance in this case. It had taken a little work to convince the Boston special agent in charge, Roxanne Donovan, that her young agent could be spared to rural Maine, but he'd had a few points in his favor. First, one of the victims was the son of a prominent Washington, DC, attorney, and he wanted help from the Bureau. Second, Rob Barrett's specialty was confessions, and the state police hadn't been able to crack a potential witness. And finally, Rob Barrett had what he'd termed a *familiarity* with Port Hope.

In the end, he suspected the last two elements

didn't matter nearly as much as the first. The Kelly family was influential in DC and angry at the pace of the investigation. When Barrett went to see Roxanne and make his case, he did so knowing that she was already getting requests from DC for some support from her office. During his sales pitch, he'd probably undersold his real interest and his history—check that; *familiarity*—with Maine.

"I didn't see any reference to this area in your background," Roxanne had said, flipping through a document that probably held more information about his life than he wanted to know.

"It was only during the summers, with my grandfather."

"But you've actually spent time in Port Hope?"

Yes. He had spent time in Port Hope. He had fallen in love in Port Hope—with the sea, with the woods, and then, of course, with a girl. All of that had happened under the shadow of a man that the residents of Port Hope remembered far better than they'd remember his grandson. Ray Barrett had been in the ground for years, but there were still cracked bar mirrors and scarred men to mark his presence in Port Hope—some of both at the Harpoon, the bar where Kimberly Crepeaux had allegedly revealed her knowledge of the Pelletier and Kelly case, the bar Rob's grandfather had once owned.

Roxanne Donovan had predicted he'd be needed in Maine for "a week or two."

That had been two months ago. Kimberly Crepeaux had not confessed easily, but when she'd broken, she'd offered a thorough account.

And now it was Barrett's job to share all those details with the victims' families.

3

They were very different families. While Howard Pelletier kept patient faith, George and Amy Kelly had hammered away with daily calls, criticisms, and suggestions. George's family had been spending summers in Maine for three generations, but George and Amy had been overseas the previous summer, so their son had gone up alone. For a time after Ian and Jackie went missing, the Kellys' summer retreat had been a base camp for the investigation. Then the tips went cold and their son stayed gone, and George and Amy Kelly went back down south but kept the calls up.

Barrett dialed their home number in Virginia. Most of his conversations had been with Amy, though George was always on the phone. He often became too emotional to speak, and then he'd mute his line and just listen. They liked videoconference calls, and in an attempt to handle his son's homicide like a business matter, George would take the calls in his office, where he could sit at the desk and turn his back to the bookcases lined with pictures of Ian playing tennis, Ian playing soccer, Ian with a diploma.

Ian with a smile. Always that hundred-watt smile.

Today, Barrett was on speakerphone but not video when he relayed Kimberly Crepeaux's confession.

"You're sure?" Amy Kelly asked, and then, before Barrett could answer, she said, "Of course you're sure."

Amy and George were attorneys, and they'd vetted Barrett as if they were appointing him to the investigation instead of accepting him from the FBI. They knew better than anyone that his expertise was confessions—getting the real ones, and cutting through the false ones. When he said he'd gotten the truth, they knew they should believe him.

All the same, they seemed to struggle with accepting the Ma-thias Burke narrative.

George and Amy had known Mathias long before he'd surfaced as a suspect in their son's homicide. For three summers, they'd employed him as a caretaker and groundskeeper at their summerhouse on the coast. Amy had resisted the early accusations, saying she had good instincts, and she trusted Mathias Burke.

She wasn't the only one to have voiced that opinion. Mathias was a multigeneration local, and he was also a local source of pride. At the age of eight, he'd been pulling weeds and raking leaves in his neighborhood; by the time he was ten he was mowing lawns; at sixteen he purchased his first truck and trailer and began to give the professional caretakers a challenge. He was only twenty-nine now but owned a caretaking business that spanned three counties and employed more than a dozen people. He handled landscaping, remodeling, alarm-system installations, paving, and trash hauling. Whatever need the summer people might have, Mathias Burke would meet it—or he'd produce someone reliable for the task. His reputation was often distilled down to a single word: *ambitious*.

It had taken Barrett a while to convince people that ambition did not prevent a man from driving erratically while high and drunk.

Kimberly Crepeaux's involvement was an easier sell. Her family had a long legacy of petty crime in an area with a nearly nonexistent crime rate, and they were even better known for their struggles with alcohol. Kimberly—or Kimmy, as she was known to all the locals—had graduated from alcohol to heroin, and her arrest rate had soared accordingly. She'd brought suspicion on herself by drunkenly telling acquaintances that the police weren't close to the truth in the case or asserting her innocence and lack of knowledge about the situation without being prompted.

By the time Barrett began his interviews with her, the dominant police theory was that an accident had turned into a body dump, and the amount of chatter coming from the heroin networks suggested drugs had been involved in the accident. The horrific story Kimberly had finally told him contained only one real shock: the identity of the man behind the wheel who'd wielded both a pipe and a knife to turn a possible manslaughter into a chilling double murder.

That was not the Mathias Burke who was the paragon of the peninsula.

After he'd shared Kimberly Crepeaux's story, Barrett told Amy and George what he was still missing.

"I do not have the truck."

The truck was the first thing Kimberly had offered up. While maintaining that it was only a rumor and certainly nothing she'd seen personally, she had described it in vivid detail and linked it to Mathias. Initially, it had seemed like a promising lead—Mathias Burke, either personally or through his caretaking company, owned nine trucks, from standard pickups to extended-cab diesels to plow trucks. Unfortunately, none of them remotely matched Kimberly's description, and no other witnesses could recall seeing him with such a truck. If anything, they dismissed it. Mathias Burke liked nice vehicles, everyone informed Barrett. A beat-up Dodge Dakota with a strange paint job on the hood was simply not his style.

But now Kimberly was firm on the story, Barrett told the Kellys, and the only other witness was dead—Cass Odom had overdosed three days after Jackie and Ian disappeared.

George Kelly spoke for the first time in several minutes then. "But you won't need the truck if you've got a confession and a..." He paused before he said, "Body."

"Not for an arrest, but I'll certainly want it for prosecution," Barrett said. The idea of a trial was intimidating when his case currently rode the skinny shoulders of one shaky witness.

"I'm sure by then you will have it," George said.

"Yes."

There was another pause, and then Amy Kelly said, "So we'll know tomorrow. When the dive team goes in, we will know for certain what happened to Ian."

"We'll know more tomorrow, yes. I will call you as soon as the dive team has results."

Results? They all knew what they were looking for: Ian's corpse.

In a distant and vacant voice, Amy delivered the inevitable words: she thanked Barrett for his time and effort.

He had no idea what to say. He had just told a father and mother that their son had been beaten with a pipe, wrapped in plastic while still breathing, stabbed, and drowned.

You're welcome.

He'd begun the call by expressing sympathy, telling them how intensely he hated to give them this news, and he didn't wish to repeat those sentiments so frequently that they sounded empty. He responded to Amy Kelly's gratitude simply by reiterating that he would call them as soon as he had information from the dive team.

Even though the divers had yet to enter the water, the conversation felt final, though he knew it wasn't. The confession was really just a new beginning. Next would come the bodies, then the trials, and the Kelly family would be in the courtroom facing Kimberly Crepeaux and Mathias Burke. They would see photographs, listen to forensic experts, watch laser pointers dance around their son's bones, and hear testimony from the accused.

When I looked up at where his head was, the plastic sucked in and moved out and then sucked in again, and I realized he was breathing.

No, this was anything but the end of the horror for George and Amy Kelly.

Having delivered news of the confession to Virginia,

Barrett hung up the phone and drove toward the Maine coast. There was no ferry to Little Spruce Island, but he knew a local who would take him.

He would tell Jackie Pelletier's father the truth of his daughter's death in person.

4

Barrett reached Little Spruce Island about an hour before sunset. The bay was tranquil, the water calm, and as he stepped off the boat and onto the dock, he could hear the sound of a hammer. It made him wince, because he knew the source.

Howard Pelletier was finishing his daughter's studio.

Howard was a third-generation lobsterman, but after his wife, Patricia, was killed in a car wreck in a March snowstorm when their daughter was eleven years old, his days on the water became a secondary concern. So did everything except Jackie.

The stories Barrett had heard about the two of them were legion and lovely: how he'd anguished over learning to make ponytails and braids, how he'd walked her to school each day with her hand in his, how he'd fished during the fall and winter so he could have more time with her in the summer, even though it meant forsaking the safer money and weather for the season when gales howled and waves threw ice over the decks. He'd done carpentry in the summer and returned to the water when Jackie returned to school. Caring for her had been the sole focus of his days, and then she was a teenager, and suddenly she seemed to be caring for him as much as he was for her. When she was fifteen, she'd signed up for cooking classes in Camden, then made every meal so her overextended father could have one less task. He'd sent her to sixth grade with a clumsy French braid; three years later, she sent him back to the water with gourmet sandwiches whose ingredients he couldn't pronounce. A father and daughter once defined by tragedy had become a testament to resilience. To say that the people of Port Hope cared about the Pelletiers was an understatement; they were beloved. And they were spoken of together, always, two halves that made a whole, Howard and Jackie, Jackie and Howard.

Some thought it was a fear of leaving her father alone that had kept Jackie from going to college. She was an aspiring artist, and though she had exceptional grades, she never submitted a college application. Howard's family had an old cottage on Little Spruce, and his daughter fell in love with the island. Upon graduating from high school, she'd moved out to the cottage. She took the ferry back to the mainland each morning to work at a grocery store and, in the summer, spent weekends behind the bar at a seafood restaurant. Jackie worked sixty-hour weeks during the tourist season and told anyone who would listen what she was saving for: an elevated studio space that would be built beside the family's old island cottage, something tall enough to give her a grand view back toward the harbor, where the sunrises lit the Maine coast.

Howard Pelletier began construction on the building five days after she disappeared.

When she comes home, he'd say, *this will help. Whatever hell she's been through, this place will ease it.*

The longer his daughter stayed missing, the more elaborate the studio design became. He redid his original roofing to provide for additional skylights, added a lofted daybed (*In case she wants to take a nap up here, you know, a little spot for when she needs a break*). Everyone understood the progressive complexities.

He couldn't stop.

If he stopped, it meant she wasn't coming home.

Rob Barrett stood on the dock at the Little Spruce Island wharf for a long time, listening to that hammering, before he started up the hill.

Howard smiled when he saw Barrett approaching.

"Agent Barrett, how are you?" he said, stepping

through the open door with his hand extended. He was just a shade over five feet tall, a foot shorter than Barrett, but thick with muscle, a fireplug build, stronger at fifty than most men were at twenty.

"It's just Rob." This was as much a ritual as the smiles and handshakes.

"It'll be Rob when you retire. Till then, you're an agent, right?"

Before Barrett could respond, Howard waved a hand at the interior behind him, which smelled of clean wood and sawdust and was lit by spotlights clamped to the wall studs.

"You can see I made a little change," he said, and Barrett saw that the staircase was gone. Howard had spent frigid winter evenings finishing the steps with coat after coat of stain, a beautiful, rich maple. Now they were missing.

"I got to thinking," Howard said, "that she was always comparing the studio she wanted to a lighthouse or a tree house, you know? She wanted to be up high, feel like she was someplace magical. That was her word. Way I figure it, walking up a straight set of stairs, where's the magic in that? But if it has that curve, that spiral, it's like you're heading someplace special. So you're not just walking up, you're... what's the word I'm looking for? You're..." He made a sweeping gesture with his small, thick hand, lifting it from belt level to eye level in a slow arc.

"Ascending," Barrett said, and Howard Pelletier's eyes lit up.

"Ayuh," he said in his old-time Yankee dialect. "Ascending. Ayuh, that's just the word. Once I get it framed in, you'll see what I mean. She'll walk up there and it'll feel like she's ascending."

Barrett said, "Howard, I've got some news."

The first flicker of fear showed on Howard's weathered face, but he blinked hard and pushed it back. He was good at this by now. While each week without answers had drained the hope from George and Amy Kelly, those weeks had given Howard Pelletier time to lay the foundation of his faith in Jackie's unlikely return, to scour the Internet for reports of those who'd gone missing only to be reunited with their loved ones years later. He knew all those stories. He'd shared them with Barrett often.

So now, hearing the promise of news, he wiped his hands on his pants, nodded enthusiastically, and said, "Good, good! A real lead this time?"

Barrett had trouble finding his voice, and when he finally spoke, the words seemed to come from behind him and far away.

"A confession."

Howard sat down slowly. Eased right down onto

the floor and sat like a child, legs stretched out in front of him, head bowed. He gathered a small mound of sawdust and squeezed it tight in his fist. Then he said, "Tell me."

So Barrett told it for the second time that day. He told Howard Pelletier as the man sat on the floor he'd laid in the building with the missing stairs, and Howard did not speak. He just rocked a little bit and kept opening and closing his small, muscular hands, crushing loose sawdust into tight packets that he would then toss idly at the door, like someone skipping rocks on a pond.

"Could be lying," he whispered when Barrett had finished. "Story like that, from a girl like that? Kimmy Crepeaux wouldn't know an honest word if it bit her on the ass."

"Maybe she is lying," Barrett said. "Hopefully she is. We'll know tomorrow, when the divers search the pond. I need you to be ready for that, Howard."

Howard had closed his eyes when Barrett said *divers*. He kept them closed when he said, "When do they go in?"

"First light. We'd have gone today, but we didn't want the divers to run out of daylight. Once the search starts, people will talk, and the media will show up fast. We want the scene secured and plenty of time for the dive team."

Howard shook his head, and then opened his eyes.

"A bullshit story," he said. "Crepeaux, she stands to gain something here, yeah? She's got other charges. You told me that. Did you offer her a deal on those?"

"It wasn't my call to make. That's the prosecutor's decision."

"Oh, but she's got a deal, don't she? You tell me the truth now."

Barrett nodded.

"There you go," Howard said. "You won't find 'em. She's told a tale to help herself out of the rest of her mess. I'm sorry you gotta investigate lies like that."

Barrett said, "I just wanted you to hear it from me first."

"You won't find 'em," Howard said, and the tears came then. He wiped them away as if they'd been a mistake, but more came, and he gave up and wept, quietly but painfully, and Barrett sat down in the sawdust with him and waited. They sat there for a long time, and even when the tears stopped, neither of them spoke. Finally, Howard got his breathing steadied and whispered, "Has Mathias Burke been arrested?"

"Not yet. The prosecutor wants the"—Barrett caught himself before he said *bodies*—"the evidence first. He's under surveillance, though. I expect he'll be in jail by noon."

Howard nodded. He was staring straight ahead, out the still-open door toward the rocky cliffs and pine trees and the setting sun, the panorama his daughter had so loved.

"You know I showed her that old graveyard," he said. "I told you that, right?"

"Yes."

"Took her up there in, it was, uh, it was her sixth-grade year. Showed her the way you could put paper over one of them old stones and rub it with charcoal and…" He mimicked the circular motion of the grave rubbings. "They came back to life. The names, I mean. She thought that was so special. Not the way most kids her age would have, like it was just a trick, but special because she knew that represented a life. Special that we could still learn their names and say them and so they wouldn't be…forgotten."

His thick chest moved in jerks as he fought for steady breath.

"So, ayuh, I showed her the graveyard."

"She loved that place," Barrett said, "*because* you showed it to her. Do not let yourself think of any—"

"I know what I think," Howard said. "You don't need to tell me how to think."

They sat there in the sawdust and Barrett tried to conceive of some words that would make Howard feel less alone. What might he say to a widowed man who'd raised his daughter and watched her blossom into a beautiful, intelligent young woman? Just what might those words be?

Did you know that there were sixteen thousand murders last year in this country? he could say. *More than a quarter of a million people have been murdered in this country since the day your daughter was born, Howard. Don't feel isolated. You're not alone. Enough people have been murdered in Jackie's lifetime to populate the city of Portland, Maine, five times over. You are anything but alone.*

Howard wiped his mouth. Sawdust stuck to his face, which was still damp with tears. "I best get this work done while there's still daylight," he said. "You just...call me tomorrow. When you..."

He couldn't finish, and Barrett didn't make him try. He said, "I'll call you."

He knew it was time to go then, and so he stepped through the open door. The wind had picked up and the smell of the sea was heavy and there was only a narrow band of crimson light, thin and bright as an opened vein, left to fight the descending darkness. Behind him, the work lamps cast a harsh white glow inside Jackie Pelletier's unfinished studio, where her father had ripped out the staircase to build something that would feel more magical.

Ascending. Ayuh, that's just the word.

Barrett walked back down the hill. The local who'd brought him out, a retired lobsterman named Brooks who'd known the Pelletier family all his life, was waiting patiently in his boat. He had not asked why they were going to Little Spruce today. He never did. But he looked at Barrett closely when he stepped down into the boat, and before he started the engine, he opened a stowage locker and removed a bottle of Jack Daniel's and held it out without a word.

He had never offered Barrett a drink before.

"Yeah," Barrett said. "Thanks." He opened the bottle and took a long drink and then tried to hand it back. The old lobsterman shook his head.

"You keep it," he said, and then he started the motor. Barrett cast off the dock lines and sat down, his eyes on the cottage on the hill and the new building going up beside it.

"Ascending," he said.

"What's that?" Brooks asked.

"Nothing," Barrett said. "Just talking to myself."

He took another drink and turned to face the wind.

5

The pond where the bodies of Jackie Pelletier and Ian Kelly allegedly lay was twenty-four acres of water fronted by only three seasonal homes. The rest of the shore was composed of marsh grass that led into the pines. At its center, the pond was approximately twenty feet deep. Between the dock and raft, it couldn't have been much more than ten.

But, as Kimberly Crepeaux had said, it was dark water, and a lonely place.

As the sun came up, Barrett stood on the shore with Don Johansson and watched the dive team gear up. A few other cops from the state police were on hand, but the divers were from the Maine Warden Service. They'd pulled bodies out of ponds, rivers, and oceans. On more than a few occasions, they'd gone through ice to do it.

Today, though, the air was already warm at dawn, fragrant with the scent of pine needles and moss. Watching the sun chin up and over the tree line, Barrett found himself thinking of the way Kimberly Crepeaux had described Mathias Burke's reaction to that unseasonably hot September day: *As if the sun had come up hot that day looking only for him, like somebody picking a fight.*

Barrett was exhausted, and he knew that Don had to be too. Neither of them had slept. After returning from Little Spruce Island, Barrett had gone directly to a meeting with the state and county police and the prosecutor and mapped out their plan for the search, the arrest of Mathias Burke, and the handling of media inquiries. It had been after three in the morning before they were done, and they'd stayed in the station, drinking coffee and talking about nothing, each distracted by his own thoughts about what had gone into this and where it would end.

At dawn, they went to the pond.

Now, after getting the thumbs-up from Clyde Cohen, the warden who was in charge of the dive team, Barrett said, "Let's bring them home."

He watched the divers vanish, one at a time, beneath the water.

Descending.

When the divers came up, this investigation would be done. When they ascended, it would all be over.

He expected it to go quicker than it did. The divers stayed down, and the minutes ticked by, and the sun arced into Barrett's eyes. He tried not to look at his watch. Don Johansson checked his plenty, but he didn't say anything.

Barrett blinked at the sun, annoyed by its brightness reflecting off the water even with his sunglasses and a baseball cap shielding his eyes. The smell of the water and the pines reminded him of fishing Maine ponds like this with his grandfather. They'd go out on a little boat with a ten-horse Johnson outboard and work Rapalas and Red Devil spoons along the weed edges, hunting bass and pike. His grandfather would drink and talk, usually about the military or manhood or all the ways his own son— Barrett's father—was an example of a culture gone soft. *The professor,* he would sneer. He always called Barrett's father the professor. *Fuckin' philosophy, you kidding me? Let me tell you about some good men who died over fuckin' philosophy, Robby.*

Twelve years after his father's funeral and ten after his grandfather's—Ray had outlasted his son; Ray had outlasted almost everyone, running fast and hard on booze, cigarettes, and venom—the smells of this Maine pond took Barrett right back to those fishing trips. Smell was supposed to be the sense most closely linked to memory, but this wasn't a day to recall the past. This day was supposed to be about moving forward—it would be painful and tragic, yes, but it would also move things forward.

And quickly. The water wasn't deep enough to hide bodies for long.

You won't find 'em.

Barrett twisted his watch so the face was pointing inward and he couldn't see the dial.

It was nearly noon when the warden in charge of the dive team told Barrett that there was nothing to be found within a hundred yards of the raft.

"You're positive? I thought you said visibility was awful down there."

"It is, but the water's shallow. We've been crawling the bottom, basically. Every square foot. They're not in this cove. I'm sure of it."

"Maybe out deeper," Barrett said, but already he was unsettled because Kimberly Crepeaux had been so clear on the location. "They weighted the bodies, but maybe not enough. They could have drifted pretty far out."

"With no current?"

Barrett looked at the warden. "Go deeper," he said. "They're down there."

The divers went deeper. By two, they were in the middle of the pond. Word of the search had leaked, and spectators began to arrive. Johansson brought in additional troopers to keep them back and secure the road. Then a TV helicopter passed overhead and filmed the divers' repeated, and empty-handed, returns to the surface. It was very warm, and Barrett's mouth was very dry.

"They'll find them," he said to no one in particular.

By four, they had worked all the way to the opposite shore and found nothing but beer bottles, fishing lures, and one rusted Louisiana license plate.

"'Came up with the Gulf Stream—from southern waters,'" the diver said, tossing the plate onto the plastic sheet they'd spread for any items of potential evidentiary value. He grinned, but Barrett couldn't match it.

"Not a *Jaws* fan, Agent Barrett?"

"Not today." Barrett worked his tongue around his mouth and tugged his baseball cap lower. The sun's glare was relentless. "No pipes, no pieces of metal?"

"Plenty of metal if you count beer tabs and Rapala hooks. But anything bigger than that?" The diver shook his head. "It's a clean bottom. Ponds like these, we usually find all sorts of shit. Refrigerators, car doors—hell, entire cars, for that matter. This is an unusually clean bottom."

Barrett nodded and tried to look impassive. The diver adjusted his mask and mouthpiece and went back in again. The television chopper took another pass, its rotors shimmering shadows on the glassy, glaring surface of the pond.

"You said every part of her story checked out," Johansson said to Barrett in a low tone. It came out more accusatory than questioning.

"It did. Every single stop. You know that. You reviewed the same route."

"Every single stop before this one checks out. This one is pretty damned relevant too."

"She was telling the truth," Barrett said. "I've spent a lot of time talking to her, Don, and I am sure that she was telling the truth about this."

"I'm aware of the time you've spent on Kimmy's stories," Johansson said, and again Barrett caught the loaded, accusatory tone. Johansson struggled to believe anything offered by Kimberly Crepeaux. *I don't want to hang my case on a jailhouse snitch,* Johansson had said. And Barrett had told him that they wouldn't have to because they'd have the bodies.

Find the bodies, close the case.

Barrett moved away from him and paced the shore, scanning the water and weeds, working south. Then he beckoned for Johansson.

"The warden's wrong," he said. "There's a current to this pond."

Johansson arched an eyebrow as he looked from Barrett out to the mirrored surface of the water, which was unblemished by so much as a ripple. "You think?"

"It's stream-fed. Water comes in at the north end and goes out the south. Let's take a look at the south end."

They slogged through the boggy soil, boots sinking six inches deep, then coming free with a wet sucking sound, the mosquitoes and blackflies buzzing. Everything at ground level was a battle, assaults by mud and bugs, by muscle aches and sweat, and everything above was a beautiful tease, pine-scented air leading up to a cobalt sky. The idea that the two worlds were joined felt absurd.

At the south end of the pond was a berm, dug out and then backfilled with gravel. The pond had been built by a man with visions of developing the property for summer cottages. The soil wasn't right for building, though; it stayed too wet for too long, and he'd created more of a marsh than a pond.

Don Johansson and one of the wardens measured the water depth on the other side of the berm, where the water worked toward the creek.

"Sixteen inches," the warden said, slapping at a mosquito that was treating his neck like a buffet line. It left a bloody smear behind. "No chance a body drifted through here even if it hadn't been weighted."

"It was a wet winter," Barrett said. "December rains,

right? Then again after the snowmelt. Would've been high back then."

The warden looked at Barrett and then away.

"Agent Barrett? Even at record flood levels, you're not going to have enough current in here to carry a body from that cove, across the pond, and through this."

Barrett watched the water flow past the berm, sparkling under the sun, melodic as it passed over the rocks. Most people would have said it was a beautiful sound, and on most days Barrett would have agreed with them, but right now the soft rippling seemed like a mocking chuckle.

"Keep at it," he said. "I'm going to see Kimberly."

6

On the day after Cass Odom's body was found, Kimberly Crepeaux climbed behind the wheel of her car with an open vodka bottle and drove the wrong way down a one-way street in Rockland near the police station. When police finally pulled her over, she made no effort to conceal the plastic bag of pills that lay in plain sight on the passenger seat. Her blood alcohol level was a modest .10, barely above the legal limit and hardly enough to create such inebriated thinking that she would fail to even attempt to hide the drugs.

"I think you wanted to be arrested," Barrett told her the first time they spoke.

She'd rolled her eyes.

Today two corrections officers brought her into the interview room, uncuffed her, and left. She was a waif of a girl, five feet—although she insisted on saying five one, the way she insisted on him calling her Kimberly even though everyone else called her Kimmy—and one hundred pounds. The orange prison garb hung off her in loose billows and folds. Her blond hair was cut just below the ears, a perky bob that enhanced the childlike look of her small face, with its splash of freckles and bright green eyes. She was the mother to one child, a daughter immediately claimed by Kimberly's grandmother, who'd explained the decision to Barrett with wide eyes and a cigarette dangling from her lips. *Why'd I take the little one from her? Mister, you've met her.*

When Kimberly entered the room, Barrett got to his feet with practiced courtesy. You showed respect from the start if you wanted to get the truth. What you had to do was encourage conversation, not force it; you wanted the suspect to talk comfortably, not feel baited or coerced. People thought that you understood them when you kept your mouth shut, maintained eye contact, and listened more than you talked. When people thought they were understood, they tended to talk more.

Another rule: You didn't sit on the opposite side of the table or desk from the suspect. Those were power dynamics in some cases, but in all cases they were literal objects placed between you and the other person. He didn't want barriers. He pulled out one of the red plastic chairs for Kimberly and made sure that she was seated first, like a guest; these small gestures of respect counted. Then, after she was seated, he brought his own chair around the table so that they were both on the same side, nothing between them. He sat with good posture, not a military ramrod bearing but also not with any slouch that suggested disinterest or dominance, and he leaned forward ever so slightly, toward her, toward the source of the words that mattered. Then he tried to clear his mind to hear her words. Tried to push back those images of the empty-handed divers and the way Johansson's face had looked when he kept checking his watch.

Kimberly said, "So it's over now?"

Almost immediately, Barrett's temper rose, and he had to still himself. *Slow down your breathing, slow down your speaking.* Slower was always better. Emotional physics; control was easier to maintain at fifty miles an hour than a hundred.

Of course, there was always black ice.

Barrett let a few seconds pass, watching the particular black ice in front of him, before he said, "It is not over. I will need to find the bodies before it can be over."

Kimberly already had a jailhouse pallor, but it seemed to whiten an extra shade, her freckles standing out stark.

"What are you talking about?"

"Where are the bodies?" Barrett asked.

"They're right where I told you. In the pond, out between the dock and the raft."

"No, they're not."

Kimberly gaped at him. Then she said, "You missed them. It's dark water. Maybe he got them out closer to the raft. Maybe the water pushed them around a little."

Bullshit, he wanted to snap. *Stop lying.* But instead he breathed slowly and kept his tone steady and his eyes on hers when he said, "We've had divers in that pond since dawn. There are no bodies in there, Kimberly."

In all of their interviews, Kimberly Crepeaux had been generally stoic. She had enough familiarity with police questioning that it didn't make her immediately nervous, and she also liked to portray herself as a willing participant in the investigation, a helpful citizen, a team player. As Barrett's questions tunneled in on her drunken references to a night with Mathias Burke and Cass Odom, she'd begun to show a slightly more emotional reaction, but even then it wasn't overt. She would avoid eye contact, pick at her nails, look at the ceiling, twirl her hair. Small, fidgeting responses. But never, not even when she'd confessed, had she seemed scared.

Now she was shaking. It was minor at first—a tremble of her right hand on the tabletop—and she clasped her hands together in her lap as if to still it. Instead, the tremble spread up to her shoulders, and then her jaw began to quiver.

"He moved the bodies," she blurted.

"Mathias?"

"Of course. That's what he did. He must have, right?"

"Mathias went out there, dove twelve feet, found bodies wrapped in plastic and pipes, brought them back to the surface, loaded them in a vehicle, and moved them?"

"He could've used ropes or something? How would I know? The last time I saw them they were right where I told you! They were sinking into that pond, out in the cove, out between the dock and the raft! *They're down there and you just missed them!*"

She'd never shouted at Barrett before. She'd been crude, she'd made jokes, she'd cried, taunted, flirted. She'd tried every tactic—but she had never shouted.

Barrett studied her quivering jaw and her hands squeezed so tightly together that those oft-injected veins pressed blue threads against her white skin, and he thought that she was telling the truth.

"Where is the truck?" he said. "If that's what happened, if he moved the bodies, then I've got to pivot. I need evidence. The truck will get me started. Blood evidence. That is—"

"I don't know about the truck!"

"Then we are back to where we started. Kimberly?

59

Without those bodies, your confession will be worthless. Mathias will get lawyers to pound away at your story, and then they'll turn to the jury and say, *If she was telling the truth, the police would have found the bodies.* And the jury will agree."

"Mathias moved 'em."

"That's a tough scenario to believe," Barrett said. "You all were damn lucky not to have been seen when you put them in, if I'm to believe that story. But now you're saying someone went back and found them, dragged them up, and relocated them without being seen? I can't sell that one."

He expected insistence that she'd given him the gospel truth. Instead, she looked down and said, "He'll still be out, then? If I get parole, Mathias will be out?"

"Of course he will," Barrett said. "You think I can arrest him based on a jailhouse confession that requires me to explain how two bodies disappeared with no physical evidence?"

There was a strange, heavy pulse in the center of Kimberly's throat, and she swallowed hard and wet her lips.

"I don't want parole then," she whispered.

"What?"

"He knows I talked by now. If he's still out...then I don't want to be."

A few silent seconds passed. Kimberly's throat

pulsed again; she swallowed again; the shaking intensified.

She's putting on a show, he thought, and then his practiced approach left him and he fell back on a technique he'd always advocated against—he threatened.

"I don't need the theatrics, Kimberly. You're a bad poker player. And you're going to make a mistake once you're out. So what I'm going to do after I leave this room? I'm going to meet with the prosecutor and the judge and have them kick you loose. You can go back home, go back to your drinking and drugging, and we'll wait until your next mistake. Then you and I can try this again."

Kimberly Crepeaux looked at Barrett with tears in her eyes and said, "You can't just take me out of jail. That's not how it works."

"It works however I want it to when there's a double murder to solve. I'll see that you're sent home by tomorrow. Then you and Mathias can get together and work on your story, polish up the lies."

Kimberly's throat pulsed once more as she stared at him. Then she doubled over in the red plastic chair and vomited onto the tile floor.

Barrett scrambled to his feet, stunned. Kimberly gagged and shook her head to cast loose a string of spit that dangled from her lip. Barrett knelt and put a hand on her small, heaving back.

"Just tell me the truth," he said. "Do that, and I can help you."

"I already did." Kimberly Crepeaux gasped, her head bowed over the pool of vomit on the tile. "I told you just how it happened."

7

He came out of the jail running hot, his thoughts torn between the expression of anguished honesty on Kimberly's face and the memory of the empty-handed divers returning to the surface. When he reached his car he stood with his palm on the door and tried to use the touch of the metal to ground himself. *Slow down, Barrett. Breathe. People screw up when they rush. There's no pressure on you. You're the one who applies pressure; you don't feel it.*

He could steady himself quickly. It was his father's skill, finding emotional calm in a raging current, and it was an ability that drove Barrett's grandfather crazy, because all he knew was the current.

My blood got up was how Ray Barrett explained his rages, as if the total loss of self-control was natural, something like fluctuating cholesterol, common and understood.

Glenn Barrett had taught his son to pause and imagine his anger as a book, to turn each moment that infuriated him into a page and then imagine turning those pages slowly, reviewing each one, before shutting the book and shelving it.

Now Barrett took a moment with each page. His blood was up, and that would not do for his next stop.

It was time to see Mathias Burke.

Mathias had been only ten when Barrett met him. Barrett was fourteen, up for one of his summer stretches in Port Hope, and he'd spent most of it fishing for mackerel off the pier in the boatyard or holed up in the tiny public library burning through its John D. MacDonald and Dean Koontz collections. Anyplace other than the dingy apartment above his grandfather's bar was just fine.

Mathias was around often, but he didn't attract Rob's attention because of the age gap between them. He wasn't a source of friendship or competition, of threat or envy, the only issues that mattered in the *Lord of the Flies* existence of adolescent males. He was, however, a curiosity—he was a young boy, small for his age, but always working. He mowed lawns, weeded flower gardens, washed windows. He advertised these services, and he'd even rigged an old wagon into a sort of flatbed trailer so he could tow his push mower behind his bike.

It was the wagon-trailer that caught Ray Barrett's

eye and thus led to the first meeting between Rob and Mathias.

"Look at that damn kid," Ray had said one hot July afternoon when there wasn't enough of a breeze to push the mosquitoes back; he'd enlisted Rob's help in filling and lighting the citronella torches that lined the small balcony off the apartment above the bar. Down below, Mathias was unloading a bulky mower in the yard of Tom Gleason, a dentist from Massachusetts who came up to Port Hope on weekends and for summer holidays. If the trailing cloud of mosquitoes bothered Mathias, he gave no indication of it.

"His father's a worthless shit pile who spends more money in my bar than on his family, but that kid..." Ray indicated Mathias with a tip of his beer bottle. "He's rigged up a damned trailer for his push mower, you see that? That kid is going to make something of himself. He already works harder than most men these days. Tom Gleason should be cutting his own grass, the lazy prick."

By then, Rob knew where this was going to go—a scathing critique of first his father, then himself.

Ray surprised him, though; he skipped the typical rant about his soft professor son and even softer grandson and instead said, "You're going down to help him, Robby."

"He won't want to split that money," Rob said.

Ray turned and glowered. "I say anything about taking his money? I said you're going to help him. That's all."

And so down they'd gone to the tumbledown shed where Ray kept an ancient mower, and although it crossed Rob's mind that Ray didn't bother to cut his own grass but somehow managed to scorn others who made the same choice, he knew better than to point it out. Instead, he'd stayed quiet, his face flushed with anger and embarrassment as he pushed the old Toro down to Mathias Burke with his grandfather trailing behind, a fresh beer in hand.

"Mathias, this is Robby, my grandson," Ray bellowed. "He's gonna give you a hand because he needs to learn about an honest day's damn work. Don't pay him a cent, you hear me? Just show him what it's like to have to get off your ass once in a while."

The little boy with the dark eyes and sunburned skin watched Ray Barrett with none of the fear that large men in bars showed him.

"Yes, sir, Mr. Barrett. I don't need any help, though."

"I know you don't. He does." Ray extended a five-dollar bill to Mathias. "Here's for putting up with him."

Mathias shook his head. "I've already been paid for this lawn, sir," he said, and a look of admiration passed over Ray's face, a look he usually reserved for linebackers or boxers.

"That," he told Rob, "is what you need to learn."

He pocketed the five-dollar bill, and Rob was interested to see the scrawny boy's eyes narrow, as if he'd just learned something important but not surprising about Ray.

Ray left them, swatting and cursing at the mosquitoes as he wandered off, and without so much as a glance at Rob, Mathias Burke fired up his mower and got back to his work, his thin shoulders straining as he pushed the mower. Rob was furious at the indignity of it all—being in Port Hope with his grandfather was bad enough, but now he was working in the heat for free alongside a kid who wasn't even in fifth grade yet—and in his anger, he pushed his mower too fast, and the dull blades cut uneven swaths through the thick grass. Up the street, a couple of girls closer to his age were working at a lemonade stand in front of the Methodist church; he could hear them laughing and wondered if it was at him.

He mowed and cursed his father silently for sending him up here, cursed his grandfather for continuing to exist, cursed the mosquitoes that feasted on his skin. He was lost in self-righteous fury when Tom Gleason came out of the house and shouted at him.

"Turn the damn mower around. You're gonna bust up my car! Look at this!"

Rob had been cutting with the mower's discharge facing the driveway. The door panels of the shiny Cadillac with Massachusetts plates were coated with grass.

"If there are scratches in my paint, I'm going to find both of your families," Tom snapped, running a hand over the doors.

When Mathias Burke said, "I'll wash it for you," it surprised Rob as much as it did Tom Gleason.

"I'll wash down the whole side," Mathias said. He'd shut off his own mower and walked up to join them. "It'll look perfect. I promise, sir."

Tom Gleason blinked at him. "Okay, but if it's banged up, I'm calling your dad down here."

"It'll look perfect," Mathias repeated.

Tom Gleason grunted and went back inside the house, and Rob turned to Mathias.

"Sorry," he said, and he truly was. The smaller boy ignored him, though. He crossed the yard, found a hose coiled up alongside Tom Gleason's house, turned the water on, dragged the hose back over, and sprayed down the side of the car. Rob ran back to his grandfather's shed and found a rag and an old bottle of Turtle Wax. He rubbed the wax on after Mathias had rinsed the grass off, and then the Cadillac was gleaming again.

That was when Mathias spoke to Rob for the first time.

"Watch the house and tell me if he comes out."

"What?"

"Just watch for me, okay?" Mathias slipped a Leatherman multitool out of his pocket. He tested the driver's door, found it unlocked, and popped the trunk release. Then he closed the door, went around the back of the car, and leaned in the trunk.

"What're you doing?" Rob said.

Mathias didn't answer. He had peeled the fabric backing away from the rear of the trunk and was using the screwdriver on the Leatherman. He moved quickly from the left side of the trunk to the right, head bowed and small hands working nimbly, and Rob realized he was loosening the taillights, and he began to grin.

"Hey," he said, "that's great. Maybe he'll get pulled over and get a ticket, the jerk."

Mathias closed the trunk and said, "Just keep your mouth shut about this, pussy."

Rob stared at him. The scrawny kid barely came up to his collarbone.

"What did you call me?"

"A pussy," Mathias said calmly in a soft, high voice that was still untouched by puberty. "Keep your mouth shut, and keep out of my way. I don't care what your drunk grandfather has to say about it, but you stay away from me, pussy."

Rob was initially more shocked than angry, but

that changed fast. "Call me that again and I'll break your nose."

For the first and only time that day, Mathias Burke smiled.

"That wouldn't end well for you," he said.

Rob glared down at him and realized that Mathias wasn't wrong. It would go very badly for Rob if he hit this little kid. Word would get back to his grandfather, and there wouldn't be a belt buckle in Texas big enough for Ray Barrett to use on Rob's ass when he learned his grandson had hit a boy half his size. Rob was grudgingly impressed—this kid knew exactly what he could get away with, and why.

Mathias looked away from him, back to Tom Gleason's yard, and his eyes seemed to go both distant and thoughtful, the sort of expression Rob was used to seeing on his father's face when he was sketching out an upcoming lecture or reading a book.

"He put the dog inside," Mathias said. "Because he knew I was mowing, he put the dog up. That would have been the way to burn his ass, though. His wife loves that dog. Probably more than she loves him."

Tom Gleason's wife had a tiny, fluffy white dog that emitted endless shrill barks that tunneled right into your brain. The dog was often outside, clipped to a lead on a tether, where it would run in hysterical circles, yipping, yipping, yipping.

"What are you talking about? What would burn his ass?" Rob asked, a little uneasy, because there was something about the kid's thoughtful expression that seemed beyond his years but not in a good way.

"I'm not talking to you. Get out of here before I tell your drunk grandpa that you're costing me money."

Hit him, Rob thought. *You're going to get your ass knocked around for something this weekend anyhow, you just don't know what yet, so at least earn it.*

But he didn't hit him. He told himself—and Mathias—that he was holding back because of the age difference, the size difference, that he wasn't going to stoop to picking fights with a little kid.

In reality, though, he did not like that kid's eyes.

That night, Tom Gleason put the little dog out again, and it ran and barked and ran and barked, and Ray Barrett cursed it and cursed Tom. The next morning, things were quiet, and then the afternoon and evening were quiet. It wasn't until the following day that Barbara Gleason showed up at the bar, teary-eyed, asking if anyone had seen little Pippa, who had somehow gotten off her tether and disappeared.

Rob didn't say anything then, but he couldn't get Mathias out of his mind.

That would have been the way to burn his ass, though. His wife loves that dog. Probably more than she loves him.

In the afternoon, Rob went over to the Gleasons' and asked if they had a photograph of the dog.

"I thought I could put up some flyers," he said.

Barbara Gleason thanked him and gave him a photo, and he walked up to the post office, which was the only place he knew in Port Hope with a copy machine, and paid for fifty copies. He put them up around the village, stapling them to telephone poles and trees, and he saved five. Those he took to the Burke house.

Mathias came outside when he saw him. Rob was stapling one of the posters right to their mailbox. Mathias walked up and studied it and didn't say anything. His expression was flat, his eyes empty.

"Did you take their dog?" Rob asked.

"Of course not."

"I think you did."

"That's crazy," Mathias said, but there was a little light in his eyes, almost the expression of someone who was telling a joke and hadn't gotten to the punch line. "I love those people. They love me. I do a good job for them, and they pay me well. Why would I do anything to them? The only one he yelled at that day was you. If anybody did anything to that dog, I'd start by asking you. But I won't snitch on you. Keep looking. If you find it, you'll be a hero."

He went back inside then. Rob stood and stared after him and then he stapled another flyer to the front door and went home.

The Gleasons stayed in Port Hope all week, walking the streets and shouting the dog's name and asking the neighbors to call, please call, if they saw Pippa. But nobody called about Pippa. If anyone ever saw the dog again, Rob wasn't aware of it.

It was twenty years after that incident that Rob heard Mathias's name in connection with a crime again, but when he did, he was prepared to give Kimberly Crepeaux more credibility than most people would.

He had no doubt at all that Mathias was, as everyone said, ambitious. He wondered a great deal about the source of the ambition, though, and about the quiet darkness that seemed threaded through him.

While the divers searched the pond, Mathias had been under surveillance, and he was working on a house in Rockland when Barrett came for him.

"We making an arrest?" the deputy from the surveillance detail asked Barrett eagerly when Barrett came up to his car. He was a jacked-up young kid who looked like he lived in the weight room.

"Not yet," Barrett said.

"Nothing happening at the pond? I kept waiting, but I—"

"Put your window up, all right? You're parked too damn close to the house."

"He hasn't so much as looked outside."

"Let's not encourage it," Barrett said, and then he left the deputy and walked up the street.

Mathias was working on a house overlooking the harbor that was probably a hundred and fifty years old and had once been a grand, three-story Colonial but now had the bearing of a strong man plagued by chronic pain—standing tall, but not easily, and not for long. Barrett could see Mathias through the front window. He was installing scaffolding along one massive wall of cracked plaster, and the floors were covered with paint-stained drop cloths. He looked up when Barrett rapped his knuckles on the glass, and he showed neither concern nor anger, just held up one finger indicating he'd be a moment. He finished tightening a bolt, set the ratchet down, dusted his hands off on his jeans, and then walked calmly to the door.

"*Special* Agent Barrett," he said. "Always a nice surprise, man. Special surprise."

He was a few inches shorter than Barrett's six one and probably weighed twenty pounds less, but he had the whipcord strength that came with a life of labor. His father had been a bigger man, but most of his size had been beer weight.

"Sorry to interrupt you, Mathias," Barrett said, "but I've got a new question."

Mathias smiled broadly. "Always one more. You need to work on your memory, Special Agent. Seems like you're always forgetting questions."

There were two Mathias Burke personalities, and he could switch between them easily. He was bright, well-spoken, and charming. He was also hard and intimidating when he wished to be. There were guys who acted hard around police because they didn't want to seem scared, and then there were the rare guys who genuinely weren't scared. Mathias Burke's confidence wasn't a facade.

"Was Cass ever behind the wheel of your truck when you went to the pond?" Barrett asked.

There was no reason to ask this question other than to test the response. Mathias was by now well aware that Barrett was pursuing leads about him and the two women. He wouldn't have known about the confession yet, though, and Barrett badly wanted to see his reaction to the information about the pond.

Mathias didn't lose his smile. He leaned on the door frame, regarded Barrett with amusement, and then said, "Her head was. I do recall that. Behind the wheel, under the wheel, however you want to look at it. For maybe five, ten minutes? Hell, I'd been drinking, so probably fifteen. You know how that goes, man." He winked.

It had taken them a while to reach this place. When Barrett first interviewed him, Mathias presented himself as he did to the people he worked for—polite, quiet, thoughtful. Only later did he drop a portion of the mask, and then the dialogue shifted, that practiced politeness moving toward the profane and the crude. *This is what you want, right?* he'd asked. *This is the white-trash guy you're looking for?* He never got angry. The closer Barrett got, the more entertained Mathias seemed.

"So what's this latest theory?" he asked. "Cass driving the truck? That's brilliant. I mean, I know you're running out of ideas, but this one would seem to *help* me. You think I was covering for her? Sure. I run a business with fourteen employees taking care of a hundred houses, I'm making more money each year, having fewer free hours each year, climbing up while everybody else is falling back, but I'd put all that at risk for a dead crack whore. I'm, what, protecting her reputation? You nailed it. I didn't want anyone to think poorly of Saint Cass. Nice work."

"What about Kimberly?" Barrett asked. "Was she ever driving the truck?"

"Kimmy can't drive a stick," Mathias said.

Mathias enjoyed floating these balloons, and they were never mistakes. He would state a fact that he knew most detectives would jump on—*How do you know the truck was a stick if you supposedly were never in it?*—and then, depending on his mood, he'd pretend to have no recollection of why he'd just made the statement or he'd take you for a ride.

Barrett wasn't going along for the ride today, though. He just nodded at Mathias as if he'd shared something profound and then said, "We're going to have the bodies by tomorrow."

"I'm damn glad to hear it."

They stood in silence for a moment, assessing each other, before Barrett said, "Do you remember Tom Gleason?"

"Sure. Dentist from Boston. Total prick. Paid late and never tipped. Say, you been out to the Harpoon recently?"

"I haven't been near the place."

"That's a shame. It's not what it used to be, but I'd think you'd want to drop in for old times' sake. Pay your respects, that sort of thing."

"It's not a cemetery or a church, Mathias."

"No?" Mathias frowned and wobbled his head side to side as if he didn't entirely agree. "There aren't many people around here who miss your grandfather, but I do. I'd love to hear what he'd have to say about your work."

"I'm more interested in what the jury will have to say about it."

"He was a foolish man when he was drunk, but

77

he was sharp enough when he was sober." Mathias continued as if Barrett hadn't spoken. "He knew liars, at least. Even if he was three sheets to the wind, he'd have known better than to believe a story spun by Kimmy friggin' Crepeaux."

Barrett nodded and turned to leave. "Don't go far, Mathias. I'm going to need you soon."

"I haven't run on you yet, have I? Tell your boy up the road to put the damn windows back down. It's a hot day to watch someone from a closed-up car. I don't want the poor bastard dying of heatstroke and adding to my body count."

Barrett tried not to show his frustration that the surveillance car had been made. He walked down the porch steps without comment and headed toward the street. He'd made it across the yard and back to the sidewalk when Mathias Burke called out to him.

"Good luck, Barrett. Don't get your feet wet."

Barrett didn't give him the satisfaction of turning around, but the statement put a little hitch in his stride, and Mathias didn't miss that.

His low laughter chased Barrett down the street.

8

"People have been talking about these divers all damned day," Don Johansson said after hearing Barrett recap the encounter with Mathias Burke and that parting shot. "Word's all over town by now. He probably got a call or a text or found it on Facebook or something. It's no secret where we're looking."

"I know it's not," Barrett said. "But I know we're in the right place too."

"Yeah? Tell that to *them*."

Johansson waved an exasperated hand at the divers, who were cleaning their gear. It was nearing sunset. A television chopper had come and gone from Portland and most of the watchers across the way had given up. Two of the divers, exhausted, sat on the shore and swatted at mosquitoes and looked at Barrett with distaste. He didn't blame them. It had been a long, brutal day, and they had nothing to show for it.

"It doesn't fit Mathias," Johansson said. "The drugs alone, nobody believes. We've not interviewed a single soul who remembers him drugging or has even heard that he might."

"Kimberly is not lying to me."

"Not *this* time, you mean."

Barrett had to acknowledge that with a nod. She'd told a few stories before she got around to confessing.

"Well, did Kimmy have a new spot for us to try?" Johansson said. "A tree to climb, maybe?"

Barrett ignored the sarcasm and said, "Get Clyde over here, please."

Clyde Cohen was the warden in charge of the dive team, and he'd supervised search efforts for Jackie Pelletier and Ian Kelly since the day of their disappearance. This day, and this spot, was supposed to have been the culmination of a lot of exhausting and fruitless hours.

"What's up, Barrett?" Clyde asked. His face was streaked with sweat and dabs of dried blood where the mosquitoes had feasted. He had worked all day without complaint, and Barrett knew that he would work a thousand more the same way.

"I want to drain it," Barrett said.

For a long time, there was no sound but the relentless droning of the mosquitoes.

"Drain the pond?" Clyde said. His accent turned the last word to *pawned*. Or maybe his disbelief thickened the accent.

"Yes."

Clyde blinked at him. "All due respect, but if those bodies were in that water, we'd have found them by now. It's not deep enough or dark enough to hide them."

"Maybe we aren't looking for bodies," Barrett said. "I'm still hoping for them, but just because we haven't found them yet doesn't mean there's not evidence down there. I want to see the bottom of that cove. I want to see it dry."

"Why?"

"To give me an idea of how they could've been moved."

Don Johansson studied the sky. Clyde Cohen studied the ground.

"It's not that big a body of water," Barrett said. "That old dam is crying for duct tape to save it already. We can breach that easily, and it ought to drain fast. The cove will, certainly. Then we'll be able to see it clearly."

"We can't just breach the dam," Clyde said. "This state, dealing with waterfront property? You know how many regulations we'll have to clear? Jeezum Crow, that'll be a mess."

Jeezum Crow was high-bar swearing for Clyde Cohen.

"I'll help you clear them," Barrett said. "I'll get federal lawyers involved."

Clyde rubbed his eyes. "We'll need an environmental-impact survey before we can so much as carry a shovel down there, let alone drive a backhoe in."

"Then get one," Barrett said.

He felt a hand on his arm, looked down, and saw that Don Johansson was tugging him away from Clyde. Away from the water's edge. Barrett followed him, and when they were far enough up the hill not to be overheard, Johansson faced him squarely.

"I'm sorry, Barrett," he said. "Nobody wanted this to be true more than me. You know that. But it's not true. Kimmy fed you—fed *us*—another lie. Maybe you'll get her to the truth at some point. But this story is not worth chasing any further."

"She's not lying," Barrett said. "Those bodies were in here once. If they're gone now, Mathias moved them. If he moved them, he probably tore up the bottom to do it. Maybe he left something down there that'll help, something the divers can't see. One of the pipes, a scrap of the plastic. A piece of bone."

Johansson didn't speak.

"We're going to drain it," Barrett said. "And we'll find something. I'll stake my reputation on that, Don. I'll stake my career on it."

"I don't think you're going to have much choice on that," Johansson said softly.

9

Upon leaving the pond, Barrett, who only twenty-four hours earlier had met with the prosecutor and agreed that no arrests should be made until the bodies were located, met with her again and told her that it was time to make an arrest.

Colleen Davis, the prosecutor, who'd been dealing with as much public pressure as the police had for failing to close this case, said she'd support bringing charges—but they'd better get something out of that pond. Otherwise it was going to amount to a short-term hold.

Roxanne Donovan was less enthusiastic.

"Even a half-wit defense attorney will have a field day with that Crepeaux girl," she told him when they spoke on the phone. "You're just teeing up an acquittal unless you have physical evidence."

"I'm going to get it," he told her. "With your support, I am going to get it."

Roxanne was a smart, tough woman with a reputation for protecting her field agents in the face of public or political pressure—provided she believed in them.

"You really think there's something down there that divers can't find?"

"The bodies were in that pond," Barrett said, "and that means either they still are or somebody took them out. The cove is empty, but so much of the water around that place is more like a bog or marsh. There's also a current to it. There will be evidence down there. But I'll tell you what else will happen if we drain it—we'll break Mathias. When he gets his TV time in the Knox County jail, turns on the news, and sees the water level going down at that pond, he'll feel it. He will feel it then."

As he explained the reasoning behind his request to drain the pond, he could hear his own bold words to Johansson going from a possibility to reality. He *was* staking his career on this one.

"I don't know if I can make that happen," Roxanne told him. "And I definitely want another pass from the dive team before I even try. But this location better not be a complete miss, Barrett."

"Am I going to be fired if it is?" he asked, only half joking, and Roxanne's response met him in tone.

"The Bureau rarely fires agents," she said. "We just bury them."

Howard Pelletier had called Barrett nineteen times since noon. Barrett had ignored the calls, waiting for the divers to make what he believed was their inevitable find. When Howard called for the twentieth time, Barrett was en route to arrest Mathias and the search had been suspended due to darkness. This time, he answered, despite every desire not to.

"You're going to arrest him?" Howard asked. "That's what Colleen said."

"Yes."

"You can do that even without finding anything?"

"The confession justifies the arrest warrant. The evidence we are going to find will do the rest."

"You still believe Kimmy's story?"

"The confession is a critical step, and I wish the evidence had confirmed it immediately, but now the prosecutor can—"

"That's not what I'm asking," Howard said. "Not about next steps or the law or anything else. I'm just asking what *you believe*."

"I think that putting pressure on him is a help. I think we—"

"Do you think he killed my daughter?" Howard screamed. The agony dragged the last word into a terrible howl: *daw-tah!*

"Yes," Barrett said. "Yes, I think he killed Jackie, and I will not rest until I prove it."

"But if they're not finding anything, then Kimmy lied. She *had* to be lying."

"She wasn't lying," Barrett said, and he realized how badly he was slipping here, defending an absence of evidence. This was precisely the sort of poor detective work he'd spent a decade studying.

"What I mean is, I think she told at least some of the truth," he said, a weak qualifier.

"Mathias knows what happened," Howard said, and this was a marked change from yesterday's resistance. Barrett had expected he might rejoice at the news that the pond was empty because it would keep his desperate hope alive. Instead, he'd accepted the validity of Kimberly's story.

Because he trusted you. Because you told him you believed in her, and he believed in you. So it better be true, damn it.

"You get him charged with it," Howard Pelletier said, "and you get his coward's back up against the wall, and you'll break the son of a bitch. I know you will."

"Yes," Barrett said. "Yes, I will."

They arrested Mathias Burke at nine p.m. Don Johansson made the arrest, and Barrett watched from the yard. There was a camera crew on the street behind a hastily erected barrier. Mathias was soft-spoken, polite, cordial. Grim-faced but not scared. A TV reporter from Portland shouted a question at him as they crossed the yard toward Johansson's cruiser.

"Mathias! Any comment?"

Johansson kept walking him forward, but Mathias turned and looked into the harsh glare of the lights without seeming bothered by them, not even squinting as they lit his face up. *Verdict lights,* one of Barrett's old professors had called them.

"I'm very sorry the Pelletier and Kelly families have to go through this," Mathias said. "They deserve better."

The TV reporter shouted another question, but Mathias just lowered his head and walked on to the cruiser. Johansson opened the door, put his hand on the back of Mathias's head to guide him into the backseat, then closed the door. He seemed more aware of the cameras than Mathias had been, or more concerned about them, at least. He kept his head down and walked around the cruiser in a hurry, and watching him, Barrett thought, *He doesn't believe we've got the right guy.*

Mathias refused to answer any questions about Kimberly Crepeaux's confession, and he refused to take a polygraph. In a steady, calm voice, he repeatedly invoked his right to counsel.

"You'll have counsel," Barrett said. "I'm curious

about one thing, though—why haven't you said 'I am not guilty' or 'I didn't do it'? Not one time have you said 'I did not do it.'"

"I'd like a lawyer now," Mathias said.

"I'd like an answer. Why don't you look me in the eye and say 'I didn't do it'?"

Mathias looked him in the eye and said, "Because the evidence will do that for me. Kimmy friggin' Crepeaux, Barrett. You believed *her*?" He shook his head. "Good luck, man. I'm not worried. You should be."

That was the end of Mathias's dialogue with police. He met with an attorney but offered no statement. To the public, there was only radio silence from the accused. Kimberly Crepeaux did issue a statement: she told the world that she stood by her confession, pledged her willingness to testify against Mathias Burke, and apologized to the families for her role in the killings.

Though very few people would know it, Barrett was now in a familiar position—he was in Port Hope, Maine, with a firm sense of the truth and no evidence to back it up. The only difference was that this time, his own family wasn't involved.

10

Rob Barrett was eight years old when he found his mother dead in the family home.

He got off the school bus and walked through the front door, surprised that his mother wasn't already holding it open. His grandfather had visited for the weekend but had left that morning, and Rob was eager for the restored peace that came with his grandfather's departure. Ray Barrett carried tension through the door with each visit.

The house was silent, and his mother did not answer his calls. He stood at the threshold uneasily and soon became aware of a single sound. A slow, steady drip. The plink of water on stone.

He crossed through the kitchen and went to the door that led to the cellar stairs, and there the sound of the drip was louder. He opened the door and saw his mother, her feet angled up toward him, her head pointing toward the cracked limestone floor, a slow-dripping leak from a pipe above adding water to the pool of blood below her skull.

The police made it to the house before Rob's father

did, and the initial assessment would also be the official one: a tragic accident.

The three floors of the home that stood aboveground were in immaculate condition, carefully restored, but that cellar hadn't been altered since 1883 and still had rough-hewn steps, sharp edges, and dim lighting.

And the leaking pipe, of course. That had been the problem. Or the *contributing factor,* as the final report labeled it, that made sense of the story. When water pooled on dark stone, trouble followed. Everyone understood that.

Except for one person, a lieutenant with the university police who was bothered by that leaking pipe.

When everyone else had gone, he came back. He wanted more pictures of the cellar, wanted more measurements, wanted to put bright lights on that pipe. Wanted to ask a few more questions. Barrett's shell-shocked father welcomed him, made him coffee, and spoke with him freely. That happened twice before Barrett's grandfather got wind of it.

Then came the storm.

He drove the three hours down from Port Hope rather than pick up the phone, and Rob hid upstairs and listened as his grandfather raged at his father. *Don't you know what is happening? That son of a bitch thinks you did it! That limp-dicked cop-wannabe who has probably never needed to draw his sidearm in his whole career got tired of worrying about drunk kids with fake IDs, and now he wants to solve a crime like a real cop. How do you not see that! How am I the only one who can see things in this fucking family!*

And in response, Barrett's father's voice would float, muted and mellow, dismissing the concern. There was nothing to be worried about, was there? Unless there *had* been a crime, unless someone *was* guilty, what on earth was there to be worried about?

I don't understand your brain, Barrett's grandfather would say over and over. *How in the hell did I raise a kid who can't think better than you? And you get* paid *just to think!*

Barrett's grandfather took to staying at the house, telling neighbors and friends that he was there for his grandson and wouldn't go until the boy was doing better. He didn't have much interaction with his grandson, though. During those days, he mostly sat alone, drinking and waiting.

The next time the lieutenant dropped by, Barrett's grandfather was there to greet him. He didn't shout at him. His voice started out low, and when it rose, it was more in timbre than volume, a resonance that boomed out of his broad chest. To this day, it was a voice that Rob Barrett wished he could match, a soft tone but one that clearly said, *You had best step out of my way.* And people did.

The lieutenant had too. Eventually. It had taken a trip by Rob's grandfather to the university police headquarters, an attorney in tow. Rob and his father stayed home and watched cartoons and played checkers for hours, game after game. Rob would always remember that day. His father had smiled and laughed but said very little. When he was convinced Rob was spellbound by the television, he'd gone into the kitchen to clean up the remnants of Ray's latest visit, not realizing Rob was watching him. He counted the beer cans under his breath as he gathered and bagged them, counted every single can, and then he had gone to the cellar door, opened it, and stared down the old limestone steps for a long time. He didn't turn on the light, just stared into the darkness, and then he closed the door and took the beer cans outside and put them in the recycling bin. The recycling bin was outside now; it had previously been in the cellar.

Then he went down into the cellar. He closed the door, and after a few minutes of silence, Rob got up and opened it cautiously. His father was standing above the old workbench not far from the foot of the stairs, a workbench that he forbade his son to go near—everything there was old and rusted. Tetanus Central, Rob's mother had called it.

His father was turning a tool over in his hands, studying it as if he weren't entirely sure of its purpose. The tool had a bright red handle and looked like a hybrid of a wrench and a vise. Rob was about to call out and ask about the tool when his father shifted, and his face moved more directly into the light of the single bare bulb at the base of the stairs. His expression was entirely unfamiliar to his son— a mask of deep anger, of hate.

Rob closed the door softly. Ten minutes later, his father came upstairs. He wore his standard semi-distant smile and said in a low, easy voice, "One more game?"

They were still playing checkers when Ray Barrett returned, took his son into the kitchen, and announced that his meeting with the university police chief had been successful and there would be no more harassment, no more bullshit. He boasted of his remarkable use of cunning and threats, and he didn't mention the attorney, as if the man had come along just to listen—or maybe to study.

Glenn Barrett didn't say a word during this tale. He just sat and watched his father as if seeing him for the first time. When Ray was finally done revisiting his triumph, he came out to the living room to say good-bye to little Robby. He'd be back in a day or two, he said, and they'd throw the football around.

It was eight months before they saw him again.

After that it had been just father and son or

grandfather and grandson; the three of them were never together again. Rob was passed back and forth in the summers like a baton in a relay.

Rob never asked his father anything about the cellar. A few days after his grandfather left, he'd gone in search of the strange tool with the red handle, but he couldn't find it. They moved three months later, to a newer home with none of what his mother had called the *special charm* of the restored Colonial but with bright lights and no basement.

Rob had intended to ask his father about that day, about the way he'd counted the beer cans and studied the strange tool, which Rob later learned was a pipe cutter. He never got around to it. There would always be a better moment than the present one, it seemed.

The last time he talked to his father was the morning after his twenty-first birthday. Rob was deeply hungover; his father spoke quietly and briefly into the phone, gave his trademark low laugh, promised a card with some cash was in the mail, and told him to buy stock in Excedrin.

The card arrived the next day. Barrett called his father but missed him and then forgot to call back in the days that followed.

He was playing pickup basketball outside his apartment when his grandfather showed up to tell him about the heart attack. It was one of the first warm weekends of spring, and Glenn Barrett had embarked on cleaning out a shed, a task that had been on his to-do list for years. The next-door neighbor had found him lying there among the old card tables and lawn chairs and toys as if he'd been preparing for a yard sale and decided to put himself out with the rest of the items.

Behind him, the once-filthy plywood floor of the shed had been vacuumed, swept, and mopped; the boards were still drying, and the smell of Murphy Oil Soap was in the air. He'd been trying to clean up everything right until the end.

Barrett probably thought about that symbolism more than he should have.

He was a junior that year, double-majoring in psychology and history. He was planning to apply to law school but was also enrolled in ROTC. Always and in everything, he was split between the competing forces of Ray and Glenn Barrett. The slim potential for combat that came with ROTC was just enough to silence his grandfather; the idea of law school keeping him surrounded by open books was just enough to make his father smile.

He never told either of them that the reason he'd chosen psychology was that it had been his mother's major.

Just before Barrett's senior year, the university started a new cadet program for its own police department, and Barrett joined immediately. It required additional criminal justice courses that would delay his graduation, but it also mandated hours around men with guns, so Barrett's grandfather made grudging peace with the news. It wasn't until later that Ray found out that the program was run by the lieutenant who'd visited the family's home in the days after the tragedy and taken photographs of the pipe in the cellar. His name was Ed Medlock, and Barrett made it a point to seek him out as a mentor.

Ed Medlock's theory, when Barrett finally got him to share it, was that Ray's temper had gotten away from him, as it had often been known to, and he'd swung at his own daughter-in-law. When Ray saw the results, he broke the pipe above the stairs. They were rough stone steps, the area was poorly lit, and if there was a leaking pipe, well, it would be hard *not* to take a nasty fall.

Ed Medlock was convinced that the pipe break wasn't from natural deterioration. There were fresh, bright nicks and scrapes on the copper right where it had supposedly ruptured. He gave Ray Barrett credit, though—that damage was hidden by plumber's tape, and the tape was coated with grease, so to the first officers on the scene, it looked like an old repair that had finally failed. Medlock was the one who'd peeled the tape back to reveal what was beneath.

His advice to Rob was to let it go. There was no prosecutor who would touch it at this point, he said. Not without a confession.

It was this last phrase that had redirected Rob's career, redirected his entire life. He didn't rush the issue. He studied it. Only when he felt confident in the art of the interview, only when he believed he understood how to apply the psychology of leverage and logic, did he finally return to Port Hope to confront his grandfather.

Ray Barrett listened, and then he began to cry. Rob had never seen him cry, had not even imagined that it was possible. Ray sat in the old armchair in his apartment above the bar and tears ran down his cheeks, and Rob sat across from him and watched him and thought, *Good, you son of a bitch.*

Then Ray lit one of his unfiltered Camels and embarked on another tale.

He told Rob that his father had called him in a panic that day, begging for Ray's help, and that by the time Ray arrived, Rob's mother was already dead. His father admitted hitting her. She'd gone down hard and cracked her head on the steps. They'd been arguing, Ray explained, about an affair Glenn had had with a department secretary.

"He called me to fix it for him, Robby," Ray said. "And I did. The pipe, the tape, the grease stains on the tape. Your cop buddy is correct about that. What he doesn't know is who did the killing. Now, what I did, was it right? No. But I was protecting my son. And my grandson."

By then, the tears were gone and Ray was getting a little bit of his old anger back.

"Remember who your old man called when there was trouble," Ray said. "That's all I ever wanted for you. For you to be the type of man who people call when there's trouble."

Rob got to his feet and called his grandfather a lying son of a bitch, promised that the police would be coming for him soon, and left.

The police had never come for Ray. Rob didn't call them. There was no evidence to challenge his grandfather's version of events. He thought he'd get him eventually, thought at some point, the old man would crack and tell the truth.

Then on an early December morning, Rob's phone rang and the police told him that his grandfather had been found in his car in the woods in central Maine. He'd been driving at night through a snowstorm when he'd apparently lost the road and flipped into the trees. It was hours before anyone saw the wreck, and by then he was dead of internal bleeding and exposure. There was a half-empty flask of bourbon in his jacket pocket and two beers left from a six-pack.

No one seemed to know why he'd set out from

Port Hope in the middle of the night in a snow-storm. Nobody knew where he'd been going, although a few people observed that he'd been driving in the direction of Hammel College in southern Maine, where his grandson was enrolled.

Whatever he'd been prepared to tell his grandson had died with him.

11

Barrett's official place of residence for the duration of the investigation had been a hotel room in Port Hope, but he hadn't spent many nights there, and he didn't go there after leaving the jail following the arrest of Mathias Burke. Instead, he headed north, to Camden.

Camden was a uniquely beautiful town even by Maine Midcoast standards, with an idyllic harbor offset by forested mountains that crowded the waterfront, sloping streets lined with brick buildings, and sidewalks chasing the Megunticook River through a series of stepped-down waterfalls that had once powered mills and, thus, the town.

Barrett had no interest in Camden's beauty tonight, though. He passed by the harbor and parked in front of the library that stood as a central feature of the town, a carefully preserved and expanded structure built on land donated by the family of a long-ago publishing mogul. He didn't get out of the car, just stared out at a sailboat that was moored in the bay and searched for lights on board.

The boat was dark, so he pulled away from the harbor and drove back through the town, past the old paper mill, and into the nearby hills. If Liz Street was not working on her boat, then she'd be at home.

Liz had been fifteen when he'd met her nearly two decades earlier, an object of desire to most of the local boys. Rob had only two advantages, but they were critical: he was from away, someone different in a small town, and he had a driver's license. Barrett had never wanted to linger near his grandfather's town in Maine before Liz, let alone return to it when his summer sentence as a ward in his grandfather's custody was done, but falling in love had the remarkable effect of making the unbearable seem little more than a trifling nuisance.

He'd come back to Maine for college, joining Liz at Hammel College, the small liberal arts school where Barrett's father had once taught.

It was Maine that brought them together, and Maine that broke them. As a teenager, he'd understood her love of the place but also believed her devotion to it wouldn't last. Sure, she'd said she'd never live anywhere else, just stay in Maine except for long sailing cruises, but every sixteen-year-old was certain of things like that—*I will live here, work there, become this, become that.* Then you met reality.

In this regard, he'd underestimated Liz Street and bruised both their hearts. To say he'd broken her heart would have been arrogant—she'd been dating someone else within months of their separation and was married and then divorced before he reached Quantico. He'd had a brief engagement that ended when his first field office was announced; Little Rock, Arkansas, did not fit into his fiancée's vision of the future. He'd gone on alone, and when he sought placement with the Boston division, he'd promised himself it had nothing to do with it being a three-hour drive from Liz Street.

He'd lasted two weeks before taking his first road trip north.

She was living in Camden again, earning her money as a reporter for the small local newspaper and spending most of it on the rehabilitation of an ancient but beautiful wooden sailboat. The life plans she'd offered to her sixteen-year-old boyfriend hadn't been jokes.

Eighteen years later, when the boyfriend returned, she'd greeted him cautiously. She hadn't been divorced for long, and she seemed wary of starting any relationship, let alone rekindling an old one. Her ex-husband had left a beautifully remodeled but never opened restaurant in the heart of downtown Camden—Liz had to pass it daily—and gone to Florida, where his next waterfront vision of craft cocktails and tapas was being built with the assistance of a much wealthier woman.

She and Rob caught up awkwardly and laughed easily at old memories, as people with shared pasts tend to do. After that first visit, she'd promised to go down to Boston sometime but hadn't. He'd gone back to Camden after she'd failed to come south, claiming he wanted to do some hiking. Instead, he'd ended up at the waterfront, looking at her new boat. She showed him the charts of her intended course for a six-month cruise, the various ports of call, everything settled about the voyage except the date of departure. He helped her sand layers of brine off the decking, and then the sun went down behind Mount Battie and an impossibly large, crimson-tinted moon rose over the bay, and they'd opened a bottle of wine and that night they'd made love for the first time in nearly a decade.

One last time for old times' sake, they'd said the next morning when they were drinking coffee instead of wine and the moonlit sex was already a memory; their bodies moving together with the gentle pitch and roll of the sailboat seemed like something from another lifetime instead of a few hours earlier. It had been a reunion, not a rekindling. They agreed that was the right approach, the *only* approach.

But, as often happened with good, right, and only approaches, they hadn't held that course long, and they'd been in the awkward dance of dating without discussing the future for four months now.

It was through Liz that he'd learned of the disappearances of Jackie Pelletier and Ian Kelly, and it was through Liz that he'd learned of rumors that a local girl currently in jail on other charges was the subject of interrogations that hadn't led anywhere. All of this was interesting, but more interesting was the source of the rumors: a bar in Port Hope called the Harpoon.

I have some familiarity with the place, he'd told Roxanne Donovan.

He was bone-weary and reeling from the day when he arrived at Liz's small house in the Megunticook River valley, the winding drive unfurling in front of him like a silver ribbon in the moonlight.

Liz was sitting on the porch.

"Long day," she said.

"Yeah."

She searched his face in the dark. "Do you have enough to keep him in jail?"

"I have a confession."

"From Kimmy. Not from Mathias."

He ran a hand over his face and leaned against the railing. A fresh, cool breeze was blowing up out of the bay, carrying the smell of the sea. Overhead, the skies were as clear as they'd been all day, but the harsh sun was gone, and that was comforting. People understood when it took you a long time to find something in the dark.

"I think he will break," Barrett said. "I think we'll find something in that pond, and between that and a few nights in jail staring at a double-murder charge, he will begin to talk. Maybe he'll blame Kimberly or Cass. He can come up with any number of stories."

"But so far he hasn't offered one."

"No. He hasn't offered anything. Just asked for a lawyer."

"People around here aren't buying Kimmy's story," she said. "Not the drugs, or the level of rage, or even him being with those two girls. They say it doesn't fit him, it's not his character."

He leaned back and looked at the stars. The night sky was so clear that you could make out the painter's brush smears of light of the Milky Way. He wondered what it looked like out on Little Spruce Island.

"He told me he'd like to hear what my grandfather would have said about it."

Liz made a barely perceptible shift in the darkness. "You can't let yourself go there, Rob. Can't conflate this thing and that one."

"I'm not. My grandfather has nothing to do with my work."

But she knew better than that, of course. She was one of the very few people who understood just how intertwined the man and the job were.

"How much credibility would you give Kimberly Crepeaux?" he asked.

She didn't answer right away, and he liked that, because it meant she was actually giving it some thought. He didn't like her answer much, though.

"Slim to none."

"That's the community consensus."

"She's a storyteller," Liz said. "A liar, to be less polite."

He nodded, still looking at the sky, and then stepped away from the railing and moved toward the door, withdrawing his keys from his pocket.

"You're right about that," he said. "But you know what? Even liars tell the truth sometimes."

"Sure," she said. "Twice a day, even broken clocks are right. But did you catch Kimmy at the right time, Rob?"

"Yes," he said.

She didn't look at him when she nodded.

"Let's go inside," she said.

He followed her. She'd already eaten dinner, but there was a clean plate and empty wineglass on the island, as if she'd expected him. The unspoken invitation that seemed to define her approach to their renewed relationship: *Pull up a chair, if you'd like.* She looked beautiful in the dim light, blond hair and bright blue eyes shining, her athlete's grace and veteran's confidence contrasting with a face that seemed impossibly close to that of the girl he'd met all those years ago.

She poured some cabernet in his glass, and he tried not to focus on the label on the bottle: THE PRISONER. He'd always liked the wine, but tonight he wished she'd picked anything else. "Want to tell me about it?" she asked.

"I want to," he said, and it was true. He wanted to tell her about how Amy Kelly had thanked him and explain the way Howard Pelletier had made that gesture with his hand when he described the ascending staircase that awaited his daughter's return and tell her how Kimberly's throat had pulsed just before she threw up. He couldn't, though, because she was a reporter.

"But you can't," she said. "We check our jobs at the door. I'll drop it."

The problem in their relationship wasn't that Liz didn't understand that situation but that she understood it too well.

She was a local newspaper's dream reporter because of her talent and work ethic and also because she seemed to know everyone along the waterfront in every little town on the Maine Midcoast. And when you knew the waterfront, you knew the towns. From itinerant fishermen to multimillionaire yachtsmen, from bartenders to bankers, all the people interacted with the waterfront in their own ways, and everyone seemed to talk to her. That was because she was one of them, a part of this place, her striking looks offset by hands that were almost always scraped or bruised from the daily work on the boat. Her father was remembered fondly in the area, and his death—he had been lost at sea—was memorialized in tattooed script that traced her collarbone and was visible along her neck when she had her hair up.

"It's fine," he said, but suddenly he hated himself for coming here tonight. He shouldn't be sipping wine with a lover when Howard was on Little Spruce Island alone and Amy and George Kelly were grieving in Virginia. Did he not owe it to those people to share some of their pain or, at the very least, hold his focus on it?

"Maybe I should stay at my hotel room tonight," he said.

"Rob, relax. I'm not going to interrogate you."

He shook his head. "It's not that, Liz. It's just…" He set the wineglass down. "I'm sorry. I've got to go."

He almost made it to the door before she caught him. Her hand gripped his biceps with the soft strength that made him immediately unsteady, wanting her now as badly as he wanted to keep his focus on the day behind and the day ahead. As he stood with his hand on the doorknob, she wrapped her arms around his chest and spoke into his ear, her breath warm, voice low.

"Stay. I'll leave you alone, and I won't ask questions. Tonight."

Tonight. That was their mantra. It had been his suggestion the first time, a hedge against pragmatic thinking, a twenty-four-hour commitment, that was all, no risk there. Of course, you could string months and years out of *tonight*. You didn't ever need to look at the horizon unless you wanted to.

"I told three people the way their children died," he said without turning, "and I haven't been able to prove it. Now I'm supposed to just have a drink, eat dinner, and wait to see what happens next?"

She released her grasp and slid around him so that they were standing chest to chest, her upturned face studying his.

"The evidence will come," she said.

He nodded silently.

He didn't sleep long. Twenty minutes, maybe thirty, and then he was wide-awake in the darkness, Liz warm against him, her breathing deep and steady, each exhalation pressing her breast against his arm and each inhalation drawing it back.

I remember that when I looked up at where his head was, the plastic sucked in and moved out and then sucked in again, and I realized he was breathing. Trying to breathe, at least.

He slid out of the bed and dressed in the moonlight.

Liz stirred but didn't wake. He watched her sleep for a few moments, wondering how homicide detectives handled nights like these over and over again. How did they balance their own lives, their own human needs, against the burden of caring properly for the victims and those left behind?

Closing this case was the real-world success Roxanne Donovan had promised. This would move Rob Barrett, the law school graduate with the criminal justice PhD and the master's in psychology, out of the classroom and into an investigator's reality. A double murder solved. He'd wanted it, hungered for it.

But what in the hell did you do while you waited for the sun to rise?

There had been no class on that, no dissertation to read. In the absence of guidance or experience, he walked down the stairs alone in the midnight quiet, opened a beer, and sat down to review a case file he already knew by heart.

12

On the morning of their deaths, Jackie Pelletier and Ian Kelly had known they were bound for a graveyard.

They'd intended to meet at what was known locally as the Orchard Cemetery because they viewed it as a romantic spot. Jackie had been painting the old graveyard for years, and her favorite time was sunrise. The manager of the restaurant where she tended bar had put one of her landscapes on display, and that painting had transfixed Ian Kelly on a June evening when he stopped by for a haddock sandwich and a beer, taking a break from his summer internship with an environmental law center. The manager had seen him admiring the painting and introduced him to the petite young woman with uncommonly dark eyes who'd done the work.

Things had gone fast from there, the way they were supposed to with summer flings. With Ian due back in Virginia by September, and Jackie having no intention of leaving her beloved island, a fling was what it was supposed to be.

However, they both realized early on that there might be more than a surface spark to the relationship, and Ian, at least, had been scared by the idea.

I told my mother about this girl, he'd written in an e-mail to a friend back in Charlottesville. I've never talked to my mother about a girl, ever, and yet within a week of meeting Jackie, I'm calling internationally to talk to my mother about her? Tell me something wise about how summer love never lasts, would you?

Rereading that on the night after he'd led the search team out to find their bodies, Barrett felt the eerie prickle that could come so easily when you looked at the last words of the dead. The living had a strange desire to believe the dead had sensed trouble in the air before it landed on them. He thought this was an almost primal response, a desperate hope that there was such a thing as precognition and that tragedy could be averted if you paid enough attention. With Ian and Jackie, though, you didn't need to cherry-pick anything to build the tragedy— their relationship had begun with the image of a grave.

E-mails, text messages, and witness interviews formed the timeline of Jackie and Ian's story, and the records always left Barrett with a feeling of voyeurism, because the two had written intimately to—and about—each other almost from the start.

On June 15, Jackie to a friend who'd gone to college in Florida:

112

Two weeks with him and I am ready to say the unthinkable—I've already thought about leaving the island for him. Crazy, and I promise I won't do it . . . but doesn't it suggest something good that I could even let that cross my mind? Leaving this place seems unbearable, but having him leave without me might actually be worse. I want both. I want everything, all the time, is that so selfish? Ha-ha-ha.

On June 19, Ian to his roommate:

Sitting on the deck out here, watching the ocean and thinking about her and I realize that the damn house sits empty most of the year anyhow, and you can finish law school anytime, what the hell harm would a year off be? I can't get the idea out of my mind. And I can't tell her that I'm thinking about it. Good ways to ruin things: say I love you on a first date . . . or propose dropping out of law school for her in the first month. Come up to Maine and talk some sense into me. We'll party and catch fish, I promise.

On July 12, Jackie to the friend in Florida:

Five Fridays, five walks at sunrise. Who does that? I mean, seriously, outside of a Nicholas Sparks book, what guy *does* that?

On July 12, Ian to his roommate:

Head . . . over . . . heels. I'm doomed.

By August, they'd made plans. Ian would go back to Virginia and complete the first semester of his second year of law school, Jackie would come down for prolonged stretches in October and November, and by December, Ian would be northbound again, transferring to the University of Maine.

His roommate objected strongly to this plan, and Ian responded with polite firmness.

I know you're right. UVA law is a perennial top 10, and Maine is a perennial...top 200. Thanks for sending me those stats! Ha. I could make an argument that I'm going into environmental law, and Maine is more appealing in that arena than you'd think. I could make an argument that law school rankings are mostly bullshit. I could say a lot of things, but I honestly can't muster the energy to even be concerned about any of that. I'm happier here than I ever was in Charlottesville, happier in one day with Jackie than I was in two years with Sarah, and I don't think statistics and rankings and analytics should govern the choice. Life is short, love is rare, and time is easy to waste.

He'd written that sentence exactly three weeks before his death.

Life is short, love is rare, and time is easy to waste.

Barrett read that and Ian's words began to blur with Kimberly Crepeaux's.

I looked up at where his head was, the plastic sucked in and moved out and then sucked in again, and I realized he was breathing. Trying to breathe, at least.

He looked at the clock: three a.m.

At three a.m. on September 10, Ian Kelly would have been in his car, probably just crossing over the state line, paying the toll down at York. He'd left at five p.m. intending to drive straight through the night so he could meet Jackie Pelletier at her beloved Orchard Cemetery at sunrise. When police searched his car, they found a speeding ticket from a Massachusetts state trooper. At 2:37 a.m., Ian had been doing eighty-four in a seventy, hustling north.

He'd no doubt dropped his speed after the ticket, and as a result, he'd been a little late. The sun was already above the water, and Jackie already walking among the tombstones.

If Ian had laid eyes on her that morning, she was already dead, according to Kimberly Crepeaux's depiction of events. The place where Jackie had been struck was below a rise, meaning that Ian couldn't have seen her until he'd crested the hill.

He was up above us a little bit. Standing there, staring. Jackie's body was between us. It was like a standoff.

If he'd regained consciousness in the truck, he might have seen her again. He would have seen her through milky plastic and a sheen of blood as the truck that carried them rattled over the rural roads. If he was coherent enough to register these things, then his final look at his rare love would have come as three strangers slid her body out of the truck and carried it toward a lonely pond where the water was dark.

I never even saw him get the knife out. I just saw him lean over and stab him through the plastic, right where his heart had to be.

Life was short, love was rare, and time was easy to waste.

Barrett closed the old e-mails, poured his beer into the sink, and returned to the chair, this time carrying the digital recorder on which he'd stored the audio file of Kimberly's confession and every other interview.

In the days when he'd thought he might remain in academia, his focus had been on interview and interrogation techniques—and particularly on false confessions. He'd come in at a perfect moment, as new technologies in the field and in the courtroom were pressuring law enforcement agencies to change their old approaches. Groups like the Innocence Project were discovering wrongful convictions with appalling ease, and while DNA evidence was often the critical element in winning those cases, false confessions made regular, concerning appearances in explaining how the innocent had ended up behind bars in the first place. Of the first two hundred and fifty people the Innocence Project exonerated through DNA evidence, an astonishing 16 percent had at some point confessed to crimes they hadn't committed.

When you studied the way detectives were trained, that number became a little less stunning. For decades, law enforcement had taught techniques that were better described as intimidation than interrogation and that focused on nonverbal communication during suspect interviews. Rookie officers and veteran detectives alike were sent to seminars that encouraged them to watch confessions with the sound off in order to hone their ability to identify a lie without hearing the words.

Barrett's thesis had been devoted to the risks of the Reid technique, one of the commonly taught interrogation methods, and then journal articles had followed, and he was asked to testify as an expert witness in a few trials. His testimony went over well with the jury because the gap between what the public expected and what the police delivered was, in many cases, shocking. In an era of iPhones and cloud computing, the nation's foremost investigative bodies had long refused to require recording of interviews, asking the courts to trust handwritten notes and memories from field agents. As more juries struggled with this and more false confessions made headlines and evening-news features, prosecutors and judges begged for a change. In 2014, the Department of Justice finally issued a mandate to record interviews, but even then there was some bitter resistance to it.

Barrett's argument was that the way a story took shape was of imperative importance, and the precise words mattered. Pay more attention to what the suspect said and worry less about whether he picked lint off his shirt or looked up and to the left while he talked. His crusade was academic, and he'd never expected his work to come to the attention of the FBI, but one day he got a call from an agent named Roxanne Donovan. She was on an internal review committee, and she wanted to discuss some of his thoughts. They'd had a good, if at times confrontational, talk, and when she told him that he might benefit from spending more time with the men and women who actually sought confessions, she'd hardly been encouraging him to apply to the FBI Academy.

The conversation had planted a seed, though. Or nurtured one. Barrett's history of curiosity about police work went back a long way and to more personal places.

Now he sat with his feet up and his eyes closed and played Kimberly Crepeaux's confession back once more, like a man relaxing to a favorite song.

Be the truth, he thought as Kimberly's distinct accent took him on the bloody ride. *Please be the truth.*

13

He was asleep in the chair when the call came in. He woke at the first ring but couldn't find the phone before it went to voice mail. He needn't have worried about that—the second call came immediately.

It was Johansson.

Barrett answered groggily, vaguely aware that Liz was awake and standing on the stairs, watching him.

"What is it, Don?"

"The bodies were found."

He couldn't have come more fully awake if he'd been injected with amphetamines. He pushed himself out of the chair and stood up.

"Who was still looking out there? Clyde?"

"Nobody was looking out at the pond."

"Then where—"

"Two hundred and twelve miles away," Johansson said. "Buried in the woods near the Allagash Wilderness, wrapped in garbage bags and stuffed in barrels."

It took Barrett a moment to find his voice. Finally he said, "And we're sure it's them?"

"Her rings and bracelets. His watch. No clothes. They're badly decomposed, and the animals have been at them, but they were both wearing synthetic clothes that day."

Barrett understood what he meant—synthetic fabrics took longer to decompose than soft human tissue did. If there were no traces of clothing, it meant they'd been stripped naked before they were buried. This was not part of the Kimberly Crepeaux story.

"What about evidence that can help us?" he asked. "Anything?"

"They pulled prints off the barrels," Johansson said. "One was a full handprint, I'm told. Seven fingers in all, clear and clean. Should get matches quickly with that quality. The autopsy is moving fast too. Everyone wants a positive ID on this in a hurry."

"He would have worn gloves," Barrett said.

"Who?"

"Mathias. If he went through the trouble of moving them, he would've had gloves on to do it." He heard Johansson's sharp inhalation but pushed past it. "The barrels are new to the story, but what about the plastic? Are they really garbage bags, or could it have been clear Visqueen?"

"I was told they were garbage bags," Johansson said, "but I'm not really worried about that."

"Well, you need to be. We're going to have to establish how they were moved from that pond. This is where we—"

"They were shot," Johansson said.

Barrett was silent. The room seemed to be growing larger and emptier, as if the walls were receding. Liz was still on the stairs, watching him. He walked to the door, slipped out into the cool night, and closed the door behind him so she couldn't hear him when he repeated the word.

"Shot?"

"Yes. Two different weapons. Each body had a shotgun wound to the front of the torso, and a small-caliber bullet wound, probably from a handgun, maybe a rifle, to the back of the head."

"We'll want the ME to try for an assessment on whether those were pre- or postmortem," Barrett said. "Whether they were the cause of death or mutilation of bodies in order to conceal the cause of death. We'll want to have them check Ian's bones for knife wounds. The skull for a fracture. The—"

"Barrett? Stop. Think. Here's what we have now: Naked bodies in barrels—not clothed bodies in plastic wrap with pipes—that were buried in the woods, not found at the bottom of a pond, several hours and several hundred miles from the pond they were supposed to be in. Multiple gunshot wounds. None of these elements were in Kimmy Crepeaux's confession. Not a one."

Barrett leaned on the deck railing. Somewhere through the trees, down along the river, a loon called. He usually loved the sound. Now the mournful tone seemed cruel.

"Who found them?" he asked.

"Warden Service. After somebody e-mailed the precise GPS coordinates to the tip line."

"*What?*"

"Want me to read it to you?"

"Yes," Barrett said, though part of him didn't want to hear it.

"Okay. It came from a Gmail account that seems to have just been set up, no history on it; the tech guys are working on tracing the IP as we speak. Anyhow, here's the message: 'None of this ever should have happened and it all got out of control fast. I do not want to go back to prison ever but I can't let you send innocent people to prison for me. You will find the bodies up in the Allagash. I will not tell you how it happened but it is all wrong, you are all wrong, and go find the bodies so you know you are wrong.' Then he gives the GPS coordinates. They were easy to find."

Barrett didn't speak right away, his mind stuck on the words Johansson had just read, playing them back and trying to imagine whose voice they came from. *I will not tell you how it happened but it is all wrong.*

"The e-mail address isn't going to lead to anyone," he said finally.

"Maybe not. But it led to the bodies. And it came in while Mathias was in custody."

Barrett didn't know what to say to that.

"Step back and tell me what you'd think of this if you were coming in from the outside today," Johansson said.

"It's a different investigation now."

"That's an understatement. And it will have different investigators as well. The discovery of the bodies moves the crime scene. We are on the sidelines now, at best. After we went all in on the Crepeaux story? Nobody's going to want us close. We're meeting with the new lead investigator in the morning."

"Who is he?" Barrett asked.

"*She* is Emily Broward. Good cop."

"Sheriff?"

"State. Major crimes, just like me." There was bitterness in his voice, but not blame. At least, Barrett didn't think so.

"I'm sorry," Barrett said, and he meant it.

"You shouldn't be. We shouldn't be. This is progress. Someone—maybe not us, but someone—is going to get to the truth now for those families. That's what matters."

"Yes," Barrett said, and he saw Howard Pelletier's smiling face then. *Ascending. Ayuh, that's just the word.*

Howard's daughter had been shot in the chest and in the back of the head, her body jammed in a barrel and dumped in the woods.

"Yes," Barrett said again. "That's what matters."

14

They didn't wait on Barrett to start the briefing. He drove like hell to make it on time but still found himself entering in the middle of the conversation, half the faces in the room familiar to him, half of them not. The woman at the head of the table looked at him as if he'd opened the wrong door by mistake.

"Agent Barrett," she said. "Thanks for coming. We'll try to catch you up."

Her words were more welcoming than her eyes. He took a seat between one of the unfamiliar state troopers and Johansson. A projector screen displayed a booking photo of a wild-eyed man with unruly hair, and the name below it was new to Barrett: Jeffrey Girard.

"Who's this?" he said.

"We got a match on the prints," Emily Broward said. "They belong to one Jeffrey Girard, thirty-six years old, originally of Rockland, now in Mechanic Falls."

"Does he mean anything to you, Don?" Barrett

asked Johansson. Johansson nodded, looking almost physically pained by the question.

"He's been arrested in the area, I know that."

"He's been arrested several times," Broward said. "Burglary, drug possession, and felon in possession of firearms are the highlights. Did his name ever come up in your investigation?"

"I don't think so, but a lot of names did."

Barrett stared at the photo of Girard. The speed at which it had all happened was disorienting, a Rip van Winkle sensation, like waking up to find the world had moved on without you.

"Don told me the fingerprints came off the barrels," he said.

"Correct."

"Considering the nature of the crime, that seems bizarre. He's packaging, transporting, and burying bodies but doesn't think to wear gloves?"

"The whole thing was done sloppily, rushed. Maybe he got spooked or maybe he wanted the barrels for transportation only and intended to leave the bodies exposed."

"Why would he have done that?"

"Because there's a low chance of bodies being stumbled across by humans in that part of the Allagash, and a high chance of animals getting at them. Exposure and the animal destruction eliminate a lot of what we can determine in specifics. Time of death, things like that."

"Cause of death?"

"Doesn't eliminate that. They were shot."

"Do we know if they were shot pre- or post-mortem, though?"

"I'm not a medical examiner," Broward said. "I won't pretend to know those answers yet. I'm sure we'll find out in due time. We have a forensic anthropologist working with the remains right now."

"Even transporting the bodies is a lot of work to go through without wearing gloves," Barrett said again, and he caught Johansson's warning look. But Barrett wasn't trying to press Broward. It seemed like a damn reasonable point.

"This fits our understanding of Jeffrey Girard pretty well, actually," she said.

"How so?"

"He's not smart, and he's nervous, jumpy. I spoke with a deputy who knows him and with his parole officer. Both of them said his IQ is extremely low and that he has difficulty processing complex situations. The PO told me that he tends to rely on television or movie narratives to give him context when he's confused, to help him in a world outside of his own."

"What's his world?"

Broward spread a state map out on the table and swept her hand over the northwestern portion, the part of Maine where there were no highways and not many towns. The deep pines of the north woods.

"This. He's an outdoorsman. Good with a gun and a fishing rod; bad with people. He claims he's never been outside of Maine, and yet he's an itinerant guy. His contacts are his family, basically. He'll bounce from mother to brother and cousin to cousin."

She tapped the map. "No sign of him recently at the trailer near Mechanic Falls that is his official address, according to the parole officer." She slid her finger north. "We're told the Girard family has a hunting camp outside of Jackman and that he'll be up there for long stretches when he's not working. There's no indication that he's holding down any kind of formal job, so Jackman is probably our best bet."

Her fingertip was resting on a speck near the Canadian border in the far western reaches of the state.

"A long drive from Port Hope," Barrett said.

"Yes, it is."

"That's strange, don't you think? We're supposed to believe that the guy was so careless and rushed that he didn't wear gloves when he dumped the bodies, but he had to cover, what, four or five hours just to get to the dump site?"

"I don't have all the answers yet, but let's remember that we're arresting a man based on physical evidence at the crime scene, not rumors."

There was a palpable shift in the room. The familiar faces turned away from Barrett, and the new ones turned toward him.

Emily Broward sensed the shift too, and seemed to regret causing it. Her tone softened and she said, "There is some interesting overlap with Crepeaux's confession, though."

"What's that?"

"There's one vehicle registered to Girard," she said. "It's a 1998 Dodge Dakota pickup, gray—similar to the one Crepeaux described. The license is Maine 727CRC."

Barrett was starting to feel punch-drunk, a fighter begging for the bell. The truck was right, but the suspect wasn't.

"Any distinguishing paint?"

"If there is, it's not noted on the registration. I'd like you and Don to check with the Girard cousin who owns a body shop outside of Biddeford. Maybe he'll know something about the truck."

"Who's the cousin?"

"Bobby Girard. It's not a very formal outfit. They do some towing and they buy and sell wrecked cars. Sporadic hours, cash clients, that sort of thing. I'd like you and Don to interview him and specifically ask about the truck."

"You said the smart money on Jeffrey Girard's location was on Jackman."

"Correct."

"Then I'd like to be part of that trip. Please."

There was an awkward, heavy silence. Emily Broward's gaze was steady and her voice clipped when she responded.

"With all due respect, I'd rather not conflate the situation out in Port Hope with the reality that we have here."

The door opened then and an older man in uniform stuck his head in and said, "Lieutenant? George Kelly is on the phone."

The desire Barrett had to walk out of the room ahead of Broward and take the call was so intense that he shifted in his chair. Johansson looked at him as Broward left the room, his jaw tight, and Barrett knew he was fighting the same feeling.

Broward was gone for perhaps ten minutes, and when she came back in, she had a tight smile and a fighter's eyes.

"Mr. Kelly just confirmed by check receipt that Jeffrey Girard was paid to pressure-wash his decks in July." She paused for a beat and then said, "That puts him at the property when both Ian and Jackie would have been there."

"Mathias Burke would have hired him, then," Barrett said. "Or found him. George relied on him for every detail of that house's care."

"We'll certainly keep that in mind. But the check

was written to Jeffrey Girard, and Jeffrey Girard's fingerprints are present at the crime scene."

There was an undercurrent to her tone that said she was running out of patience. Barrett stayed silent for the rest of the meeting. When it broke up, Emily Broward headed northwest with an arrest warrant in hand, and Barrett headed southeast to talk to the suspect's cousin.

"It's bullshit that they're sending us south," Barrett said to Johansson.

"Yeah."

"The idea that Girard worked on the Kelly property puts him in Burke's realm. If he moved those bodies, he'd likely have needed help. I don't think this discredits Kimberly's confession. Not yet."

Don didn't answer.

"Maybe the cousin will have something," Barrett said. "Want me to drive?"

"I'll just meet you there," Don said, and then he walked to his car without a look back, leaving Barrett alone in the parking lot.

15

He was on I-95, headed for Biddeford, when Johansson called.

"They got something from the autopsy," Johansson said.

"They've already done the autopsy?"

"This morning, I guess. Don't know how much help it will be, because the decomposition was advanced, but...they did get something." He cleared his throat. "I, uh, I thought you should hear it from me."

"What is it?"

"She was pregnant," Johansson said.

For a long time, there was no sound except for the tires of Barrett's Ford Explorer on the asphalt.

"Pregnant," he said finally, as if he were unfamiliar with the word.

"Yeah."

"How...it couldn't have been far along."

"Two months, tops," Johansson said. "The ME found a, um...the start of a pelvic bone. I guess that's the first one to form. Who knew that? I've got a kid, but I never knew that."

For a while they were both silent, and then a horn blew, and Barrett snapped his eyes to the rearview mirror, saw a Cadillac hugging his bumper, and realized he'd let his speed fall from seventy to fifty without even being aware of it.

"Do the families know?" he asked as the Cadillac passed him. "Does Howard know?"

"Yes. County sheriff called them. A stranger. Somebody they'd never met in their lives, never talked to. He beat Broward on it, even. Said he felt it was his duty to tell them as soon as possible."

"Fuck that," Barrett said, and now his own voice was hoarse, his throat tight and thick.

"Yes," Johansson said. "That was my sentiment as well."

More silence. Barrett realized his speed was dropping off again. He felt light-headed. He shifted into the right lane and looked for an exit sign. He wanted to get off the interstate. He wanted to get out of the car and into fresh air. Wanted to punch something. Wanted to lie down and close his eyes.

"I'll see you in Biddeford," Johansson said, and he hung up without another word.

Barrett put the window down and let the wind rip into the car, grateful for the way it stung his eyes.

16

Bobby Girard's auto-body shop was outside of town, located down a dirt road beside a hay field. A modular home sat across the street from three prefabricated garages. A hand-painted sign on the gate said only GIRARD's, as if anyone who made it this far should already know what kind of business it was. That assumption wasn't a bold one; there was nothing else on the road.

Behind the garages, abandoned and gutted cars fought a losing turf war with the hay field. A tow truck was parked alongside a battered pickup with a snowplow attachment. The high sun gleamed off the snowplow blade, a reminder not to be fooled by summer in Maine—there would be snow again soon enough.

The fence around the property was gated and locked; a dirty NO TRESPASSING sign dangled from the chain. Barrett parked and got out into the dust that rose when Johansson pulled his cruiser in. It was a windy day, and the breeze pushed the dust into Barrett's eyes and mouth. For a moment, he smelled paint on the wind. Then the gust died down, and only the fresh-cut-hay smell lingered.

Johansson got out and looked from the garage property over to the house. He wasn't wearing a hat, and in the sunlight, his close-cropped blond hair showed a lot of gray. He'd put on weight in his months working the case. The waistband of his uniform pants should have been earning hazard pay.

Neither of them spoke at first. Barrett knew they'd both been thinking about the autopsy result for the entire drive. He took a breath and tried to clear his head, focus on the task at hand, and not think about the arrest that was taking place in the western mountains.

"What was it Broward said about this outfit?" he asked. "Informal operation? Guess so. Closed for business at one o'clock on a Friday."

"Chop shop, maybe." Johansson sounded as distant and detached as Barrett felt, and he looked like he'd been a long time without sleep. He didn't have sunglasses, and he kept blinking in the brightness as if he were confused.

The killings had gone into motion on a Friday too, Barrett remembered. A hot and windy Friday, not so different than this. Here the hay rippled and the barbed wire hummed, but back in Port Hope there would be whitecaps on the bay, and down past the old orchard and the graveyard, the pines would be swaying above the pond.

"Barrett?" Johansson said.

"Huh?"

"I just asked if you want to try the house."

"Oh. Right. Sure."

They walked across the road and knocked on the front door. Nothing. They stood on the porch and looked back at the property. Nothing moved among all those cars except for a starling that hustled in and out of the shadows of a windowless Oldsmobile resting on cinder blocks in the weeds.

"Did you call Howard?" Johansson asked.

"No. Not yet. You?"

Johansson shook his head. He was staring at the old cars without any focus.

"Pregnant," he said. Then, when Barrett didn't respond, he added, "Jackie was an only child."

"I know."

Johansson blinked, shook his head as if to clear his vision, and said, "Do we wait or go looking for him?"

Barrett was about to suggest they leave to find a neighbor when the wind gusted, whistling over the wire fence and lifting dust from the dirt road, and he smelled the paint again. This time the wind held long enough that he was certain.

"He's working over there. Somebody is, anyhow. Smell that paint?"

Johansson cocked his head, hesitated, then nodded. "I do."

They crossed the road and walked past their cars and up to the gate. It was chained shut and padlocked, but here the smell of the paint was even stronger, and there was a faint, staccato thumping from inside one of the garages. Barrett cupped his hands and shouted a hello. No response. Tried again; same result.

"Climb the fence?" Johansson asked.

"Why not." Barrett slid his badge case out of his pocket and folded it over his belt so it was visible. The fence was basic chain link, and the gate had a crossbar that made climbing easy. He went up and over and dropped to the gravel on the other side.

The closest of the three garages had an office built into one corner. He went over and checked the narrow window. It was dark inside, and the cluttered space was filled with stacked furniture, the file-cabinet drawers hanging open as if they'd been ransacked.

"They're out back," Johansson said. "I can hear them now."

They walked down the rutted, hard-packed dirt lane. There were a dozen old cars between the garages, jammed in at odd angles, as if they'd been spilled there instead of parked. As they neared the last building, the thumping sound resumed, and now there was an undertone to it, a soft hiss.

"What the hell is that?" Johansson said.

"Air hammer, maybe?" Barrett said. "They're also spraying paint."

The biting chemical smell was strong back here. There was something about the hissing sound and the clatter of the air hammer amid all the empty, broken cars that made the place feel ominous even under the bright midday sun.

He looked the cars over, trying to assess why they had not been hauled into the field with the others. Maybe they needed to be scavenged for parts, and the others already had been? They were missing hoods or doors or wheels, wounded soldiers on a forgotten battlefield.

"Chop shop, maybe," Johansson said again, walking toward the back building. He'd gone about ten paces before he realized Barrett was no longer beside him and turned. "What are you doing?"

Barrett was staring at a truck that rested in the weeds behind the garage. It was missing its wheels and its body seemed to be suffering from a skin disease, gray flesh pocked with rusty sores. The chrome grille was bent and one headlight was cracked, but the square face of the truck was intact, and you could read the word DODGE stamped into the top of the grille.

They made a million of them, Barrett thought, but he left Johansson and walked to the truck. The color was right except for the hood. No black-on-white, no Halloween cat. Nothing that matched Kimberly's story. Of course, that could have been painted over. If anyone had painted over this truck, though, he'd done one hell of a job—it was tough to match thirty-year-old paint and rust spots.

He came around to the back of the truck and then pulled up short, his blood seeming to thicken in his veins.

The weathered license plate was Maine 727CRC.

"Barrett, what in the hell are you doing?" Johansson called in a low voice.

Without speaking, he motioned for Johansson to join him, then pointed wordlessly at the plate.

"Son of a bitch," Johansson whispered. "He's here."

"Or he's long gone and driving another vehicle. But the plate is right." Barrett stepped forward and looked in the bed. It was filled with junk, old cinder blocks and some scrap lumber and a chain. On the inside of the tailgate, a splash of rust-colored stains was visible.

His pulse began to speed up again. Slow warmth spread into his fingertips as he rounded the truck and looked at the hood. It had not been replaced, and it had not been repainted.

"Right truck," he said. "But what in the hell was she talking about with the paint?"

"I think we can forget about Kimmy for the moment," Johansson whispered. "Let's call this in."

The soft clattering resumed from inside the garage, *thunk-thunk-thunk,* as the air hammer pounded metal. The smell of paint rode heavy on the wind. Barrett walked to the passenger door, pulled his shirttail free, wrapped his fingers in the fabric, and tried the handle. Unlocked. The door creaked open and he looked in at the long bench seat.

There was no extended cab, only a bench seat in front. I usually get stuck in the middle because I'm small, right? But Cass took the middle that night. She wanted to be close to Mathias.

"It is the right truck," he said again under his breath.

There was no sound except for the hiss of the paint gun.

"We need to call this in," Johansson repeated.

"Yeah." But Barrett didn't move. He was scanning the cab now, looking at the collection of fast-food receipts and candy wrappers and *Uncle Henry's* trader magazines that littered the floor and seat.

"Hey!"

The shout was so loud that Barrett rocketed up and smacked his skull on the door frame, a brain-rattling shot that left him dizzy as he stepped back.

A short, muscular guy with unkempt hair and uneven stubble was walking toward them with swift, officious strides, like an umpire hustling across the diamond.

"What the hell are you doing inside my—"

The man stopped short when he saw Johansson's uniform. Barrett fumbled his own badge loose from his belt, still wincing from the blow to the head.

"We're police," Johansson said. "I need you to calm—"

"I know why you're here," the man said, his voice going high and unsteady. Barrett could see him clearly now. It was Jeffrey Girard.

"Calm down," Johansson said.

But Girard was retreating, backing toward the garage, where a pedestrian door stood ajar.

"Stop moving," Johansson barked. "Stop moving!"

"I know why you're here," Girard repeated, and then he turned and moved to the door with that odd, urgent walk.

"*Stop right there!*" Johansson shouted, and then he drew his gun.

Girard ducked through the open door and vanished.

Johansson swore and rushed forward, his gun raised, but Barrett caught him by the arm.

"Easy! We don't need to escalate."

Johansson was buzzing, his eyes wide, muscles tensed, jaw locked.

"He said he knows why we're here."

"He ought to," Barrett said. "Now call it in. We've got Girard and we've got the truck. Let's not screw this up."

His eyes were still on the doorway where Girard had vanished. Against the sunlit day, it was just a square of blackness. Somewhere beyond, the hissing sound continued.

Johansson lowered his gun. He kept it in his right hand and used his left to key the radio that was just below his collar. He'd only had time to say "Unit one-forty-three" before there was motion inside the door and Jeffrey Girard stepped out of the darkness and into the daylight with a shotgun in his hands.

"Put that down!" Barrett shouted, sidestepping to get behind one of the gutted cars as he drew his Glock nine-millimeter duty pistol, the first draw he'd ever made in his career. Before he'd even cleared it from the holster there was the double-clap of two gunshots.

Girard had been holding the shotgun across his chest, not pointing it at them—at least not yet—but now he fell back against the door and slid down, leaving a bright streak of blood against the white paint on the door.

"Damn it, hold your fire!" Barrett shouted at Johansson, who was standing in place, gun leveled out in front of him in one hand like an amateur pistol shooter at the range. He'd fired so fast he hadn't even gotten into a two-handed grip. He'd just lifted and shot.

And hit.

"I thought he was shooting!" Johansson said, still holding the odd pose, as if the scene were frozen until he broke it, as if this could be rewound. "I heard shots!"

"That was the air hammer," Barrett said, and he could see a little of the color drain from Johansson's cheeks.

"Oh, *shit,*" Johansson said, and then he finally lowered the gun.

Barrett looked at the writhing, bleeding man in the grass just in front of the garage and said, "Give me cover, and *do not shoot unless you have to.*"

He stepped out from behind the car and advanced on Girard with his own gun held in front of him. Shooter's stance, two-handed grip, careful stride. Just like he'd been taught at the academy, which was not all that long ago.

Girard was holding his stomach with both hands. The shotgun was just in front of him. He looked from Barrett to the shotgun and then back.

"Do not move," Barrett snapped. "Just stay down. We're going to get you help. Do not move, though."

The paint fumes wafting out from the open door stung his eyes and made them water as he advanced. He didn't want to blink, was afraid of what might happen in that brief instant. Jeffrey Girard watched him approach and tried to speak. Instead of words, though, he made a sound like a stifled yawn and then bright blood ran over his open lips and down his chin. He looked at Barrett plaintively, the sort of look you could give only when you understood that you were badly hurt and were helpless to fix it.

Then he reached for the shotgun.

Barrett tensed his finger on the trigger, but Girard didn't try to pick up the shotgun or even close his hand around the stock. Instead, he pushed it with an open palm, sliding it a few pitiful feet closer to Barrett, like an offering.

"Thank you," Barrett said, understanding that this meant surrender. He kept his Glock trained on Girard while he reached out with his left hand and pulled the shotgun away, out of reach. Then he waved Johansson forward. Johansson had been speaking into his radio, but now he hurried forward—moving too fast, too upright. Everything about him had been too fast today.

"Sheriff and state en route. And an ambulance," he said.

Barrett wanted to help Girard because that level of bleeding would kill him fast if it wasn't stopped, but there were others inside to worry about. A swirl of training and assault simulators spun through his mind as he tried to steady his breathing and bring his heart rate down.

"We need to clear that building and then help him," he said. "I can't turn my back to that door to help him until we clear it, do you see?"

Johansson nodded. He face was awash with sweat, and his breath was coming fast and ragged. It was not the face you wanted to see on someone who might need to provide cover fire for you.

"Whoever is in there is probably just working on a car, okay?" Barrett said. "Be alert but not anxious. You got me?"

Johansson nodded again, crab-walking closer, and when he brought his gun up, Barrett almost wanted to tell him to put it down. Barrett took a breath, gathered himself, and then went through the door and spun toward the light, keeping low, gun drawn. Almost immediately he saw a bulky figure in the center of the room.

"FBI! Hands in the air, *hands in the air!*"

When the big man in the bulky suit and mask turned toward him and pointed the gun, Barrett nearly shot him. The visual was simply *Gun, he is pointing a gun, shoot him now, kill him now,* but the gun was blowing blue paint into the air.

The man was dressed in a heavy protective suit,

wearing a mask and ear protection, clueless to the chaos outside. In front of him was a half-painted car, its windows covered in clear plastic and tape. He stared at Barrett for a second, blowing the paint into the air between them, and even through the mask, Barrett could see his wide eyes, the absolute confusion in them.

That was when Johansson whirled in and screamed, *"Drop it, drop it!"*

"Not a weapon, it is not a weapon!" Barrett shouted back, and he was reaching for Johansson's arm when the man in the suit dropped the paint gun and stumbled back, hands in the air.

"Stay there! Do not move!" Johansson's hands were shaking, and Barrett sagged against the wall, thinking of what could have happened in here. He'd been through dozens of close-quarters simulations at Quantico, each of them designed to be challenging scenarios, but nobody had ever dreamed up a paint gun and the staccato clap of an air hammer. Even the simulator programmers weren't that sadistic.

"Go get him, and be easy," Barrett said. The man in the suit was down on his knees now, hands held so high he had to be close to dislocating his shoulders. He was terrified. "Get him secured. I'll be with Girard."

He went back outside and into the daylight. The

hot copper smell of blood was mingling with the chemical odor of paint now, a sickening pairing, and he had to swallow against the rise of bile in his throat. Jeffrey Girard was curled up like a child, hugging his abdomen. There was blood all over. It shone ruby-colored in the sun.

Barrett holstered his gun, unbuttoned his shirt, and peeled it off, no other material to hold pressure with in sight. He had a first aid kit in his car, but it was for cut fingers, not gunshot wounds. He balled the shirt up and knelt beside Girard. There were sirens in the distance now.

"Let me help you."

Girard didn't want to take his hands off his wound. He made a low moan and pressed them harder against himself, and blood bubbled between his fingers. He looked at Barrett's shirt with doubtful eyes. He knew he was bleeding out and he was afraid to let up on the pressure even for an instant. So primal—*I can't afford to lose any more of this.* Barrett put the shirt over the wounded man's hands. It was not going to matter much either way. Unless those sirens closed the gap awfully fast, it was not going to matter.

He leaned over Girard and said, "Did you kill them? Jackie and Ian? Did you kill them?"

Girard stared at him. His eyes were glassy and distant. Barrett wanted to smack him, get his attention.

It was past that point now, though. So far past that point.

"Did you do it? Or did you help Mathias Burke?"

Nothing. Barrett could feel the warmth of the man's blood even through the shirt.

"Please talk," he whispered. "Please tell me how it happened."

Girard's head drooped forward, his neck muscles loosening. His mouth fell open and a thin stream of blood ran out of it.

"Fuck," Barrett said, speaking in a calm, reasonable voice into this day gone mad.

He stood and went over to the shotgun. It was a heavy black Remington twelve-gauge. He broke the barrel and looked for the load.

Empty.

He closed his eyes for a moment. Took a breath. Then he snapped the barrel shut so that it would look better when they found it in the grass. He wanted to do that much for Johansson. It was a mean-looking gun when you thought it was loaded. It was a mean-looking gun and it had been in a suspected murderer's hands and the air hammer had been clattering like a semiautomatic weapon.

It had been tougher out here than people would understand.

Barrett was kneeling by the body again when Johansson came out to join him. The sirens were louder now and they could see the first cars up on the hill. Two cruisers, running like hell.

"It's his cousin inside," Johansson said. "Bobby. I cuffed him. Just to...I didn't know what the hell to do with him."

Barrett nodded. He didn't tell Johansson that the shotgun hadn't been loaded. It was better that he not know that detail when the incident-review team asked him how it had happened.

"I didn't know what the hell to do," Johansson repeated, his voice urgent, almost pleading. "I've never been in a firefight before."

"We still haven't," Barrett said, and then he walked to the gate to meet the oncoming police, shirtless and bloodstained, his badge held high.

17

Mathias Burke addressed the media on the jail-house steps after his release.

He faced the cameras with poise and reminded the reporters that everyone's heart should be with the families of Jackie Pelletier and Ian Kelly today and that the injustice Mathias had endured was nothing compared to what they were going through.

But what if the bodies hadn't been found? a reporter asked. What if there had been no tip, and they'd pressed on with the prosecution based on Kimberly Crepeaux's confession?

"That's God's hand," Mathias said.

They asked Mathias if he was angry.

"I'm angry with the FBI agent," he said. "Rob Barrett. Barrett didn't want the truth. He just wanted to hang me. He accused me of terrible things, and probably a lot of people believed him. Now people know the truth. I'm grateful for that. For myself, sure, but mostly for the families of those two who were killed. As far as what was said about me, the accusations that were made…if you ask me, that's criminal."

When questioned as to whether he would pursue civil charges for libel or slander, Mathias demurred.

"I'd win if I did, but I just want to get back to my own life, keep my head down, and put this behind me. It was a nightmare while it lasted, but I'm awake now."

Kimberly Crepeaux didn't give a press conference, and she wasn't released, still serving time for her unrelated charges. Instead, she issued a written statement through her public defender explaining that she'd made up her horrific tale to appease the relentless pressure of Special Agent Rob Barrett.

I was coersed, she wrote. *I talked to him over and over and told the truth but he didn't want to hear the truth. Barrett wanted to hear a spacific story and finally I just told him what he wanted to hear, because I didn't want to spend my life in prison. He told me if I gave him that story, the one he wanted to hear, then I'd be able to stay out of prison and see my little girl grow up. Who wouldn't be willing to make that trade?*

The dead man's defense consisted of a single hollow excuse from his cousin.

Bobby Girard claimed that a man in Rockland had borrowed Jeffrey's battered Dodge Dakota sometime in the summer or fall a year earlier because his own vehicle was in the shop. There was no evidence of this, but even if there had been, it wasn't a threat to Mathias Burke, who personally owned a truck, a car, and a motorcycle and through his company owned an additional eight trucks and two cargo vans. He was hardly hurting for a vehicle.

The idea that the truck matched most of Kimberly's description led to theories that she'd been with Girard at the time of the killings. She denied this, and the dead man couldn't say otherwise.

Barrett's requests to talk to Kimberly Crepeaux again were denied by Kimberly, Emily Broward, and Colleen Davis. As soon as the police in Maine were through reviewing the shooting at the body shop, he'd been recalled to Boston.

"Do not go back to Port Hope," Roxanne Donovan said. When he said he still had to clear out his hotel room, she promised to have an agent from the Augusta field office ship his things south.

Boston felt loud and distracted and detached to him. He wanted everyone he passed on the streets to know of the case, the way they had in Maine. He wanted strangers to approach him and tell him a story about the time Howard Pelletier had made Jackie a rocking chair out of busted lobster traps or the time they'd seen Ian and Jackie walking hand in hand down the pier to the Marshall Point Lighthouse.

He wanted people to care.

Considering the kind of publicity he was getting for his role in the case, though, he should have been grateful that they didn't.

Roxanne Donovan, who'd brought him to Boston because of his expertise in interviewing, interrogation, and confessions, now told him she needed him on document review for a case involving a pharmaceutical company that had endured a wave of citations from the FDA and drawn interest from the Department of Justice. His assignment: read seventy-three thousand pages of e-mails.

"Don't rush," she said.

He spoke to Amy Kelly once, and George Kelly didn't join the conversation. Amy gave Barrett five curt minutes, and this time she did not thank him for his time and effort.

He called Howard Pelletier repeatedly. The phone was never answered, and none of his calls were returned. Barrett left a final message.

"I believed her, Howard," he said. "And I'm sorry."

He had questions that he was not allowed to ask, most of them for the medical examiner and some for Emily Broward, but any inquiries to those

MICHAEL KORYTA

sources would boomerang back to Roxanne Donovan. He told himself to let it go, to respect the chain of command, but on one of his first days back in Boston, he found himself making a call to the only person in the Bureau he trusted to keep quiet about his interest.

Seth Miller was the first agent Barrett had worked with in Little Rock, and he had IT expertise. He also was due to retire, which Barrett hoped would make him more cooperative. Seth had less to lose than other agents from hearing him out.

"They sending you back to Little Rock?" Seth said, immediately removing any hope that he wasn't aware of the mess in Maine.

"Not just yet."

"Good. I'm gone in six weeks, off to the happy hunting ground otherwise known as Florida. It won't be any fun here without me."

"I don't doubt that. Listen, Seth, I've got a question, and it needs to stay between us."

"Oh boy."

"If you don't want to hear it, I'll understand."

"What are they gonna do, fire me? Let's have it."

"How could a man in custody who has absolutely no access to a computer or a phone send an e-mail?"

He was expecting Seth to either laugh at him or lecture him for going on a fool's errand. He wasn't prepared for the immediate answer.

154

"Easily," Seth said.

"Really? How?"

"A half a dozen ways, but the most effective would probably be a dead man's switch. You put your message and its recipient into an automated system and instruct it to be sent if you disappear. So every day or every twelve hours, whatever you want, the system sends you a link. If you activate the link, the system knows you're good, and the e-mail stays on the shelf. But if you fail to interact with the link within a given time frame, the e-mail goes out."

"Where do you find systems like that?"

"They're all over. I believe one is literally dead-manswitch.com or something close. Google provides the service for free. You can pick what they call your *digital heirs* to receive your data, or you can have it all removed. They call that the Inactive Account Manager, which is a term I've always loved. So polite, considering the only people who need it are either dead or in prison."

"In that case, though, I'd know who sent me the e-mail, right?"

"Sure. But it's amateur hour to reroute that. And somebody good is going to code the switch himself using the same idea. You pick a system to interact with. Could be a text message, an e-mail, or a web page. Could be your Facebook or Twitter account. Then you write a code that watches for your interaction on the site, and if that stops for a prolonged period, an alert goes out. This alert could be an e-mail to one person, or it could be a file dump. You'd better believe the big-time hackers, Snowden, guys like that, have these set up. It's a beautiful form of protection. *If I go missing, your personal e-mails will appear on Facebook*, that sort of thing. Makes people think twice about trying to take you out."

"That sounds pretty sophisticated."

"Sounds harder than it is. Is your suspect up there a techie?"

"I don't think so. But he's smart."

"Then he could have done it. Give a smart person some time on YouTube, and they can learn how to do a lot of shit that seems out of reach."

"It came in pretty quickly when he was arrested."

"Would he have smelled you guys coming for him before the arrest?"

Don't get your feet wet.

"Absolutely."

"Then he could have set it up on a short timer, anticipating things. How much investigation have they put into that e-mail?"

"I don't know. I'm being boxed out."

"Well, all I can tell you is that the answer to your question is yes, it could have been done. But there's another possibility too."

"What's that?"

"Someone outside of the jail walls sent that e-mail."

"An accomplice."

"Possibly," Seth said. "But that's not what I was suggesting. I mean the guy outside of the jail walls was the guilty party, Barrett. I'm not in the mix up there, so you tell me: Is there any evidence to suggest what you're asking about is actually the way it went?"

"No," Barrett said. "Not yet."

He made it through the week in Boston, dodging some calls and making others. Liz gave him updates. She told him that Jackie Pelletier's funeral would be on Saturday and was closed to the media. She was going out to take a few pictures of the headstone afterward.

Barrett knew better than to consider trying to attend. He bought tickets to a Red Sox game and tried to scare up some colleagues willing to go along. Out of pity for him or a love of Fenway, a few agreed.

On the morning Jackie Pelletier was to be laid in the ground beside her mother, Barrett rose early after a restless sleep and went for a run, five miles instead of his usual three, trying to purge all thoughts of Port Hope out in sweat. Afterward he showered and got in the car and turned the air-conditioning on high and angled the vents toward his face, as if he could blast prudence and good sense into his brain.

Then he called his co-workers, said he was feeling under the weather and would have to miss the baseball game, and put the car in gear.

It was a perfect summer weekend and people were scattering out of the city, loading up luggage and kids, throwing kayaks or bicycles onto roof racks, and heading north, some going up the coast, others into the cooler reaches of the mountains and pines. I-95 northbound to Maine was a logjam of Massachusetts plates.

His blended right in.

18

The cemetery where Jackie Pelletier was buried was between Port Hope and Thomaston, and while it was nicely landscaped and lined with pine groves and rhododendrons, it offered no view of her beloved ocean. There were police in the parking lot to protect the family's privacy, but a few members of the media waited for a glimpse of the mourners anyhow, cameras at the ready. Barrett was pleased to note that Liz wasn't among them. You could cover the news without being a vulture; you could convey the day's anguish without needing a photograph of Howard's tears.

He drove by without slowing, and then he stopped at a flower shop and bought a single bouquet and went to the forgotten graveyard by the tidal flats that Jackie Pelletier had loved so much. This cemetery was overgrown and untended, and while some thought that was a shame, Howard had once told Barrett that Jackie preferred that feel in a cemetery, that she'd always hated the idea of lawn mowers and weed trimmers buzzing above her mother's bones.

She liked the Orchard Cemetery, where Howard had taught her to make charcoal rubbings of the crumbling faces of faded stones. In this place, long before she'd painted her first landscape, she'd walked with her hand in Howard's, sounding out antiquated names and wondering over the various Bible verses chosen in memory of the dead. Once, she had discovered the tiny matching headstones of infant twins, and it made her cry.

Barrett parked on the same ground where police had found Jackie's Subaru sitting empty. He took the bouquet and walked by the sloping, moss-covered stone walls, making his way carefully among the dead. You had to be cautious with your steps here, because some of the stones had sunk into the earth as if in pursuit of the bodies they'd been placed there to honor.

While Barrett remembered where police had taken castings of tire imprints and samples of bloodstains, he didn't want to stand there. He wanted to stand someplace where he could see the water, the spot Jackie liked best. A few of the graves were always visible out of the corner of your eye, yes, but most of your focus was on the sea and the sun. That was what she'd loved about the place, Howard had told him. Juxtaposition, she'd called it, and when Howard had told her he wasn't familiar with the word, she'd said, *Balance.*

Barrett found a spot on a hill that looked reminiscent of several of Jackie Pelletier's paintings. He laid the flowers on the grass, but the wind off the tidal flats was brisk and it pulled apart the bouquet and scattered the flowers.

When he left, he intended to drive to Liz's house. He certainly didn't intend to turn south instead of north, bound for Port Hope instead of Camden.

But he did.

He tried to drive like a tourist, aimless and intrigued, and not like a detective, hunting and seeking. He told himself that if he found Mathias Burke's pickup truck or his panel van with PORT HOPE CARETAKING SERVICES on the side, it would be merely an unpleasant coincidence and not the end of the search.

When he found Mathias's pickup parked in the crushed-stone lot outside the Harpoon, though, all pretenses faded away. He pulled his Explorer in directly behind it, pinning the truck in, and then he got out and walked toward the bar where his grandfather had held court for so many years.

Maine was populated by more than its share of taverns, and each sent a different message. There were the waterfront bars with wide decks and brightly colored umbrellas; microbreweries with stainless-steel vats or aged wooden casks displayed in wide plate-glass windows; ramshackle joints with nets and buoys adorning the walls, promising that nostalgic Maine feel; sports bars with televisions and chicken-wing specials. And then, generally off the water, priced out of the view but never too far from a workingman's wharf, there were bars that didn't bother with so much as a single neon sign, bars that could have been on a street corner in Cleveland or a wind-blasted butte in Wyoming. You wouldn't hear anybody asking what local beers were on draft, but you would hear the crack and clink of a pool game. The message these bars sent wasn't one of vacationland or nostalgia or craft spirits or sports but something far simpler and more lasting: *We'll pour you plenty, and we'll pour it cheap.*

That was the Harpoon.

That had been, for a decade, Rob's boyhood summer home. In the two-bedroom, one-bathroom apartment above the bar, separated from it by a thin floor that did nothing to dull the noise below, he'd received a more profound education than he had at any of the universities he'd attended.

Now he pushed the heavy, dented steel door open and stepped out of the sunlit day and into the dimness of the bar, the trapped smells of spilled beer and sweat and old mop water rising toward him, and he half expected to see his grandfather towering behind the bar.

Instead, the man facing him was Mark Millinock,

a fisherman whose drug habits had washed him out of every crew he'd ever joined. He'd finally given up on the water and bought the Harpoon off Ray Barrett with an unimpressive stack of cash, the origins of which were unknown and unquestioned.

Mark Millinock glanced up without interest when the door opened, then did a double take and straightened. At the corner of the bar, Mathias Burke noticed and turned with curiosity. Mark Millinock's face looked hateful, but Mathias smiled.

"Pour me another, Mark," he said. "This man owes me a drink."

Barrett crossed the room, conscious of two on-lookers to his left and two to his right. Everyone in the barroom was male, which wasn't uncommon at the Harpoon. Women who came into the Harpoon either realized their mistake quickly and left or were there precisely for the sort of trouble the place invited.

Barrett recognized only one of the other men in the room. Ronnie Lord was a heroin addict from Rockland who'd been one of the first people to report Kimberly Crepeaux's self-implicating statements about the disappearances. He was also a part-time employee of Mathias Burke and had scoffed at Barrett's questions about a possible intersection between Kimberly and Mathias.

"Oh man, he came back!" Ronnie said, and Barrett

could see from his bright eyes and dilated pupils that he was high. "That takes some balls!"

Barrett ignored Ronnie and took the stool beside him as Mark Millinock cracked a can of PBR and set it down beside Mathias.

"I'll take one too," Barrett said.

"That was my last one," Mark said.

"Then I'll take a Budweiser."

"Also out of that."

Barrett leaned across the bar and smacked the tap handle forward. Beer splattered down and Millinock swore and slammed the tap back off, his stubbled face darkening with anger, powerful forearms tensing as his fists clenched.

"Pour me the beer, Mark," Barrett said.

"Fuck you. It ain't your—"

"Pour his drink," Mathias said quietly.

Mark glanced at him, surprised, and Mathias made an impatient gesture with his hand. "Come on. His money's still good, and he's buying. Aren't you, Barrett?"

"Sure."

Millinock poured the beer into a mason jar and set it on the bar. Then he took a bottle of Glenmorangie off the shelf behind the bar, poured two tall ones, gave one to Mathias and kept the other for himself. At the Harpoon, a ten-year-old Glenmorangie was top-shelf liquor.

"So long as you're buying, I'm drinking too," he said. "Wouldn't mind hurting your wallet. Ronnie, you want one?"

"I'll take a double," Ronnie Lord said. He was a scrawny guy who inexplicably wore muscle shirts, and he was bouncing on the balls of his feet now, pool cue in one hand. Buzzing and high and convinced that he was hard by whatever was in his bloodstream. Barrett glanced at him and felt a strong desire to knock him to the floor.

"We're all buying," he said. "My salary comes from the taxpayers. But by all means, drink up, boys." Barrett turned to Mathias and lifted his beer. His pulse was thumping and the skin along the base of his skull felt tight, the nerve endings alive.

"Here's to Jackie Pelletier and Ian Kelly," he said.

Mathias didn't move. His dark eyes were steady on Barrett's.

"No respect for the dead?" Barrett said.

"No respect for you. But, sure, here's to the dead." He clinked his beer off Barrett's and drank, never lowering his eyes. "How about another toast? To the truth."

"Amen."

They clinked glasses again.

"And one more," Mathias said. "The last one. Here's to you saying, *I'm so sorry, Mathias. I apologize for fucking with your life over a crack whore's lie.*"

"Before we get to that one, I've got a question."

"You never run out of them, do you, Barrett?"

"Well, I used to be a teacher."

"I hope you didn't teach police work."

Ronnie Lord's high, keening laugh came over Barrett's shoulder and entered his brain like the sound of breaking glass, but Barrett managed to ignore him and stay focused on Mathias.

"It was in the theories of police work, at least. I had one rule I just hammered into my students—theories are to be tested, not protected."

"Cute."

"So my theory about you, in this case, seems to be short on evidence."

"Just a touch."

"It's my job not to protect it, then. Not to cling to a falsehood, to deny that I could have gotten it wrong. But…" He drank some of the beer, and it sat thick and flat on his tongue. "It is also my job to test it."

Mathias had set his beer down and both of his hands were resting on the bar.

"How good are you with computers?" Barrett asked. "I've never been much of a tech guy. I was learning some new things recently. Simple stuff, but new to me. Dead man's switch coding, for example. You ever heard of something like that?"

Mathias didn't blink. "No. I don't spend much time in my cubicle."

Ronnie Lord tittered.

"The police took my computer," Mathias continued. "And my phone. Back when I was falsely accused and under arrest, they did that. Do you remember when that happened?"

Barrett nodded. "I didn't think you had much time to spend playing around on your computer. Not as hard as you work. You told me once that every dime you made was based on your reputation for hard work. You explained all the character references you could provide and all the damage I could do to your livelihood."

Mathias waited.

"George and Amy Kelly were two of those references," Barrett said. "You told me to ask George and Amy what they thought of you, of how you'd taken care of every problem they ever had and billed only for the work you'd done, never trying to skim a nickel, the definition of an honest caretaker."

"That's the truth," Mark Millinock said, but both Barrett and Mathias ignored him.

"You got quite the memory," Mathias said.

"I record everything. I like to go back and listen. Keeps me from letting my instincts get the better of me."

"With your instincts, I can see where that would be a concern."

Again, Ronnie Lord's laugh brayed. Barrett

leaned toward Mathias, trying to hold his focus. "Here's my question," Barrett said. "How does a man who takes such meticulous care of a client's property, with such unflagging attention to *every…last…detail,* miss something as simple as washing and sealing the decks?"

Mathias didn't speak. Behind them, Ronnie Lord shifted the pool cue in his hands, and one of the men Barrett didn't know took a step closer to the bar. Mark Millinock had picked up a bottle opener, a massive cast-iron thing in the shape of a mermaid that had been here since Barrett's childhood and had broken plenty of glasses and a couple of noses over the years.

"Do you not own a pressure washer?" Barrett asked.

"I own ten of them."

"But your company didn't clean the decks for a long-term client? And you didn't hire Jeffrey Girard?"

"This is bullshit," Mark Millinock said. He was tapping the heavy bottle opener on the bar with a tense hand. "I want you to get the—"

"You don't deserve an answer," Mathias told Barrett, interrupting Millinock, "but there's a part of me that almost feels sorry for you. So I'll give you an answer. The last one." He leaned close to Barrett, eyes aflame. *"Ian Kelly wrote that check.* The kid made the hire, okay? I don't know how he met a worthless shit-brain like Girard, but here's what I do know—I had to fix the work for him. And, oh, Barrett? I didn't bill anybody for that either. Why? Because my reputation is my livelihood."

He stood up, leaving the beer unfinished and the whiskey untouched. "I don't know what empty places you're trying to fill, staying stuck in the same rut of bullshit that Kimmy fed you, but keep spinning in it, man. It'll take you down now, not me."

He turned to Mark Millinock and said, "Make sure he tips you well," and then he walked out of the bar. Millinock was still drumming that ridiculous but dangerous bottle opener on the bar, and Ronnie Lord and one of the strangers were circling behind Barrett with pool cues in hand.

Barrett drank his beer and waited, watching the dusty mirror behind the bar. He fixated on a place in the corner where his grandfather had once kept a family photograph tucked between the glass and the frame. The picture had been taken when Barrett was seven, the last time he'd ever been in Port Hope with his father, and the last time he'd been anywhere away from home with his mother. She'd been thirty-four years old then, the same age as he was now, healthy and beautiful, with eyes that seemed set in permanent laughter, and in the photograph she'd had the full confidence of youth.

She was dead five months after the photo was taken.

Barrett thought he could still make out the lines of the old masking tape that had held it to the glass. He was staring at them when the door opened again and Mathias stepped back inside. Barrett watched him in the mirror, not turning.

"You blocked me in? What in the hell is the matter with you? What are you trying to do?"

Barrett didn't answer.

"Move your car," Mathias said, and the first glimpse of his temper showed, his self-control beginning to curl up at the edges from the heat beneath.

"Just let me finish my beer," Barrett said. He didn't like how familiar it all felt, this room and his face in the mirror and his absurd words and actions, each one the choice of a fool spoiling for a fight. Most of all he didn't like how much he was enjoying it. His blood was up, and it did not feel bad. Not even a little bit.

Mathias Burke laughed with disbelief and shook his head. "You're a stupid man," he said. "You think you can push me until you find the right spot, don't you? But you're the one at risk. Keep pushing."

Barrett didn't answer, just drank his beer.

"Get up, asshole," Mark Millinock said, starting to come around the bar, and Barrett pivoted to meet him with an odd sense of relief, as though this was what he'd always needed.

Mathias Burke said, "Let him be, Mark," but it wasn't Mark Millinock who reached for Barrett first. Instead, Ronnie Lord grabbed a fistful of his shirt.

"Get out of here," he said. "You got no reason to be here anymore."

Barrett stood still for a moment, looking first at Ronnie's hand bunched around his shirt and then into his face, this social disease putting his hands on him and telling him to get out.

"Ronnie, damn it, back up," Mathias snapped, and he stepped forward, but he was too late.

Barrett's first blow felt like something watched through a window or heard through a closed door. Anything but intimate. He drove his right fist into Ronnie Lord's sternum, watched the man's green eyes go wide and white with pain, and then slammed him against the bar. A glass fell and broke and then Mark Millinock was coming toward them as Barrett smashed his elbow into Ronnie's throat, taking the man's breath out high and low, then pushed him into Millinock.

They fell into the bar together, Millinock cursing and Ronnie wheezing in strangled gasps as he fought for air, and Barrett lifted his fists and felt a smile rising to his lips as he saw Mark Millinock reach for the pool cue.

Good. Have a weapon, have two, I don't care, because I don't mind getting hit today . . .

Mathias Burke caught the pool cue before Mark brought it home across Barrett's chest.

"Nobody's hitting him, damn it!"

"What in the hell is the matter with you?" Mark roared at him. "The son of a bitch is in here busting up people in my bar, and I—"

"Go back behind the bar and call the police."

Mark stared at him, dumbfounded. "Call the *police?* I'll put his ass out into the parking lot, I don't give a damn if he's an FBI agent or the pope, it's my bar and I want him gone!"

"Let's see you put me out, Mark," Barrett said, still wanting the fight, the release of physical contact working on him like a drug. Then he looked down at Ronnie Lord, who was hunched over on the barroom floor, one hand on his gut and one at his throat, still fighting for breath, his face contorted in pain. The sight of him brought Barrett back into the moment, carried him through that sealed window and shut door and returned him to a shameful reality.

What are you doing? What in the holy hell are you doing?

"Call the police," Mathias repeated, his voice low and calm. "He's disturbing the peace in your business, don't you think? That's for the police to handle."

A stupid grin slid over Mark Millinock's face. "Sure it is."

"Then call them."

Mark stepped back behind the bar and picked up the phone, and Mathias Burke looked at Barrett and spread his arms.

"I guess you wanted it to go like this."

"I guess so," Barrett said, and then he went outside to wait for the police.

19

The responding officer spoke to Mark Millinock and Ronnie Lord and made some references to rumors he'd heard about their drug habits, and then it was swiftly agreed that nobody wanted to press charges. The officer came back outside and looked at Barrett with a mix of confusion and contempt and told him to get the hell away from the bar before he embarrassed the badge.

When Barrett left, there was a small crowd of on-lookers in his rearview mirror and he saw clearly on their faces that they believed they were watching a fool, and he knew that they were not wrong. By now he felt ridiculous and ashamed and could not understand how he'd gotten so far along such a stu-pid path.

He gets my blood up. That son of a bitch Mathias gets my blood up.

The voice in his head was not his own. It was his grandfather's, and he knew that. So why was it there? How had he allowed it in and then let it take control, like a tumor?

You were wrong. Kimberly lied to you, and you were wrong, and you can't admit that. So instead, you're acting like a fool.

He was only five minutes away from the bar when Liz called.

"Please tell me it isn't true," she said.

"Where are you?"

"Home. Rob? Come here now, and don't stop along the way."

He'd lost his ability to listen to his own good advice today, but he could still follow hers.

She was waiting on the front steps, scratching the cat she'd named No Smarts. He was a stray she'd found along the road, and although she'd had him neutered, the vet had apparently forgotten to notify the cat of the procedure, because No Smarts remained prone to fights and feral behavior and held a deep distrust of anyone other than Liz. He flattened his ears when he saw Barrett, hissed, and retreated beneath the porch to watch from the shadows with flicking green eyes.

"Sweet," Barrett said.

"He knows trouble. You'll be in the paper tomorrow."

"You wrote about that? With no charges, no arrest?"

"I didn't write about it. I'm not allowed to write

about you." She gave a humorless smile. "Ethical concerns. I disclosed my relationship with you to my editor."

"I'm sorry," he said.

"It's hardly a story I'd have enjoyed writing. What in the hell were you thinking, Rob?"

"I don't know. I wasn't thinking. I was...I just wanted to see him. I wanted to see him and look in his face and..." He shook his head. "Know the truth."

"How'd that work out for you?"

He sat beside her on the steps. She didn't move toward him or look at him. He wanted her to put her hand on his leg in the way she often did, or lean her head against his shoulder. Instead, she ran her palms across her thighs as if smoothing wrinkles out of her jeans. Her jeans were covered with paint and dust and he knew she must have been working on her boat when she'd heard about his near arrest at the Harpoon.

She still didn't look at him when she said, "You were lied to. You believed it. That happens to all of us. Don't self-sabotage like this because you're embarrassed that it happened to you."

He didn't answer. He sat there beside her and looked out at the pines and the outline of Mount Battie beyond them. If you hiked to the top, you had an astonishing view of Penobscot Bay and its islands and peninsulas and lighthouses. When he was seventeen, he'd made his first visit to see Liz in the winter, and they'd hiked up there with a sleeping bag and a bottle of wine pilfered from her father's boat and made love in the snow, her breath fogging the air above him, snowflakes in her hair. Neither of them had liked the wine, so she'd poured it out in the snow in the shape of a heart, but by then the storm was picking up and the islands were lost to fog and soon the red wine was covered by a blanket of white.

It remained one of the most vivid memories of his youth. There was only one image that floated to the surface more readily, and that one was far less welcome, though still marked by a crimson stain.

"He's not your grandfather," Liz said.

"What?"

"You're lumping them together. Your grandfather trusted Nate Burke and liked Mathias, and you hated your grandfather, and now—"

"My grandfather killed my mother, Liz. It's not a matter of personal dislike. He killed her and got away with it."

"You're sure of that?"

"Yes," he said, and looked away. He was sure of it. He'd just never proven it.

"The mess today wouldn't have happened if it wasn't at the Harpoon," she said. "If you'd seen

Mathias anywhere other than in that bar, you wouldn't have been so damn dumb."

He agreed, but somehow he couldn't imagine the encounter taking place anywhere else. It was as if Mathias had known he was in town, had gone to the most vulnerable ground, and waited.

She leaned forward and her hair fell across her face like a shield to keep him from seeing her eyes. "The evidence isn't there, Rob. In either case."

He didn't have a rebuttal. Maybe he was blending the two. He was definitely blending some things; this afternoon, he had not only failed to reverse the family legacy in Port Hope but embraced it. He'd gone into the Harpoon with his blood up, spoiling for a fight. Meanwhile, Mathias had kept his cool. Played peacemaker, even.

"Roxanne is keeping me out of Maine," he said.

"I don't blame her."

"But I'll be in Boston. Boston's not that far from you."

"No, it isn't," she said, but she occupied herself with scraping paint off her jeans with a thumbnail.

"You'd still have to make the trip, though," he said.

She nodded without comment.

"So it's not far," he continued, "but it's still too far?"

"Do you *want* me to make the trip?"

"Yes. Of course."

"Then I'll make the trip." She still wasn't looking at him.

"That's exactly the enthusiasm I was hoping for," he said.

She looked at him finally, and there was something so sad in her eyes that he had to will himself not to turn away.

"Do you remember what you told me back at Hammel when I said I wasn't leaving Maine? You said that people returned to their little hometowns for one of only two reasons—family or failure."

"Come on, Liz, I was in college!"

"So what reasons do you see for people returning to their little hometowns now?"

He spread his hands in exasperation. "Work, relationships, opportunity, weather, beauty, family, cost of living, I don't know. Any combination of those. They're countless."

Her eyes searched his. "You know what you never say? That it's the *right place* for someone, plain and simple. That the person feels like they belong there."

"Wouldn't that fall into one of the combinations I just mentioned? Why in the hell are you bringing up some conversation we had when we were kids? Did you hear me ask you to move? I never came close to asking that, and I wouldn't. I'll be only four hours away. I'm asking if you even want to try, that's all."

"That's not my point," she said. "I was just thinking…back then, I heard what you said about needing to leave Maine, and I thought, *He doesn't understand me*."

"Fair enough. I didn't. I'm trying to now."

She put her hand on his leg then, but the touch wasn't the welcoming sensation he'd wanted. It felt more like a farewell.

"I was wrong back then," she said. "Self-absorbed. I heard what you said, and I thought you didn't understand me. What I left out was you. I left out the possibility that you understood yourself very well."

"What does that mean, Liz?"

"This place isn't good for you," she said. "I think you've known that for a long time."

He was trying to form an objection when his phone rang. It was Roxanne Donovan.

"Shit. This won't be good."

"Take it," Liz said, and she removed her hand from his leg.

He stood up and walked into the yard and answered. He was expecting to catch hell, to hear that knife-edged voice that Roxanne was capable of producing when provoked, but instead she was calm and clipped.

"Sounds like you had a bad day, Barrett."

"Yes."

"In my experience, bad days are often the product of bad decisions. Let's see if my theory holds up. Tell me what happened."

He told her, and she didn't interrupt, and when he was done, the expected tirade still didn't come. Instead she simply told him to return to Boston immediately and produce a written account of the incident with Mathias Burke.

"Of course," he said. "I'm sorry. It was a mistake, and it won't happen again."

"Not to worry," she said. "It's actually done you some good."

"Pardon?"

"You've been promoted."

He stood staring at the shadowed slope of Mount Battie and trying to comprehend what she'd just said.

"Can you explain that?"

"You're the boss of Butte."

The FBI's Butte field office had closed in the 1980s, but nevertheless a Hoover-era joke lingered in the Bureau that if you pissed off the director, you were sent to Butte.

"Bad joke, Roxanne," he said.

"Wish it were one. You have been promoted and reassigned to the Bozeman, Montana, field office. I'm told that Washington feels the new SAC out there could use some help getting his feet under him. Apparently, and I quote, 'Rob Barrett's recent expertise with rural task forces makes him an asset.'"

"You've got to be kidding me. Because I had an exchange of words with some idiot in a bar, I'm being sent to *Bozeman*?"

In his peripheral vision, he saw Liz rise and stare.

"It wasn't a product of that exchange, no matter how ill-advised that was," Roxanne said. "I caught wind of it this morning, well before you ignored my instructions and showed up in Maine." She paused, and then her voice softened. "For whatever it's worth, I will tell you that my protest was completely disregarded. I shouldn't share that with you, but I will."

"Bozeman," he said, numb. He remembered her comment on the day of the pond search—the Bureau didn't often fire agents, they just buried them.

"With any luck, it will be temporary. Go out there, work hard, keep your head down, and let time do what time does."

"What is it that time does, Roxanne?"

"Heals all wounds, is what they say. And what they say is bullshit, I know. But what time really *does* do? It lets things cool off. Once the heat dies down on you here, I'll get you back."

He hung up in a daze, pocketed the phone, and

turned back to Liz. She was standing on the bottom step of the porch, as if she'd started toward him but then stopped.

"That wasn't some kind of a joke or a threat?" she said. "It was real? Bozeman?"

"Yes," he said. "Bozeman. It was real."

Part Two

STORYTELLERS

Now every day is numbered
And so are the words.
—Matthew Ryan,
"Hustle Up Starlings"

20

H e'd been in Montana for six months when Kimberly Crepeaux was released from the Knox County jail without much fanfare. Liz wrote an article noting the release and recapping her role in the murder stories, but by then police and public opinion had been settled: samples of blood taken from the bed of Jeffrey Girard's truck matched Jackie Pelletier's and Ian Kelly's DNA. Kimberly was viewed as a liar, not a murderer, and the only national attention the case got had one theme: Rob Barrett. He didn't read the stories. The headlines were enough.

False Confession Haunts Port Hope Residents

FBI Confession Expert Charged Innocent People with Murder

Families Struggle After False Confession Exposed

The good news was that his colleagues in Montana either weren't aware of the case or didn't give a damn. They had thousands of square miles to cover and no shortage of investigations—there was real estate fraud, regulatory fraud, and all flavors of embezzlement; there were interstate opioid traffickers, motorcycle gangs, and militias. The Wild West had not quite been tamed. He tried to throw himself into the work. Give it time, Roxanne Donovan had said, and he was trying his best to do that.

Then, five weeks after her release, Kimberly Crepeaux called.

Barrett was driving through the flatlands between Billings and the Beartooth Mountains en route to interview a high-school student who'd been making repeated bomb threats to the sheriff's department, which was interesting because the sheriff was his uncle. Then the phone rang and he saw the 207 area code, which covered the entire state of Maine, and his mind was out of the mountains and back on the coast.

He let the call go to voice mail, then played the message.

"Barrett, it's Kimberly Crepeaux. I wanted to ask you about something. You're not the right person but I gotta figure out who the right person is." Her voice was shaking and slurred. It was evident that she'd been drinking and that she was scared.

"Nobody believes me, and nobody cares," she said. "Call me back, please."

He didn't call back. He'd already been taken for a long and painful ride by Kimberly. He knew better than to give her another chance.

* * *

She called again two weeks later, and again he didn't take the call but listened to the message.

She was sober this time, and she had clearer requests. She demanded compensation for the way she'd been badgered and intimidated and coerced by the FBI—by him, specifically—and in exchange, he would avoid a "big-ass lawsuit."

All she wanted, she said, was a decent house and a decent job someplace warm. Oh, and ideally the house would have a fence. She'd like to bring her dogs, and Sparky and Bama needed room to run.

He did not return that call either.

In March, a blizzard swept down out of Canada and blasted Bozeman for three straight days, a howling, relentless wind that seemed determined to peel the houses right off their foundations. It was during the worst of the storm that Howard Pelletier called, and Barrett never saw the number, just received the message once his signal was back.

Howard wanted to tell him that he thought people were wrong about Girard and that maybe Barrett had been right the whole time.

For an instant, this was a whisper of validation for the theory that Barrett had never been able to clear completely from his mind. Then Howard explained his reasoning.

He'd had a dream, he told Barrett. In the dream Jackie was in the water, not a trash bag or a barrel, she was down in the water and the water was still, not like the ocean but more like a pond. She was down in the weeds and even the tops of the weeds didn't move, so Howard knew that it was calm, inland water. A fish had passed by in a flicker of white belly and dark spine, and he was sure that it was a smallmouth bass and not a saltwater fish. Jackie's eyes were wide and alert, and right before Howard woke up, she'd opened her mouth to speak to him but only bubbles came out.

"I'm thinkin' maybe you were right all along," Howard said. "Maybe she was down there, and then he moved her."

That night Barrett walked to a bar and drank bourbon with beer chasers until the floor was unsteady beneath his feet, and then he stumbled back home through the drifting, blowing snow and fell asleep on the living-room floor, still wearing his boots and his jacket. In the morning, he threw up, chewed Excedrin, and went back to work.

He did not call Howard Pelletier.

The snow had melted and spring rains fell and then burned off beneath an ever-warming sun before he heard from Maine again.

First, it was Kimberly.

"Barrett, I don't blame you for not wanting to talk to me, but...he's gonna come for me. He's angry because I told the truth, and he's gonna kill me for it." She was crying, her voice low and choked with tears. "If you could just...if there's anybody who could help me out here, I really need it. I really need some help."

He didn't call her back, but this time he made a recording of the message so it couldn't be deleted or lost.

For three nights after Kimberly's call, he played her message back, listening to the panic in her voice and wondering whether there was any legitimacy to it, then cursing himself for being fool enough to let her words drag him back in.

On the fourth night, he found himself playing old recordings of their early interviews. Only the first rounds; he couldn't listen to the confession again. Not to her *coersed* words. Not yet, at least.

Then, on the fifth night, Liz called.

"Kimmy Crepeaux was arrested yesterday," she said. "Up in Bangor. She tried to buy heroin from a police informant."

He felt strangely pleased by this report, because if Kimberly was using again, then he could dismiss all her paranoia as a product of the drugs.

"I'd love to say I'm surprised," he said. "But I know better by now."

Liz went silent. Where he'd expected agreement, there was only a pregnant pause.

"What?" he said.

"She's out on bail."

"Of course she is. Her grandmother will go bank-rupt getting her out of jail. She probably has a reverse mortgage on the house by now or some high-interest line of credit with a bondsman."

"Her grandmother didn't bail her out," Liz said. "That's why I'm calling. I thought you'd want to know who put up the money to get her out of jail."

"Who was it?"

"Howard Pelletier."

21

He returned to Maine on the first weekend of May.

By the time he reached the Port Hope Road it was just after midnight and the wind was cold and the moonlight choked by clouds. When he was a boy, the Port Hope Road had been a name that amused him as he sought to get his bearings and learned that inevitably the main thoroughfare to any of the little villages would bear the name of the village. The locals had a habit of putting *the* in front of each name, as if to differentiate the road from the town. How to get to Camden? Head north on the Camden Road. Which way to Searsmont? Take a left on the Searsmont Road. The naming of the roads to match the towns was a distinctly Mainer trait—practical and unpretentious, no need for creativity when the landscape was so creative on its own.

The Port Hope Road either began in Port Hope or ended there, depending on which way you were headed.

On this night he headed northwest along the peninsula, the bay visible at points, dark pines filling the gaps, and two miles outside of town, out of sight of the water but still smelling of the sea, stood a house with shake-shingle siding and a detached garage. In front of the garage a flatbed trailer was parked, stacked eight feet high with lobster traps. The traps were green; the buoys piled beside them were a yellow so vibrant they returned the glare of Barrett's headlights when he pulled in. He shut off the car but the buoys seemed to hold the glow, an ethereal mass of light in his peripheral vision, like an aura.

The door to the garage opened and a silhouette joined him in the darkness.

"Go back to your car," Howard Pelletier said.

Barrett stopped walking. "Pardon?"

"Pull her in the garage so I can put the door down. Ain't many people passing by this time of night, but those who do will notice your car, and remember it."

Barrett went back to his car and kept the headlights off when he started the engine and waited for one of the overhead doors to go up. Then he drove into Howard's garage. The door was already going back down by the time he stepped out of the car, closing behind him like sealed lips.

"Anybody seen you?" Howard asked.

"Not yet. But they will."

"Ayuh, and they'll be talking soon as they do."

The garage had three bays and a large workshop with a woodstove and a homemade drafting table where Howard had once sketched out designs for his daughter's studio on Little Spruce Island.

Howard sat on a stool beside a pile of mangled lobster traps. He'd been mending them, bending and tightening wire and replacing torn lines until the traps were functional again. When they were done, he would offer them back to the sea, where they would gradually be thrashed out of commission again, and then brought back into the garage. This was the constant cycle of a lobsterman: tend and mend, tend and mend.

Barrett sat on a low wooden bench and turned so that he wasn't facing the drafting table because he did not like the memories of Howard proudly showing him various designs and asking for his thoughts on what Jackie would think of the place when she came home.

He'd called Howard from the Portland airport to tell him he was on his way. That was all he'd said. The rest he'd wanted to discuss in person. He wanted to see the man, not just hear his words. He'd taken two weeks of personal leave for what he'd described to his SAC as a family problem. At this point, the only person in the world who knew that he'd flown to Maine was sitting across from him.

"Tell me why you bailed Kimberly out," Barrett said.

Howard nodded without any trace of surprise at Barrett's knowledge of this event. He'd lost weight since Barrett had last seen him, maybe fifteen pounds. His hair was hidden by a camouflage Cabela's cap, but there was more gray in his beard than Barrett remembered, and it was thicker and more unkempt.

"Sure, that's what brought you back," he said. "I didn't know whether you were still payin' any attention. Figured if you were, that would make you sit up straight. I guess I figured right too."

"Why'd you bail her out, Howard?"

"Because she isn't a liar." Howard's jaw was set, and his gaze never wavered.

"What about Girard?" Barrett said. "The truck, the blood evidence, the overlap with Girard and Ian and Jackie, the—"

"That don't mean there's nothing else to it!" Howard cut in. "Nobody asks questions anymore. I'm just supposed to believe everyone got it right. For a time I was okay with that, I was getting by believing the right man was dead. But then..." He shifted and sucked in a shallow breath through his teeth. "Then she came to see me."

"Kimberly?"

"Yes. One night there's a knock on my door, and

I open it and she's standing out there and she starts crying before she says a word. I figured she's come to say she was sorry for lyin', you know, and I figured her grandmother had put her up to that, but what she said was…"

His voice went hoarse and he had to stop and clear his throat.

"What she said was *I want you to know that she was dead before I ever touched her, Mr. Pelletier.*"

He wiped his eye with a thick, gnarled thumb. "If I said anything to her, I don't remember what it was. I think I was just standing there. Then she told me that she…that she only stabbed Ian, not Jackie. *We only used the knife on Ian.* That's how she said it. Talking about all three of them, just the way she'd told it to you.

"And then I started getting angry. I mean, here's this cruel little lyin' bitch standing on my doorstep and starting back in with the same story I'd been trying to put out of my mind, you know? So I shouted and swore and she just stood there and took it. She was crying all the while, but she took it. She's just a little thing, but she don't so much as flinch when you come at her."

This time he used his whole hand to wipe his eyes, and it took him a few seconds to get his breathing steady.

"When I'd burned myself out, she said, *I told*

Barrett the truth. I thought it was over, because I told him the truth. And somehow, I found my-self...found myself inviting her into the house. Kimmy Crepeaux, who said she put my baby girl in plastic and sank her in a pond, and I brought her into my home." He shook his head as if he still couldn't fathom why he'd made that choice. "I said, *Tell me what happened. No more lies, just tell me the truth, for once, tell someone the fuckin' truth!*"

He shouted the last words, then gathered himself and looked up at Barrett, and when he spoke again his voice was soft.

"She gave me the same story she gave you. If she got a single word different, I don't know what it was. She sat at my kitchen table and told me how she'd been there when my daughter was killed, and how she'd helped hide the body, how she'd stabbed Ian, and how she'd lied. And I...I believed her."

Barrett leaned forward and braced his elbows on his knees, keeping calm, while Howard watched him with what looked like hunger.

"You believed her too," Howard said.

"Yes, I did, once. But the evidence—"

"You're supposed to be the best at it too. Colleen Davis told me that. Don Johansson said the same. Everyone did. You were sent here because you'd know who was lying and who was telling the truth."

It was why he'd been sent here, yes.

"I remember the day you came out to the island to tell me the story," Howard said. "I didn't want to believe you that day. But I came around. Then it all went to hell, and I was trying to get back to believing something new, but Kimmy showed up and..." He shook his head. "Agent Barrett? I *believe her*."

Barrett heard himself say, "I do too." He hadn't wanted to say it, but the words left his lips as if pulled forth by some force beyond his control.

"I knew you did," Howard said triumphantly. "I knew you still did. I don't hate her, not anymore. Do I hate what she did and how long she stayed silent? Of course. But she was scared. That ain't so hard to understand. Then she did what was right, she finally told the truth, and that got her nothing. Got her in a worse position, really. But what reason does she have to lie now? Not a soul around here will hire her, and she's got the little girl to raise too. A daughter of her own. So she needs cash, and I got Jackie's life insurance—you think I can touch that money? Ain't no way in hell I can touch that money. What am I going to buy with that? The only thing I want in this life, I can't ever have back. But for the truth? I'd pay plenty for the truth."

"She's not going to be able to get it for you, Howard."

"Then help her. I'll pay you."

"I'm not taking your money."

"She needs help," Howard Pelletier said plaintively. "Police here don't trust her. But if anyone listened, I think maybe she can prove what he did. What she did."

"Have you asked the police to talk to her again? Johansson or Broward?"

"They don't want to hear it! To them it's done, and Kimmy's like...she's like a cancer. She walks down the sidewalk and people cross the street to avoid her. They watch and they whisper, but nobody talks to her, and if they did, they wouldn't believe a word she said."

He leaned forward and grasped Barrett's shoulder with a grip so fierce, his tendons bunched.

"I see Mathias Burke every week. It's a small town; I can't help but cross his path. I see him buying groceries, see him going into the Harpoon, see him at the lumberyard or the wharf, or I pass him on the road. I watch people shake his hand, I hear people share their friggin' *sympathy* with him, talking about what he went through, and I...I think he might've done it. Agent Barrett? I don't know how much longer I can go like that. It's a lot to hold up against, seeing him and wondering."

It was cool in the garage but a few beads of sweat lined the creases in his forehead, and his eyes looked feverish.

"Can't you listen to her at least?" he asked. "Can't you do that much?"

"I already have, Howard." Barrett had trouble getting the words out, because the intensity of Howard's eyes and his grip felt like an anchor pulling him down into a deep and troubled sea. "Listening to her cost me dearly. Cost you dearly, cost us all."

"One more time," Howard said. "What's the harm in that?"

There was plenty of harm in it, but Barrett found himself nodding instead of objecting.

"One more time," he echoed, his voice little more than a whisper. "I'll listen one more time."

Howard released his shoulder and exhaled in a way that came more from the soul than the lungs.

"Thank you. I can run you out to see her tomorrow."

"I'll need to be alone. When I see her again, when I listen to her again, I cannot have someone else with me. That's a deal breaker to me, Howard."

"That's fine. Can you run a boat?"

Barrett cocked his head. "Yes, but why do I need to? Where is she?"

"The island."

The garage seemed to chill another ten degrees. Barrett stared at him. "She's staying in Jackie's place? You let her stay in—"

"No!" Howard snapped. "She's staying in the cottage. The studio is locked. That'll stay locked too. But she needed to get away from Port Hope. So I took her out there and put her up and told her to just…just lay low for a bit, right? Until we could get someone to listen. Get you to listen."

Two distinct realizations came at Barrett like rolling swells: the depth of anguish that would allow Howard Pelletier to turn his daughter's sacred cottage over to the very woman who'd confessed to hiding her bloodied and broken body, and the depth of conviction he must have in her words.

"I'll go see her tomorrow morning," Barrett said.

"Good. I'll leave my skiff at the public landing. It's a little thing, but it'll make it to the island in calm water."

Barrett nodded and stood. He'd flown out of Bozeman at noon and he should have been feeling the fatigue and the jet lag but instead there seemed to be a fresh, kinetic energy in his blood, his nerves sparking like live wires.

A mistake, he thought, *this is a terrible mistake,* but then Howard Pelletier grasped his hand and said, "I'm glad you came back," and when Barrett said, "Me too," he knew that he'd never spoken more honest words.

22

He never checked into a motel. He spent the remaining hours of the night driving, got halfway to Liz's house before he turned around and worked his way back along the coast, chasing moonlight along the back roads, and as dawn broke he went to a Dunkin' Donuts in Rockland and drank coffee and thought about calling Liz, or Roxanne Donovan, or Don Johansson. He knew that he should make someone aware of his return and of what he'd just been told by Howard Pelletier.

He didn't make any calls.

I'll speak to Kimberly first, he told himself. *I'll do that much, and then let people know.*

It could cost him his job. That idea should have seemed threatening, but after all the months in Bozeman, it didn't. The career he'd anticipated with the Bureau was gone, and he saw his FBI future clearly: a succession of satellite offices, waiting to become pension-eligible in someplace like Iowa or Indiana.

There were other options. The damage he'd done

to his future as an agent wouldn't reach back to his reputation as a professor. But he'd wanted to do the work, not write about it or lecture about it.

He'd wanted to close cases.

Most of America was still asleep by the time he reached the wharf at Port Hope, but there the day was already well in motion—the only fishermen who hadn't headed out were the ones who wouldn't last more than a season or two. Howard Pelletier's boat—the *Jackie II,* named after her as a reminder of what he was working for, what kept him heading out on rough water and in harsh winds—was gone from its mooring, but his skiff remained. He'd have rowed out so Barrett could have the skiff, which was a fourteen-foot aluminum boat with a small outboard, not so different from the one that Barrett's grandfather had owned.

The water was different, though. Even on a calm day in a sheltered bay, and even across so short a distance as Port Hope to Little Spruce, the North Atlantic could remind you of what it really was beyond that pretty face.

As Barrett cast off from the dock and motored away from Port Hope, farther out into the bay, toward the open sea, the morning sun was winning the fight with the fog and the breeze had come to its aid, pushing back the fog in long gusts like strokes of a whisk broom. Each gust seemed to reveal a little more of the coast—high, packed pines that appeared black where they grew thickest, and gray granite cliffs carved jagged by wind and water. This ocean always whispered reminders of its power. It was beautiful, but it was also brutally honest. There were few sandy beaches; there were many battered rocks. It was an ocean that seemed intent on announcing that it hadn't been conquered, only coped with. Anyone who told you that it had been conquered had not sailed out of Bar Harbor or Belfast in foul weather.

It took him twenty minutes to make it to Little Spruce, and he was freezing in his jeans and chambray shirt and sneakers, the lazy casual attire of the airport rendered ridiculous out here on the water, as if he were wearing a sandwich-board sign identifying himself as a rube. The good news was that all the locals had headed out earlier, leaving nobody to gawk at the sight of a tourist stealing a working-man's boat.

When he arrived at Little Spruce, the dock was empty. The island was home to only summer cottages and a dozen diehards like Jackie Pelletier, but it was too small to offer any of the year-round potential of Vinalhaven, Islesboro, and Monhegan, with their fishing communities and ferries. Little

Spruce was about beauty, plain and simple, and it held no shortage of that.

The last time he'd been on the island it was to notify Howard Pelletier of Kimberly Crepeaux's confession. Now he tied up and climbed the ladder to the weathered pier and headed back up the slope to find the same woman and tell her that he was going to listen again—just one more time, that was all.

Just once more.

The studio looked as he remembered it except for the addition of a set of gleaming padlocks on steel hasps. The ancient but solid cottage beside it offered no trace of change, and when he knocked, there was no sound inside, and for an instant he thought that either she was gone or she'd never been here at all, that it was all a cruel tease designed by Howard Pelletier as repayment for the one Barrett had given him. Then the door opened and he stood face-to-face with Kimberly Crepeaux for the first time since he'd visited her in jail on the day the divers had searched the empty pond.

Unlike Howard, who'd seemed to age years in the past few months, she looked unchanged, the short and slight girl with a fragile, almost birdlike bone structure. She seemed likely to blow away in a strong wind, but she was also the only person who'd ever sat across from Barrett and confessed to plunging a knife into a wounded man's stomach before drowning him.

"You're back," she said matter-of-factly. The lack of surprise gave him a sudden realization.

"How does Howard contact you? There's no cell reception out here."

"He gave me some kind of radio. He called it ship-to-shore or something? That way I can talk to him and to my little girl, you know?"

Ship-to-shore phones were expensive. Howard's investment in Kimberly Crepeaux was growing quickly.

"I guess *he* can get your attention," Kimberly said with a touch of petulance. "I never got a call back when I needed help."

Her tone-deafness was astonishing. Barrett said, "Your story and your recanting—do you understand what those meant to people other than you? Do you even think about that, Kimberly? Ever?"

She blinked her pale green eyes at him in confusion. "Of course I do. It's why I went to see him. To make things right."

"To make things right."

She nodded. Her pupils were pinpoints, and he wondered if she was using again.

"I thought my only option was to pretend I'd lied. Once you couldn't find the bodies, what other choice did I have?"

She said that like an accusation, like it was Barrett's fault that she was in this fix.

"I could not find the bodies," he said, "because they were not where you promised they would be. I am also now supposed to believe that your original story was the truth, despite all the evidence to the contrary, despite the fingerprints and DNA linking Jeffrey Girard to those murders."

"Oh, I think I understand that now." She leaned against the door frame, regarding him with pride. "He might've helped move them. See, I heard all sorts of stuff you don't know about."

"Where did you hear all this?"

"In jail, mostly."

Barrett nodded and looked away from her, out to the glittering sea, the adrenaline fading into fatigue. *Here we go again. Kimberly and her jailhouse stories. What sort of idiot do you have to be to come all the way back out here and listen to more of them?*

"Mathias is going to kill me," she said. "Or have somebody do it. Just because he got out of it, that doesn't mean he'll let it go. Me talking to you, telling you how it happened? That'll get me killed." She rubbed her arms, shivering in the wind off the ocean. "Come on inside so I don't freeze, would you?"

"No."

"What?"

"Go get a jacket if you need one. We're taking a field trip, Kimberly."

She looked more fearful at this prospect than she had when she proclaimed that Mathias Burke intended to kill her.

"What are you talking about? I don't want to go talk to more cops. Nobody listens, and they'll just—"

"We aren't going to see any cops. We're going to the pond."

She stopped rubbing her arms. "I don't want to go back there. Not ever again."

"That's why we're going," he said. "It's what I should have done the first time."

He'd made his academic reputation by critiquing the police obsession with physical reactions of suspects. He was convinced that he needed only the words. Now, in practice, he was not so sure. Kimberly was a fine storyteller, but he didn't think much of her as an actress. If that place mattered to her, he thought she would show it.

"I'm not going," she said, jutting her chin like a pouting child, but her eyes were wide and truly afraid.

"Then I'm leaving."

She bit her lower lip and stared past him, back toward the mainland. The wind picked up and tousled her hair and she reached up and pushed it back from her face. Her shirtsleeve slid up when she did that, and he looked for needle tracks but didn't see any. That didn't mean much, though. She could be snorting or smoking.

"Okay," she said then in a soft but firm voice. "I've got her ghost all around me out here already. If I can stand it here, I can stand it out there."

23

They didn't speak much on the boat. He watched her grow progressively more nervous as they neared the Port Hope landing. She kept her head down as she climbed off the boat but her eyes were active, darting. Barrett didn't recognize anyone except one woman who was smoking a cigarette outside the general store. She worked the breakfast and lunch counter inside, and she knew him and certainly knew Kimberly. She turned away as if she hadn't recognized them, but he knew that she had, and he knew that she would talk.

He pulled away from the wharf and then drove up the hill and turned right, onto the Port Hope Road. Kimberly took out a cigarette and lit it. She jiggled her left leg, jittery, and turned her cell phone idly in her hand, but he never saw her touch the screen. When they turned onto the Archer's Mill Road, the speed of her nervous gestures increased, her leg hammering like a piston. Barrett watched her carefully as they drove past the Orchard Cemetery. She kept her face away from it, and in the bright morning sun, she looked as pale as some of the limestone grave markers.

When they reached the dirt drive that led to the camp above the cove, Barrett pulled onto the shoulder and parked in the grass. Kimberly's leg had gone still. She kept her head turned toward the window so he couldn't see her face.

"All right," he said. "Let's have a look."

She set her cell phone in the console but tucked her cigarettes into her pocket and pushed open the door with grim acceptance, like someone entering a booking room.

When they got out of the car and started down the drive, he realized that his own heart was pounding. He'd been curious if the place would trigger any authentic emotional reaction from Kimberly, but he hadn't counted on it doing it to him.

The drive curled around the massive boulder that was nearly as tall as the cabin beside it and then they were facing the cove.

There was no evidence that anything had ever disrupted the peacefulness of this spot. It was as tranquil as ever, the sky clear and the air scented with pine needles. The water was flat and still and dark, its surface reflecting the trees and sky but denying any glimpses of what lay at the bottom.

There was no raft in the cove, and the cabin windows were boarded over, but that was no surprise—

this far north, most people didn't open up their seasonal camps until after Memorial Day. Barrett remembered where the raft had been, though. He had no trouble at all triangulating its position and was just about to point it out to Kimberly when she walked away from him.

She went down to the water's edge, where cattails were beginning to grow in, and he saw that her thin shoulders were shaking. He walked up onto one of the boulders so he could see her face.

She was crying without making a sound. Crying and shaking and staring into that water like something was going to emerge from it and grasp her by the throat.

She's a better actor than you thought.

But he couldn't make himself believe she was acting.

"So...so this is where he parked," she said. She wiped her eyes with the back of a trembling hand. "The first time, he pulled in facing the water. Because it was dark, you know, and he needed the headlights. The next time, he backed down."

Barrett watched in silence.

"If he'd gotten the tires any lower, he might've gotten stuck," she said, staring down at the muck beneath the cattails. "But he didn't. He parked it just right, where he could open the tailgate and we could slide them out and..."

She lost her words to tears then. The shaking intensified, and she breathed in sharp, fast gasps. He was staring at her, entranced, when she suddenly took another step forward and entered the water.

At first, he was too surprised to speak. She simply stepped off the shore and into the frigid pond, the water soaking her sandals and rising up on her jeans.

"Kimberly," he managed finally, "get out of the water."

She gave no indication that she'd heard him. Her pale face was angled toward the north side of the cove—precisely where the raft had been anchored. She was walking right toward it, shaking and crying but showing no reaction to the cold water at all.

He watched her and remembered what she'd once told him.

We took him out into the water. Same way, same place. As far as I can wade up to my neck, and I'm five one, and then Mathias swam him out maybe ten feet farther. They're down there between the raft and the dock. Closer to the raft. You'll find them there. I don't know how deep. They aren't down there very far, though. It's just dark water, and a lonely place.

You'll find them easy.

"They were right here," she said. "It's like I can still see them here. Still *feel* them, how heavy they were when we went into the water and how light they became the deeper it got."

She took two more steps and suddenly the water was up around her shoulders. It got deep fast.

"Kimberly, get out of the water, damn it!" Barrett snapped, and it was his grandfather's voice, the one that usually lived only in his head. It got her attention, though. She emerged from the water like something from a myth, as if she belonged to the pond itself. She was shivering, her thin sweatshirt plastered against her small breasts. Fresh tears chased the old ones as she came toward him.

"They were here," she said. "I promise you, they were here."

He didn't mean to embrace her. Didn't even mean to move. But he'd never seen anyone look so utterly broken. He came down off the rock and put his arms around her as her thin body heaved and shuddered against his, and he rubbed his hands across the wet fabric that clung to the small of her back and said, "I believe you, I believe you," without even pausing to think of the weight of the words.

She tilted her face up toward him, that pale face with the pug nose and freckles that would always keep her looking girlish, at least until she had a knife in her hand, and said, "Bullshit, Barrett. Nobody does."

"That was a stupid thing to do," he said. "It's too damn cold to go in the water like that."

"It's what you wanted, right? To bring it all back to me?"

"No! I just wanted to…"

"What?" she said. "You just wanted to what?"

"I wanted to see if you responded to the place."

She was trembling against him. The lower edge of her hair was soaked and resting against his arm, the rest still dry. Her tiny, taut body seemed even smaller due to the wet drape of her saturated clothes.

"Well?" she said. "Did I *respond* right?" She choked back the tears and said, "His eyes were open, Barrett. His eyes were open and he was trying to breathe. I can't go back to that island either. I can feel Jackie all around me out there. I can't take that again, not after being back here."

Her shaking intensified, either from the memory or the cold water or both. He put his hand on her shoulder to calm her, and that was when he looked beyond her and saw Liz.

24

She was standing halfway down the driveway, in the shadows from the pines, dressed in jeans and a thin fleece and holding a camera. For a moment they were trapped in a silent stare, and then Kimberly Crepeaux, who'd been oblivious, followed his eyes and turned to see Liz. She stepped back quickly.

"What's she doing here?" she snapped, shooting Barrett an accusatory stare. "She's a reporter!"

"I didn't call her," he said.

"No," Liz said, stepping toward them and speaking to Barrett. "He certainly didn't."

She let that remark hang in the air for a moment before returning her attention to Kimberly.

"I got a call this morning from someone saying that you two were out at the Port Hope wharf together. I said, *There is no way*."

"I was going to call you today," Barrett began, and Liz lifted a hand as if to repel the words.

"I'm sure you were."

"No, really. I got in last night, near midnight."

Kimberly was looking from one of them to the other, and Barrett saw some understanding flicker in her eyes.

"It's my fault," she said, speaking to Liz. "I kept calling him."

Liz didn't even look at her. "What are you doing, Rob? What in the world are you doing?"

"Hearing her out. Will you do the same?" He stared hard at her, trying to remind her with eye contact alone of all that lay between them and across the years. "Liz? Please listen to her. Please do that much."

For a time there was no sound but the rustle of the pines in the breeze as he and Liz stood there with Kimberly Crepeaux shivering between them.

"She needs dry clothes," Liz said at last. "She'll fit in mine. They'll be baggy, but she'll fit in them."

"I've even got to hem petite jeans," Kimberly announced. "Can you believe that?"

Liz stared at her for a few seconds as if trying to comprehend a new species, then looked back at him.

"I'm sure I'm not the only one getting calls. Somebody else is going to check the tip out soon enough."

"We'll talk to you. She'll do that." Barrett nudged Kimberly. "Right?"

"I guess," Kimberly said softly. "I guess I'm talking to everybody again. It didn't do much good last time, though, did it?"

No one answered that.

25

When she told them her latest story, Kimberly Crepeaux was sitting at Liz's kitchen table with a cup of coffee that she didn't drink, just pressed between her hands. She was also wearing Liz's jeans, which flapped around her feet like she was a child trying on her mother's clothes, and a sweater that was a closer fit, too long but snug enough.

Vehicles had followed her since the day she got out of jail, she said. Different types, sometimes a car, sometimes a truck, sometimes a van. But they were always there. She'd been free for six days before the first window was shot out at her grandmother's house—her *mémère,* as Kimberly called her, the French-Canadian word for "grandmother"—and then someone started coming by in the night, shining flashlights in the windows, and that scared her grandmother and made Kimberly's daughter cry, and she knew she had to leave.

"They hadn't done anything wrong," she said. "Ava, she's just a little baby girl. And Mémère, she's only wanted me to be better than what I am, my whole life. They didn't deserve this. I mean, Mathias is keeping me from getting a job even!"

Barrett and Liz exchanged a look—this was the Kimberly everyone knew, the sob story, the excuses, the tall tales.

Kimberly shook a cigarette out from a saturated pack and reached for her lighter.

"Please don't smoke in my home," Liz said.

Kimberly sighed and tossed the damp cigarette down.

"How has he kept you from getting a job?" Barrett asked, trying to keep this thing moving.

She told them how she'd applied for jobs up and down the coast, always with employers who had a history of working cooperatively with the parole office. Some showed interest, but by the next day the job was gone. For all of this, she blamed the outsize—or outlandish—influence of Mathias Burke. People in town didn't understand Mathias like people in jail did, Kimberly explained. Everybody on the outside liked him, respected him, or didn't know him. People on the inside, though? "He scares them shitless," she said. "Men who aren't scared of anybody, they're real careful using his name. He's never been arrested, never been inside once, but he scares people."

This was pre-confession Kimberly, the prolific source of rumors that couldn't be verified, and

Barrett knew that Liz's fuse was burning down fast.

"Tell me something new, Kimberly," he said. "I can't go to bat for you with the same old shit."

She did that jutting-chin gesture of the only child that she resorted to so often and said, "Jeff Girard sold drugs. He didn't just use them. He and his cousin sold them."

"Okay. What does that have to do with the murders?"

Kimberly shrugged.

"Something new," he said, trying to keep the fatigue out of his voice, "that has a *connection to the murders*."

"Um…well, that's harder. Oh, hang on—you know those parties Ian Kelly would throw? Down at the private beach by his house?"

Barrett nodded. Ian enjoyed hosting, particularly for the locals, liked presenting himself as a man of the people as opposed to the privileged outsider.

"The bonfires?"

"Yes! Exactly. Well, there were drugs at those bonfires. That girl who drowned earlier in the summer, Molly Quickery? I heard she might not have drowned at all. That she was dead before she went into the water because she'd OD'd at one of those parties. Which would *not* have surprised me. Molly Quickery was a wicked mess. I mean, she made

Cass Odom look, like, *classy*. Guys liked her because of her boobs, but she was a slut. Molly Quicker-Lay, that's what the guys used to call her. I heard so many stories about her, you wouldn't even believe it. I heard one story about her giving a blow—"

"It was in the paper." Liz's voice was tight with anger.

Kimberly cocked an eyebrow. "The story about her blowing two guys at the same party was in the paper?"

Liz put her hands to her temples. "No. The story about the cause of her death was in the paper. She was dead before she went into the water, and I know that because I wrote that, and therefore anyone who can read might know it too. So let's stop pretending like that is some sort of an insider tip."

Liz was close to losing her temper, and Barrett felt the same way. They were watching Kimberly spin her tires now, hunting for traction, but she didn't have anything new.

"What does any of this have to do with Ian?" he asked.

"Well, they were his parties. He might've been selling the drugs."

This was unlikely—Ian Kelly had no arrest history and no need for money, so the risks and rewards of drug dealing were a very poor fit for him.

"You told me that Ian died because he was a witness to a hit-and-run," Barrett said. "That's the whole story, which you now insist is the truth again."

"Right. It is the truth."

"Then why do we care if he did drugs or sold drugs? What does that have to do with you three taking his body down to the pond and stabbing him after an accident?"

"I'm not saying one has anything to do with the other, but, it's, like, proof that I'm still trying, right? I'm the only one trying to keep people interested in the truth, Barrett."

He wanted to slap her. All of the pity he'd felt watching her in the water was gone again; she was just the same old Kimberly, taking him along for the ride.

"Girard left evidence," he said. "Nobody else did. That's a problem, Kimberly."

She shrugged.

"Why did you even tell me the story?" Barrett asked. "You'd been lying to me for weeks. Why did you decide to tell the truth?"

She stared at the table. "The card," she said. "That stupid old card. I don't know why she kept that. I didn't even...I mean, it wasn't even a very nice card. I just wanted her to know that she'd been lucky, right? She'd had a good mom for a while, which was more than I had. And she still had a good dad. She was lucky."

Her voice had gone faint, and she lifted her hand as if to wipe away a tear but scratched the side of her face instead. "I just remember the way Howard looked at her," she said softly. "The way he held her hand so tightly that day when she came back to school, and the way he looked at her when he finally let her go...you could just tell how *scared* of her he was. Because he loved her so much. And we took her from him. Everything he was afraid of back then, we made true."

She looked up again, eyes bright. "I'm sorry I waited, but now I'm *trying,* at least. Everyone says, *Prove it, prove it, prove it.* But I don't know how to do that! All I know is that I was there when Mathias hit Jackie, I was there when he cracked Ian's skull with that pipe, and then their bodies were in my *own hands in the water!*" Her voice was rising, high and shrill now. "I can tell you that I picked up a knife and *stabbed him* through that plastic and he was still trying to breathe and he was looking right at me, I can tell you that, but you don't want to listen! Because I'm a liar, I'm Kimmy Crepeaux and all I do is take drugs and lie! That's what you people want to believe! But I held their bodies in my own hands and I carried them into that pond and it is the truth! So *you* fucking prove it!"

She emphasized each word of the last sentence by smacking Liz's glass-topped table with her palm.

For a moment, nobody said anything. Then Liz gathered herself and said, "You were arrested trying to buy heroin last week. If you want to improve your credibility, that's not the best way to go about it."

"Fuck you."

Liz took that with only a slight widening of the eyes. "In my house and wearing my clothes, no less," she said. "Charming."

"And staring at me like I'm nothing more than shit on your shoe the whole time. Did I try to buy drugs? Absolutely. You want to know why? Because I'm *scared*." She reached for the damp cigarette and twisted it in her fingers. "And because I know what I saw! What I did. I know what I did." The cigarette broke and spilled wet tobacco onto the tabletop. "He was breathing," she said, her voice desperate and imploring. "He was breathing, and his eyes were open. He was looking at me."

She swept the broken cigarette aside and stared at Liz. "Think about that, and then tell me you wouldn't want to take something that could make that memory go away."

She was mesmerizing. If she was a liar, Barrett thought, she really was the best.

"What about the truck?" Kimberly said. "That

helps me, right? I was right about the truck, except for the paint. Don't you think that's strange? That I had the right truck, if I was making it all up?"

"*Except for the paint* is a big problem," Barrett said, although she was hitting a nerve here, the memory of the body shop, when he'd opened the door of the old Dakota and looked at the bench seat and thought that she'd described it just right. "I've talked to people about this, Kimberly—nobody re-painted that hood. It was old and rusted and gray. It was not what you claim to have seen."

She blinked and her eyes suddenly filled with tears that didn't spill.

"I know," she whispered. "I was scared when you didn't find the bodies, but then I thought, well, Mathias moved them, that's all. But the truck paint was..." She swallowed. "The paint makes me think I'm crazy. I'm telling you all these things, and I *know* they happened, right? I was there. I saw them. I *did* them. But the police brought me pictures of the truck, and they explained all of this scientific bull-shit about how the rust that was there couldn't have been painted over or whatever. I didn't know what to tell them. The hood was real bright white, too bright, and there was a black cat on it with red eyes. Who makes something like that up? But then they tell me it's not possible, and they had pictures and paint samples and rust samples and..."

She ran out of breath. Reached for the broken cigarette and then stilled her hand.

"Maybe they're right," she said. "But if they are?
Then I'm crazy, not a liar. Because I know what
happened that night." She looked up and stared first
at Liz, then at Barrett. "I know who I killed."

26

She drank two beers and then fell asleep on Liz's couch. They stood above her until they were sure she was asleep, like parents watching a child, and only then did they move to the kitchen.

"She can't stay here," Liz said.

"I know that. I'll put her up in a hotel or something."

"What are you doing, *begging* to be fired?"

"I don't know what else to do with her. She won't go home, and she won't go back to…"

Liz arched her eyebrows. "Won't go back to where?"

He blew out a long breath, glanced at the room where Kimberly was sleeping on the couch, and said, "She was staying on Little Spruce. In Howard's cottage."

"Kimmy Crepeaux is staying where Jackie Pelletier lived?"

"Shh!" He held up his hands against her rising voice, and she lifted her own in response against her rising temper, then she turned from him, pressed her fingers to her temples, and shook her head slowly.

"The studio is locked," he told her.

"What difference does that make!"

"It makes one to Howard, I can assure you of that."

He told her about the phone calls then, and his trip to see Howard in the middle of the night.

"Howard believes her?" she asked, staring at the diminutive form of Kimberly Crepeaux curled up on her couch. Kimberly was snoring softly.

"Yes," Barrett said. "Howard believes her. And now you've heard her out in person. So tell me: What do you think?"

Liz leaned on the kitchen island, looked at him, and then away. "I don't want to tell you what I think."

If he hadn't known her so well for so long, he might have misinterpreted this gesture, this statement. But he was remembering the way she'd responded when he'd told her about the lies his grandfather had offered. She had looked away from him that day because she hadn't wanted to disagree with him. She was looking away from him today because she didn't want to agree with him. In both circumstances, she saw risk for him on the horizon. There was no reason for him to have such certainty except for the familiarity of people who had long understood each other in the darkness.

"Liz?" he said. "I need to know."

She turned to face him, her hair sweeping across her cheek.

"I understand now why you believed her."

"But you still don't?"

She bowed her head. He could see the top of the tattooed script that traced just below her collarbone. "Two hours ago, I'd have said no chance. When I got the first call saying you'd been seen with her down in Port Hope, I was devastated that you'd come back to listen to *that,* to *her.* But…"

She crossed the kitchen and stepped into the small sunroom that served as her dining room. She sat down and stared at the pines, looking exhausted.

"I certainly believe this much of what she said— the truck is the biggest problem. It's one thing to say that her whole story rests on bodies in a pond that turned out not to be in that pond. It's one thing to say that they were shot, not stabbed. We can believe that happened later, right? We can believe Girard helped Mathias move the bodies, maybe. But the truck is harder. You put out that bulletin for a white truck with a black cat painted on it, but the truck you found at Girard's with their blood in it was completely different."

"Yeah," he said. "That is a problem."

"There are plenty of people around here who still think she told part of the truth, actually," Liz said.

"What part?"

"That she was an accomplice to murder, and that she was in the Dodge Dakota when it happened. The rest of it—who was with her, how Jackie and Ian were killed, and what was done to them—is still up for debate."

He nodded. He'd had plenty of time to think of those options himself. To wonder whether he had gotten to the right woman but extracted the wrong story from her.

"She believes what she's saying," Liz said. "I never saw that before, I only heard it from you. But she *believes* her story."

"Yes, she does." He leaned against the kitchen island and they studied each other in the fading light. "So I'm back where I started."

"Prove her story?"

"Right." He glanced at the couch. "And figure out what to do with her."

"One night," Liz said. "She can stay for one night."

"You don't have to do that. I haven't asked you for that, and I won't."

"If you'd asked, I would have said no," she said, and she gave a familiar wry smile with only the corner of her mouth. "When was the last time you slept, Rob?"

"It's been a few hours."

"You look like shit. Go get some rest. I'll stay down here and keep an eye on your girl. I probably should hide the knives."

"Bad joke."

"Who said it was one?"

He stepped down into the sunroom and knelt before her, put his hands on her thighs, and looked up at her. "You know why I'm doing this. I've got to put some certainty behind this one. For Howard, for Amy and George."

She leaned down and touched his forehead softly with her lips, then rested her face against his.

"I know why you're doing this," she said. "And you can keep telling yourself those are the reasons. In the meantime, Rob, be careful listening to that girl's story. Whether it is true or not, it can burn your life to the ground."

27

Liz woke him at four in the morning with the news that Kimberly was gone.

"What do you mean, gone?"

"Walked out of my house wearing my clothes, that kind of gone."

He sat up, moving to push the covers back but catching nothing but air. He hadn't even undressed, just gotten his shoes off before lying back on the bed and falling into a deep and troubled sleep.

"I heard her go out the side door and when I went to yell for her, she started running up the drive," Liz said.

Barrett pulled on his shoes and went down the steps and outside. He couldn't see anything but trees and shadows. The drive was a long winding path through the woods that led out to the rural, two-lane highway that ran between Camden and Augusta. There was never much traffic on it, and at this time of morning, it was completely silent.

He got into his car and started down the drive, figuring he'd have to gamble on turning east or west and guessing that she would have gone east, back toward the coast, when he came around a curve and she was pinned in the headlights. She was standing at the end of the driveway, trying to light a cigarette while staring at her phone. Her face was lit a ghostly blue from the screen. When he got out of the car, she looked back at him and wiped her eyes with the heel of the hand that held the cigarette, blotting fresh tears.

"What are you doing?" he said.

"Got a ride coming. I know she doesn't want me there, and I don't want to be there either. Can't sleep there, can't sleep out at Little Spruce. I just need some friggin' rest, Barrett. That's all."

"Where are you going to rest?"

She made a dismissive gesture. "I got a friend coming."

"Who?"

"None of your damned business."

He reached back through the open window and shut off the engine.

"I'll wait with you, then."

"I don't need you to wait with me. Go on back to bed." She was looking up the road uneasily. "I'll call you tomorrow, tell you where I am."

"No, thanks. You called me all the way back from Montana. Remember that? I'd rather know where you are. I don't have time to waste finding you."

Headlights interrupted them, winding up the

road from below. They were both silent as the car approached—an old Saturn that sounded like a steam locomotive. The car pulled up beside them, the window slid down, and a voice from inside said, "Yo, Kimmy, who's your friend?"

It was a young white kid with a thin beard tracing his jaw, most of his face hidden by the shadows from his Red Sox cap, but Barrett knew the car. The last time he'd seen its driver, he'd been fighting for breath on the floor of the Harpoon.

Barrett leaned down so Ronnie Lord could see his face.

"Aw, shit," Ronnie said. "What are you doing to me, Kimmy?"

"Where are you taking her, Ronnie?" Barrett said.

"I'm not taking her anywhere. This is bullshit. This is entrapment, man. You had her text me— that's not legal. That's not…nothing you find is legal." He was already putting the car in park, prepared for the inevitable search.

"It's your lucky night, Ronnie. If you tell me the truth, you get to drive out of here with no searches. Where were you taking her?"

"Nowhere. Seriously. I was just…" He wet his lips, studied Barrett, and decided that honesty was the lowest-risk option. "I was dropping off for her, man. She hit me with this address, and I was dropping off what she needed. I don't know what you're asking about, where I was taking her, all that. I'm not a damn cabdriver."

"Of course not. It's legal to drive a taxi." Barrett stepped back from the window and smacked the Saturn's door. "Get out of here. I'd dump whatever shit you've got, though. Cops can hear you coming from Belfast to Bangor. And, Ronnie? If I learn that you told anybody about where you stopped tonight—"

"Nah, nah, nah." He held up his hands, the picture of innocence. "I don't remember a thing, bro."

"Go home, Ronnie."

Ronnie Lord shifted the car back into drive. The exhaust clattered like a sawmill and he pulled away. Barrett watched his taillights disappear, and when he turned to look at Kimberly, he saw Liz standing in the driveway behind her.

"That was Ronnie Lord?" she said. "At my home in the middle of the night?"

"Yes," Barrett said, feeling a building rage like distant thunder. "Kimberly needed a package. Strange, considering she told me she's been clean."

"I *have* been clean! But then you took me to the pond and made me remember it again, and now all I can see is them! I close my eyes and I see the way the blood bubbled up in all that plastic and how it got caught in his mouth when he tried to breathe! I just wanted something to make it go away."

"We're leaving now," Barrett said. He was hearing Kimberly but it was Liz's voice that resonated with him—a drug dealer had pulled up to her driveway in the middle of the night, and it was, ultimately, Barrett who'd allowed that. "Pick a destination, Kimberly. Pick a bus station, pick Ronnie's basement, I don't give a shit. But you are leaving."

"Take me to Mémère's, I guess."

"Fine."

"I don't know if she'll even open the door for me."

"I guess we'll find out," Barrett said, suddenly exhausted. He went around the car and pulled the passenger door open and waited. Kimberly finally walked over to it. Just before she climbed inside, she stopped and looked back at Liz.

"Miss Street? I'm sorry. I just…I just needed to make it stop for a little while, that was all. If you'd seen the same things I did, you'd understand."

She ducked into the car without waiting for a response.

28

They made the drive in silence, with Kimberly facing away from him. Only when they were back in Port Hope, closing in on her grandmother's house, did she speak.

"I've been clean, Barrett. I've been trying real hard."

"You've tried to buy at least twice this week."

"That doesn't mean I haven't been trying hard!"

He'd been around enough addicts to know that wasn't a lie.

"We'll get you help," he said. "There are good programs."

Her face told him that was a nonstarter, but she nodded and said, "All I need is a little bit of rest. Get to see my baby girl. She always puts a smile on my face, you know?" And her face did brighten a touch, just thinking about it. "I'll see her, and I'll get some rest, and I'll be okay."

They were two blocks from her grandmother's house when she said, "Stop here. Mémère isn't really a fan of yours. I got enough trouble without letting her see you."

He didn't argue, just pulled up to the curb and watched her climb out, still wearing Liz's too-long jeans. She'd rolled them up before she made her break for the road and Ronnie Lord's promised fix, and now she looked like a little girl who'd been out wading.

"When I call, you need to answer," he said. "Promise me that, Kimberly."

"I will. Same goes for you."

"Yes."

She hesitated before closing the door. "Where you going now, Barrett?"

He looked at the band of pink light that was clawing up along the eastern horizon. "I'm going down to see Bobby Girard. I've got some ground to make up with the truck."

"Be careful with him," she said. "He might not be as bad as Mathias, but I haven't heard anything good about the Girard family."

"I'll be careful," Barrett said. "And you'll stay clean. Deal?"

"Deal." She stepped back from the car and closed the door. He watched her walk past the old saltbox houses and occasional trailer that lined the less-tourist-friendly backstreets of Port Hope, a lost child off to reunite with her own child, and he thought of Ronnie Lord driving out in the middle of the night with a needle for her arm or powder for her nose and wished he'd hauled Ronnie out of the car and kicked his ass once more.

Don't get your blood up.

He wasn't here to roust small-time dope dealers. He was here to put Mathias Burke in prison for two murders.

He pulled away from the curb and headed for Biddeford, to the salvage yard where just nine months earlier his life had spun out of his control. When he passed Kimberly, she turned and waved. It was such an odd, cheerful gesture—like one friend bidding another farewell after a long and raucous but ultimately fun night—that he didn't even react. He just stared at her as he passed by, and then she was facing back toward her grandmother's house, and he was pulling away.

Girard's body shop and salvage yard seemed to be decaying at an accelerated rate. The weeds were taller, the cars were fewer, the siding on the garages more dirty and mildewed. Business had not boomed for Bobby after the revelation that his cousin was a multiple murderer.

He was there, though, and he was at work. When Barrett got out of his car, he heard the high shriek of a saw cutting through metal, and he remembered the staccato clatter of the air hammer and winced.

The gate was unlocked today, so he didn't have to climb the fence, but he felt a sick sense of déjà vu. Although he knew the Dodge truck had been impounded, he still glanced at the spot where it had been.

Unlike his first advance on the property, this time the garage doors were up, and he could see a man moving around a car that was chained to a frame rack. He wondered how much of a difference it would have made if the doors hadn't been down and the air hammer hadn't been in use. What might have happened? And what might Jeffrey Girard have been able to tell him?

Bobby Girard was cutting a crumpled hood off a prehistoric Cadillac, sparks flying, goggles over his eyes. He was facing the front of the garage, though, so he saw Barrett approaching and shut off the saw and lifted the goggles. He looked relaxed, even friendly, until Barrett was almost inside the building. Then he recognized him.

"Get off my property."

"I understand that reaction," Barrett said, "but I think you'll want to hear me out."

"I want to use this saw on your spine, actually."

"I didn't pull the trigger on him, Bobby."

"I don't give a damn. You were here when it happened."

Barrett glanced to his left, at the spot where he'd knelt over Jeffrey Girard as the man tried desperately to keep his life from leaking out. The grass was tall and bright and green where he'd died.

"I also don't think he murdered those two," Barrett said. "And I've come back to try and prove it."

"Bullshit."

"Let me ask you something, Bobby—how'd all this work out for me?"

"A hell of a lot better than it did for Jeff. Or my family."

"Better than that, yeah. But I lost my job over this case," Barrett said, which wasn't entirely untrue because the transfer to Bozeman had felt like a firing. "Now I come back and tell you that I want to set the record straight, and you're sure you don't want to hear me out?"

Bobby Girard stood behind the wrecked car, glowering at Barrett, the goggles perched up on his head like the eyes of an insect.

Barrett said, "I think he was trying to give us the gun."

Bobby blinked at him. "What did you say?"

"He came out holding it across his body. It was never pointed at us."

"That's not what you pricks said to defend yourselves!"

"It's always been what *I* said, at least. He came out

here holding it like this..." Barrett mimed the position of the shotgun. "And then later, after he had bullets in him, he tried to push it toward me. He couldn't talk then, but he was trying to communicate through the gesture. I think he was trying to show me that what he'd always intended to do was give up the gun."

At the description of his cousin dying on the ground, Bobby Girard clenched his jaw and looked away. "He'd gone to jail before on the same charge," he said. "Felon in possession of a firearm. He'd have wanted to give it up to you, yeah. I bet he thought that's what you were here for. He'd pulled it out of a wrecked car and was talking about selling it. That's probably what he was going to admit to before you shot him."

Barrett wanted to say *It wasn't me* again, but what was the point? "Or maybe he was going to admit to being involved in heroin," Barrett said. "I heard he was part of the trade."

"You wanna talk drugs, go get a warrant."

"I don't give a shit about your drugs, but I'll be more than happy to use them as leverage if I need to. The only thing I care about, Bobby, is making sure the right man goes down for those murders. Now, we can talk about that, or I can find ways to get your back up against the wall and see if you're more talkative when you're looking at charges of your own."

"I don't talk to cops," Girard said.

"Actually, you do. You told them that Jeff had loaned his truck to someone up around Rockland."

"That's right."

"But you don't know who?"

Bobby shook his head. "He'd had a bad summer up around there, was feeling guilty about some shit he'd gotten into with a friend, and I didn't ask many questions. That doesn't mean I'm lying, though. I just don't know, plain and simple. All I know is I had to give Jeff a loaner because he'd taken money from somebody to give up his truck for a few days. To be clear, he didn't loan it to anybody. They paid him to use it."

"That's not a truck many people would pay for," Barrett said.

"Exactly what I told him. But he had cash in hand, and his truck was gone."

Barrett stepped into the garage, and Bobby didn't attempt to stop him. There were tools scattered around the concrete floor, and workbenches overflowed with parts, and the chains on the frame rack were coated with thick, coarse grease. The impression was chaos, but Barrett bet that Bobby Girard knew where every wrench was and which old coffee cans held which bolts.

"There's a lot of evidence that isn't explained just by the truck. Fingerprints on the bags, the barrels."

"Man, I don't know. Maybe that shit was stolen."

"Mathias had to have a partner," Barrett said. "He was in custody when the bodies' location was reported. Someone on the outside was helping him. That person knew where they were too. Would Jeff have helped him with the bodies? Let's say Jeff didn't kill them, wasn't even around when it happened. Fine. Could he have been talked into moving those bodies or sending that e-mail? Maybe Mathias paid him, maybe bribed him with drugs, maybe threatened him. Would he have helped hide the bodies?"

Bobby took one of the chains on the frame rack in his hand and squeezed. The tension seemed to ripple up his body, hand to shoulder to neck.

"I don't want to believe it, but *maybe*. If he was high? Yeah, maybe. He was feeling so guilty about what had gone down with this dude in Rockland...I don't know. Jeff was a good guy, man. When he wasn't high, he would give you the shirt off his back, let you track it through the mud, and then put it back on without complaint. Which is pretty much how everybody treated him, because he was slow. People picked on Jeff from the time we were kids. He never learned how to guard against that. Jeff trusted everybody. From the day he was born until the day he died, he couldn't believe anyone he met had bad intentions."

He stopped talking. His gaze had gone distant and sad.

"You really think he was trying to give you the gun?" he asked. "I didn't see any of it, you know? I just saw you come in, and I was so scared I damn near pissed down my leg. But all of my family, they keep asking me how it went, and I got no idea."

"I don't think we'll ever know for sure," Barrett said. "But what I can tell you—*all* I can tell you—is that I saw the way he looked at me, and I saw what he did with the gun. He was trying to push it toward me. I think he wanted me to understand something that had been miscommunicated."

"That would be just like Jeff. It always took him a couple swings before he made contact."

Barrett leaned on the frame of the old Cadillac.

"He never painted that truck hood?"

"Jeff never touched the truck with any paint. That whole story about the way the hood looked had to be bullshit."

"Kimberly talked about how bright it was," Barrett said. "If you listen to her specific words, she talked about the way the *paint* looked, not just the design. She thought the paint itself looked strange. Too bright. That was her phrase. Could that have been done with some type of sticker, a vinyl logo, like the kind with the company name that Mathias Burke uses on his trucks and vans?"

Bobby Girard reached out and touched the hood of the old Cadillac as if imagining the method Barrett had just suggested.

"It's possible, I suppose, but I think it would be hard to get the whole hood just right." He ran his palm across the expanse of metal and frowned. "But if you actually believe what she said, then it almost had to have been done that way." He looked up, eyes bright with surprise. "You really believe that girl's story, don't you?"

"Yes," Barrett said. "I do. So the truck is a problem."

They silently stood there beside the gutted Cadillac, and ten feet behind them the wind ruffled the grass where Jeffrey Girard had died. There would be no answers coming from that place. It was doomed to memory and questions now.

Barrett finally broke the silence by saying, "What was he feeling guilty about up in Rockland?"

"Huh?"

"You said he'd gotten into some shit with a friend up there."

Bobby's chest filled with a deep breath and then he said, "He'd sold a sick batch. Wasn't his fault, but he couldn't get it out of his mind."

"Heroin?"

"With fentanyl, yeah. Jeff didn't even know what he had. Fool's luck saved him. Most times, whatever he had went into his own bloodstream, but this time, he sold it to some buddy of his up in Rockland, and that cat was dead the next morning. I remember when he wasn't going on about feeling guilty, he was carrying on about feeling lucky. Think about that, right? A couple months before two cops show up and kill him and then a murder rap gets hung on his neck before his funeral, and he's talking about good luck."

"Did this guy in Rockland die before or after Jackie and Ian disappeared?"

"Around the same time."

"You know his name?"

"Something with initials. J.R. or J.D., maybe?"

Barrett nodded, filing this away. "How often did Jeff sell?"

"Not much. You'll hear other talk, I'm sure, because that's what people do once a guy is dead, but he wasn't some regular dealer. He didn't sell as much as trade, really."

"With who?"

Bobby bowed his head like a battered boxer, closed his eyes, and gripped the chain on the frame rack again, as if to take strength from the steel. "I don't know the names, just the place, but it's only going to make you think he's guilty because of where it is. Some dive bar in Port Hope. I know that's close to where they went missing, but I still don't think—"

"What bar?"

The intensity in Barrett's voice drew Bobby's attention. He looked surprised. "The Harpoon, I think?"

For a moment Barrett couldn't find his voice. Bobby seemed to take his silence as confusion, so he said, "Maybe that's not what it's called, but it was something like that."

"Yeah," Barrett said finally. "That's what it's called."

"You know the place?"

"I know the place."

29

If the FBI ever got serious about improving efficiency, they'd do well to hire librarians.

Barrett had been in the beautiful Camden Public Library beside the harbor for less than fifteen minutes before the woman at the reference desk found the case he was looking for.

"There were at least forty-two overdose deaths in Maine in August of 2016, but only four in Knox County," she said, clicking away at her keyboard while the printer hummed beside her.

"Forty-two?" Barrett said.

"That's right. It was a very bad summer. For the year, Maine averaged about one overdose death per day, but that summer it was even higher."

It was moving around like a fever that summer, Kimberly Crepeaux had said.

In the year of their deaths, Jackie Pelletier and Ian Kelly had accounted for 10 percent of Maine's murder rate, two of the state's twenty homicides. In the same year, 368 Mainers had died from drug overdoses.

Dealers found lucrative ground in the state. A tenth of a gram might fetch five dollars in Queens or Newark, but it would pull fifty dollars in the rural reaches of Maine. Supply and demand were the age-old arbiters of price, and out in the deep woods or along the lonely coast, supply was scarce, and demand was high. In areas where police resources were overstretched and addiction resources nonexistent, the drugs held sway. One of the state's more uncomfortable problems was the prevalence of drug abuse in its famous lobstering industry, an industry essential to both the state's economy and its identity. Maine lobstermen were portrayed as tough and tireless, the cowboys of the sea, up before dawn and out on the water in all weather, hauling their traps with rugged relentlessness. All of this was true. Also true was that plenty of the men hauling traps now were high while they were doing it. In a business that required bruising work through brutal conditions, prescription painkillers were a valuable aid, and when their cheaper, easier-to-acquire cousin heroin was made available, it found willing customers.

Drugs were taking more lobstermen's lives than the sea now.

"A fisherman with the first initials J.R. died at his home in Tenants Harbor two years ago in July," the librarian told Barrett. "Full name was Julian Richard Millinock."

The punch that Bobby Girard had landed with

the first reference to the Harpoon now felt like a jab, and the librarian had delivered the big right cross hiding behind it.

"Millinock," Barrett echoed. "I know the name. But the one I know is named Mark. I don't know anybody named Julian or J.R."

She was scrutinizing the story. "There's a Mark mentioned here. An uncle. It says Julian was the beloved son of Adrian and Lucille, brother of Mary, and nephew of Mark."

Barrett had a vague memory of Adrian Millinock—he'd been a fisherman, and he'd kept his distance from his brother.

"I guess I'll catch up with Mark, then," Barrett said, a cold stone in the pit of his stomach. He hadn't wanted to find his way back to the Harpoon.

The librarian handed him the printout of the obituary. It showed a muscular man with a bearded face split into a smile. Julian Richard Millinock, dead at twenty-six.

He paid for the copies and was walking out, his head down, reading, when she said, "Have a good afternoon, Agent Barrett."

He looked back with surprise, and she regarded him without a hint of judgment.

"I remember you," she said.

"Okay," he said, unsure of how to respond to the flat statement.

"Mind if I ask you a question?" she said.

He waited.

"Do you think they got it right? I know that's also to ask if you got it wrong, but that's not my point. People still talk about them so often, you see. Jackie and Ian, they were our tragedy. People still wonder."

"I didn't get it wrong," Barrett said, and he left before she could ask any more questions.

The Harpoon had been an operation of arbitrary hours when Ray Barrett owned it, the locks turned according to his moods and sobriety, but Mark Millinock ran it with more consistency—he opened every day at four, and he closed whenever the last drink was paid for.

It was just after three when Barrett arrived, and the parking lot was empty and no one answered his knock. Mark's battered Jeep Wrangler was in its spot behind the building, though, so he couldn't have gone far.

The Harpoon wasn't waterfront property, but it wasn't far from the water either. In Port Hope, nothing was. The public landing, with its tourist-friendly bars and quaint general store and ice cream shop, was only a mile away from the Port Hope boatyard, which was just down the steep hill behind the Harpoon, but it felt like the two were much farther apart than that. The boatyard offered no entertainment value for visitors from away—it was about function, not form. The people who used it didn't care that the dumpsters obscured the water view because nobody gave a damn about a photo op when he was hauling garbage on an icy February morning.

Barrett had always liked the boatyard. As a kid he'd spent hours fishing with mackerel jigs off the short pier and talking to the men who came and went. Several of them had taken a special interest in him because they knew his grandfather, and they knew that it couldn't be much fun to be Ray's grandson.

Today, the boatyard was quiet, and Mark Millinock was alone on the pier. He was in a lawn chair at the end of the dock, smoking a cigarette with his feet up on one of the wharf pylons, and when he heard footsteps on the dock boards, he turned without much interest. Then he recognized Barrett and swung his feet down and straightened up.

"Look who's back," he said. "I thought they sent your ass to Missouri or someplace."

"Montana."

"How was it?"

"Cold."

Mark laughed. He was showing none of the animosity that Barrett had expected, but there was no mystery to that—he seemed to be riding a good high.

"So they sent you back to Maine to get warm?" he said. "That doesn't make much sense."

Barrett leaned on the wharf pylon and watched the boats at mooring in the bay rise and fall gently in water that glittered like broken glass.

"They didn't send me back," he said.

"You quit the FBI?"

"Not exactly."

"You get canned?" Mark asked with hopeful enthusiasm.

"No."

"Oh, mutual breakup, then. Yeah, that's what I've called every one of mine."

"I've got some questions for you," Barrett said, "but it's important for you to remember that I don't have a case here anymore. I'm vacationing, right?"

"Vacationing. I like that. Came back to see old friends?"

"Sure."

"Then the questions shouldn't have anything to do with Ma-thias, 'cause he's no friend of yours. Now that I think about it..." Mark made a show of pretending to count on his fingers before closing his hands into fists. "I can't think of any friends you've got here anymore."

"That might be true," Barrett said. "But I still have my questions."

"That'll be on your tombstone," Mark said.

"'Here lies Rob Barrett—he still has his questions.'"

Mark gave a too-loud, too-jittery laugh. Whatever was coursing through his bloodstream was an awfully cheerful substance. Barrett wondered what he'd be like when he came back down and the laughter stopped.

"My point," he said, "is that I can't do anything to you, no matter what you say. Understand? I'm just passing through. You could tell me what you're using right now, for example, and I wouldn't arrest you or even show any interest."

Barrett was expecting either denial or distrust, but instead Mark snorted and said, "Shit, you sound just like your partner. That mean you want the same thing?"

Barrett cocked his head. "My partner? You mean Johansson? He's come around?"

Mark nodded, seeming surprised that Barrett didn't know and a little regretful that he'd mentioned it. "You guys can't let it go, can you? You'd think nobody had ever been murdered before."

Barrett felt an odd flush of pride and camaraderie, his surprise giving way to admiration. He'd thought Don would try to leave it behind. Nipping at the heels of that admiration, though, was a touch of envy—was Johansson already out in front of him?

"Did he ask about your nephew?"

Mark Millinock's amused face went cold and dark.

"You speak about my nephew, asshole? J.R. was a good kid, and he didn't have shit to do with those murders."

"I know he didn't. He was dead before they happened."

They held a stare until Mark's jumpy eyes couldn't take it any longer, and he turned and spat into the water angrily.

"You need to leave. I don't know what makes a man foolish enough to come back around the same fire that burned him before, but I don't want to be a part of it."

Barrett said, "Do you want to know who sold him the bad batch?"

Mark lit a fresh cigarette and blew smoke toward the water.

"Will it matter to me?" he asked finally.

"Maybe. It was Jeff Girard."

Mark Millinock turned and stared at him through the wafting smoke.

"You're serious?"

Barrett nodded.

Mark took a long pull on the cigarette and then released the smoke without seeming to exhale. It framed his face like a ghostly sketch.

"This is news to you," Barrett said.

"If it's not bullshit, then I suppose it could pass as news, yeah."

"It's not bullshit. Came from Bobby Girard, down in Biddeford. He said that Jeff was tight with your nephew, sold him a bad batch, and felt like hell over it. Does that sound believable?"

Mark leaned forward and braced his elbows on his knees, looking suddenly weary.

"He bought a few grams of that DC from somebody, no question about that. That was back before people were really talking about it, though. And I'd seen Girard. He was around Rockland and out in T-Harbor that summer. Was the drugs that led him here, I think. Hard to find a consistent fix out in friggin' Jackman or wherever he was from. Until the moose start cutting heroin, you'll have to come out of the woods for it. I never knew Girard to sell, but, shit, everybody'll sell if the price is right. My nephew…"

He stopped, shook his head, and took a sharp, almost fierce drag on the cigarette. "My nephew was a good kid when he was straight. My brother got him a job working as sternman on Brian Wickenden's boat, and Brian got him off the pills and onto beer, which was progress, believe me. But the heroin…that shit is hard to quit."

Barrett looked out at the boats and buoys, thinking of Kimberly Crepeaux's reference to the killing drug that worked up the coast like a fever, leaving a trail of death behind. The wind came up and the water sparkled beneath it and somewhere beyond the farthest reaches of the light, old rigging creaked like footsteps on the stairs of a haunted house.

"Does Mathias still come around?"

"I told you, do not ask me questions about Mathias."

"What do you need in order to answer them?"

Mark spat into the water again. "You still do not get it."

"What don't I get?"

"Anything about him. Or about this place. You remember being up here in nice weather as a kid, and you think that shit was real. It wasn't. You got no clue what this is really like. When it's twenty degrees and the wind is sitting down out of the northeast and the plow drivers are in my bar at noon and there ain't a soul on the roads to miss them. That's fine, man. Nobody ever begrudges you summer people coming here with your dollars. We need 'em. But don't pretend you understand us."

"You started with Mathias and ended with *us*. All I'm asking about is him. What's it matter where I was as a kid?"

"It matters because you think you understand things, and you don't. You thought you got it, and you were wrong. Divers went into the water and proved you wrong. Why can't you let it be?"

"Because she's not lying."

Mark blew cigarette smoke with exhaustion and hung his head in near despair. "The people who will talk to you? You should be smart enough not to listen to them. The people who won't talk to you? Listen to the silence, brother. It's a lot more important."

Mark flicked the cigarette. The sparks flew in a pinwheeling arc before hitting the water with a soft hiss.

"How do you know the drug came from DC?" Barrett asked.

"Huh?" Mark frowned at him with genuine confusion.

"The batch that killed your nephew. You said it was a DC batch."

"No, I didn't."

"I heard the words come out of your mouth."

"You heard them wrong. I didn't say anything about where the shit was from. *DC* has nothing to do with a place, man. It's for the *devil's cut* or the *devil's calling*."

Barrett had heard plenty of nicknames and jargon for drugs, but this was new.

"Who started calling it that?"

"Survivors, Barrett. They're who started calling it that. The ones who *took* the devil's cut? They never had a chance to say a word about it."

"Kimberly thought it was from DC."

"Exhibit A of what I keep saying—your trusted

source has no clue what she's talking about. What she doesn't invent, she gets wrong."

"You hear a lot of talk, standing behind that bar. It's been almost a year now. Do people in your world really think Girard killed those two?"

Mark's high laugh cut the air again. "Man, you're really doing it, aren't you! I saw you and thought, *There's no way he came up here for anything other than another pass at Liz Street's lovely ass—*"

"Easy..."

"Fuck you, *easy,* I'll say what I want. I sincerely hoped she was all you were after. I sincerely hoped that Ray Barrett's own blood wasn't dumb enough to still be asking about this bullshit. The pond...was...empty. Kimmy lied. What's left to say?"

"You could tell me about Girard. You started to, because you cared about your nephew. Why not give me a little more?"

Mark looked at him and smiled. "I wish you could've seen yourself the day you came up here looking for Mathias. Man, your face...you've never looked more like your grandfather than that day. Had your ass hanging out for the world to see."

Mark laughed a little louder, and the sound seeped into Barrett like heat, warming his blood and quickening his pulse.

"Was Girard in the bar much?"

Mark kept laughing for a minute, then stopped and wiped his eyes. "Sorry, man. I don't mean to laugh in your face, it's just that I'm sitting here thinking of how the person you decided to believe was Kimmy, and you *arrested* Mathias, and then the pond was empty. I mean...there's screwing up a case, and then there's *that*."

Barrett's greatest asset in interviews was patience. That ability to see each page of anger and then close the book. For some reason he was struggling now.

"Don't laugh too hard, Mark. I still know plenty of locals with badges who will be happy to drop in on your bar."

"Sure. Like your old partner?" Mark laughed again as he pulled out a pack of cigarettes and shook one loose. "Go ahead and give him a call."

Barrett cocked his head. "Why all the teasing bullshit about Johansson? What's going on with him?"

"That's private," Mark said. "That's between me and a man who has some authority in Maine, not Montana." He was sitting below Barrett, cigarette halfway to his lips, face upturned, a smile on it. "You remember those kind of men?"

"I remember them." Barrett's quickening pulse had moved into his temples. "Now you mind answering my question?"

"What difference will it make? I could tell you the

truth, could tell you a lie, it won't matter, because you never know who to believe, not even when everybody else in the whole damned town—"

Barrett's backhand slap smashed Mark Millinock's cigarette into his teeth, and for an instant Mark seemed too stunned to respond, the cigarette stuck sideways to lips that were now leaking blood. Then he bolted out of the chair and swung a big, looping punch at Barrett's head that never had a chance of contact because Barrett drilled him in the eye with a closed left hand and then smacked the side of his skull with an open right, knocking him back into the chair, which fell sideways beneath him, spilling him onto the dock.

Mark pushed upright on his hands and knees, looked at the blood dripping onto the deck boards in disbelief and then up at Barrett. Again, Barrett felt that odd distance from his own violence, just as he had when he'd hit Ronnie Lord in the bar all those months ago. His hands acted, his thoughts receded, and some dark part of him felt at peace.

It was a dangerous feeling, because it wasn't a bad one.

"You need to be careful taunting a man," he said. "You got my blood up."

He didn't like the sound of his own voice. He took a step back and circled, his hands still raised, expecting Mark to come at him again. Almost wanting him to. It seemed like Mark was considering it, but he didn't move, just spat blood without taking his eyes off Barrett.

"I asked you a question," Barrett said. "What's Don Johansson doing on this case?"

"You're a lunatic," Mark Millinock said, licking blood off his lips.

"That's not the answer I—"

"He's not doing anything on *this case,* you stupid son of a bitch!" Mark shouted. "There is no *case!* It's over!"

The heat flushed inside of Barrett again; his hands curled back into fists.

"You said he and I were both the same, that we couldn't let it go. So what is he asking about?"

"Nothing."

Barrett grabbed him by the shoulders and lifted him and drove him backward, slamming him into the wharf railing so hard the security lamp rattled above them. He was about to throw another punch—or many punches; it felt as if things were going to get away from him fast, pull him under and hold him there in a red haze—when Mark shouted at him.

"He just wants a friggin' *fix!*"

Barrett released him and stepped back. Mark hung from the top rail, wincing and breathing hard.

"That's the truth?" Barrett asked.

"Yes, it's the truth, you prick. The two of you are the same because you can't let the damn thing die, you're all twisted up by it, can't just accept that you were *wrong!*"

"What does he buy?"

"Pills." Mark spat blood into the water. Looked at Barrett with hate. "Oxy, Percocet, Vicodin, whatever. He's in pain, he says. Bad back. But he's just like you. Coming apart, because you got it wrong."

30

Barrett drove out of Port Hope with Mark Millinock's blood drying on the hand that held the steering wheel.

You got my blood up, he'd said. That phrase so etched in his memory had risen easily to his lips as his heart thundered and his muscles bunched and he saw the pain he'd inflicted on another human being.

You got my blood up.

He stopped at a Dunkin' Donuts in Thomaston, washed the blood off his hands in the bathroom, and looked at himself in the mirror as if assessing damage, although Mark had never landed a blow on him.

What in the hell had he been thinking? Mark was an addict and a ne'er-do-well, deserving of sympathy, not rage, and Barrett had just delivered painful news about his nephew's death. Then somehow at the first taunt, the first provocation, Barrett had swung on him. What in the hell had happened?

Mark had reminded him of Mathias, that was the

problem. He'd called Barrett out on failure and he'd laughed.

Don't get your feet wet.

Barrett shut off the water and dabbed his face with his damp hands as if trying to cool a fever. It had been two days since he'd had any real sleep. He thought that he should get a hotel room, pick some national chain where everything looked the same. He'd close the blinds and sleep the day away until he was rested, until his mind and fists belonged to him again.

He bought a large coffee instead. Then he got back in the car and called Don Johansson.

He's just like you, Mark Millinock had said. *Coming apart, because you got it wrong.*

Johansson answered his call with good humor and a touch of wariness.

"Hey, Barrett. How's Montana?"

"I'm not sure. I'm in Maine."

There was a long silence. Then Johansson said, "Why?"

"I'd like to meet in person to talk about that. Grab a beer, maybe?"

"If this is about Kimmy, I do not want that beer. If it's about anything else, I'll buy."

"What if it's about both?"

Johansson's sigh was soft and sorrowful, like a mourner's at a wake.

"Barrett, I can't step back to that. And you should know better. You should—"

"I saw Mark Millinock today," Barrett said. "He mentioned you."

The silence stretched on and out like an unfamiliar highway.

"Come by the house," Johansson said finally, and then he hung up.

Johansson lived in a charming ranch with cedar flower boxes under the windows. The flower boxes, usually overflowing with beautiful color, were empty today, the remnants of last summer's soil beaten down.

Johansson opened the door before Barrett knocked. His fleshy face was now hollow-cheeked, his double chin converted into a sharp angle of bone as if at the hand of an aggressive plastic surgeon. His rounded gut had closed inward, and his belt, once straining to keep his pants closed, was now overworked trying to keep them up.

"How's it going, Barrett?"

Barrett gave him a long look and said, "I was going to ask if Mark Millinock had fed me a lie about you. I don't think I need to, though."

"He's a failed fisherman and a bad bartender with a pill habit," Johansson snapped. "You believe anything he has to say, you're even more gullible than I thought."

Barrett didn't answer.

"Last few times I've seen that junkie, he was higher than a giraffe's asshole, and now you're telling me he's reliable? Come on."

Still, Barrett didn't answer. Just watched and waited.

"What'd he tell you?" Johansson asked finally.

"That you've got a bad back."

"I hurt my back. That's true enough."

For a moment they faced off, Johansson defiant, Barrett patient, and then Johansson stepped back from the door and said, "Ah, screw it. Come on inside."

Barrett stepped in and was stunned by what he saw. The interior of the house looked more like a dorm room than a family home. The only furniture was an old couch and a coffee table facing a television that sat on the floor. Two empty beer cans also sat on the floor, and there were stains on the carpet where previous members of their battalion had fallen wounded. The walls were bare, but nails and hooks that had once held family photographs and childhood artwork still protruded from them.

"Let's have that drink," Johansson said, and he walked into a kitchen that smelled of old sourness. Barrett stared around, thinking of the last time he'd been here. It was for a barbecue, and Don's wife, Megan, had put out a spread of fine food while Don and his son manned the grill and shot unsuspecting attendees with squirt guns.

Johansson came back into the living room and handed Barrett a can of Budweiser. He'd already cracked his own. He lifted it in Barrett's direction.

"Cheers."

He sat on the couch then, and Barrett felt ridiculous joining him there, the two of them sitting side by side in the empty house, staring at the blank TV on the floor, so he remained standing and leaned against the wall.

"Where are Megan and David?"

"Florida. Living the good life. Fun in the sun. But don't get to feeling sorry for me—it isn't as bad as it sounds." He gazed around his home. "Or looks."

"No?"

"No. I'm headed down there myself. They just went ahead of me, that's all."

And went in a hurry, Barrett thought, but he said, "You're quitting the police?"

"Retiring, yeah."

"You're five years from retiring with a pension, Don."

"I'll get work easily enough down there. Florida police departments, are you kidding me? Security guards in the gated communities make as much as me. It's just time for a move."

Barrett said, "How many people know about the pills?"

Johansson looked like he was considering denial, but instead he sipped the beer and said, "A few people know about the pills. I don't think many know that I've…gone to outside sources. If anyone in the department knew that, I'd be fired."

"Have you tried cleaning up? Getting to a clinic or a counselor or—"

Johansson waved him off. "Yes, yes, yes. I'm working on it, Barrett. Shit, I don't need you showing up at my doorstep like a missionary. Leave your tracts and go, if that's what this is about."

"That's not what I came for, but I'd like to help you. Seriously."

"Right. What else is on your mind, old boy? Let me guess—you finally figured out how Mathias moved the bodies."

"Not yet."

Johansson's eyes tightened. "But you're trying? You came back here to try *that*?" Johansson gave a little laugh and shook his head. "Tenacious," he said. "You are tenacious." He tipped the beer back, realized it was empty, and set it down on the carpet beside one of the stains.

"We fucked up the wrong case," he said. "Too many people cared too much. And then with Girard…" He shook his head. "I really did a number on that one, didn't I? The man's gun wasn't even loaded. Lead suspect in the most famous murders this state has seen in years, I killed him before the courtroom, and the son of a bitch was *unarmed*."

"You didn't know that."

"No. But I can tell you exactly how much that meant to people. Ask Howard Pelletier about it sometime, see what it meant to him. Ask Amy and George Kelly."

Barrett finished his beer but held it in his hand, unwilling to set it on the floor the way Johansson had.

"Did you know that Girard sold the drugs that killed Mark Millinock's nephew?"

Johansson's face registered more interest than he probably wanted to show, because all he said was "You don't say?" without looking up.

"Yeah. And Mark said something interesting. He called the drug that killed his nephew DC. It's the same term Kimberly used, but she attached it to a place. She thought it was from Washington. Mark told me that it was a nickname. Devil's cut or devil's calling. Have you heard of it?"

Johansson closed his eyes and shook his head again, slowly and emphatically.

"Bear with me," Barrett said.

"'Bear with me,' he says," Johansson said sarcastically, as if talking to someone else in the room.

"'Bear with me while we search this pond. Hell, let's drain this pond!' If Girard hadn't had a good guilt complex, I'd have been breaching dams with you and wandering around in my hip waders, sorting through old beer cans and babbling about items of evidentiary value. I shouldn't have shot the son of a bitch—he saved me a lot of embarrassment."

"You're sure he was the one who e-mailed the body location?"

"Yes."

"He seemed startled to see us, in my opinion. If he gave up the location, he should have known how fast it would move from there. No gloves, the truck still parked with their blood in it, but all he could bring himself to do was direct police to the bodies? Why? Because he felt guilty seeing Mathias take the fall? If he really did, why not go all the way and come forward? He knew it wouldn't take long."

"The guy was hardly a Rhodes scholar. Maybe he thought the scene was old enough that there'd be no evidence to attach him to it, and he'd bust Mathias loose without paying the price."

Barrett didn't like that idea and never had.

"I'd like to see the forensic reports from the body-dump scene," he said, ignoring him. "I was never given that access. If I can prove—"

"What you can prove is that none of what that

trailer-trash tramp told you was the truth!" Johansson shouted. "We already proved that, Barrett!"

Barrett let silence hang for a moment, and then he said, "I didn't come out here to draw you back into this."

"Sure as hell sounds like you did."

"I came out here to tell you that people will be talking now that I'm back. Mark Millinock may be one of the people doing the talking. You follow me?"

Johansson didn't respond.

"I don't want to drag you down," Barrett said. "So I'm giving you fair warning. Be ready for some attention, okay?"

"I'm fine," Johansson said.

"You're not fine, and more people than Mark know it."

"Let 'em talk. I'm done here, anyhow. Florida, brother. And once I'm gone, unlike you, I won't be stupid enough to come back."

Barrett crossed the room and set the empty beer can down on the stained carpet where the other cans were accumulating.

"If you need me, call me."

Johansson didn't answer.

Barrett let himself out.

31

He left Johansson's house and headed for Port Hope, feeling sick about how far and fast Don had fallen and trying not to blame himself. That was easier said than done, though—Johansson's vision of how things could have gone if they'd proceeded with draining the pond was vivid. And probably not inaccurate.

He couldn't allow Johansson's addiction to distract him from what he'd come here to do, though. He'd heard a lot today, and he needed a fresh round with Kimberly based on this fresh information. But before he spoke to her again, he wanted to hear the old story, the original confession. Specifically, he wanted to hear her talk about the drugs from DC.

He reached in the glove box, moved his gun aside, and found the slim digital recorder that held all his audio files of his interviews with Kimberly Crepeaux. He paired the recorder with the car's Bluetooth so that the tinny, scratchy sound flowed through the speakers. There she was again; Kimberly's wry, heavily accented voice filled his car.

Am I supposed to say his full name in this one, like we don't all know it? Mathias Burke. You know what's funny? Your eyes get tight at the corners when you hear his full name. That's really weird. Every time I say it, I can see you tighten up. Like you're bracing for a punch. Or want to throw one. Which is it? Hey, you said to tell it in my own words, right? Careful what you wish for, Barrett.

He had come to a stop sign at an intersection, and when the car behind him honked he realized he'd been waiting even though there was no cross traffic. He pulled across the road, and only once he was on the other side did he remember that he'd needed to turn right to catch Route 17 on its winding way toward the coast.

He thought he remembered this new road, though, and the map on the rental car's navigation system showed it running parallel to 17. Lower speeds, but the same destination. That was fine by Barrett. All he wanted was a quiet road and an open mind.

And Kimberly Crepeaux's voice.

Now, I hadn't done much all summer but drink. Maybe a little weed, but that was about it. I mean, I guess a few pills. But nothing serious, because, you know, people kept dying last summer, even before Cass. It was all over the news. There was bad heroin somebody brought up from Washington, DC. A black guy, I think. Or maybe he was Mexican. But I know it was from DC, because people kept calling it that. It was moving around like a fever that summer. People were dying without even OD'ing because of what it was cut with, some chemical thing I never really understood.

That chemical thing she'd never really understood was filling emergency rooms—and coffins—from Maine to New Mexico: synthetic heroin mixed with fentanyl. In the right mix, fentanyl played nicely with heroin, each increasing the potency of the other, like a perfect dance partner. In drug parlance, that little beauty had originally been known as China white.

Get the mixture even a little skewed, though, and the dance became very deadly very swiftly. The recent versions floating around and adding to the national death toll had other nicknames—theraflu, bud ice, income tax. And, maybe, devil's cut or devil's calling.

If the ratio was wrong, users died before they had any sense that something had gone wrong. An overdose death from pure heroin usually required somewhere around thirty milligrams; an overdose death from fentanyl could be caused by as little as three milligrams. If you didn't know the heroin was laced, good night and good luck.

And good riddance, many people said, because they saw only a dead druggie, and what loss was that? Then it landed in your neighborhood or on your street or in your house, and perspectives changed fast.

Barrett was listening to Kimberly and thinking about Mark Millinock as he followed a curve around a wooded hillside and water appeared to the left, a bog lined with high cattails and dark moss. His grandfather would have called the spot a mosquito farm. He was fond of fishing those areas to test his grandson's ability to endure the hateful, droning swarms. If Barrett missed a fish because he was swatting at the bugs, that was a grand excuse to tell the boy how soft he was and how little he knew about real trouble, about bullets rather than bugs.

We were all over the road, Kimberly's voice declared. *The worse the curves, the faster he took them...*

Mostly what I remember from that ride is staring at the cat. It started to look a little crazier to me on that ride.

It was such a vivid story for a fabrication. That didn't mean it was true, of course; some people liked elaborate lies. Barrett didn't think that Kimberly Crepeaux was one of them, though. She typically pretended to be confused or she diffused blame, saying she'd heard a story from someone else—and usually she couldn't recall that person's name. She always wanted to have a fallback position if she was caught lying.

She took full ownership of this story, though, and offered a depth of detail that she'd never brought to a lie with Barrett before.

Barrett rewound, fidgeting with the recorder and glancing up here and there to make sure that the road ahead was empty. Dangerous, like texting and driving, the kind of thing that got people killed. He knew he should pull over, but the road here had no shoulder, it was flanked by the marsh on either side, so he just slowed down as he looked at the recorder.

The sound of the roaring, accelerating engine caught him totally by surprise.

He'd been driving with his attention divided between the recorder and the road in front of him, where any threat would be coming from, but he hadn't checked his mirror. It showed a black truck with a reinforced grille guard like the kind ranchers in Montana had. The truck was burning up the road, death-wish speed, so instead of trying to pull away, Barrett cut the wheel to the right so he could clear out of the idiot's path.

The truck turned with him.

Then into him.

It wasn't a glancing impact; it was a devastating one, glass shattering, the head restraint slamming into the back of his skull, the front wheels driven off the pavement and into the mud. The rental car slid down the embankment as Barrett mashed on the brake pedal and got it stopped a few feet from the water, dazed and angry.

"Son of a bitch!" he shouted, fumbling for the

seat-belt release. The rearview mirror offered nothing but the spider-webbed glass of the broken back window. He glanced at the side mirror and saw the truck, its grille protector giving it the look of an animal with bared teeth. The driver backed the truck up and cut the wheel, and Barrett's first thought was *The prick is going to flee the scene,* but then the tires realigned and that protected grille was facing him again and Barrett understood two things with sudden, sharp clarity: the first crash had been intentional, not accidental—and there was about to be a second.

He couldn't go backward fast enough to avoid it, and to go forward meant driving into the water, so he released the seat belt, slammed the emergency brake on, and reached for the glove compartment, going for his gun. The black truck's engine howled behind him. He had the glove compartment open and his fingers were closing around the stock of the Glock when the second impact came.

The emergency brake was his worst decision. Without it, the momentum of the crash would have driven the rental car forward, down the hill and into the water. With the brake engaged, instead of sliding forward and giving him the chance to turn and fire, the vehicle fought physics, and lost. It didn't just slide forward; it flipped.

The gun came out of his hand as the world spun.

He was slammed into the dashboard, his body angled sideways, and he watched a tall, dark pine tree go from upright to upside down. That was his only clear sense of the rotation. Physically it was just chaos, pain and noise, but visually he saw that lone tree going from logical to deeply wrong.

Then his head smacked against something hard and unyielding—roof or dashboard or windshield—and he was aware only of the taste of warm blood and the shock of cold water as the light faded.

32

*I*hadn't even thought of you guys yet, to be honest. *Hadn't thought about anything bigger than that little stretch of road. That was the whole world right then. The world was gone and it was just that road and the truck and Mathias. That's all that was left.*

People won't understand that.

Kimberly Crepeaux was sitting in the backseat, the legs of her orange prison pants soaked. If the water bothered her, she didn't show it. Barrett looked at her and tried to tell her that she was wrong, that he *did* understand. He couldn't seem to find his voice, though, and then he remembered that was the point, that he was just supposed to listen. *Don't think, don't speak, just listen.* That was his job.

All we would have had to do was drag them down to the tidal flats and let the current do what it does, she told him. *Instead, we went back to that camp, and that pond. We waded out until it was up to my neck and then he swam a little farther, dragging her out toward the raft. Then he let her go. She sank pretty easily. I remember you could see some blood in the water, but it was gone fast.*

Barrett was trying to concentrate but her words were becoming hard to follow. She wasn't making any sense. Even the way she was sitting didn't make sense; the floor of the car was above her head, and that was confusing.

He knew that she had to be cold, but she didn't show it, didn't react even as the water rose, covering the baggy orange prison pants and plastering them against her legs. The water was murky with silt and mud. A broken cattail floated right past her, an empty beer can behind it, but Kimberly didn't so much as glance at them. Her eyes were locked on Barrett's, even as the water rose and flattened the baggy prison orange against her, giving her body shape, like a slowly developing photograph.

The rest of it, I don't know about. What he did after, and what happened to the truck, I don't know. I can't even make guesses about that stuff, no matter how many ways you try to get me to.

He didn't know how she kept talking through the cold. There wasn't so much as a tremble to her fine-boned jaw as she spoke. The water rose higher, and her breasts showed beneath the wet fabric, small and taut as closed fists, and then the water reached the base of her throat, and her thin red lips parted in a smile. Her lips were the only touch of color on her pale face other than the splash of freckles across her nose and high on her cheeks, like flecks of rust.

Barrett didn't like that smile.

That is how it happened, Kimberly told him. *Can we stop now?*

Barrett wanted to tell her to stop smiling. Why was she smiling?

When she moved for him, it was without so much as a tensed muscle of warning. Just a flash of motion in the water and the silver glint of something in her hand as she lunged for his belly. He felt the sharp bite of pain when the knife found him. For an instant he was face-to-face with Kimberly, her smiling lips so close to his that he could feel her breath on his mouth. Then he looked down and saw the handle of the knife.

She'd buried the long, glistening blade in the middle of his chest. He knew his life would end quickly, and he opened his mouth to scream, but cold, dank water filled it before he could make a sound.

33

He came to consciousness coughing and choking, his legs pinned in the backseat, his torso jammed over the center console in the front. The car was three-quarters submerged, water seeping in from all directions, and he'd woken only when it reached his lips. Kimberly was gone—of course she was gone—but there was still the eerie droning of her voice, and when Barrett lifted his head, the digital recorder slid away from him. He'd come to rest with his head against it, Kimberly whispering into his ear as the car filled with water.

The recorder slid down his body and entered the water and then Kimberly's voice vanished. Disoriented, he watched the recorder sink with fascination. It settled by his feet, which were braced against the headrests of the backseat. The world was pain and confusion, and he wanted to sink like that recorder, twirling gracefully into the peacefulness of the dark water.

He was fading again when a piece of the roof gave way with a snap and a stream of cold water poured onto his neck. He blinked and coughed and clawed back against the pain and the fog.

Have to get out. Have to get out fast.

The problem was how to get out. He could see the sunroof below him, crushed against black mud and weeds, and the doors above the sunroof were buckled. Not options.

Look above, then. Go higher.

When he twisted his head, pain rose like a choir in full voice. Blood dripped off the dashboard and into the water around him, where it diffused and lost its color. He wondered what was bleeding and how badly.

Doesn't matter. Not yet. Won't matter at all if you don't get out.

He twisted his head again, the pain overwhelming him temporarily, and when his vision cleared he realized that he could see the sky through the driver's window. The glass was fractured and the metal frame was bent, but the sky was there.

I can't make it. Not all the way up there, and not alone. I need help from above. Need someone to...

To what? Drop a net? Nobody was going to cast for him from above. He had to do some of the work, at least.

He reached up and wrapped his hand around the steering wheel. His right arm worked. It hurt, but it worked. He gripped the wheel tightly and pulled himself forward, using the wheel like a chin-up bar to haul his legs out of the backseat and draw closer to that one window where the sky remained.

When he flopped into the front seat, the car shifted, and for one terrible second he thought it would tip and then he would be underwater and out of time. The car didn't overbalance, though. It just settled deeper into the mud at the bottom of the marsh, like an old man adjusting in a recliner, getting comfortable. The water rose but didn't fill the car. Behind the front seats, there was no air, only water, but up here, balanced on the driver's seat as if he were sitting on the top step of a ladder, he could breathe, and he would be able to unless the car tipped. The marsh was shallow, which was the only reason he was alive.

He leaned over to try the door handle, and that brought his face closer to the driver's window, and he saw the man in the black mask.

The man was standing on the embankment below the road, almost at the water's edge, and he held a shotgun at belt level, the muzzle pointed at Barrett. They were no more than ten feet apart. Point-blank range. The man in the black mask had his finger on the trigger, and if he pulled it, he would not miss. Not from there. Barrett thought vaguely of the handgun he'd been trying to draw before he'd gone into the water, but he knew there was no point in trying to find it now. He was trapped and he was helpless, so he just looked at the man and waited. There was a row of cattails between them, and they swayed left and right, like a crowd turning to watch the action.

The man in the black mask glanced up at the road, then back at Barrett. He lifted the stock of the gun a little, bringing the muzzle down for a better firing angle.

Then he slipped his gloved finger off the trigger.

He lowered the shotgun, still looking at Barrett, who had to blink blood out of his eyes to see him, and then he shifted the shotgun to his left hand, turned, and scrambled up the embankment and out of sight.

A few seconds later, an engine roared to life, then disappeared.

It was very quiet then. Barrett lifted his right hand to his face to clear his eyes and when he lowered it, his palm was filled with blood. He tried the door handle. The door didn't move.

He pondered this as he looked at the bent metal and broken glass. It seemed unlikely to him that the door would ever move again. He thought about the window, and he knew that wasn't going to open without a little help. His vision clouded with blood and he palmed it away again and thought about making a fist and punching that window. He needed to get something open somehow, and that was the best option he could come up with, but he would have to hit it very hard, and any violent motion might tip the car.

If he could find his gun, he could shoot the window. Logic said that the gun was below him, claimed by gravity and drawn to the back of the car, which was filled with water. He could make it there, but he wasn't sure he could make it back up here. Not quickly, at least, and not without tipping the car.

When the voice said *Don't move, buddy,* he thought it might be coming from inside his head. His grandfather, or his father, maybe. Then he heard it again and understood that someone was up on the road. He heard a series of splashes, and then a gray-haired man in jeans and a shirt with cutoff sleeves was up against the window, his face stricken with fear. He reached for the door handle tentatively, and Barrett whispered, "Careful."

It was the first word he'd spoken, and it brought blood onto his lips, but it also came out clearly, and the gray-haired man nodded and withdrew his hand.

"I don't want her to tip," he said.

"No," Barrett agreed, licking the blood from his lips. "Do not want to tip."

The gray-haired man looked at him. "Can you hang on? Just for a minute, fella?"

"I can wait," Barrett said, though he wasn't sure of this. His head was pounding and the blood kept clouding his vision.

"I'm gonna get some help," the gray-haired man said. "It'll come fast, buddy, I promise. You just hang on. You stay as calm as you are right now, and you'll be fine."

"Yes," Barrett said, because it seemed like a good idea to keep agreeing with the gray-haired man. He was very nervous and Barrett didn't think it was good to have anyone that nervous around the car.

"I'll be right back, and you'll be fine," the man said, and then he was gone, and this time when the blood got into Barrett's eyes, he just closed them instead of wiping it away.

With his eyes closed, all that was left was the smell of the water and the blood and the sounds beyond the darkness. He could hear a faint voice, and he thought there was a siren behind it, but he wasn't sure. He could hear a cricket trilling. He tried to count the trills, thinking it would be a good idea to have a task, something to keep him awake and alert. His grandfather had told him that you could tell the temperature by counting the number of times a cricket trilled in a minute. Or was it thirty seconds? He couldn't remember. But his grandfather had told him that the number of trills increased with the temperature. Barrett wasn't sure if that was accurate.

As the siren grew louder and he lost the sound of the cricket to it, he thought that he should try to find someone to ask about that old story about crickets. As the red tide carried him toward blackness again, he wanted very badly to know if the story was true.

34

When consciousness returned, it was driven by an urgency of memory, a sense that he had forgotten something critical and needed to remember it fast.

The memory did not come, though, and awareness of his surroundings pushed it down the ladder of priorities. He saw the hospital room and felt how dry his mouth was and knew from the creaky, ponderous way his mind worked to put these things together that there must be a drug involved—and a damn fine one at that. He felt no pain, and he was pretty sure he should be feeling pain.

He looked himself over as best he could, taking inventory, but he lost track of the inventory a few times and had to start over. Tubes in right arm, leading to intravenous fluids or medications. Legs bandaged, but functional. Toes wiggled, knees flexed. All good. There was something strange that he wasn't catching, though. Some odd feeling along his skull that had nothing to do with whatever painkiller was dripping into his blood. When he touched his head gingerly with his right hand, he discovered nothing but stubble.

He was pondering that when the doctor came in. He was a tall and thin man with very dark black skin, and he had a trace of British diction in his voice when he introduced himself as Dr. Abeo and asked how Barrett was feeling.

"Bald," Barrett said. "And thirsty."

Dr. Abeo smiled and brought him water and said he was sorry about the baldness.

"We were in a bit of a hurry," he said as Barrett sipped the water. "There are thirty-seven stitches and five staples and some glue in your scalp. It's hard to do that and keep the hair."

Barrett acknowledged that was likely true and said he did not blame anyone for the bad haircut. The doctor was watching him with both compassion and curiosity, and Barrett had the sense that he was not expressing himself as articulately as he believed.

"There are some drugs," he said carefully. "Right?"

"You are on medications, correct."

"Well. That's the reason."

Dr. Abeo nodded patiently. "You will be good as new soon. No worries now. When you came in? The liver scared me."

Barrett thought that was harsh. Sure, he drank

a little more than he should, but how bad could his liver have been? He tried to inquire, missed the proper phrasing a few times, and finally got the word *whiskey* out. The doctor laughed a beautiful, rich laugh that made Barrett smile. This was not so bad. With these drugs and that laugh, why would any man need hair?

"You have a healthy liver," Dr. Abeo told him. "I wouldn't have guessed at the whiskey. I was afraid your liver was lacerated. Do you understand?"

Barrett said that he knew lacerations, yes. Dr. Abeo told him all was well now. The liver was fine. There hadn't been any surgery. He'd been given a few units of blood, and then they'd closed his scalp wound. Barrett was tired and he liked the sound of the man's voice and particularly the sound of his laugh. Dr. Abeo talked some more and laughed some more and adjusted a dial on a monitor.

Then the blackness returned.

The next time he woke, he was more coherent, and this was viewed as fine news by the doctor because the police had been waiting to talk to him.

"Rather impatiently," Dr. Abeo said.

"I've known that type."

The cop wasn't anyone Barrett had worked with before. He was a short but muscular Hispanic man with a shaved head and penetrating, intelligent eyes.

He introduced himself as Nick Vizquel but did not share his department or title.

"State police?" Barrett asked him.

"No. DEA."

"MDEA?" Maine had its own drug enforcement agency.

"Federal."

"You mind telling me why my attack has attracted a DEA investigation?"

"Let's talk about that attack. It's a little murky to me right now."

Vizquel pulled up a chair and explained that the story Barrett had offered in the ambulance, before blood loss and painkillers knocked him out, hadn't given them much to work with; he'd spoken only of a masked man and a truck with teeth.

"I thought you might want to try that one about the truck again," he said with a faint smile.

Barrett gave him what he could. It wasn't much. He could clarify that the truck did not in fact have teeth but a ranch-style grille protector, and that it was black, and so was the mask, and so was the shotgun. His memory was scattershot, which was logical because of his concussion and blood loss.

Vizquel said, "And you're back in Maine because..."

Barrett shrugged, and Vizquel nodded as if this was the response he'd expected.

"Sure. Just passing through, getting body-shop quotes from Bobby Girard."

"Want to explain why *you're* here?" Barrett said. "Or am I supposed to believe that the locals were overstretched and you volunteered?"

"I'd like you to talk to Crepeaux for me."

"The DEA wants to talk to Kimberly? About what?"

"About the death of Cass Odom," Vizquel said, and now Barrett felt more confused than he had when he'd first woken up.

"What's interesting about Cass?"

"Where she bought her drugs, maybe." Vizquel leaned forward, studied Barrett, and said, "You're really still looking at those murders? That's honestly what brought you back? If it's a lie, I'll find out, and that will become a very big problem for you."

"It's not a lie, and I don't like to be threatened while I'm in a hospital bed."

"Fair enough. Your interest in Port Hope is certainly not mine. I'm not worried about Jackie Pelletier and Ian Kelly or any stories about them."

"Compassionate."

"Call it what you want. You're losing sleep over two dead. I'm losing sleep over two hundred and fifty-seven and counting."

Barrett stared at him. "Want to say that number again?"

"You heard it."

"Explain it, please," Barrett said.

Vizquel obliged. He was out of Miami originally and had been in New Hampshire by way of Dayton when he heard about Rob Barrett's return to Maine. He was in these disparate places because he was following the spread of a deadly strain of heroin that had taken, to the best of his knowledge, more than 250 lives already.

"Fentanyl?" Barrett asked.

"Carfentanil, actually. Heard of it?"

"No."

"It's an elephant tranquilizer. I kid you not. Now it's coming out of labs in Mexico and China and into the U.S., mixed with heroin. It crosses the blood-brain barrier with ease and produces an incredible euphoria—right before it kills you. Fentanyl can be fatal at minuscule levels. Two milligrams. The size of a few grains of sand, literally. Consider that. Now consider the fact that carfentanil is approximately one hundred times more potent."

Barrett said, "Devil's cut?"

Vizquel arched an eyebrow. "Pardon?"

"Is that what it's called? Or devil's calling? I've heard those names."

"New to me, but drug names change often, and regionally." He took out his iPhone and made a quick note. "Who told you those?"

Barrett didn't answer, and Vizquel sighed. "Come on," he said. "Cooperate with me, Agent Barrett."

"Happy to, if it's a two-way street. What's this have to do with Kimberly Crepeaux and Mathias Burke?"

"Nothing." He lifted his hands before Barrett could argue. "Honestly, nothing. I've read about the case. I believe you were given a false confession, and frankly, I don't care. It's of no interest to me. What is of interest to me is the drug. I'm following a distribution map. Or trying to build one. Some areas are making sense. Port Hope, Maine, is not. Usually this thing kills in waves. I go to see a coroner who has seen two dozen dead in two weeks. In Ohio, they had fifty in one county. Up here, that's not the case. Toxicology reports are showing matches, and Cass Odom is one of them. The matches are sporadic, and the path of entry isn't clear. That's what's important to me. I chase this cancer all around the country, talking to coroners and cops and watching the bodies stack up, and what I need to know is how it's coming in. Maine's intriguing to me."

"Why?"

"Because Maine has plenty of harbor towns, and my job is to determine how the drug is arriving. A lot of it has been flown into Dayton or Indianapolis, centrally located cities with major interstate systems. Maine is usually a final destination for heroin, not an entry point. But it's not killing many people up here either. A handful of dead in tiny coastal towns doesn't make sense for this shit. Which makes me wonder...did it arrive here, and did some enterprising soul pilfer a little before they let it bleed out into the rest of the country?"

"Interesting questions," Barrett said. "But I can't answer them. And I'm still curious about my questions. Someone tried to kill me, and you seem to know more about it than I do, but you're not sharing that."

"Who do you think did it?"

"I'm not sure, but it seems safe to assume it was someone who doesn't want me asking questions about a murder case that was closed too early."

"I think you're halfway there but facing the wrong way."

"What?"

"They don't want you asking questions, but that's because your questions are changing. You're not asking about the murders anymore. You're asking about the drugs."

"How do you know that already?"

Vizquel smiled and shook his head. Barrett wondered who his informant was. Millinock? Girard? Johansson?

"How's your relationship with the state police up here?" he asked.

"Aces," Vizquel said, "but you're still facing the wrong way."

"Then set me straight, and stop throwing the curveballs. I clearly can't hit them, and I can't help you unless I can hit them. Who's your source, Vizquel?"

Vizquel gave a dry little smile. "No source. Oh, by the way—there was a GPS tracking device attached to the frame of your car. That's why I'm here. Cass Odom matches the drug profile, and Rob Barrett nearly gets killed with a tracker on his rental car, and this is what brings Nick Vizquel hustling up to Maine to chat at your bedside, understand?"

Barrett stared at him, trying to catch up. "Is the tracker clean or do you think you can get something from it?"

"We'll try, of course, but unless someone got lazy, it'll be clean. You've honestly got no idea who might have put that on your car?"

"I don't. My first thought is Mathias Burke, because he's the—"

"Stop thinking about the murder case. That's small ball."

Barrett pointed at Nick Vizquel, dragging IV tubes across his body as he did it.

"Tell that to Howard Pelletier, asshole. Tell him that his daughter's murder is small ball."

Vizquel sighed. "I was hoping you'd get it. You're a fed, not a local."

"Sorry to disappoint."

"You are disappointing. I could use the help, and you're still talking about caretakers and addicts and old murders. Get past that. Think about money. Somewhere, somebody is making big money on this drug."

"I'm sure they are. But it's not Kimberly Crepeaux."

Vizquel looked disgusted. "You're right about that. Listen, I'm leaving my card and my cell number. You get better ideas than that, share them, would you? You scared somebody pretty good by coming back to Maine. I'd like to know who it was."

"Yeah," Barrett said. "You and me both."

Vizquel left his card on the table beside the bed and stood. "You're a lucky man."

Barrett gestured at the rack of IVs beside his hospital bed. "Really?"

"Absolutely. You wandered into the ring without knowing what weight class was punching in it. Most guys like you? They don't see a hospital bed. They see a morgue."

35

Dr. Abeo came and ran him through his tests and paces and proclaimed him fit for release—and bed rest.

"That must be taken very seriously," he said. "You're not to lift anything heavier than a frying pan. You stay in bed, you get bored and miserable, and you get better."

Barrett nodded and promised the doctor that he would adhere to the bed rest. He said he'd have to call a cab to get him home, and Abeo looked surprised.

"The ladies have been waiting," he said.

"The ladies?"

"Two of them, yes." Abeo smiled. "They do not seem to like each other very well, though."

Barrett was puzzled by this statement until he made his way out to the waiting room, dressed in blue hospital scrubs, and saw Liz Street and Rox-anne Donovan occupying opposite sides of the room, each on her phone, pretending not to be aware of the other. Liz glanced at him and then back down at her phone. He caught a blend of relief and anger in her eyes before she looked away. Roxanne came over to him and gave him a head-to-toe look followed by a chagrined shake of the head.

"You've looked better, Barrett."

"I've felt better."

"I was told you shouldn't be driving. I thought you might need a ride to the airport."

Liz cleared her throat. "I thought you might want one heading back north."

Dr. Abeo watched this exchange with amusement. He winked at Barrett and said, "I will see you next week, yes? And—bed rest. North or south, you stay in bed."

Roxanne rolled her eyes. "Nobody's fighting over the man with the staples in his head, Doctor. The outside of his skull is actually more appealing than the inside."

"I've missed you too, Roxanne," Barrett said.

"I know it. And before you follow your guiding light toward another bad decision, let's talk." She glanced at Liz. "Alone."

She walked toward the door and he followed. When they were outside and alone, her hard-ass approach softened, and she put both hands on his shoulders.

"What...are...you...doing?"

"Ending my career, I'm sure."

"Good news—medical leave will buy you some time. It's poor form to fire an agent who was nearly murdered. But seriously, Barrett, what do you think you're doing?"

He told her about the calls—Howard's and Kimberly's—and how he'd ended up on a plane to Portland, needing to see them for himself.

"And this"—he pointed at his wounded head—"actually suggests I'm not crazy. Before, it was all instinct, right? No proof, no proof, no proof. But somebody just tried to kill me, Roxanne, and it's because they do not want those tired old questions asked again."

"DEA says it's not about that," she said.

"You've talked to my friend Vizquel?"

"Yes. He told me about the tracker. Asked if it could have been ours, since he knew you'd, to quote him, 'fallen out of favor' with us."

"Interesting. He didn't suggest to me it was the work of the beloved Bureau for whom I serve so tirelessly. I probably should have thought of that myself."

"You think we knew you were back? Please. You'd have been grabbed at the airport and put on the next plane out. And you should be now. Screwing with a DEA investigation, intentionally or not, is the red line."

He didn't answer.

She regarded him sadly. "You could be a great agent, Barrett. I regret ever sending you up here. I thought it was the right case and that you could use your knowledge of the area. I didn't think you'd get hung up on a lie. You didn't seem like that type."

"Fooled you," he said.

She didn't smile. "When someone with a higher rank than me calls you in the next few days, you need to understand exactly what you and I discussed: your medical condition, and my concern for your health. That's all. Got it?"

"Sure."

She put her sunglasses on, so he couldn't read her eyes when she said, "Has anyone disclosed that the investigation was already active without your helpful nudge?"

"The drug investigation or the homicide investigation?"

"The latter. Both, apparently, but I'm talking about the latter. Maine State Police do not consider the case closed, no matter what they've said publicly."

"If it's active, then why haven't they told the families? Howard Pelletier is sitting up there in Port Hope losing his mind. That's wrong, and cruel."

"If they're keeping him out of it, maybe there's a reason."

"What does that mean?"

She spread her hands. "I don't know. You've heard what I understand about this; it is more than I should have told you, but it's also all I've got. Okay?"

"Okay. And thank you."

"Make good choices, Barrett," she said. "I know that would be breaking new ground for you, but there's never been a better time to start."

With that, she turned and walked to her car.

36

When Barrett stepped back into the hospital, Liz rose to greet him, but she didn't reach for him. Even Roxanne Donovan had touched him, but Liz did not. She just floated close, tantalizingly close, but kept the distance between them.

"Your old boss doesn't like reporters," she said.

"It's why I may quit."

She held up a hand. "Spare me." Her eyes drifted up from his, and her face darkened and he knew she was looking at the ghastly wound across his skull. "How you feeling?"

"Conspicuous," he said. "I would like a hat."

"What about a ride?"

"I'd like both."

"You know the right woman."

They left the hospital and walked to the battered Ford Mustang that was the worst possible car for a Maine resident, rear-wheel drive and torque-heavy. Naturally, Liz had persisted with it for years.

"I didn't think to bring your suitcase down here

with me," Liz said, "but you've got some clothes at my house. Until then, I can help with a hat."

The backseat of the car looked like a cross between a mobile office and an abandoned storage center, and it took her a few minutes of rooting around before she emerged with a New England Patriots cap.

"There you go."

He stared at it and shook his head. "You know better."

He'd been a Giants fan since birth.

"You look like someone from *The Walking Dead,* but you won't put on the hat?"

"No."

She sighed, tossed the cap into the backseat, and found another.

"This is the other option." She held it out— it featured a cartoon moose in a yoga pose and said NAMOOSTE. "You tell me what you'd rather be seen in."

He took the moose hat.

When they were in the car, she gunned the engine to life—it made a clatter more befitting a boatyard than a parking lot—then turned to him and said, "Kimmy's in the wind."

"What?"

"Howard Pelletier told me. As soon as word spread about you, the media came looking for her.

She took off. Stole her grandmother's car and went AWOL."

"Shit."

"Media scares her."

"Media scares her, maybe, but that's not why she ran. She's afraid of Mathias."

"He's happy to give quotes. He told me that the police should be awfully interested in what happened to you after you visited Bobby Girard."

Barrett closed his eyes and took a breath. "And Howard?"

"He told me to wish you well," she said. "He didn't want to be on the record."

"Right."

"Rob, who do you think came after you?"

"I don't know." He was checking the side-view mirror compulsively and wondered how he'd do the next time he was behind the wheel, whether he'd be able to keep his eyes off the mirror, his mind off memories of the black truck with the grille guard that looked like bared teeth.

"The state police haven't bothered to talk to me," he said, "but the DEA dropped by, apparently because they found a tracking device on my car."

She turned to him, wide-eyed.

"Watch the road," he said. "My last wreck was enough to hold me for a while."

She turned away. "The DEA."

"Yeah. And I was encouraged to think bigger. To ignore small-ball issues like the murders of Jackie Pelletier and Ian Kelly. Bigger, to them, is drugs and money. They didn't mention sex or rock 'n' roll, but I assume those are in the mix."

"Mathias has no drug history. Girard did."

"I'm aware," he said, and then realized that he sounded like a total prick and added, "Sorry. I'm trying to get my head around it. You've listened to Kimberly, and you came away with the same thought as me: She's not lying. Not completely."

"No."

"But..."

"But she's telling a story that doesn't fit with the rest of it."

"Exactly." He paused. The Maine landscape loomed ahead, dark and shadowed as storm clouds moved in, meeting a thin fog that was drifting in from the coast. This state of impenetrable fogs and deep woods and deep snows and deep oceans could hide a lot from you when it wanted to. He thought about what Roxanne and Nick Vizquel had told him and he felt the old fear again.

"Maybe Kimberly did lie," he said softly. "Maybe she told me what I wanted to hear and so I believed her, just like every cop who has ever put a conviction ahead of the truth."

"You haven't stopped asking questions," Liz said. "If you were a bad cop, Rob, you wouldn't bother."

"I'm asking the wrong ones, according to Nick Vizquel."

"And you almost died because of it. I hate to say it, but...they can't all be wrong."

He watched the road pass by and wondered about that, about which question had been right, or closest to it. A few raindrops big as nickels splattered off the windshield, and Liz turned on the wipers as the sky darkened around them and they headed farther north.

"I hadn't thought about Cass Odom in a while," he said. "She wasn't much use to me, considering she was dead when I arrived. Maybe I was wrong about that."

Liz glanced at him. "I don't follow."

"I'm not sure that I do either," he said. "But the DEA thinks there's only one question I'm supposed to ask Kimberly, and it's about Cass."

The preliminary raindrops revealed themselves as harbingers then, and a drenching, car-wash rain welcomed them north. Liz slowed down while setting the wipers at their highest.

"You have sources with the medical examiner, don't you? I remember your stories."

She'd won an award for a series of articles

about the overwhelming burden overdose deaths put on medical examiners and coroners. "I've got people who will talk to me," she said with a touch of wariness. "What am I supposed to ask them?"

"I need the medical examiner's reports on Cass Odom and J. R. Millinock. Julian is his full first name."

"Why do you need that?" Liz asked.

"Because Vizquel said that he's interested in the drug that killed Cass and wants to know where it came from. I already know where the drug that killed Millinock came from—Jeff Girard. If they match...that would answer his question, maybe. Or tie some loose ends together, at least."

"The tox reports would show that?"

"I don't know. That's why I need to see them. Think you can work some magic for me?"

"I can try."

"Remember what she said about...shit, what was the name?" The pain meds were putting up a fog between his mind and his memory. "I don't remember the name. But Kimberly told us about some girl who'd drowned, but it turned out she really hadn't drowned...something like that. You said you wrote about her?"

"Molly Quickery. Her body washed up on the beach out by Owls Head. Nowhere near the

Kelly family place, which is what Kimmy was telling us."

"But she was in that group."

"What group?"

"Users. Addicts."

"Yes."

"Do you think you can pull that one too?"

"I'm not sure they did a full toxicology panel. I just know the coroner said Molly was unconscious when she went into the water or something. There was no evidence of drowning. He was sure of that."

Barrett had more questions, but the pills he'd taken were settling into his brain now with a comfortable numbing, like a soft whisper telling him that he didn't need to stay in this moment, didn't need to worry about a thing, just needed to close his eyes, and the drugs would take it from there. He didn't like the feeling, but those whispering voices were powerful persuaders.

The rain was pounding on the car in a ceaseless staccato, and Liz's attention was on the road, so he allowed his eyes to close just for a moment. No more than that, he promised himself, because he needed to think of the memory that had eluded him in those early minutes in the hospital. The memory came from being in the water, from a faint, dizzy thought that had come to him as the blood ran down his face and he looked for help, but he couldn't identify it. Think harder, then. Concentrate.

He wasn't sure when he fell asleep, but he stirred awake just before she stopped the car. It was nearing sunset and they were pulling into her driveway.

"Sorry," he said. "Drifted off, didn't I?"

"Just a bit."

She got out of the car and he followed, moving stiffly, every muscle seeming to have its own twinge and ache. She unlocked the door and led him into a small but bright kitchen and a room with a wide bank of windows that caught the fading sunlight.

"I was expecting you'd get a lot of calls, but I gather your phone was confiscated," she said.

"I'd say so. It sank first, so it doesn't matter either way. Problem is, that'll be the number Kimberly tries. I need to find her. Need to talk to Howard too."

Liz touched him for the first time then, stepping close and clasping her hands together behind his neck.

"You could've died over this," she said. "Do you actually realize that?"

He thought of the way it had felt in the car with the water rising up and his blood pouring down, and he nodded. "I got pretty acquainted with the idea."

She leaned her face against his, cheek to cheek, like they were dancing. She didn't speak. He put his hands around her lithe lower back and closed his eyes and felt at home in a way he had not felt in months. His throat was tight, nerves tingling. He'd known her for nearly twenty years and she could still do this to him. Hell, the thought of her could do it to him, let alone actually having her in his arms.

"Bed rest was prescribed," she said. "I heard it straight from the doctor's mouth."

She stretched up and kissed him then, and at the touch of her lips, the idea that he'd just been asleep in her presence or ever could be again seemed laughable, every nerve ending awake now, awake and urgent. He was pulling her closer just when she pulled back, shaking her head, and for a terrible moment he thought she was going to say being with him was a mistake that she wasn't willing to make again. Then she said, "I'm sorry, but you've got to take off that stupid hat."

He laughed and took off the baseball cap with the moose logo. Her eyes went to his scalp, a tender glance at the ghastly wound.

"You're supposed to be taking it easy," she said. Then she reached for his hand. "So I'll have to be careful with you."

She was. Excruciatingly, exquisitely careful, in graceful erotic motion while telling him to lie still, lie still, lie still—instructions he followed for as long as he could, and when he finally disobeyed, there were no objections until after they were done, her head on his chest and their bodies damp with sweat. Then she said, "You need to work on your patience."

"I promise I will. A second chance, maybe?"

"I suppose that's only fair."

37

Barrett woke in a state between pain and pleasure. Liz's body was curled against his, the swell of her hip pressed against him, and the feel of her was wonderful, but in his shoulder and along his neck the clarion tones of pain were rising. His whole sensation was one of rising, in fact, floating up from unconsciousness and the darkness as the room took dim shape around him and awareness and memory joined his surroundings.

It wasn't until she groaned and moved that he realized what had woken him—her phone was vibrating facedown on the nightstand. She picked it up, blinked at the display, and then answered.

"Hello? Yes, he's fine. Or alive, anyhow." Pause. "He's with me, that's how I know." Pause. "Why don't you tell me instead?" Pause. "Okay. Hang on."

She turned to him, the sheet slipping off her breasts, her face lit on one side by the blue glow of the phone. "Howard Pelletier wants to talk to you."

He took the phone and put it to his ear. "Hello, Howard."

"Barrett, I'd have been at the hospital if not for...well, the attention."

"I know."

"You're okay, though? You're gonna be fine?"

"I'm fine."

"Ayuh, I hoped so. I'm sorry."

"Did you try to kill me?"

"What? No!"

"Then don't apologize."

"You know what it means, though. You hit a nerve because you were right. We were right. She wasn't lying. But now she's gone. I'm scared for her, Barrett. I can't get hold of her anywhere, and she won't call me back. She's always called me back. I think when she heard what happened to you, she ran."

"Any idea where?" Barrett sat up and pulled on his pants, each back muscle feeling tight as piano wire.

"I don't know. And I'm not the guy who can get people to talk about her, you know? People...freeze right up when I say her name."

When Barrett stood, the pain radiated through his body, as if it were excited by the opportunity to find new pressure points. He left the bedroom and went downstairs to where he'd left the bottles of painkillers. He took two pills with a full glass of water while he listened to Howard list and then dismiss possible locations for Kimberly Crepeaux. He heard them all, but his mind was elsewhere. He'd awoken with the memory that had eluded him in the hospital. It was lurking there in that sense of a rising from someplace down below, some-place dark and lost. He remembered now what he'd imagined as his savior in those moments when he knew he couldn't make it out alone.

"I'll find Kimberly," he said. "I promise, Howard. But can you put that aside for a minute? I've got a technical question for you."

"What's that?"

Barrett was grateful he did not have to see Howard's eyes when he said, "I've been wondering about a net."

"A net?"

"A trawling net. Don Johansson and Clyde Cohen weren't wrong when they told me how much trouble it would have been for one man—or even two—to get those bodies back to the shore once they'd been sunk. I was wondering if you thought it would have been possible to toss one out there and…and drag it back in. All the problems that men would have diving and wrestling that weight back to shore, they could fix with a net."

He listened to Howard Pelletier breathe as he imagined a man tossing a net into the water to come up with Jackie's bludgeoned body.

"Wouldn't work," Howard said finally, and the cost of the imagined scenario was evident in those two words. His voice was choked with pain.

"No?"

"A net would settle around them. On top of them." Howard cleared his throat and spoke with effort. "The nets are weighted, so they settle down, and then they bring up what's above. You see? If what you were after was already on the bottom, then you wouldn't bring in anything but weeds and maybe a fish. The net would drag right over the top of what was already on the bottom."

Barrett saw the clean logic of this now and was embarrassed that he'd forced Howard to explain it to him and, worse, envision it.

"I'm sorry, Howard. I'm a little out of it. When I was down in the water myself, I got to thinking...to wishing...never mind. It was a dumb question and I'm sorry."

"You just need some time on a fishing boat," Howard said, searching for good humor. "You sure you're feelin' okay?"

"I'm fine."

"And you'll find Kimberly?"

"I'll find her," Barrett said.

He hung up after promising that he'd call Howard as soon as he had news, and then he found himself wincing with pain and eyeing the pill bottles speculatively. He hated the need for them, the emotional and mental relief that came before any physiological effect possibly could have, his brain eager for these new chemicals with which it had so rapidly and easily formed a friendship. He thought of Don Johansson's hollow-cheeked face and purple-ringed eyes. *Hurt my back*. Maybe he had, once. That was how it started for plenty of people. Then it ended with you sitting alone in a house you'd once shared with your family, beer cans collecting on the living-room floor.

All the same, Barrett was hurting, and one more pill tonight wouldn't guarantee he'd take one more tomorrow. As long as he was paying attention, he was in control.

He was reaching for one of the bottles when Liz spoke from across the room.

"A net?"

He stilled his hand just above the pill bottle and turned to face her. She'd pulled on shorts and a T-shirt and was leaning against the door frame, studying him.

"Crazy idea," he said. "But when I was down in the water trying to figure out how to get back to the surface, I was hoping someone up there was already tossing a net down for me. I don't know why that was the image. Basically, I felt beaten, and I wanted to know someone was up there trying to help me. Or aware of me, at least. That was all. Just aware. I thought I was going to die, and all I wanted to believe was that someone was watching my place in the world when my place in the world ended." He shrugged. "Like I said, just a crazy thought."

She was quiet, arms hugged beneath her breasts, her eyes on the floor.

"A good friend of my dad's died on a boat they built together," she said. "Same storm that took the *Andrea Gail,* the one they made the movie about? You remember watching that?"

"Yes." He remembered it vividly. It was the first time he'd seen her cry, and he'd been stunned that it had been prompted by a George Clooney movie about men on a fishing boat. Later, when her father drowned, he'd recall that moment uncomfortably, as if she'd had a premonition.

"It hit my dad hard, of course," she said. "Not just because he'd lost a friend but because he'd built the boat. As if altering the stern line or spending more time on a joint would've gotten the boat through the perfect storm, right? But on his worst days, he'd get caught up thinking about what it felt like to be alone in the water like that. One of the things he kept wondering about was how you saw the sky. Whether it looked like it was joined with the water against you, or if it was...I don't know, friendly."

She ran a thumb below her left eye. It would have looked like an insignificant gesture if you didn't know her.

"Don't do it for Kimmy," she said. "Or for your grandfather, or your father."

"Don't do what?"

"Stop asking questions like you don't understand what I mean!" she shouted, and he was taken aback because she wasn't a woman given to shouting, or to any display of excess. She was always controlled, always contained.

"You almost died yesterday," she said, fighting for a lower voice. "I want to hear you explain why it's worth that."

"To know," he said.

"Know what, Rob?"

"The truth."

"Yes, of course, the truth. But why is it worth it?"

He was embarrassed that he had to think about this for a moment, that an answer wasn't already teed up, something he could swing at with full conviction. He thought about it and then he said, "It beats wondering, Liz. Trust me. If I can take the wondering away from Howard, from Amy and George? Then it's worth it."

She gave a fatigued nod. "So you're off to find Kimmy? Is that what I overheard?"

"I need to find her, yes."

She offered him her slim hand but kept her eyes down. "Can it wait until morning?"

"Yes," he said. "It can wait until morning."

They didn't make love, and they didn't talk, but she slept curled tight against him in a way he remembered only dimly.

After a long time, he slept too. His last conscious thought was that she'd kept him from reaching for the pill bottle an extra time, and he was grateful for that, because he was feeling no pain now.

38

L iz was in the shower when he woke again, and the sun was up. He got out of bed and tried to stretch and loosen his battered body, without much success, then sat on the floor with his back against the wall, staring at himself in the full-length mirror she'd mounted on the bathroom door. The mirror had once made him laugh, because she'd mounted it before she'd hung the door and managed to put it on the outside of the door instead of the inside as she'd intended. Rather than take it off or reverse the hinges on the door, though, she'd just shrugged and moved on. It was beautifully symbolic of Liz's approach. You could spend time fixing things or accept them as they were. She favored the latter.

Today, the mirror brought no laughter. His torso was lined with bruises and superficial cuts, and the area over his liver was so dark it looked more like a birthmark than a bruise. The stitches in the long gash across his freshly shorn scalp made the segmented wound look like a night crawler. Without hair on his head, his blue eyes looked brighter. And colder.

He touched the wound with grim wonder. Someone had tried to kill him. Someone had nearly succeeded.

His image pulled away from him as Liz opened the door, and then it disappeared as steam covered the glass.

"Taking stock?" Liz asked. She stood with a towel knotted loosely over her breasts, running a brush through wet hair, the full script of the tattoo along her collarbone visible: *Fair winds & following seas.* The old nautical blessing for a sailor's voyage— a wish for all things visible on the surface to be in harmony with all things unseen, the movement of the water, wind, and tides working together.

The same phrase was on her father's tombstone. There was no body below it; when the Coast Guard recovered his capsized boat off the coast of Halifax, it was empty. Liz had been eighteen that year. She and Rob had both lost their fathers in college. There'd been a time when he'd believed that shared grief brought them closer, added a layer of undesired maturity. Later, he wondered if they'd begun to think they'd marked each other somehow, that bad luck stalked them closer when they were together than when they were apart.

"Not much to take stock of in the mirror," he

said. "The view I've got at the moment, on the other hand…"

"Take a longer look in the mirror, pal. You're way out of your league now. Always were, but at least you had hair."

He smiled and nodded, then said, "So, a few dilemmas have occurred to me. Not insurmountable challenges, but challenges nonetheless."

"Oh boy."

"I have no car. You, however, have two cars that, when combined, become nearly one functioning automobile."

"Just for that remark, you get the Mustang."

"Oh, come on." She had a Jeep that rivaled the Mustang in years but not in noise.

"I've never been convinced you can drive a stick," she said. "Go prove it."

They went downstairs and she gave him the keys to the Mustang and then frowned. "You also have no phone. I don't like that."

"I'll get a burner and call you."

"Okay. Go to U.S. Cellular. They seem to hold a patent on bouncing cell signals off lobster pots or something. Better out here than any other carrier."

For a moment they stood awkwardly, not wanting to separate, and then she laid her palm on his chest. "Rob? Be careful today."

"Don't worry. I'll be watching the mirrors now."

He stood in the yard while she backed the old Jeep out of the garage and drove away, and then he fired up the Mustang and left in a cloud of exhaust fumes in search of Kimberly Crepeaux.

Kimberly's grandmother lived in a small but tidy home not far from the concrete plant where her husband had worked for thirty years. He'd died six months into his pension, a victim of a heart attack that came only a few hours after bailing his eighteen-year-old granddaughter out of jail for the third time.

Jeanette Crepeaux opened the door, looked at Barrett, and then slapped him with an open palm. He stepped back, rubbed his jaw, and said, "Hello, Mrs. Crepeaux."

"Think you didn't deserve that?" she said. She was about her granddaughter's size, and so she'd had to rise up on her toes to hit him. The fierce set of her face promised that she was ready to do it again too.

"I'm not sure that I did, but I don't intend to debate it with you. Is Kimberly here?"

There was movement behind the older woman, but it wasn't Kimberly—it was her daughter. The girl was four years old and had her mother's eyes and freckles.

Jeanette stepped outside and pulled the door shut.

"Kimmy will never be right again. Any chance

she had, you ruined it, making her tell a story like that. Think that little one in there won't hear the stories? Think that won't be hard on a child? Then you have to come *back*? I guess you didn't do enough damage the first time, or maybe you thought you had to finish the job."

Barrett waited her out.

"And if you think I give a single sweet shit about that new gash on your head, you have me confused with another woman."

"Do you know that she's been in touch with Howard Pelletier?" he asked.

She nodded. Her lips were a thin, tight line.

"Then you know why I came back," he said. "We can stand here and carry on about the things I made her say, or we can deal with the reality that she said them, and now she's missing, and she's scared. I think I can help."

"*You're* going to help!" She laughed bitterly.

"I intend to, yes."

Jeanette Crepeaux kneaded her hands together and glared at him. She was scared, but she covered it up with anger. Barrett's grandfather had been the same way. It had taken Barrett a lot of years to understand that a fast temper wasn't the product of confidence but evidence of a lack of it.

"Where might she have gone?" he asked.

"I don't know. She was here when you made the

news. We were watching the TV, and somebody called and told her to change the channel. They were showing your car."

"Who called?"

"She didn't say. She got real scared, though. She was talking nonsense about loading all of us up in my car and going to Florida. I...I got to arguing with her, and then Ava was crying, and I took Ava and went into the bedroom, and I was in there when Kimberly took the keys right out of my purse and drove off in my car."

Her anger had tipped to fear. There was a tremble in her thin lips. "She does things like that, you know, but...not for long, usually."

"What was the argument about?"

"None of your business."

Barrett studied her and said, "She called a kid from Rockland before I brought her here, looking for drugs. She didn't get them, but she was trying."

Jeanette Crepeaux closed her eyes. "She wanted some of my pain pills. I didn't give them to her."

"But she was looking again."

Jeanette nodded, steeled herself, and opened her eyes. "My guess would be that's what she set off for. By now she'd usually have phoned, though. Even if it was to call me names that nobody should ever hear from their own granddaughter, she'd have phoned by now."

She looked up at him, hot with anger again. "It's *your* fault she's out looking for pills or needles, you know that? She's trying to block it all out. Hide from the world. That's all because of what you made her—"

"I get the idea," Barrett said. "Where could she be, Jeanette?"

She hesitated. He knew that she wanted to order him off the property, but she was worried about her granddaughter, and some part of her still believed that he was a potential source of help. In the end, she gave in to that part.

"If not her daddy's, then at the Odom girl's, probably. She goes there now because she's still got a key, and nobody's moved in after that girl died. That's what you've turned her into—a girl who hides in a dead person's trailer."

"If she comes home or calls, you make sure she doesn't leave until I see her," he said. "Don't let her leave without me."

"I don't know why I should do that."

"Yes, you do," he said, and then he left.

39

After finding Cass Odom's trailer empty, Barrett drove along the coast to look for Steve Crepeaux, the car's windows rolled down. The rain had tapered off overnight and given way to a gorgeous day, the sky and sea competing for the deepest blue, a light wind pushing off the water, temperature nearing eighty. The air was scented with ocean breezes and pines and held only the faintest trace of humidity. A quintessential Maine day, more suited to July than May.

If you weren't looking for a drug addict and self-confessed murderer, it would be a day to treasure.

Kimberly's mother lived in Lowell, Massachusetts, and had little contact with her daughter. Kimberly had been raised by her paternal grandmother, which gave her at least sporadic contact with her father, Steve Crepeaux. Steve had never married but had sired four children with four women. None of the children or mothers had lived with him for long, but despite this—or maybe because of it—he maintained pleasant relationships with all of them. He was one of those likable losers, a man who brought nothing but problems to friends and family but somehow was always welcomed back, like a dog who wandered off to chase cats or pursue bitches in heat and then returned with a limp, fleas, and *I meant no harm* eyes that promised you that a good meal was all that stood between him and changed habits. *That's just Stevie* seemed to be the peninsula's mantra.

His place was between Port Hope and Cushing, three overgrown acres with a scattering of slumped outbuildings and a house that was a bizarre blend of an ancient mobile home and a stick-built addition. The old trailer was off-white; the house was brown cedar-shake shingle. The stairs leading up to the porch were untreated deck boards; the porch itself was stained a deep red. A gutter ran down directly beside the front door and through a hole that had been cut out of the porch. Ugly as it looked, the carpentry of the marriage was solid enough, and the steps didn't yield or creak when Barrett went up them. There were no cars in the drive, so Kimberly probably wasn't around, but it was still worth a stop.

The front door was part of the old trailer. Barrett knocked on that and got no answer. Through the window he had a clear view of the kitchen. There was no one in sight, but dishes were stacked in the sink and an open bag of barbecue potato chips sat on the table, a few empty beer cans beside it.

And a spoon and lighter. Barrett cupped his hands and leaned forward so he could see. There was a clear brown residue on the spoon.

Steve Crepeaux had no shortage of faults and vices, but drugs weren't among them. In fact, he'd told Barrett that hard drugs terrified him. He'd been drinking a forty-ounce beer at ten in the morning when he'd said that, but he'd been sincere.

"Kimberly?" Barrett called, and he banged on the door again. Nothing.

He walked off the porch and around the framed portion of the house and looked in at the living room. A couch and two recliners, woodstove, and television. The TV was on, Johnny Depp strutting around a pirate ship, but nobody was in the room.

Barrett moved away and walked through the weeds to the opposite side of the house and the next window. He could hear music playing faintly through it.

The ground sloped away here, so he had to stand close to the wall and stretch to get a look. This room was a small bedroom, and on this side of the house, the sunlight worked against him, putting a glare off the glass. He shielded his eyes. The first thing he saw was that the footboard of the tiny bed was an old ship's wheel. A child's bed, though he wasn't aware of any children having been raised here. The rest of the room was cluttered and cramped but there was no sign of human life except for the music. The same song played on a loop, something both beautiful and sorrowful, a woman's gorgeous voice singing about flying sparks over a haunting guitar riff. He was looking for the source of the music when he finally saw Kimberly.

He'd looked right over her the first time. She was so small that her body was scarcely visible among the tangled blankets. He noticed her feet before anything else—bright red flip-flops poked up out of pale blue blankets. She was on her back and her hair was splayed out over the pillow and she looked like she was sleeping.

"Kimberly!" He banged on the window. The single-pane glass was so thin that he was lucky he didn't crack it. Kimberly didn't react.

He stepped back from the window and ran to the front door. It was unlocked. Most doors out here would be. There wasn't much crime to speak of on the peninsula, and people knew their neighbors. Kimberly Crepeaux wouldn't have left her doors unlocked, though. Not after the panic she'd shared with her grandmother.

He entered the small, musty room and called her name again, but the only answer was a soft voice on the television. The house smelled of flat beer and old cigarette smoke, more like a long-closed tavern than a home. He crossed the living room and turned left and found the bedroom. Kimberly hadn't changed position. She was wearing shorts and a tank top and those red flip-flops, and she looked incredibly small.

He reached for her shoulders. Her skin was cool. "Kimberly."

No response. He rolled her toward him, and her head flopped bonelessly. Her cell phone rested beside her cheek, and soft music played from it, that pure and starkly beautiful voice: *A disaster, dignified...sparks fly.*

He knew by then that it was hopeless but couldn't allow himself to accept it yet. So he searched for her wrist in the tangled bedding, wanting to check for a pulse, and it was only by an inch that he missed sticking himself with the syringe that lay beside her.

He jerked his hand back like he'd brushed by a coiled rattlesnake. The steel tip gleamed with cold menace against the pale sheets.

Float on my back, watch the purple sky the woman sang through the phone, as if she were serenading Kimberly. *I know you don't recognize me. But I'm a live wire, finally. Sparks fly...*

Barrett wiped sweat from his face and said, "Damn it, Kimberly," as if chastising the dead girl, but then his voice broke and he went silent again. He took a moment to collect himself and then, carefully this time, he found Kimberly's right arm. It was so thin that he could encircle her forearm with his hand. He pressed his index finger to her wrist.

No pulse.

He put his fingers on the tip of her chin and, very gently, turned her head to face him. Against the pale cast of death, the spray of freckles across her nose and cheeks looked red as blood. Her green eyes stared at his, and though he knew he was imagining the accusation in that unseeing stare, it didn't make the feeling any less real.

When he moved his hand from her chin, her head immediately rolled back to the left, as if she were turning away from him.

He picked up her phone and hit the home button. The screen told him the source of that haunting voice: Waxahatchee. The song was "Sparks Fly," and Kimberly had died with it playing on loop. Beyond that, there was no information. No missed calls or text messages were visible because the phone was locked, asking for a pass code. It was a cheap smartphone and he wasn't familiar with the make or model, but it looked like an iPhone, and his iPhone unlocked with one of two methods: a pass code or a thumbprint.

He looked at Kimberly's hand. He didn't know whether it would work. It had been a while since blood had flowed through her hands. But maybe...

When he picked up her cold hand, her skin was

the texture of a raw scallop, and he had to look away and swallow hard. Then he brought her cold thumb to the home button and pressed the soft flesh against the phone, his own thumb on the back of her thumbnail.

The screen blinked away, and for a moment he thought it had worked. Then the screen refreshed and told him once more to enter a pass code. No biometric lock on the knockoff phone, evidently.

He wiped the phone down to remove his prints and considered muting the sound, but then decided against it. She'd chosen the song as she went out. She should have it as long as possible.

He put the phone back by Kimberly's cheek as the singer sang *I take it back, I was never alone,* and then he covered her with the blanket to ward off a chill she would never feel again.

"I'm sorry," he told her. Then he went outside to stand in the warm sea breeze beneath the stunning sapphire sky while he called to report the corpse.

40

The man who'd once arrived in Port Hope, Maine, to get people to talk to the police now refused to do so himself.

"I hate to do this to you," Barrett told the state police lieutenant who'd come in after Barrett declined to make a statement to the first officer on scene. "But I will need a lawyer present before I talk."

"What in the hell for? You're an FBI agent! You know all about this shit!"

"You just answered your own question," Barrett said. He knew enough to understand that he had left physical evidence behind at a death scene, that it would not be hard for someone to imagine a motive for his desire to settle old scores with Kimberly Crepeaux even before he'd been driven off the road by a man with a shotgun in hand, and that he probably had more enemies than friends in the Maine law enforcement community.

"It looks like just an overdose, man. All I need is for you to explain how you got there and walk me through the scene," the investigator implored.

"I'll do that through an attorney," Barrett said. He'd taught this class long before he'd become a cop. No matter how badly you wanted to believe otherwise, there was legitimate risk for an innocent person eager to help an investigation.

Kimberly Crepeaux could have testified to that.

They didn't charge him with anything, although they threatened to. Once his Boston-based criminal defense attorney, Laura Zaltsberg, got through with her first phone call, Barrett found himself being escorted quickly out of the police station. This was not unusual for Laura's clients.

"You'll be back here," the state cop promised him. "With Zaltsberg or without her, you'll be back."

"I intend to be back," Barrett said. "But it will only be with her."

After he drove off, he made a few extra turns and watched the mirror, and when he was sure he was not being followed, he pulled to the curb and got out of the car. He lay on his back on the pavement and checked the frame, feeling with his hands for another tracker. When he was certain there wasn't one, he got back behind the wheel and drove to Howard Pelletier's home.

He knew that word of Kimberly's death and his presence at the scene was circulating by now. Roxanne would know, and the police he'd worked with in Maine and those he hadn't, and Colleen Davis, the prosecutor who'd put such faith in him, and Jeanette Crepeaux, whose slap he could still feel on his cheek—all of them would know by now.

And maybe the man who'd driven the black truck with the grille guard and held the shotgun at point-blank range would also know. In a perverse way, Barrett was grateful to that man. He had dozens of stitches and a few pints of strangers' blood in him because of that man, and he was also lacking a few things he'd once had: his own cell phone, his rental car. He'd been put adrift by that attack, but right now, that didn't feel so bad. The tether between him and the real world had been severed, and at this moment, he was glad. He didn't want to hear rational, reasoning voices. Standing above Kimberly Crepeaux's tiny, lifeless body, he'd felt the real world recede and a black, comforting rage surge forward.

He didn't want to let go of that just yet.

Howard came out of the house at the sound of the Mustang's engine and looked at the car with suspicion until Barrett got out. Then he hurried down the steps. When he drew close enough to see Barrett's head wound, he stopped and studied it with interest.

"You go through the windshield?" he asked,

curious but not horrified. Lobstermen were rarely impressed by wounds.

"Nope. I'm not quite sure what was responsible for the redecorating of my dome. The roof of the car, maybe. It got smashed down pretty well."

"You have any luck finding her?" Howard asked, and the question took something out of Barrett, like a bloodletting. Howard Pelletier had lost his mother, his wife, and his daughter. He seemed like a man who truly had nothing left to lose, and yet here Barrett was, about to take something else away from him.

"Howard, can we go inside?"

"Sure, sure."

He led Barrett to the garage instead of the house. He seemed more comfortable there. Howard took the stool by the workbench and slid another one over to Barrett. A stack of traps was piled near the door, and they smelled of salt water and old bait.

"I thought she'd have called me," Howard said. "After what happened to you, I was sure that I'd hear from—"

"Howard, she's dead."

Howard Pelletier blinked at him as if he'd misheard. "Ayuh, I know. But that don't mean there's no point in trying. I thought we all agreed on that."

"I don't mean Jackie. I mean Kimberly."

Barrett hadn't believed this could be worse than

the trip he'd made out to the island to share Kimberly Crepeaux's confession. Somehow, though, the look on Howard's face made this one worse. That day, he'd resisted. Today, he merely accepted, and Barrett couldn't remember seeing a man look more broken.

"Aw, no. Aw, shit, no."

Barrett sat there in the garage that smelled of salt and rust some ten miles from the studio that had smelled of fresh primer and clean sawdust and watched a tear work its way down Howard's wrinkled cheek and into his beard. He was crying over the loss of a woman he believed had helped hide his daughter's body.

Barrett understood it. Others wouldn't, but others didn't know what it was like to live with questions of innocence and guilt. They didn't know how much hope you could put in anyone who promised to replace the questions with answers.

"I shouldn't care," Howard said, as if reading Barrett's thoughts. "After what she did and what she put me through, I should be happy to hear it. But she seemed to want to make it right so bad. She seemed to be trying, and it wasn't any good for her to try. It was worse for her to tell the truth than to just be a liar. But she decided to tell the truth."

Howard blew his nose into a rag and then shook his head savagely, as if he needed to rattle something loose in there, needed to knock silent some tired, creaky gear that simply wouldn't stop turning.

"How'd Mathias do it?"

"I'm not sure he did it."

"Oh, bullshit! Stop with the damned dancing and say what we both know! That son of a bitch—"

"The DEA tells me I'm looking the wrong way," Barrett said, and that silenced Howard.

"DEA?"

Barrett told him about the hospital visit from DEA agent Nick Vizquel and about the one question Vizquel had hoped for help with.

"Kimberly can't answer that anymore," Barrett said. "But if the toxicology report matches Odom's, then she's still got answers." He felt a little sick, and then for some reason he found himself holding his head in his hands and telling Howard Pelletier the details of the scene, right down to the child's bed with the ship's wheel and the phone by her cheek and the soft, gorgeous song it had been playing when she died.

"It doesn't matter to me whether she put the needle in her arm or someone else did," he continued. "Either she was murdered and it was made to look like an overdose, or she took her own life because she wanted to go on her own terms, and she didn't think she'd have that option for long. You tell me, Howard, does it really matter?"

"No."

Barrett nodded and rubbed his jaw and stared at the floor. "It could be hard to inject somebody and make it look like an accident," he said. "If they were resisting, you'd have to fight them. But what if they weren't resisting? What if they didn't know what they were taking, but you did?"

Silence. Howard watching him.

"I need to find out who she got it from," Barrett said. "That is what I need to do."

"There are four of them now," Howard answered.

"What?"

"My daughter and Ian. Then both of the girls who helped Mathias. And you damn near made five yesterday, didn't you?" Howard tugged on his beard. "He's going to have an easier time now, with Kimmy dead. Your way of settling this hasn't worked. I don't believe it ever will. But that doesn't mean there's no way to settle it." He released his beard, and his voice was exhausted when he said, "I've tried to give you time. Tried to do it the right way. But I got nothing left. Not with Kimmy gone too. There's nobody to say the truth in the courtroom, and the evidence you find only *helps* him."

"Howard, before you let yourself even think about doing something, I need you to make me a promise."

"No! I'm not giving you any more promises, no patience, and I don't want to hear any more of the 'Give it time, it's a process' bullshit. Don't ask me for that again!"

"I'm not. I'm asking you to let me help you if you decide to settle this in a different way."

"You don't get what I'm sayin'."

"Oh yes, I do. And if it comes to killing him," Barrett said, "then we'll do it together."

Howard Pelletier stared at him, mouth agape.

"We will bury him," Barrett said, "and walk away clean. People may wonder. They may talk. But we will walk away clean."

"You don't sound quite like yourself." Howard's eyes were locked on his, and they were hungry. "You ain't kidding. You mean to do it."

"Yes. Will you promise me that you won't do this alone? If he's got to be killed, then we kill him together."

He hadn't intended to say this. Hadn't believed himself capable of saying it. And yet it felt good. Felt more natural than any words he'd ever said.

"Okay," Howard Pelletier whispered. "We'll kill him together."

"I need your help, though. You've got a cell phone and a landline, right?"

"Yes."

"I'll need to borrow the cell if that's possible."

"No problem."

"And I'll need a gun."

Howard didn't question him. He left the garage and went into the house and Barrett stood beside the stack of battered lobster traps, breathing in their scent, until Howard returned and gave him a cell phone and a Taurus nine-millimeter with an extra magazine.

"That work for you?" Howard asked.

"That works."

"Where are you headed?"

"To take a last swing at doing this the way I always wanted to. I'll call tonight. Stay close to the phone."

4 1

His first call was to Liz, and she answered her phone by saying, "Hello, Howard."

"It's me. I took his phone."

"Rob? What in the..." He heard her take a breath, and the background noise told him she was in the newsroom and didn't want to be overheard. "Oh, Rick. Sorry, your connection's terrible. I was confused."

It was an awkward cover, but he knew that she sat four feet from a colleague. He kept his voice soft when he said, "You know the gist of today, I take it?"

"The gist, yes. Details, no."

"I found her at her father's house. She'd been dead for a while. Needle at her side. A song playing on her phone that I can't get out of my mind." He cleared his throat. "She was an addict, Liz, but not a suicide case. On the same day someone tried to kill me, she randomly overdoses? I'm not buying it."

She was quiet, and he said, "I'm hoping you had some luck with the ME reports. I really want to see the toxicology on those, Liz. I need to."

"Hang on a minute, would you, Rick? I want to get outside. Maybe it's my phone and not yours."

He waited in silence while she left the newsroom and found a quiet spot, and then she spoke again, her voice hushed. "I've got a call in to the medical examiner, but I also received a call this afternoon. For you."

"What? Who was looking for me?"

She took a deep breath. "I feel like I shouldn't even tell you this, because it's bound to get you in deeper trouble, but it was Bobby Girard."

"Why did he call you?"

"Because he heard I might know you. He wants you to call him. Says it's important. Wouldn't say why."

"You get his number?"

"Yes."

She read it to him, and he scribbled it down on the back of a receipt that was jammed in the cup holder of the Mustang.

"You've gone from an emergency room to a police station in under twenty-four hours, Rob."

For a long moment there was nothing but white noise on the line, and then she said, "Right. That won't discourage you. So when you go missing today, I'll tell the police you were headed to Bobby Girard's before you disappeared. Got it."

"I'll be fine."

"Sure."

She hung up, and he wanted to call back and say something better, but he didn't know what that was. Instead, he called Bobby Girard.

"It's Rob Barrett. Heard you wanted to get in touch with me."

"And I heard you nearly got clipped."

"What's up, Bobby? I don't have time to waste."

"Ain't no wasted time here, man. I got something to show you."

"You're two hours south of me. Just tell me what you have to say."

"It's not something I can tell you. I gotta show you." When Barrett didn't answer immediately, Bobby added, "Trust me, it'll be worth the drive."

"Isn't much that'll make Biddeford worth the drive for me."

"I think I know how he did it. Still not worth the drive?"

42

It was near dusk when Barrett arrived, and the gates at the salvage yard were locked, but Bobby Girard appeared immediately from the house across the street, keys in hand.

"You don't look so bad for nearly getting murdered," Bobby said as he unlocked the gates.

"I'm doing fine," Barrett said, though in truth his skull throbbed and the light in his peripheral vision was a floating gray ring that had made the drive down exhausting. "Would've been nice to have an idea of what this is about, though."

"You'll see."

Bobby was buzzing, moving fast and with confidence, like a ballplayer sure he's going to have a good night at the plate. They walked through the wrecked cars to the garage at the back of the property. Bobby unlocked the pedestrian door, and the smells of grease and paint and trapped sweat enveloped them as they stepped into the darkness. When Bobby swung the heavy steel door shut and it closed with a clang behind them, Barrett had the uneasy sense he was walking into a trap. He had to talk himself down from drawing Howard's gun— guns hadn't worked out for him on this property before.

"Mind turning on a light?"

"I'll turn on the light. Go on out into the shop."

Barrett fumbled through the workbenches and toolboxes and out toward the open area of the shop. The overhead fluorescents came on with their trademark hitch between initial glow and full brightness, and then his unease was swept aside by astonishment.

He was looking at the truck hood that Kimberly Crepeaux had described.

The hood was resting on a pair of aluminum sawhorses in the center of the garage. It was a vivid, glistening white, almost unpleasantly bright beneath the fluorescent lamps, and in the middle was the outline of a black cat, jagged lines sprayed along its arched back to indicate raised fur. The cat's eyes were a strange, glowing red with a textured finish that gave them an unsettling depth, as if they were actually watching him.

"What do you think?" Bobby Girard said.

"Where in the hell did you find this?"

"Right here." Bobby grinned with pride. "I did it myself. That hood's off an old Silverado, not a Dakota, but I figured it didn't really matter for this test run."

Barrett felt a wash of disappointment. A test run. At first, he'd thought he'd stumbled on the actual hood.

"Okay," he said, circling the paint stand, taking in the striking glow of the white, and, for some reason, trying to avoid looking directly at those deep red eyes. "You did a real nice job with the paint, but that's not much help, Bobby. I need to explain what happened to it, not show how it looked."

"Hang on."

Bobby crossed the garage, grabbed a pressure washer from the back of the room, and wheeled it over. He flicked the battery on and pulled the starter cord until the little two-stroke engine caught and filled the room with echoing, clattering noise.

"Time me," Bobby said over the sound.

Barrett gave him a curious look, but Bobby didn't offer anything other than a tight smile. Barrett took Howard's cell phone out and opened the stopwatch application.

Bobby stepped away from the pressure washer, withdrew a knife, and flicked the blade open. He put the tip of the blade against the hood and then popped his wrist upward. A small, pocked hole appeared in the paint. He pocketed the knife, grabbed the nozzle of the pressure washer, turned on the water, and adjusted the setting to a narrow jet before he turned it on the hood.

When the water contacted the pockmark he'd opened in the paint, the tiny hole widened and the adjacent paint seemed to rise, as if the water were sliding beneath it instead of over the top.

The hood blistered, swelled, and burst.

Bobby shut off the pressure washer, and silence returned to the garage. The white paint was gashed, and the blistered areas now showed red underneath, as if blood had been drawn.

Barrett started to speak, but Bobby Girard lifted a hand.

"Just watch. And keep timing."

He stepped forward and grabbed an edge of the white paint, which was tattered near the pressure-washed gash but still tight across the rest of the hood. Bobby took the edges with both hands and lifted, and the paint came up in long strips, like sunburned skin. When they tore loose, he discarded them on the floor and grabbed another handful, moving fast, peeling, tearing, tossing. The red hood showed itself like an original painting hidden beneath a false canvas.

When the floor was littered with white strips, there was nothing left of the previous paint job but a thin layer near the windshield. Bobby fired up the pressure washer again, turned the nozzle against the hood at a forty-five-degree angle, and blasted the remaining white off in one smooth stroke. Then he killed the pressure-washer engine. The hood was now all red, dripping water into the tangle of white strips below.

"Time?" Bobby Girard asked.

Barrett looked at his phone and hit the stop button.

"Four and a half minutes."

Bobby nodded, pleased, and then he lowered the pressure-washer nozzle and turned to face Barrett.

"Plasti Dip," he said.

"What is Plasti Dip?"

Bobby went to the workbench, grabbed a can, and tossed it to Barrett. It was the same size and shape as a standard can of spray paint.

"I was thinking about your sticker idea. You've got to have good equipment and know what you're doing to make a whole hood look good with a vinyl wrap like that. And even then, it's hard for me to believe that somebody would confuse a sticker with actual paint. But *this* shit?" He nodded at the can. "What'd it look like to you?"

"Paint. Bright, clean paint."

"Exactly. It sprays on like paint, but it's actually just putting this rubber layer over the top, almost like a new skin. Guys started using it to coat their nice chrome wheels in the winter to keep them from getting torn up from salt or sand, and then in spring they'd pressure-wash it off. Over time, people started doing more with it. You ever see cars done up to look like something out of *The Fast and the Furious,* all neon, that dumb crap?"

"Yeah."

"Okay, that would cost you five grand to have painted, and maybe twice that if you cared about detail. But you could Plasti Dip it for maybe eight hundred bucks and then just blow it back off when you got tired of it and wanted a new color. It gives gearheads ways to play around like that. And it comes off *fast*."

Barrett studied the can. "It actually holds up to weather?"

"It can take rain, snow, hail, go through the car wash, whatever. But I'd heard that if you got a pressure washer working under it the way I did, it would peel off fast. And you saw it—four and a half minutes." He waved his hand at the original red hood. "Now your new truck hood looks just like the old one again."

Barrett knelt and picked up one of the loose strips. It felt like a piece of a burst balloon. He rubbed it between his fingers and then dropped it. He was interested in the possibilities but also not sharing Bobby Girard's buzzing enthusiasm. Not yet.

"How long did it take you to put it on?"

"Less than three hours. I did four coats, gave each one thirty minutes to cure, and then tried painting the cat. That took longer than it should have, just because I didn't know what I was doing."

Barrett fished among the white strips until he found one with the odd red sheen.

"What gave the eyes that glow?"

"It's a different texture. Called a metalizer. The color was black cherry." Bobby shrugged. "I figured I'd give it a try. Stuff is only eight bucks a can."

"It's interesting," Barrett said.

"It's more than interesting! If she wasn't lying to you, man, then *this* is how he did it. Guarantee you. That hood wasn't repainted. I'm sure of that, and so was your police lab."

This was true. The evidence techs had dismissed the possibility of any repainting.

"So Mathias could have painted it with this and he could have cleaned it off in—"

"Five minutes."

Barrett nodded. "Five minutes, sure. So by the time Jeff picks it up from him, he's seeing the same truck. No alarm bells go off."

"Exactly." Bobby looked at him with a proud smile, like he'd cracked the case.

"I'm just wondering why," Barrett said. "Even if this stuff is fast and cheap, why would he have spent any time and money at all on a truck that wasn't his."

Bobby's smile wavered.

"Man, I can't answer all of the questions! I'm only

saying that this would have worked." Bobby pointed at the dripping red hood that had once been white.

"I'm just trying to wrap my head around the idea that he'd have gone to all the trouble to paint your brother's truck so memorably just before he happened to get in a hit-and-run."

He walked back to the hood, knelt again, and probed through the strips of peeled rubber until he found one with a splash of that metallic red.

Kimberly Crepeaux hadn't liked the cat's eyes. They'd bothered her more than the rest of it. She'd thought the eyes looked mean. She'd also thought that was the point.

"He wanted it to be noticed," Barrett said. "The only way it works is if he *wanted* it to be memorable."

"So he planned it."

"It's one thing to believe Mathias planned a murder," Barrett said. "I can buy that. But would he be dumb enough to take two witnesses along?"

Bobby frowned and picked up a ratchet and spun it, as if the question were something he could solve with torque.

"Maybe he didn't take them along. Maybe you got lied to and don't want to admit that. Listen, I was trying to help you, that's all. My original theory was that the Crepeaux slut lied and then—"

"Kimberly Crepeaux is dead, Bobby, and if you

call her a slut one more time, I'll take that wrench out of your hands and lay it upside your skull."

Bobby Girard stared at him, then set the ratchet down.

"What is your problem, man? I didn't know she was dead. And my cousin is dead too. Don't forget that."

"I won't. Sorry. You just…"

Don't say it, damn it. Do not say that he just got your blood up.

Barrett pulled in a few breaths, feeling the tingle along his scalp wound. The threat he'd just made to Bobby Girard was bad-beat-cop behavior, precisely the sort of thing he'd have highlighted in the past while prepping lectures about police mistakes for students who had no intention of participating in fieldwork. Today, though, he'd meant the words, and he'd said them to a witness who was only trying to help him.

"I'm sorry," he said again. "This could be big, Bobby. Thanks for tracking me down to show me this." He sat back on his heels, turning the thin plastic skin with the dark, metallic red over in his fingers. "I appreciate it."

Bobby Girard was nonplussed now. "It's the only way he could have done it," he said petulantly. "I'm sure of that." He stared forlornly at the damp red hood above its sheath of peeled white skin. He was convinced he'd found a puzzle piece, but he had no idea what the other pieces were, let alone how they might fit together. All he could do was turn this one over and wonder.

"Waste of time," he muttered. "You got me thinking about it, and I was curious. But it was a waste of time, wasn't it?"

"There's only one guy who can answer that question for us."

"Mathias Burke is not going to talk to you."

"Maybe not," Barrett said, "but it's time to try again. If you're right, and this is what he did to the truck, then he won't like to be asked about it."

He pushed away the creeping memory of the last time he'd wanted to test Mathias's reaction, when he'd told him that divers were at work in the pond.

"I think I'll be able to tell if you're right," he said, but he said it more for himself than Bobby Girard.

43

He called Mathias Burke from a cell phone he borrowed off an elderly man at a Dunkin' Donuts in Wiscasset. He told Burke he'd just moved to Rockport but was leaving town for a month and was having trouble with his caretaker. He had plenty of projects, he said, but he wanted to be sure he found someone reliable. He then asked if Mathias could guarantee a job done by the end of the week as a test run and offered to write him a check for it right away.

"What's the job?" Mathias asked.

"Pressure-wash and seal," Barrett said.

Mathias agreed but said he was on a job site in St. George, checking on a wall his crew was building, and he couldn't pick up the check until the next day. Barrett said he was headed to St. George anyhow, for a stop at Luke's Lobster, and he could deliver the check in person and before five.

Mathias appreciated that.

When Barrett reached the job site at St. George, a van with the PORT HOPE CARETAKING SERVICES logo was pulling away, leaving a truck behind. Two men were in the van, but Barrett saw that Mathias was still on the property, standing alone, his back to the road, surveying a half-completed fieldstone wall that spanned most of the distance between the main house and the guesthouse. Penobscot Bay was visible beyond him, and on a clear day you'd see islands and the Owls Head Light and maybe even Marshall Point. It was high-dollar real estate. The new wall alone would cost more than many homes in Maine.

Barrett cut the engine of the Mustang and sat there for a moment, watching Mathias. He knelt and checked the top of the wall with a level, then rubbed his thumb along the mortared edges between the massive, rounded rocks. It was a fine wall, a beautiful piece of work, and whoever owned the place would be pleased with it. Mathias Burke's clients were always pleased. Barrett had heard that from plenty of them.

Only when he slammed the door did Mathias glance back his way. He recognized Barrett—that was evident—but he didn't react to him, didn't speak or even move from his kneeling position. Instead, he just waited until Barrett was standing next to him.

"Pressure-wash and seal," he said then. "You probably think that's funny."

He stood up unhurriedly and dusted his palms off

on his jeans before picking up the level and sliding that into his back pocket. He looked just as Barrett remembered, although his chest seemed even thicker, as if he'd added another slab of muscle during the winter, growing harder while others stayed indoors and went softer.

"I knew you'd take a simple pressure-wash job. It's so easy, and your reputation is so valuable."

Mathias leaned back against the new wall. "You look like shit, Barrett."

He was utterly calm, studying Barrett's recently disfigured scalp with a casual glance.

"It's been a hard couple of days."

"But you came back looking for trouble, right? Otherwise, why come back?"

"New leads," Barrett said. "It's a hassle, but it's my job. You know that feeling. Things need to be fixed, and we come when there's trouble, right?"

"Sure. The two of us, we're just alike."

"I think so. People call us when there's trouble."

Out beyond the wall, the lawn gave way to landscaped grounds featuring massive boulders that had to weigh hundreds or thousands of pounds each, and none of them were natural to the yard. They'd all been dug up, hauled out, and then carefully placed by men like Mathias for sums that would seem unthinkable to most but that wouldn't earn a blink from the people who owned homes like this one. It was this kind of work that so impressed Barrett's grandfather. People out here *really* worked, he would say, and his grandson would be well-advised to pay attention to them. Rob lived out there in a different America, a country populated with thinkers and talkers but not doers, and if he fell into place among them? Well, he'd be no better than his father. A soft-hand man, paying others to do what he would not, or could not.

Ray would inevitably be pouring himself another drink while he delivered this lecture, and whatever needed to be done around the Harpoon would be sitting neglected, waiting for someone else's handiwork. The irony never seemed to register with him.

Mathias said, "So what got Kimmy so scared that she opened up whatever vein she hadn't already tapped?"

Barrett's pulse filled his ears like horizon-line thunderheads. He looked away and breathed in the salt-tinged air of the sea. Finally, he looked back at Mathias.

"Kimberly was telling me about this thing called Plasti Dip paint," he said. "It was very interesting. Now, what the lab guys can do with it, I don't know, but…" He shrugged. "At least she got them started."

Mathias turned his back to Barrett and knelt and

set the level atop the rock wall. The green-tinted bubble in the level floated left, then right, then crawled back to the center.

"It's plumb. It's taken me a long time to find the boys who can do it right. Usually, they screw up one way or the other. Now, though...I've finally got the right crew."

He didn't turn around. Just studied that level as if it held every fascination the world could offer. The bubble didn't move. It held a perfect center.

"Here's the way I understand it," Barrett said. "You took that truck from Girard, marked it up, then sprayed it clean and gave it back. That's a good trick. Lab techs will confirm, and we'll go from there, but I'm curious—what was the extra step worth to you? Why not just borrow the poor bastard's truck and set him up that way? It's the extra flourish that got you in trouble. That, and taking the girls along for the ride."

Mathias didn't speak or turn. He moved the level a few feet farther down the wall. The bubble bobbed, swayed, and returned to center.

"I understand the reason you went back to the pond," Barrett said. "There's a lot about it that is easy now. I see the mistakes I made before. But what was the idea with the paint?"

Mathias slid the level down another foot. He brought both hands up to shield his eyes, just the way Barrett had done when he'd looked in the window and found Kimberly Crepeaux's corpse. The bubble swayed left to right, found the center again, and held.

"You know what makes me happy?" Mathias said. He spoke easily yet with a patronizing tone, like a friendly teacher talking to a hopeless pupil. "Hard work done right. That has always pleased me. And this?" He tapped the wall with his knuckles. "That house will blow into the ocean before this wall moves an inch. Because I know how to see that hard work is done right."

He straightened, slipped the level back into his pocket, and turned to Barrett. His face was too weathered for his years, but his hair rose in the light breeze and gave him a boyish look. "Plasti Dip paint," he said. "That's beautiful."

It had taken him a while to arrive at this familiar scorn, and he'd needed to turn away first. Barrett had interviewed him on many occasions, and this was the first time he'd seen Mathias turn his back to him.

"Never heard of it?" Barrett asked

"Sure, I've heard of it. When I first saw it, my dad was dipping tool handles into it, replacing the grips so he didn't need to buy new ones that weren't built to last. Now druggies and rich kids like it for their cars. But, yeah, I've heard of it."

His gray-blue eyes didn't betray any emotion, but Barrett didn't recall him volunteering his father's memory in their previous conversations. Barrett had tried to nudge him there a few times but always pulled back because he did not want to guide the interview. You got to the truth by listening, not talking, by following, not leading.

Today, he was struggling to hold that approach.

"You've come a long way," Mathias said, "not to have any better ideas than that."

"I didn't have any ideas, period. Kimberly had a few, but mostly it'll be the lab guys. I don't pretend to know their side of the business either. That's elite science."

Again, he was becoming the cop he'd promised never to be. Now he wasn't just steering the interview to the places he hoped it would go, he was outright lying to push it there.

"If I painted the truck," Mathias said, "whether it was with Plasti Dip or Rust-Oleum or finger paints, I'd still like to know *why* I did it. Can't you tell me that much, Special Agent Barrett?"

"Here's what I'm wondering," Barrett said, ignoring the question. "Who was your real partner? Somebody helped you out the night I had you arrested. Somebody who knew where the bodies were. Girard?"

Mathias just smiled.

"Or maybe Mark Millinock. I don't think you'd have trusted Girard that much. Was it Mark?"

No response but the smile.

Barrett shrugged. "That's fine. I'll wait on the evidence."

"Of course you will. What about the motive, Special Agent? Found one of those yet?"

"I assume it had to do with the drugs, but I could be wrong. So I'll wait. I can be patient. You know that by now."

Mathias smiled. "Ah, the *drugs*. What was I doing with the drugs again?"

"Selling or transporting—you tell me."

"Selling or transporting now? Damn, I've moved up in the world! Major leagues, eh? I *love* that. Back when you had me charged with murder—*double* murder, at that—I was just *using* drugs. Now I was selling or transporting! Look at me go! Here's a question for you: I'm not a legal expert, but at some point, don't you have to stick with a story?"

"It's a process. And I'm patient."

Mathias grinned. It seemed like a genuine smile, the infectious kind that could change the mood in any room.

"I like your choices. In one option, I'm a drugged-out maniac willing to kill with a truck, a pipe, or a knife. In another, I'm, what, a crime boss? Drug kingpin? And in the third option...*I didn't do a damn thing.*" He pushed away from the wall, stepped toward Barrett, and stopped just a few inches from him. "There's only one constant in all those. No matter which version you believe—maniac, crime boss, or innocent man—they all go to the same place. They mean the same thing."

"How do you figure?"

"No matter which one is true, I'm a serious threat to your future."

He shouldered his way past Barrett and walked to his truck.

Part Three

CLEAN TRAGEDY

Skin and bones, you never did come
  home
Crashing on my heart through the
  telephone.
I remember the tall grass waving,
In past lives, old poems.
                    —Brian Fallon,
                    "Nobody Wins"

44

He had told Howard Pelletier to stay close to the phone, but he decided to talk to him in person. New information and old information and something still submerged in the subconscious were swirling together, but he felt he was close to an answer that required revisiting an old idea. The old idea would be hard on Howard, and it deserved more than a phone call.

Howard opened the door when Barrett pulled in, just as he had that morning, as if he'd been waiting for him. Then again, the Mustang didn't let you sneak up on anyone.

They went back into the garage workshop, Howard's preferred meeting space. He had a beer in hand and offered one to Barrett, who shook his head.

"Probably had one too many myself," Howard said, and it was evident from the way he worked on the words that he'd had more than one too many. "I was just...strugglin', after hearing about Kimberly. There was a lot riding on her, you know? Without having her around to tell a jury *This is the truth, and this is why I changed my story,* it seems like it'll be harder to convince them. Don't you think?"

"We're going to convince them."

Howard didn't argue, but it was clear that he didn't believe it either.

"Howard, do you remember when I asked you about the trawling net?"

"Sure. Wouldn't have worked." Howard tugged on his beard, one of the edgy tics he always displayed when discussing his daughter's corpse.

"You said it wouldn't work because the net settles on the bottom and pulls up what's above."

"Right."

"Would it have worked if someone set it down there first?"

"Well…sure. But a good net ain't cheap, and it's not likely someone just happened to leave one down there in a pond and…"

He got it then. He stopped talking. He looked like he might have stopped breathing.

"If he put a net down there," Howard Pelletier said slowly, "then you're saying he knew what he was going to do."

"I'm wondering if it's possible."

"But that doesn't make any—"

"Don't worry about anything else yet. Just think about whether it could have worked. If he'd used the raft as a guide and laid the net down below, could he have gone back and gathered them up quickly?"

Howard seemed to be receding within himself. He wet his lips and then said, "Yes. In fact…the raft would make it easier. He could have stood on it and cast the net out in front. Watched it settle down, and he'd have known just where it was."

We waded out until it was up to my neck and then he swam a little farther, dragging her out toward the raft, Kimberly Crepeaux had said.

"Would he have had to dive for them later?"

"No. If he knew what he was doing, he would have laid a line back toward shore. Then he could have just…could have just winched them out."

Barrett nodded. It was how he'd envisioned it, but he'd never handled a fishing net.

"What you're talking about," Howard said, "doesn't fit with nothin' we've ever said. What you're talking about means he planned it! And that ain't nothin' like what you've ever told me to believe!" He slapped his palm on the workbench hard enough to rattle tools.

"I know."

"If it's true, then she lied, and you keep telling me she didn't! If he laid a net down, he knew he was gonna use it, and then none of what Kimmy said was the truth!"

"Maybe it was. Maybe he wanted it to look like an accident when he did it."

Howard fell silent, slack-jawed and staring. Barrett could feel a tight tingle along the stitched flesh in his scalp again.

"What in the hell are you thinking of?" Howard said, voice low.

"I believe Kimberly. And to believe her story, I've got to explain some very dumb choices made by a very smart man. I've also been told I'm thinking too small. I'm trying to widen my mind a little."

He leaned forward, searching for eye contact that Howard didn't seem to want to grant him.

"What Kimberly described was an accident that turned into a murder," Barrett said. "She described a man who was high, drunk, and raging. Then he got calm. Do you remember when Mathias finally calmed down in her version of things?"

"After it had happened," Howard said tonelessly.

"Yes. And then, in his calm, he made a mistake. A very stupid mistake. So stupid that Kimberly recognized it from the start. They were alone with the bodies not a hundred yards from the tidal flats, and the tide was high. They could have dragged them in there and let them drift out to sea. But Mathias Burke didn't choose to do that. He chose to put the bodies in his truck and then take them to a pond. The ocean was right there in front of him, and he chose a pond?"

Howard hunched forward as if struck by a stomach cramp. "I don't understand what you're saying."

"I am wondering about that mistake," Barrett said.

Howard remained hunched over, staring at the cracked concrete floor.

"It doesn't make sense. Even if it was like you say, and he'd gotten the net down there, the tidal flats were still smarter."

"No, they weren't."

"How do you figure that?"

"Because he had two witnesses with him. Their testimony would have put him in prison. I was going to do it with the testimony of just one, in fact."

"Why not kill the two of them too? Dump 'em all in the flats and get out?"

"He'd been with them all night. He was the last person in the liquor store with Kimberly. He'd have been a suspect before sundown."

"If he was worried about them being witnesses, why let them walk away?"

"Ultimately, he didn't," Barrett said. "But I also don't think he was worried about them talking."

"Why the hell not?"

"Because he knew where they'd lead the police," Barrett said. "He knew that if the girls told the truth, then some poor dumb bastard with a badge would walk out to that pond and point at the water and say, *This is where we find them.*" He could hear his heartbeat in his own ears again. "But they wouldn't be down there. Then what would that poor dumb bastard with the badge have?"

Howard was rubbing his hands together like he was trying to warm them.

"It's a stretch," he said. "The net *could* be done, but unless you can show somethin' else..."

"I'm going to," Barrett told him, and he felt a confidence in that statement that he had not felt since he'd gone out to Little Spruce Island at sunset to tell Howard that his daughter's body would be found the next morning. "He'd paid to borrow a truck he didn't need and then he'd prepped it to look a certain way. It was supposed to mean something. Now I just need to learn what it meant and who it meant something to."

Barrett's cell phone rang, and he moved to silence it, but Howard said, "Check who it is," and Barrett remembered that it was actually Howard's phone. He was prepared to hand the phone to him when he saw Liz's number on the screen. Then he answered.

"We've got to talk," she said without preamble.

"Sure."

"Not on the phone."

"I'll come by."

"Not to my house. I've got the ME reports on

Odom and Millinock for you, but if you come here, you'll never see them. A lot of people are looking for you, Rob."

"Who?"

"Your boss, the state police, and the DEA. They're all pretty intense too."

"I can call Roxanne and back them off you."

"Let's talk first. I'll be on the boat." She sounded a little breathless, and he couldn't tell if she was rushing or excited.

"You get something from those toxicology reports?"

"No idea. Haven't even looked at them. But I got something else. The drug you said Millinock called the devil's cut or devil's calling? They have another name for it."

"What's that?"

"Devil cat."

45

It was dark by the time he reached Camden, the soft lights around the library and harbor park glowing beneath the shadow of Mount Battie. Out on the water, more scattered lights represented occupied boats. Liz's wasn't one of them, though. If she was on board, she was in the dark.

Barrett thought that was likely after what she'd said about the police intensity. He didn't drive down to the harbor but instead went a few blocks up into town and parked on the street below the long-defunct paper mill's smokestack. From here he could see the local police station and watch the traffic coming toward him. All seemed quiet.

He got out of the car, cut across the street, and went through one of the public parking lots to a walking path that wound along the Megunticook River and followed it past a series of short waterfalls and toward the sea. The harbor was only beginning to pack in boats, a few dozen at mooring floats now. By July there would be a few hundred. The waiting list for a mooring in

Camden Harbor was long—it took years to work your way to the top.

Liz's mooring had belonged to her father, and it was prime real estate, central to the harbor. A lot of people used dinghies with small outboards to reach the moorings, but she always rowed to it. Her ancient but beautifully maintained dinghy was tied up at the wharf, oars stowed, which meant either she wasn't on the sailboat or she'd grabbed a ride to it from someone else in the harbor so Barrett could use her boat.

He stepped down into the boat and fitted the oars into the oarlocks and then cast off from the dock and started out. Liz rowed with practiced grace, each stroke a study of economic muscle movement, whereas Barrett always felt as if he were fighting the wind and water. As he got closer to her sailboat, he saw absolutely no light, and he began to worry, this journey joining with memories of his trip to find Kimberly. Then Liz's voice floated out of the darkness.

"I wasn't sure it was you until you started rowing," she said. "You've still got that seagull-with-a-broken-wing style."

"Hilarious," he said, his fear evaporating into relief at the sound of her voice.

She stepped out of the shadows and tossed him a line, which he missed, naturally. It landed in the bottom of the boat and he found it and pulled the rowboat in and she tied him off. Then he climbed up into the sailboat and faced her. She was wearing dark jeans and a black top, blending with the darkness, and he didn't think that was by accident.

"You think someone's watching you?"

"It wouldn't be surprising. Not after the runs they took by my house today. Nobody followed me down here, but…" She shrugged and cast a speculative eye back toward the harbor.

"Where's your car?" he asked, thinking of the tracker that had been on his own.

"Back at the office. I figured I'd rather take a long walk than leave it anywhere that pointed out here."

"You'd make a hell of an FBI agent."

"I hear there's a shortage of good ones around here," she said, and then she pulled him close to her in a fierce hug. He squeezed her tight against him. After a long time, she took a deep breath and stepped back.

"Let's go below. Can you make it down in the dark without breaking your land legs?"

"We'll see."

The sailboat was a forty-two-foot, wooden-hulled beast with a cutter rig, originally built in the 1920s in England as a lifeboat designed for rescue missions in heavy seas. She'd had a sleek, fiberglass-hulled sloop when her father died off the coast of

Halifax. The wooden lifeboat was more work and less fun, but Barrett suspected its history of pulling lost sailors from hostile oceans meant more to her than she'd ever say.

He followed her below deck, and she closed the hatch and turned on a dim battery lantern. All of the curtains were closed. There was a knife and a can of pepper spray on the table.

"Who put the scare into you, Liz?"

"You. Kimberly. Everyone I talked to today." She sat down on one of the cushioned benches that ran the length of the table. "You're circling something that I don't understand—and I don't think you understand it either. But it's getting people killed."

"Who told you about the devil cat name?"

"Theresa—the medical examiner who's my source. I asked if she'd heard of the other two, and she said no, but she'd heard of devil cat. Heroin mixed with fentanyl, she thought."

"Fentanyl or carfentanil?"

"Does it matter?"

"Maybe," he said. "You met my friend Vizquel from the DEA, right?"

"Yeah. He was looking for you."

"That's all? No questions about Kimberly, Mathias, anything else?"

She shook her head. "All they want is you, Rob. Three different agencies, all asking me one thing—where's Rob Barrett? FBI, DEA, and Maine State Police. Oh, guess who showed up from the staties? Emily Broward. She was all business, and all she wanted was a way to contact you."

"Why?"

"Because you're knocking the hornet's nest around, I'd assume."

"There's more to it than that," he said. "They're looking at some level of a case that I never saw, never even heard rumors about. The DEA guy, Vizquel, made it patently clear that he does not care about Mathias Burke or Kimberly Crepeaux. So what do they understand that I'm still missing?"

She laid her hand on his arm, and only then did he realize his voice was rising with frustration.

"You made one good guess, at least," she said. "The same drug killed Cass Odom and J. R. Millinock." She slid a pair of manila folders across the table to him. "Theresa gave me these. I can't get any details on Molly Quickery. They never ran the toxicology there. Just settled for the fact that a known drug abuser and alcoholic passed out and ended up in the ocean, evidently. The coroner's office seemed a little embarrassed about that, but, and I quote, 'There were so damn many of them last summer.'"

Almost exactly what Kimberly had told him during her confession.

He started with Cass Odom's file, though he'd already seen it. He'd reviewed it more than a year ago, when she was first mentioned as an acquaintance of Mathias Burke. The medical examiner's report hadn't been completed until four months after her death, a typical delay for an overdose report lately.

In Odom's death, the toxicology report had shown the presence of both synthetic heroin and carfentanil. The first time he'd seen this, it hadn't given him much pause—opioid overdoses were epidemic. Now, though, he was left to consider the question he'd asked Howard Pelletier: What if you knew exactly what drug you had? Users were expecting euphoria on the other side, not death. If the provider knew the reality of the drug and the user did not, then it became murder.

And if your victims were known drug users, it became murder that was likely to escape investigation. Family and friends of opioid abusers treated the news of an overdose death as believable, if tragic. Some of them treated it as inevitable. Very few responded with suspicion of foul play.

He closed Cass Odom's file and moved on to J. R. Millinock's. Five months after J.R. had been buried, the toxicology analysis, conducted in a Pennsylvania lab, showed a perfect match to the drug cocktail that had killed Cass Odom.

"Well," Barrett said, "I could tell Nick Vizquel

that much, at least. I don't know where Cass got her final fix, but Millinock's came from Jeffrey Girard."

"Are you going to call Vizquel?"

"I guess I should. I'd like to stay in front of him, but if I'm honest, I need to admit that I'm already way behind. The guy rubbed me the wrong way, though. He was a little too emphatic in telling me that Jackie and Ian were small ball. People like Kimberly don't matter to him. People like these."

He moved the toxicology report aside and pointed at the death-scene photographs of Cass Odom. There were only two for her, and three for Millinock. Neither police nor coroners treated cases like these as crimes, because they knew them so well by now. A drug overdose, one more on the scoreboard, take a few photos, take the body out, let the lab in Pennsylvania confirm, and move on to the next one. There was always a next one.

"I want them to matter to him," Barrett said. "I know the distribution network is critical, but I want him to care about the victims too." He tapped the photo.

Even in death, J. R. Millinock looked strong, his shoulders thick and rounded, his arms layered with muscle. He no doubt would have felt invincible when the needle went in. He might not have even had time to feel vulnerable before he died. In a strange way, Barrett hoped that was true.

He looked at Millinock and thought of Kimberly, curled up in bed, cell phone at her ear, syringe at her side.

"Did they both inject?" he asked Liz.

"Yes." She reached past him and flipped to the next photograph, a close-up of the syringe. There was nothing unique about it. Just another hypodermic, one of a million, and its contents had been in the dead man's blood by the time of the photo.

"I wish I'd taken her phone," Barrett said. "Just so she couldn't have made the call to whatever dealer she found. But you can't keep the phone out of her hand forever, can you? She'd have found another, or just walked down the right street and..."

When his voice trailed off, Liz said, "Rob?"

He didn't answer. He just pointed at the bottom corner of the photograph. Beside the syringe, there was a bottle of vodka resting on a plastic bag on a cluttered coffee table.

"What does that look like to you?"

She leaned close. "You mean the baggie?"

"Yeah. What's on it?"

"It's like something was drawn on it with a Sharpie, maybe?"

"Yes. What was drawn on it?"

She tilted her head. Her hair fell across her face and she pushed it back, tucked it behind the row of small silver hoops in her left ear. Her eyes narrowed as she pulled the photo closer to her. Then they widened as the image registered.

"It's a cat."

"That's what I thought."

"It's a cat with its back arched. Like a—"

"Halloween cat," he finished.

She looked up at him. "Like she described on the truck."

Barrett nodded, feeling a prickle of gooseflesh along his neck. He stared at the photo and thought of Bobby Girard pressure-washing that paint off while Barrett timed him.

Less than five minutes.

He'd painted the hood real bright white, and then in the center there was this black cat, a bad drawing of one, like a little kid would do of a Halloween cat, you know? Kimberly Crepeaux had said. *Fur sticking out, back arched, tail up. All these black squiggles.*

Barrett pulled the photo close, squinted at it, then shook his head. "It's too small and it's catching some shadow off the bottle."

"What are you trying to see?"

"Whether there's any red on the eyes."

"You think that matters?"

"It might matter a lot."

"Why would someone have drawn anything like that?"

"Street value is determined by quality. People tag

drugs with a logo or a color or initials. Then buyers know they're getting what they paid for, and if dealers learn that someone is selling something that isn't tagged…that's when people tend to get killed."

He set the photo down and sat back, feeling an adrenaline buzz that left him both energized and light-headed, as if he'd had a few too many drinks too quickly.

"The medical examiner who called it devil cat—did she mention a logo, a stamp? Or just the name?"

"Just the name. But it made me think of Kimmy's story, of course. Do you think maybe she saw that…" She pointed at the image on the baggie. "And then, once the drugs were working on her, she hallucinated the same thing on the truck or something? Or maybe there was a bag inside, on the dash. Would a reflection of it have confused her if she was drunk and high?"

"I don't think she imagined it. I think it was painted on that truck. That's what Bobby Girard wanted to show me—how it could be put on and taken off easily and quickly. I think it was on the hood that night, and it was supposed to mean something to someone. But I don't know what or to who."

The boat rocked lightly beneath them, and above them the rigging creaked in the wind. They regarded each other in silence for a moment.

"What are you thinking?" Liz asked.

"I'm remembering the parties that Kimberly talked about."

"The ones Ian threw at the house?"

"Those, and the bonfires on the beach, yeah. We know people were using heroin down there. Never determined the source. It was just around, Kimberly would say, and then she'd shrug. It was no big thing to her. But if Mathias painted his truck like that, he did it for a reason. And ever since her confession, I've been working off the theory that Jackie was an accident, and Ian was collateral damage, a witness removed."

"You think Mathias was coming for them?"

"Everything he did seemed choreographed. Not the result of panic, but planning. When I look at it like that…" He nodded. "Maybe. Coming for one of them, at least."

"He'd have had to be in communication with one of them, then."

"Why?"

"Because they were on a rural road at sunrise, and nobody but Jackie knew Ian was coming to Maine, let alone where they were going."

She was right, and it was a damn good point. Still, the logo on that baggie bothered him. Kimberly's wild fabrication suddenly had a place in reality.

"I need digital copies of these photos," he said. "I

need to see that blown up. Do you know who took them? Coroner or cop?"

"No."

"It depends on the area, but around here, they're usually not sending out a death investigator or deputy coroner. It would be the police." He flipped through the file, looking for the initial incident report. "The on-scene officer was..." When he saw the name, he lost his voice.

The on-scene officer was Lieutenant Don Johansson of the Maine State Police.

46

In full summer, there'd be a few bars open late on-shore and maybe a few boats with parties in the harbor, but it was a weekday in May and the night air was cold and the harbor was silent when they went above deck to sit together in the darkness. The wind had freshened and it whined through the rigging cables, and the mooring line creaked.

"He either didn't notice the cat logo to begin with, or he didn't remember it later," Liz said at length. "It seems critical to us now, but to him back then, Millinock would have been just another overdose call, and he probably never even looked at the photos. By the time Kimmy told her story about the truck, he wouldn't have remembered."

"The truck was the first thing she ever described," Barrett said. "Johansson worked those leads, and he worked the Millinock family, but he didn't remember that one of them had died that summer, even though he was at the scene? No way. He's too smart of a cop and it's too small of a community."

"Maybe he just didn't see the overlap."

"Maybe."

"You don't buy it."

"I'd like to."

"But you don't."

The clouds had peeled back and the sky was a mist of starlight that seemed determined to reach the mountains.

"I asked him about J. R. Millinock, and he acted like he'd never heard of him," Barrett said.

"Maybe he forgot him. If he's as strung out as you say—"

"No." Barrett shook his head. "He would not have forgotten Mark Millinock's nephew. He was the one working leads at the Harpoon. He was seeing Mark on a regular basis. Now he is again, although the circumstances are different." He shrugged. "Or maybe they're the same. I don't know when he started on the pills. I'd like to give him a chance to tell me, though."

Her silence told him she didn't love the idea.

"He was my partner on this case," Barrett said. "Closest thing I had to one, at least. And it's torn his life apart, Liz. I'd like to see him alone before I make any calls."

The wind rose in a long gust and blew Liz's hair across his cheek. They were sitting in the stern, down on the decking with their backs against the bench seats. The moon gave the bay an ethereal light that seemed to come up from within the water instead of down to it. The boat rocked steadily and gently and he wanted to hang on to the night.

"I wish she'd stayed," Liz said suddenly.

"Who?"

"Kimmy. Kimberly." She leaned forward and wrapped her arms around her knees and rested her chin on them, staring up at her beloved Mount Battie, the flattened summit a dark line against the starlit sky. "I wish she'd stayed at my house. That's my fault. I didn't want her there, and she knew it. So away she went, and now..."

"She was going to leave. You couldn't have kept her there."

"Maybe not. You can't say that for sure."

He couldn't say it for sure, so he didn't say anything at all. He rubbed her shoulder and tried not to think of how small Kimberly had looked in the tousled sheets of the child's bed on which she'd died.

"When will you go see Don?" she asked.

"Morning. I've got a few calls I need to make first, a few things to run down before I see him, but I want to be off the boat before first light."

"DEA could be watching him."

"Could be."

It went silent again.

"Howard claims he's going fishing tomorrow, but I'm worried about him," Barrett said. "Any chance you can check on him? Just see that he's actually out there hauling traps? I don't want to lose track of Howard for long. He's supposed to wait on me, but I don't know that I trust his patience."

"Wait on you for what?"

"I said some crazy things, that's all. I'd just seen Kimberly and…and things got away from me a little."

"Said some crazy things," she echoed. "Such as?"

He didn't answer.

"You should have stayed in Montana," Liz said. "You were safer from yourself there."

He looked at her in the darkness, but she was facing away from him. He leaned back to stare up at the mountains. "Do they still put the star up on Battie in the winter?"

When they were kids, there was always a massive Christmas star placed on the summit of Mount Battie in December. You could see it from well out in the bay if you were on a boat and the skies were clear. When they were dating, he and Liz always made one frigid night sail to see the star from the water.

"Yes," she said softly. "They still put up the star."

He nodded and studied the shadowed mountain and thought about the times they'd shared up there or out on this bay. She was the person who'd made him love this place that he'd once loathed. Many of his memories of Maine were wrapped up in fear or failure. When he thought of her, though, the place always felt like home.

"I love you, Liz," he said.

For a moment, he thought she was going to hit him.

"Not tonight. You kidding me? You say that *tonight*?"

"Sorry. But I'm going to say what I need to say tonight. You don't need to answer it, but you need to hear it. I love you. I always did. When we were together, and when we weren't. When you were married, and when you weren't. I always will."

In the moonlight he could see her face but not her eyes.

"I've got nothing to say to that," she told him in a low voice.

"That's fine—" he began, but she interrupted.

"Quiet. Please, Rob. Just be quiet. I've got nothing to say."

She got to her feet and stretched out her hand for his. He rose and took her hand and she guided him below deck. She had not lied—she had nothing to say. She undressed him silently in the dark, and then he felt her mouth on him, and then her clothes were off and she was above him, then beneath him, but she never said a word. All he heard was her rapid, ragged breathing and then a soft, suppressed moan as a long shudder ran through her body and her fingernails bit deeply into his skin. And then, later, he heard her heartbeat as they lay chest to chest in the sweaty darkness while the boat rolled beneath them.

She offered no words, though.

When she finally spoke, her heartbeat had slowed and their sweat had dried and the trapped heat below deck had given way to chilled, predawn air.

"You'll need to leave now if you want to beat the sun," she said.

He didn't want to move.

"Or you could stay," she said. "And let Vizquel and Broward and the rest of them do their jobs."

His chest filled and emptied beneath her weight, and she nodded as if he'd responded. Then she shifted away from him in the darkness, her warmth immediately missed, that unique loneliness that you could feel from an altered position in a shared bed.

When she began to dress, he finally sat up and did the same. While she went up to the deck, he found his jacket and Howard Pelletier's gun. Then he joined her.

Above deck, the faint gray light of dawn allowed him to see her clearly for the first time in hours, but she felt farther away because of it.

"Put the rowboat back in the same spot," she said. "I'll make sure people see me leave this morning and that they see me leaving without you."

"Okay. Listen, Liz—"

She shook her head. "Get going, Rob. Get going before I say something like *Be careful,* or *Please call,* or *Stay with me.* I don't want to be the woman who tries to say those things to you."

She turned away from him and went below deck, alone.

He climbed down the stern ladder and got into the small boat and cast it loose and began to row across the harbor. He was focused on the task, looking over his shoulder toward land, and when he heard the words *I love you,* he was facing the wrong way.

By the time he turned back to the sailboat, he couldn't see Liz, and the only sound was the water and the creaking oarlocks. It was as if he'd imagined the words.

47

The sun was up by the time he reached his car. He lay on the pavement on his aching back and checked the frame for another tracker. It was clean. He climbed behind the wheel and drove out of town headed west, away from the coast. He watched the mirrors. No one was following him.

At a gas station where the early risers were coming and going with coffees and breakfast sandwiches, he parked in the back of the lot and made a call to the one person affiliated with the FBI whom he trusted not to question his motives.

Judging by the sound of Seth Miller's voice when he answered, Barrett figured his retirement gig in Florida had a later start time than the Bureau. Once he was fully awake, though, he was the same genial partner that Barrett remembered.

"You're doing PI work down there, right?" Barrett asked.

"As little as possible, because it interferes with golf."

"Do you have fast access to Florida property records?"

"Sure."

"Try a couple names for me, please?"

Seth ran the requested searches, and ran them fast.

"House is in her name. Megan Johansson. DOB July ninth, 1971?"

"I don't know for sure, but it's close, and that's the right name."

"SSN is from Maine."

"That's probably her, then. She was born here."

"Okay. She's not far south of me. Lakewood Ranch. Close to Sarasota. Kind of a bedroom community, gatehouses and golf courses."

"When did she buy the house?"

A pause, a few clicks. "January of this year."

"Price?"

"One point two million. Nice spread. I'm looking at the pictures right now. Pool, hot tub, lanai, wet bar. Not bad. Go up to Maine in the summer when this place gets hotter than a whore in church, and then come down to Florida when Mainers start lacing up their snowshoes. That's good living."

"It sure is," Barrett said through a tight throat.

"What'd you say the husband does?"

"He was a cop when I knew him."

"I guess that's been a while, then," Seth said, and laughed.

"Yeah," Barrett said. "Seems like it has been."

He was about to end the call when Seth said, "Megan has a nice truck too."

"Pardon?"

"Registered to her in Maine. F-250 diesel, last year's model. Those aren't cheap. Has to run, what, sixty grand? Seventy? Big trucks are big dollars. I've always liked a woman in a truck, Barrett, got to tell you. Smaller the woman and bigger the truck, the more it works for me. I'm telling you, the smaller the—"

"What color?"

"Huh?"

"What color is the truck, Seth?"

"Black."

"And it's registered in Maine, not Florida."

"Yeah. She bought the truck the same month as the house, it looks like. She's also got active registration on a Honda CRV."

Barrett remembered that car, and he remembered Don Johansson's battered Ford Ranger pickup. A truck so old they didn't make them anymore. The Ranger had been parked in the driveway when Barrett visited Johansson last, and no F-250 diesel had been in sight.

Not then, anyhow. But later, in his rearview mirror...maybe then.

He thanked Seth, disconnected the call, and started the Mustang. He tilted the rearview mirror and studied the night crawler–looking ribbon of stitches, glue, and knitting flesh that traced his skull. He threw the hat in the backseat, put Howard Pelletier's nine-millimeter into his jacket pocket, and then pulled out onto Route 17 heading west across the hills to see his old comrade.

48

The windows were open when he arrived and a radio was on inside, sports-talk guys breaking down the early-season woes of the Red Sox, who'd been pounded by the Indians. The house was bucolic and peaceful. Barrett left Howard's gun in his jacket pocket but kept his hand around it as he walked to the front door and rang the bell. The radio went off and footsteps approached and then the door was open and Don Johansson was smiling at him.

Barrett pulled the gun out and put the muzzle to Johansson's forehead. The gun jabbed Johansson hard enough to snap his head back, but all Don did in response was what most people did when you put guns in their faces: he stopped moving and started listening.

"You remember my rule about interviews?" Barrett said.

Johansson was trying to look at the gun instead of Barrett, which gave him the look of a cross-eyed man imploring the heavens.

"Which rule?"

"No guns in the interview room. You remember why I put that rule in?"

"Because guns intimidate people," Johansson said. His focus was on Barrett's trigger finger.

"That's right. I've decided I don't give a damn about that anymore."

Barrett walked into the house, forcing Johansson to backpedal, the gun still pressed to the center of his forehead. Barrett kicked the door shut with his foot.

"Where were you while they were stitching my scalp back together and pouring other people's blood into me to keep me alive?" he said.

"Sitting right here."

"Sure. Sitting on the floor of his empty house, poor old Don, down on his luck, head full of guilt, blood full of pills."

Barrett stepped back and pulled the gun away. The muzzle left an imprint on Johansson's pale skin. A thin sheen of sweat formed around it.

"You were right, Barrett, I got a problem with pills, but I would never have—"

Barrett lifted the gun again. "Stop talking."

When Johansson had been silent for a few seconds, Barrett said, "Now start again. Do it better this time. More truth, less bullshit. Where's your truck?"

"Right out front."

"I misspoke. Where is Megan's truck?"

Johansson's mouth worked but he didn't get any words out. He reminded Barrett of Jeffrey Girard dying in the grass, an untold story trapped behind his lips.

"Why didn't you pull the trigger on me, Don?"

"I don't know what you're talking about. I never—"

"You had me at, what, ten feet? Finger on the trigger too. So why not pull it?" Barrett moved his own finger to the trigger of the Taurus. Johansson's eyes followed. "Was there enough blood that you thought I was already done, so why turn an accident scene into a homicide scene? Was that it?"

"I didn't try to kill you."

"Bullshit."

"It's the truth," Johansson said. "I wanted to back you off, not kill you. You got knocked around, that was all."

"Knocked around. I was ten minutes from bleeding out."

"You were conscious when I left. I could see that. If you hadn't been, I'd have called it in. It's the only reason I took the risk of getting out of the truck."

"That was real thoughtful of you."

Johansson was starting to get a little confidence back now that the gun wasn't pressed to his forehead. "You want to solve the big mystery, man?

You've already done it. Donny's got a drug problem. Ain't that tragic?" He sneered at Barrett. "Blow that one out of the water if you want. Have your girl put it in the paper, let everybody know that I lost my family, my job, lost everything I cared about to pills."

"*Wife took the truck and took off.* Who wrote those lyrics, Waylon or Hank? Worked out well, though. That's a nice house she's got down in Lakewood Ranch."

Johansson went as rigid as he had when the gun was in his face, but it was a different type of tension this time—less cowered, more coiled.

"You leave my family out of this."

"*You* put them in it, you corrupt son of a bitch! Think they'll just keep floating along down there, nobody noticing? You got a *kid,* man, he has friends, has Facebook and Instagram and I don't know what the hell else. At some point, somebody back in Maine is going to notice the Johansson family found a real soft landing place. They probably already have. The DEA is involved in this now."

Johansson looked like he'd just been given a terminal diagnosis. Too numb to be angry or scared. Yet.

"Last time I was here," Barrett said, "you told me that you'd never heard of J. R. Millinock, but in fact you were at his death scene."

Don rubbed the gun imprint on his forehead. "There were lots of death scenes with guys like that. If you think the Millinock family is worth something, then you are truly lost."

"I don't think I am. You took some pictures that day. The drugs that killed him were marked with a cute little logo. The logo was awfully similar to what Kimberly described on the truck. Did you not notice that?"

"I've got no idea what you're talking about, Barrett."

Barrett didn't like standing with the wide bay windows at his back, so he sat down on the couch, then checked the hallway again, the Taurus pointed at Johansson, who was still standing in the middle of the room.

"The DEA agent told me to think bigger," Barrett said. "Drugs and money, he said. I didn't like him, but he wasn't wrong. Now...I can get you on the black Ford alone. I don't know where you've got it tucked away, but I'll find it. If you want to tell me about your role with the drugs, though, you can buy yourself some time."

Johansson shook his head wearily. "I've got nothing to do with drugs."

"Come on. All of this"—Barrett waved a hand around the half-empty house—"is one hell of a front, I'll give you that. You even committed physically.

That was brilliant. Start peeling off the pounds, then the family moves out, then you're buying pills from a guy you *know* can't keep his mouth shut. You built yourself a beautiful lie. When you disappear, it'll all make sense. You're another sad victim of addiction."

"It's not a lie."

"Damn it, Don, I—"

"It is not a lie!" Johansson screamed, and for a moment Barrett thought he was going to charge him despite the gun. Johansson stared at him with hate, his chest rising and falling. "You've always got to be so damn smart. Always think you see all the things other people miss. You don't see *shit*. Never did. Back when they first sent you up here to look over my shoulder, it was obvious—Rob Barrett thinks he'll solve this thing by seeing things differently, hearing things differently. You never understood *anything*."

"Did the money come from looking the other way on investigations or from actively helping?" Barrett said. "What's your role?"

Johansson gave a contemptuous laugh.

"Killing Girard probably helped, right?" Barrett said, and Johansson's smile went away. "How much was that worth?"

"All of it."

The words came so softly that for a moment Barrett didn't believe they'd actually been said.

"What's that?"

Johansson squared his shoulders and stared at Barrett like a man refusing to back down, the military cadet who couldn't be broken. There were tears in his eyes, though. He cleared his throat wetly and then said, loud and clear this time, *"All of it."*

Barrett leaned forward, letting the muzzle of the gun drift toward the floor, and stared at his old partner. Twin rivulets of tears ran from Johansson's tired blue eyes.

"You think the rest is all a lie," Johansson said. "You *prick*. Megan left me. David won't talk to me. I have lost my wife and son. She's trying to figure out how to unload that damned house without implicating me. She doesn't want me arrested, even though I deserve to be. And you know what helps me? Drugs. It doesn't clear the head, but it..." He made a gesture with his hand like he was petting an invisible dog. "Pushes everything back. For a little while."

He wiped his face with his shirtsleeve.

"You got paid for killing him," Barrett said, remembering the way blood had bubbled out of Jeffrey Girard's mouth while he lay there in the grass, trying to push the gun toward Barrett, trying to set this terrible misunderstanding straight.

"Yes. One million dollars."

"Whose money was it?"

Johansson ignored him. "You know I actually told Megan the whole deal? I was that convinced what I'd done was righteous. We had Girard's fingerprints with the bodies, and then we found the truck...I felt good about it. I was afraid he'd get off in a trial because of us. Because we'd put Kimmy's bullshit out there, and a defense attorney would use that confession and get him off somehow or get his sentence reduced, and he killed two innocent kids and one of them was *pregnant,* Barrett. She went out walking that morning with a new life inside her. Girard took all of that. He deserved to die."

"And you deserved to get paid?"

Johansson shrugged.

"Whose money?" Barrett asked again. He wasn't expecting any answer, and he certainly wasn't prepared for the answer that came.

"George Kelly's."

Barrett took his finger off the trigger and set the gun down on the couch beside him. He leaned back and stared at Johansson, who nodded with grim pleasure.

"One of the good guys," Johansson said. "You hate that, don't you? You're always looking for bad guys, Barrett. In real life...you got all kinds. It's not so clean."

"George Kelly paid you to hit Girard," Barrett said. He felt numb.

"No. He promised me a reward if I hit the *person who did it*. Nobody knew who Girard was at the time. I was at the Kellys' house one night, before you showed up from Boston, back when I was dealing with those families and seeing all their hope die, and George looked at me and said that if I ever found the man who'd killed his son, he didn't want a trial. He wanted him killed."

"You agreed to it?"

"Not that night. He repeated it a few times. *One million dollars,* he said, *if you kill the son of a bitch when you find him.* I never said yes or no."

"But when you had a chance, you killed Girard for the money."

Johansson looked reflective. "You know...I'm not sure. You won't believe that—hell, nobody will—but I am still not entirely sure. These things are true: I killed him, and I took the money. But did I kill him *for* the money?" He swayed his head side to side. "Maybe. I might have, but in that moment...I might have just killed him because I *wanted* to. That really might have been all it was that day."

Barrett remembered the sun and the smell of the paint and the sound of the air hammer, and he remembered the way Johansson's voice had broken when he told Barrett that Jackie Pelletier had been pregnant. He thought what Johansson had just said might be the truth.

"I have a son of my own," Johansson said. "He even looks a little like Ian Kelly. Younger, but same kind of build, same goofball smile. Always laughing. I'd go talk to George, and I'd come home and look at David, and I would think…I would think that what he was asking for made some sense."

"You took the money, though," Barrett said. "You could have avoided all this, but you took the money."

"I *kept* it, actually. He transferred the money into an account he'd set up for me. Online bank account, funded with a wire transfer from overseas. I just let it sit for a while, and time went by, and I thought, *Nobody noticed, and nobody cares.* I wanted out of this place. Wanted my family out of here. I needed…" He took a ragged breath. "I needed a new start."

"Don," Barrett said slowly, "whatever your reasons were? You killed the wrong man."

Johansson turned from him and walked into the kitchen. When he reached for a drawer, Barrett reached for his gun.

"Easy," Johansson called. "I'm not getting a piece, Barrett. If I use one today, the barrel will be in my mouth, not yours."

"You're not using a gun today. On anybody."

"We'll see. But first I think we ought to take a ride."

He came back from the kitchen with car keys in

his hand. Barrett didn't like the look in his eyes or the way the thin sheen of sweat was beginning to turn to thick beads that found creases where his fleshy face had hollowed out.

"Where're we riding, Don?"

"George's house."

"Why?"

"Because George is there."

Barrett cocked his head. "I thought George and Amy decided to sell their place here."

"George came back."

"When?"

"The day you hit town." Johansson jingled the keys, walked to the front door, pulled it open, and said, "You want to call it in instead and have my own people come out here and cuff me, that's your choice. I wouldn't ask you to hear me out, but I will ask you to hear him out. That man's no different than your buddy Howard Pelletier."

"He's plenty different."

"Not so much," Johansson said. "One has money. The other's got a gun." He nodded at the Taurus. "Howard bought that one two months ago. No one around here had any illusions about who he meant it for."

Barrett didn't say anything, torn between wanting to deny it and not wanting to lie, and Johansson saw his struggle and laughed.

"You see what I mean, Barrett? You want us all to be so different. We aren't. Howard and George, you and me? We aren't so different."

We will bury him, Barrett had told Howard Pelletier, *and walk away clean.*

"Talk to the man," Johansson said. "Look him in the eye the way you look Howard Pelletier in the eye and listen to him, and then you make your decision."

49

To access the long ribbon of blacktop that led to the Kelly house, you had to pass through a gate. Johansson keyed in an entry code, the gate parted, and they drove in and followed the winding lane through the tall pines until the immaculately landscaped lawn came into view, resplendent with large, artfully placed boulders and flower beds. An old sailboat mast converted to a flagpole stood in the center of the yard, the flags snapping in a strong sea breeze, chased by tendrils of inbound fog that moved as fast as smoke.

They went around one more curve and then the North Atlantic came into sight, the bold open ocean as it could rarely be seen, even in Maine. The Kelly family truly had a million-dollar view. More like five million, Barrett guessed.

There was a carriage-house-style garage with guest quarters above that connected to the main house through a glassed-in breezeway. The main house was an imposing structure with a chimney on each end and cedar siding stained to a grayish blue. George Kelly opened the door and stood at the threshold with no trace of surprise.

Barrett had spoken to the man countless times on the phone and in videoconferences, but he'd met him in person only once, in the conversation that left Barrett with the sense that he hadn't so much updated them on the investigation as auditioned for a role in it.

Maybe it had felt a lot like that to Johansson too.

Barrett got out of Johansson's truck with the nine-millimeter held openly. Johansson looked at him and said nothing, just shrugged and led the way up the curving front steps to where George Kelly waited. He, too, was looking at the gun, but he didn't comment on it either.

Don Johansson had lost too much weight since the investigation, and Barrett's skull looked as if it had been redecorated by a horror-movie makeup artist, but George Kelly was remarkably unchanged. He was wearing a crisp white polo shirt and gray chinos that seemed an exact match for the house's siding. His hair was as white as his shirt, but there was plenty of it, combed straight back. He seemed to stand perfectly straight at all times, as if military posture were a natural, comfortable thing.

George Kelly's eyes followed the gun. "Hello, Agent Barrett. Come on in."

They followed him into a sunlit expanse of house that was designed to funnel all attention to the banks of windows and sliding-glass doors that fronted the bay. It was an astonishing view of a gorgeous but intimidating stretch of ocean. You could see some of the islands and a few lighthouses, but while it was waterfront property, there was no water access. The home had been positioned above towering and jagged granite cliffs, built like a monument to dominance over nature.

If the ocean was impressed, it didn't show it. The swells threw spray up at the deck before retreating with the unique bass timbre of deep water. That high, fast-running fog was blowing in as if it were late for an appointment.

"How often do you have to replace the shingles?" Barrett asked.

George Kelly blinked at him. "You want to talk about shingles?"

"I'm curious."

Kelly apparently decided to consider this an interesting opening salvo. He said, "A few every year. It's a well-built home, but that wind?" He nodded toward the sea. "It gets cruel in the winter. It takes its toll on the place."

Barrett was oddly glad to hear that.

"If you're here, then Don has told you about his financial incentive," George said in a calm, clipped voice. "He suspects you won't be interested in the same sort of terms."

"He suspects correctly."

"Then you intend to alert your few remaining friends in law enforcement to the situation. Roxanne Donovan, perhaps."

There was something troubling about his use of her name, as if he already had a list of potential adversaries and plans to deal with them.

"I don't think it's quite that simple," Barrett said.

"No? It seems very cut-and-dried to me. Either you stay silent or you don't."

"I'm more concerned with getting it right first."

George looked at him strangely. His eyes were red-rimmed, like he'd been crying not long before their arrival.

"Getting it right," he echoed, as if the words made no sense.

"Yes. As in finding out who killed your son, and why. Are you no longer interested in that, George? Or do you already know?"

George stared into the distance for a few moments. Then he said, "This doesn't help anyone, don't you see that? They are dead. They will remain dead. They are also beloved. They will not remain beloved if you tell this story."

"I didn't write this story," Barrett said. "You two did."

"But you came back to help, theoretically. You believe the truth will help someone."

"I do, yes."

"Who? Don's family? Mine? Jackie Pelletier's?"

"Jeffrey Girard's, for one," Barrett said.

"How does it help them? Financially, I suppose. They could sue me. They could sue the state. But their son is still dead, and their son is still complicit in a murder."

"*Complicit*. That's an interesting term. He's not guilty, then?"

"Not solely, no."

Barrett was astonished by how matter-of-factly he said that.

"How did it happen, George?"

"I'm not exactly sure."

"But you know it didn't happen the way everyone thinks."

"If it did, that was only the surface. If Girard was involved, he was certainly not a lone actor. And I have trouble believing he was involved at all now. The more I learn about him, the less he fits."

"So what's beneath the surface?"

"I would like to show you something before you make any decisions. I think it's important that you see it."

"What am I going to see?"

"A confession," George Kelly told him, and then he turned on his heel and walked out of the room and down a hall.

Barrett looked at Johansson.

"Have you seen this?"

"No."

"Okay." Barrett waved the gun at the hallway. "Then let's go see what he's talking about."

50

George Kelly was at a desk, a modern affair of glass and stainless steel that didn't suit him nearly as well as his polished mahogany one in Virginia. When they entered the room, he glanced back at them just once, to make sure they were watching, and then returned his attention to the computer. He opened the downloads folder and went to a video file named Badtimes1. When he double-clicked on it, the monitor filled with an image of a deck overlooking dark pines and granite cliffs. You could hear the water, but you couldn't see it. The image seemed to be from a high-resolution security camera, and there was a time and date stamp in the corner: 1:43 p.m. on August 9, 2016. The deck looked familiar to Barrett but he couldn't place it immediately. He was about to ask about it when Ian Kelly walked into the frame like a conjured ghost.

Barrett knew the place then. It was directly above him. The house had an expansive main deck and then a small private deck off the master bedroom.

Ian was up on the high deck, where you could see for miles across the bay.

Watching him move was surreal and sad. He looked exactly like what he'd been—an intelligent, attractive kid with the confident, natural smile that suggested he knew he had the whole world ahead of him and he couldn't wait to experience all of it.

"Listen," George said, and he turned the volume up. On the monitor, Ian was reacting to a phone ringing, the smile fading as he withdrew his cell phone and looked at the screen, then put the phone to his ear.

"He's *dead?*" Ian Kelly said, his voice surprisingly clear. Barrett leaned forward, staring at the video, and Johansson watched intently, but George was half turned from the screen, as if he'd watched it too many times or didn't want to face it directly. Or both.

"You're sure?" Ian said, and then he leaned on the balcony railing and covered his handsome young face with his left hand, crumpled and defeated. "Oh, shit," he said, and now he sounded less like a young man and more like a hurt boy. "Oh no, *oh, shit.* Do you have any idea what happens if they trace that back to me?" There was a pause as the caller on the other end of the line spoke, and then Ian straightened and shook his head. "No way. This isn't something my dad can *fix.* Are you kidding? You think my *daddy* should be called?"

Barrett glanced at George Kelly. He had closed his eyes.

"Wait it out?" Ian said, his tone of voice suggesting he was repeating what he'd just been told. "What if it's still on the street? I've got to communicate with somebody, right? Somehow?" Another long pause, then: "You're sure of that? Man, you need to be *positive* of that. I might not have invented that stuff, but I shared it, didn't I?"

Ian Kelly was now standing with the phone to his ear and his left arm lifted high above his head, as if trying to signal for help from somewhere out at sea.

"You've got to be sure," he said. "I mean, if you're *positive*..." Pause, followed by: "Of course I don't want to go to prison!"

This time the pause went on longer, and Ian lowered his hand and started to pace. Whoever was on the line was putting forth a strong argument.

"Okay," Ian said after the caller finished. "If it's off the streets, what's done is done. I'll find a way to live with myself." He said that doubtfully, and then his voice rose, heated, in response to the next comment. "No, I haven't told Jackie! You know what this would do to her? That would be the end. She's not going to be understanding about something like this. She's not that type of person." Then, softer: "She's a lot better than me."

Barrett felt some relief hearing this. He'd wanted

to believe that their love was authentic, that it hadn't been romanticized after they'd gone missing. He'd had to consider all the other scenarios—affairs and fights and arguments—but he'd always hoped that the one true thing of that sunrise in the graveyard was that two people had set out to meet each other because they were in love.

Ian muttered something unintelligible, ended the call, and put the phone back in his pocket. He reached out and gripped the balcony rail in both hands as if he needed help to hold himself upright, and then his shoulders began to shake, and you didn't need to see his face to know that he was crying.

George Kelly didn't open his eyes again until the screen had gone black. Barrett guessed he'd probably watched it enough to know the timing. George said, "How much do you understand about that?"

"They were talking about heroin. Devil cat, if you're familiar with the term."

George nodded. "I'm familiar."

Barrett eased into a chair. He suddenly felt very tired. He looked at the gun in his hand and then set it down on the desk beside him.

"Ian brought it up from Virginia?"

"From school, yes. One of his undergraduate roommates was the original source, I believe. A really pleasant young man from Dayton who died at his parents' home that summer." He paused. "Ian wasn't a user, but he enjoyed hosting. He enjoyed throwing a party and giving people something special." George gave a disturbing smile. "This certainly was special, wasn't it?"

"He never talked to you about it?"

George shook his head. "Daddy couldn't fix things like that," he said, and his voice broke faintly.

"When did you get that video?"

"About two weeks after Ian's body was found."

Barrett didn't like that answer, and not just because of the obvious withholding from police. He thought a man like George Kelly would be certain of the date that video arrived. He wouldn't need to generalize or guess.

"That would have been an asset to investigators, don't you think?"

"At that point, I thought it was worth any amount of money to protect my family, actually."

"Hang on—you *bought* that video to keep it from the police?"

"*Police* were never really threatened," George said. "There was a list of media contacts. That's how it was going to start. And more videos. You've only got a taste. Want another?"

George swiveled his chair back to the computer, opened another file, and typed in a password, and the screen filled with an image from the lower deck.

The time and date stamp was 7:03 p.m., August 24, 2016.

This time, Ian was not alone. Jackie Pelletier was with him.

George turned his back to the screen and closed his eyes. Johansson leaned forward, and there was fresh sweat on his forehead and above his upper lip, his complexion waxen and gray as a dirty, melting snowdrift.

For what felt like a very long time but was only forty-five seconds according to the clock at the bottom of the screen, Ian and Jackie just stood at the deck railing, looking out at the sea. His arms were around her, and his chin rested on the top of her head. They were both smiling. Every trace of the tension and fear Ian had shown in the video from August 9 was gone.

"Two weeks?" Jackie said, her voice so low and muffled by the wind that it was scarcely audible.

"Yeah. I'll take Monday off."

"We have time," Jackie Pelletier said. "There's no need to rush."

"I think there is," Ian told her. "Get family involved early. It'll be better that way. If I drive straight up that Friday, the ninth, we'll have a full weekend."

"You won't get in until Saturday."

"I'll get in early. Hey—" His voice rose with

sudden enthusiasm and he took her by the shoulders and turned her. "We'll meet at the Orchard Cemetery. Sunrise."

When the smile lit her face, Barrett's breath caught in his throat.

"You're serious?" Jackie Pelletier said.

"Yeah. Why not? It's the right place to start."

She stretched up and kissed him, and Barrett wanted to look away, feeling voyeuristic and horrified as they planned their last day alive with such enthusiasm.

"Then to my father first?" Jackie Pelletier said, pulling back from him.

Ian's smile wavered, but he nodded. "That's the right way. I don't know if he's going to like me much when he hears the truth, though."

"My father understands real life. He's had some trouble of his own."

"Sorry. I'm thinking of my own parents. They've had less trouble. The problem will be keeping them from wanting to...manage it all. My father is a fixer. Always, in everything. So I just need to make it clear that he's not going to be wanted in this. I'll make him understand that. Just know that he'll blame me, right? He'll say terrible things. You'll have to let him say those things about me."

George Kelly sat in his chair, motionless, eyes still closed. On the screen behind him, his son was staring out at the sea, his good humor gone. Ian's face was almost hostile when he began to speak again, but Jackie Pelletier silenced him with a finger to his lips.

"It's cold out here," she said. "Let's go inside."

She took him by the hand and guided him out of the frame and into the house.

It was August 24 at 7:07 p.m. and Ian Kelly and Jackie Pelletier had seventeen days left to live.

5 1

George Kelly shut off the monitor after that video, but then he sat and stared at it, able to confront the blank screen but not the images of his son.

"Do you understand that one?" he said.

"They're making plans for the last trip," Barrett said. "The morning it happened."

"Do you understand the rest of it, though? The reason the file was called Confession when it was sent to me?"

Johansson had turned away and was back to his pacing and jittery fidgeting. He looked as if he were on the verge of being sick. George wouldn't look at either of them, just that blank screen. Barrett paused before he said, "I think they're talking about breaking the news of her pregnancy."

"Why?"

"The timing's right. They're stressed but not scared. Not like he was in the first video. They're not talking about police, just family."

George Kelly stiffened a little bit.

"The kind of trouble Howard had seen in life," Barrett continued, "wasn't drugs-and-jail trouble. It was family trouble. The unanticipated. Becoming a single father overnight. I think that's why she believed he'd be understanding. If they were talking about drugs and dead people, she wouldn't expect her father to be so supportive. She also wouldn't be excited by the idea of a romantic sunrise walk."

"Very good," George said softly. "I suspect you're right. But do you know how you got there?"

"Because I'm aware of her pregnancy."

George pointed at him without turning from the blank monitor. "Ah, there you go! You have the advantage of looking at the past with the knowledge of the present. That is one hell of an advantage, I can assure you."

Barrett didn't say anything.

"Now," George said, "imagine that you saw this video without that knowledge. Imagine that you watched it on the day it was taken and that your only knowledge of Ian's *troubles* involved deadly drugs. What would you have guessed then?"

Barrett felt a cold fist open and close in his stomach. "Damage control," he said.

"Explain."

"In that case, it would sound like Ian was getting ready to seek help. She was there to support him, to offer her family as support, even. But you'd assume he was talking about the drugs."

George Kelly finally turned from the monitor and looked at Barrett with a sad smile.

"Excellent work," he said. "Really fine deductive reasoning. Where was that skill when we needed it?"

"Where were those videos when I needed them?"

"Fair enough. Fair enough." George glanced back at the darkened monitor as if the video were still playing.

"Mathias thought he was being threatened," Barrett said. "He watched that video, and he thought he was being threatened."

George Kelly sighed with utter exhaustion. "You simply can't let the girl's story go, can you? You think too small, Barrett. You've got to remember that Port Hope is part of a bigger world. The problems of Port Hope come from outside in, not inside out."

"I'm growing tired of people withholding information and then telling me that I think too small," Barrett said. "First the DEA, now you."

If George was startled to hear that the DEA was involved, he didn't show it.

"Mathias Burke is part of this—" Barrett began, but George cut him off.

"Mathias Burke is absolutely part of this."

Barrett felt a momentary victory just before George added, "But only as an ally."

"Excuse me? An *ally?*"

"That's right. He was a help to me with Ian's initial situation and with the aftermath. I have no intention of discussing his role with you. He deserves better than to be chased by you. He's a man who understands loyalty and its rewards in the long game."

"The long game," Barrett echoed, incredulous. "I always thought that was solving your son's murder."

"You're quite right about that. I'm getting closer all the time."

"I don't think you are."

George Kelly ignored that and turned to Don Johansson. "Did you bring the camera?"

Johansson looked confused, then blinked and nodded as if he were just rejoining them. "In the truck."

"I asked for the camera," George said. "Rob deserves to see it."

"I'll get it," Johansson said, and left the room.

"What camera?" Barrett asked.

"The ones that were used to create these videos. Very sophisticated little things. Good resolution, good audio. They did a fine job." George gave that disturbing smile. "I look forward to finding out who capitalized on them. I've learned they aren't so difficult to hack. What people do in the name of security can so often become a weakness."

"Mathias Burke put the cameras in, didn't he?"

"You're a tedious man, Barrett. I have real enemies, powerful enemies, and I'll admit they have real motivation to hurt me, and yet you never spoke to any of them. You remain obsessed with my caretaker." He shook his head with disgust and got to his feet. "Let's walk out to the deck. I can show you where the cameras were."

Barrett picked up his gun and followed George back down the hallway and across the vast open great room. The instant George rolled back one of the sliding doors, the smell of the sea entered the home. The fog seemed to give the smell a texture.

"This is a truly stunning place," George said, wandering onto the deck and surveying the granite cliffs and breaking water below, eyeing the drop onto the rocks as if it seemed inviting. "My grandfather found it. Paid fifteen thousand dollars for the property back in 1946. Right after the war. Built the original house two years later. I tore that down and built this one in 2001, when Ian was a boy."

He turned his back to the ocean and gave the house an appraising stare.

"I suspect I could get six million for it today. Maybe seven. It's time to sell, that's for sure. There is nothing but pain here for me now."

Barrett thought of Howard Pelletier, who had to

motor out past Little Spruce Island each morning to haul lobster traps.

"Do you think you understand who killed them?" Barrett asked. "Are you actually equipped to tell me a believable scenario?"

"Not yet. But I'll get there. I pay the son of a bitch, but that's fine, because it protects my family and makes him feel content. Whoever he is, I want him to feel content. Right up until the moment I arrive on his doorstep."

"You're still making payments?"

"Monthly," George said. His level of calm was disorienting. "Through Bitcoin and Ether. I've learned a good amount about digital currency. It's hard to trace, but not impossible. I'll get to him. As I said, there's real value in having him feel content, untouchable."

"You know who might have been able to help you trace digital currency? The FBI. You hid all this just to protect Ian's reputation?"

"You say that as if it's nothing. But for his mother, his brother, his sister, it is worth an enormous amount. Right now Ian is a tragedy to the world. That's as it should be. That's the truth. But if those videos were shared? Then Ian's no longer a victim. He's a perpetrator. An overprivileged child who tried to play with drug dealers and got hurt. Then the lawsuits would start. I would face criminal charges, wouldn't I? Obstruction or the like?"

"Yes," Barrett said. He was almost in awe of the clinical detachment with which George had broken this all down.

"Then I'd say it's a prudent investment, wouldn't you?" He looked at Barrett with hard eyes, and Barrett wondered how many boardrooms he'd dominated in his day, how many deals had been handled in just this fashion.

"There's also Howard Pelletier to consider," Barrett said.

"He's living like my wife—with the clean grief of tragedy. I hardly see how this knowledge would help him."

"I think he might disagree. And I don't think he's living with *clean grief*. He's haunted, and broken."

"Our children are dead either way. Right now, they are remembered and they are loved. Why would you take that from them? What purpose does it serve?"

"It serves the truth, you selfish prick. It serves justice for a lot of people who are still waiting on that and for a lot of people who believe it's already been done!"

George Kelly waved a disgusted hand. "I intend to serve justice, but I will also protect the things that matter to me."

Barrett looked back into the house, wondering if Johansson was listening, if this was the pitch that had caught him before he pulled the trigger on Jeffrey Girard. Johansson still hadn't returned with the camera.

"If you could move on from the Crepeaux story," George said, "and listen to more reasonable theories, then we could make this an ideal situation for both of us. You are, in fact, a partner I would love to have. Your FBI position is an asset. You could do more for me than Don, certainly. In matters overseas, for example, where this extortion may have begun? You could be a valuable resource."

A resource.

"I'm not joining the team, George."

George Kelly looked at him with sad contempt, nodded, and then stepped away and said, "Don," in a sharp voice.

Don Johansson appeared around the side of the house, and though he wasn't wearing a mask this time, the black pump shotgun was very familiar. He'd aimed it at Barrett's blood-covered face through the cattails not long ago.

The nine-millimeter was in Barrett's hand but pointed down. He could lift and fire and probably hit Johansson. Johansson hadn't pulled the trigger yet, though, and Barrett didn't think he would here.

Not on George Kelly's deck. If it happened, it was going to happen somewhere else.

"You didn't pull the trigger last time," Barrett said. "Don't do it this time."

Johansson glanced from Barrett to George Kelly like a child checking for instruction. Barrett willed himself to keep his gun down. He didn't think Johansson wanted a firefight, but it was one thing to think that and another to know it. If he was wrong, he was going to be dead very soon.

"Nobody wants to kill you, Barrett," George Kelly said.

"Sure. That was a real love tap he gave me in the truck."

"You have options. We're not in a different place right now than we were last year. Three men with a shared goal."

"It feels like a different place to me."

Johansson said, "Put the nine down, Barrett. Please."

The request sounded heartfelt. Johansson's finger was on the trigger but Barrett was more interested in his eyes, trying to find the truth in them. The decision he made now was going to have to be right. There weren't going to be any second chances.

He lowered the gun and set it on the table.

"Now you," Barrett said, and Johansson shook his head.

"Right," Barrett said. "Somebody always has to keep one, don't they? Otherwise there's chaos."

"You were given opportunities," George Kelly said. "You could have gotten exactly what you returned for and become a wealthy man in the process."

George looked legitimately disappointed.

"You don't know anything about family," he said, "or what a man will do to protect his son."

"If I've learned only one thing in this life, it is that," Barrett told him. "And I knew that long before I ever heard your son's name." He looked back at Johansson. "Well, Don? Why so slow? You've done it before. Just pretend I'm Jeffrey Girard."

"Down the steps." Johansson gestured with the shotgun.

Barrett turned from him back to George Kelly. "How much am I worth? Girard was a million. What am I?"

"Get him out of here, Don."

"Yes, Don," Barrett said. "Let's not shed blood on the family estate."

Johansson walked up the steps. Barrett was still staring at George Kelly when the shotgun stock hit him high in the back and drove him to his knees.

"You were a cop once," Barrett gasped out. "Remember that, Don?"

This time the shotgun hit him in the head, sending fresh pain through not-so-old wounds, and the combination threatened to pull him under. He was facedown on the deck when the world swam back into focus, pain radiating through his skull. He was barely aware of Johansson's hand on his shirt collar, hauling him upright.

"Give me his gun," Johansson said, and George Kelly picked the Taurus up. Johansson traded him the shotgun for the pistol, which he jammed into Barrett's back as he shoved him down the porch steps and into the yard. The ocean shone and glittered to their right as the fog raced across the top of it, hiding everything as quickly as it could. Barrett thought he was being walked to the cliff's edge until Johansson redirected him toward the truck. Through the haze of pain, Barrett was hopeful. If they'd gone toward the cliff, he'd have known putting the gun down was the wrong choice. A ride was better. A ride meant time.

When they reached the truck, Johansson slammed him against the hood so hard that Barrett gagged and slumped to the ground. Johansson let him fall, then grabbed his hands, and something sharp bit into Barrett's wrists. Plastic flex cuffs.

Johansson dragged him around the truck, pulled open the passenger door, and shoved him inside. Barrett fell against the seat, breathing in thin gasps. George Kelly stood directly in front of the truck, the shotgun held with familiarity, his eyes filled with the distant sorrow of an executioner overseeing unpleasant but required work.

Johansson took the shotgun from him, opened the back door of the truck on the driver's side, and tossed it inside. Then he pulled open the driver's door. "He'll be gone fast," Johansson said.

George Kelly offered only two words of instruction.

"Deep water."

52

You know he's lying to you," Barrett croaked from behind teeth gritted against pain.

Johansson was backing down the long drive, and he kept his eyes on the mirror, cutting the wheel.

"He got those videos before the bodies were found," Barrett said, fighting past the pain for the last argument he might ever make. "He was compromised before it started. It's the reason Ian is talking about his father being a fixer. He thinks the drugs have already been sorted out."

"Shut up."

"How many times did you search that house? You were there the day they disappeared, Don. You didn't notice security cameras? George forgot to mention them or suggest that they be checked? Bullshit. He'd had them pulled down before his son went missing."

Johansson didn't respond. The Taurus lay on his lap, and his eyes were on the mirror, but Barrett couldn't try for the gun with his hands cuffed behind his back.

"Were you involved that early?" he asked. "Were you working for George before they were even killed?"

Nothing.

"Deep water," Barrett said, and almost laughed. "Kimberly was always right. It would've worked with deep water and the right tide. George learned that much from her."

Johansson was driving dangerously fast, and Barrett had the numb thought that he was in Kimberly's role now, on the same ride, just pointed in reverse.

They emerged from the long drive and out onto the lane that bordered nearly a hundred acres of oceanfront real estate but was home to only nine houses. No help would come out here.

Don took them down the lane and turned right and then they were on a hard-packed dirt road leading down toward the water. Signs claimed it as private property and warned against beach access. Barrett remembered the stories of Ian Kelly's private-beach bonfires and figured this was the spot.

They went down the narrow lane and the trees parted and then the beach showed itself—a thin band of gravel and sand.

There was a boat tied up just off the beach, a Boston Whaler with twin engines and plenty of horsepower.

Deep water.

Johansson cut the truck engine. For a moment he sat in silence, staring out at the sea, and he did not look at Barrett when he said, "I didn't think George would take it this far. Killing an FBI agent?" He shook his head. "I was supposed to run you off by any means necessary, but…I thought he'd pull up short of killing. But I guess all he sees is the cliff ahead of him now. However you can slow down when you're headed right toward one, you take that chance, right?"

"You can stop this," Barrett said.

Johansson laughed softly. "You got no idea what *this* even is," he said, and then he got out, walked around the front of the truck, and opened the passenger door.

"Make it easy or make it hard. I don't give a damn."

Barrett made it easy. He stepped out of the truck and walked down the beach, past the cold remnants of a rock-lined fire pit. Johansson nudged him into the water. It got deep fast. One moment the water was slapping at Barrett's knees, the next at his waist. He wondered how well he could swim with his arms behind his back, but then Johansson's hand found his shoulder and the muzzle of the pistol found his spine. The tide was coming in and the water was clearly deeper than

443

Johansson had anticipated—but struggling left the option of being shot, and it left all his questions unanswered. Instead of struggling, Barrett almost helped Johansson get him into the boat.

Johansson started the fuel-injected outboards, sending a thrum under the boat. A winch cranked an anchor up, Johansson cast off the bowlines that had been tied off on shore, and then they were free and motoring toward the open sea.

When they were about a hundred yards out, the Kelly estate took shape above the cliffs, visible for only a moment before the fog claimed it.

Barrett sat in the stern, feeling the boat vibrate beneath him. "Do me a favor, Don. Someday, somehow, let Howard Pelletier know the truth. Do that much for him, you cowardly prick."

Johansson hit him so hard that Barrett's head smacked back off the stern rail and he fell onto his side, gasping, on the bottom of the boat. Johansson knelt above him and pressed the nine-millimeter to Barrett's forehead and leaned down. Their faces were only inches apart when he whispered, "You got a camera on you, so you sure as shit better make this look good."

Barrett's vision was clouded and he was choking on the fuel-tinged salt water and he couldn't make sense of Johansson's words.

"George is watching?" he asked.

"Oh, no. The real boss is watching. And we're going to see him." Johansson was using his gun hand to shield his mouth. His posture was aggressive, and if you were watching him from afar—or on a video stream—you'd certainly believe he was making threats, but his eyes were imploring Barrett for trust. For help.

"Who's the real boss?"

"You've always known who. You just don't understand how."

Barrett stared at him. Johansson gave a sickly smile.

"Yeah. And if you help me, you might even live to talk about it."

Johansson shifted position and smacked Barrett hard with an open palm. A fresh cut opened up on his lip, and Barrett sucked in the blood and tried to tell himself that Johansson was playing a role. That was easier to accept when you weren't handcuffed and taking blows to the face, though.

"Anything you said to George on that deck, Mathias probably heard," Johansson whispered. "Just remember that. You're totally exposed to him. That's how he works."

His eyes were nearly desperate now, begging for Barrett to understand.

"It was George's money," Barrett whispered. "That's who paid you."

"George rents. Mathias owns. And only one guy needs to spend any money to do it."

"You need to make a little more sense," Barrett said, and when Don winced as if he'd shouted the words, he lowered his voice and asked, "When did Mathias come at you?"

"After I took the money. That's when I got *my* first video. He has a perfect recording of George making his pitch to me. He knew I was going to get paid, and once it happened, he was ready. Everything you learned about Florida, he's known for months. That's how I ended up working for the big boss."

He had the motors running hard and loud, and his voice was low, but even so he kept glancing around as if there were a listening ear nearby.

"He understands how to own people," Johansson said. "He finds their secrets and threatens to share them with the people they love the most."

He slapped Barrett once more, then whispered, "Can't chat too much."

He wanted Barrett to put on a show of anger and hate, and that wasn't hard to achieve when you kept getting hit in the face. Johansson leaned over him again, switched the gun from one hand to the other, and jammed it into Barrett's ear this time.

"You've got to stay in the bracelets, okay?" he whispered. "Whatever he's seeing now, it has to look right. I'll cut you loose when I can. I don't know when that will be. But when it happens? You better be ready to move fast and shoot straight."

He shifted and said, "Take this," and Barrett saw that he was pressing a hypodermic syringe into Barrett's jacket pocket, blocking the gesture with his body. "Naloxone."

Naloxone was what police and paramedics carried to reverse opiate overdoses.

"What am I going to need that for?"

"Stay down," Johansson shouted, his voice too loud, another performance for the camera, then he smacked Barrett twice more in the face with his free hand and returned to the wheel.

He took the boat farther out, weaving around a few brightly colored buoys that marked the lobster traps down below. The high fog was descending and thickening, and the buoys were visible for only twenty or thirty feet before they vanished in the gray mist.

Barrett fought into a sitting position in the bottom of the boat, recognition of all Johansson had said seeping slowly into reality. Move fast and shoot straight, he'd said.

Shoot with what?

If Johansson thought there were cameras and microphones on the boat, then Barrett needed to make it look right. That wasn't hard—he was hurting, he was bleeding, and his hands were bound behind his back. He let his head sag and watched drops of blood fall from his lips and diffuse in the puddled seawater. He wanted to look beaten, defeated, but there was also a gain to keeping his head down—it helped his shoulders and neck stay as loose as possible, stretching the upper back so that when he did have his hands free, he'd be ready to use them. He was desperate to ask Johansson for more information, for some idea of where they were bound and what waited there, but he knew he couldn't speak, so he continued to watch his blood fall in fat droplets that thinned around the edges first before losing their center and fanning out into the water, and he tried to reverse the visualization skill his father had taught him all those years earlier, the pages of the book of rage, reviewed and then closed. This time, he flipped back and forth through the pages—images of Mathias Burke smiling at him and saying, *Don't get your feet wet;* images of the reward-for-information posters with photos of Jackie Pelletier and Ian Kelly that had plastered the Maine coast, images of Kimberly Crepeaux wading into the pond and Kimberly Crepeaux lying dead in a child's bed, cell phone pressed to her ear, syringe at her side. Back further, then, back to the image of an eight-year-old boy opening the cellar door and finding his mother crumpled on the steps.

He called them all up, the pages in the book of rage, and this time he did not close the book.

His breathing steadied and his pulse slowed and he began to take pleasure from the pain and enjoy the sight of his blood in the water.

Suddenly Johansson was back with the gun in Barrett's face, whispering.

"I thought we had it right," he said. His eyes were fevered. "I thought we had it right, and so...so all the rest came from that. The things I shouldn't have allowed to happen, I did because I believed it was Girard."

Barrett said, "I know."

Johansson stared at him for a few seconds as if assessing the truth of the statement, and then he gave a short nod and returned to the helm. He was blinking and muttering about the fog, and he kept staring at a GPS unit mounted near the wheel.

"Rocks all around us, and I can't see a damned thing."

They cruised past Little Spruce on the northern side of the island, the Pelletier cottage and Jackie's dream studio obscured by mist. Johansson changed course once they were past the island, angling north by northeast, farther into the bay. The granite cliffs looked like broken bones, the reason that the Maine coast was lined with lighthouse after lighthouse, erected following shipwreck after shipwreck. A freighter was way out on the eastern horizon, headed north, probably toward Halifax, and a single, distant sailboat cut through the water off the stern, visible only briefly, then gone into the gray.

They motored along for another twenty or thirty minutes in absolute silence and thickening fog, the world closing in on them like a tightening fist. Johansson changed course again, cutting the wheel hard to starboard, eyes on the GPS. Spray flew over the side and soaked Barrett, the salt stinging his bloodied lips. The morning sun now seemed like an impossibility; this was a land of gray, water and sky and fog all the color of gunmetal. He had no idea where they were, just that they were well out into the bay. Somewhere with deep water.

When the rocks appeared off the starboard bow, he was surprised by how close they were. For a moment he thought he'd lost his bearings and that they were coming in to shore, but then he realized it was a barren island. There were more than a thousand islands in Penobscot Bay, but most were of this breed—a stretch of cruel, cold rock, uninhabitable and absent vegetation. They were islands only for navigation purposes, but not for sustaining life. Rather, they took lives, claiming ships and sending sailors spinning toward the depths.

Johansson swore and slowed the boat, the rocks evidently coming up on him with as little warning as they had for Barrett.

Johansson looked at the GPS, then cut the wheel again, and suddenly a narrow, V-shaped cove appeared in the rocks. At the far end of it, another boat rested at anchor.

It was the *Jackie II*.

Howard Pelletier's boat waited for them, and Mathias Burke was standing in the stern.

53

Johansson throttled down as they approached the *Jackie II,* letting the Whaler ride the waves.

"Grab hold of her," he called. Mathias didn't move, but another man emerged from the fog. He was wearing a sweatshirt with the hood up, and it took Barrett a moment to place him—it was Ronnie Lord.

The sterns thumped against each other, the fenders preventing damage, and then Ronnie looped a line over the cleat and drew it taut, binding the two boats together.

Mathias was silent, his eyes locked on Barrett's, a hint of a smile playing across his face. Behind him the fog crawled up from the water and moved over the rocks as if in search of something. The world beyond the immediate radius of the two boats and the rocks was lost to webs of white and gray. You could have pointed in any direction and promised a mountain or open sea, and Barrett would no longer have been able to dispute it. If he made it out of this place, he'd never be able to come back and identify it. The weather seemed to have come in at Mathias's instruction.

Johansson cut the engine on the Whaler and turned back to Barrett, gun in hand.

"Get up, asshole." There was such emptiness in his eyes now that the words he'd whispered to Barrett earlier were hard to keep faith in.

Johansson pressed the gun against the side of Barrett's head as he helped him to his feet. The swells were running higher and faster out here, and with his hands bound behind his back, Barrett struggled to keep his balance. Johansson shoved him forward.

"Give me a hand," he called, and Ronnie Lord helped drag Barrett out of the Whaler and into the lobster boat. When they had him inside, Ronnie picked up a twin of the shotgun Johansson had used and stepped toward the cockpit. Mathias was holding a revolver in one gloved hand. Barrett turned to him and was about to speak when his eyes caught motion in the bow.

Howard Pelletier was bound at the wrists and ankles, his hands tied over his head to the anchor line. Each time the boat rocked, it pulled at his shoulders cruelly. Both of his eyes were swollen and blackened, and dried blood crusted over the duct tape that covered his lips.

Barrett started for him instinctively, but both Ronnie Lord and Don Johansson grabbed him and held him back. Mathias watched with a languid grin.

"The bruises are his own fault. For an old bastard, Howard can put up a tussle."

Howard's eyes searched Barrett's with no trace of hope.

"You have a story ready for it," Barrett said. "I'm sure of that. Am I supposed to be the one who did that to him? You really think you can sell that, Mathias?"

"I think there will be competing theories. Maybe you killed him, sure. Maybe you both died when the boat ran aground, and it was nothing more than bad luck. It happens on days like this. But I think the more popular theory will be that he killed *you*. It's no secret that Howard Pelletier hasn't been a well man since his daughter died."

"You won't be able to sell that one."

"No?" Mathias raised one eyebrow. "Time will tell, but I think once they search Howard's garage and find tapes of the two of you plotting a murder, it might make him seem a little less stable."

He finds their secrets and threatens to share them with the people they love the most, Johansson had said.

"The security business has been good to you." Barrett was talking largely to buy Johansson time. Johansson was standing behind Barrett, but the promise that he'd cut him loose wasn't so reassuring now—with the shotgun in Ronnie Lord's hands, the revolver in Mathias's, and his own hands still cuffed behind him, Barrett wasn't loving the odds.

"All business has been good to me," Mathias said.

"I wouldn't have figured you for a Bitcoin guy," Barrett said. "And, clearly, George Kelly hasn't either."

For the first time, there was the flash of some anger in Mathias.

"That's why it works," he said. "What you *figured* about me, what everyone like you did, *that* is why it works." He dropped to one knee and withdrew a plastic case with a clear lid from beneath one of the stern cushions. The case had once held drill bits; now it held five hypodermic syringes.

"Wouldn't want any swimmers," he said. "It's a long way to shore, but you hear crazy stories sometimes. Some people just don't know when to die. We'll make it smooth and sweet, Barrett. Hell, you'll enjoy it."

He removed one of the syringes and set his revolver down to take off the cap.

Barrett was thinking, *Now, Don, do it now,* with such intensity that he almost didn't realize that the pressure on his wrists had loosened.

"Get up there," Johansson said. He'd been standing close to Barrett, and now he shoved him forward, then made a show of stumbling, saying

"Shit!" just as the Taurus fell to the deck, as if he'd dropped it.

The gun clattered out into the bulkhead, into the middle of a triangle between Barrett, Ronnie, and Mathias. Absolutely perfect position—somebody was going to have to reach for it, and only two parties thought they were in the mix.

Mathias started to rise, then seemed to think better of it on the rolling boat with the deadly syringe in his hand. He nodded at Ronnie instead.

Ronnie had to break his shooter's stance to move for it. When the shotgun muzzle swung toward the deck, Johansson gave Barrett a nudge and then stepped sideways.

Johansson had cut the flex cuffs while he stood close to Barrett, and Barrett's hands were finally free as he dove for the Taurus. He landed on the deck boards and used his left hand to knock the Taurus toward his right, all of his focus on coming up shooting. He was convinced that the pistol was their last hope, only hope, right up until he heard the staccato claps from above.

He looked up in time to see twin roses bloom in the center of Ronnie Lord's chest. Ronnie staggered backward and lifted the shotgun, and Barrett reached for it with a desperate, grasping hand, trying to keep the muzzle down as Ronnie's finger landed on the trigger.

He missed.

The blast of the shotgun was cacophonous, a thunderclap inches from Barrett's ear, and it felt as if the force of the sound itself drove him down.

Ronnie Lord stood for a moment with odd rigidity, then looked down at his chest, wobbled like the last pin between a spare and a strike, and went over backward, the shotgun tumbling from his grasp.

Barrett rose to his knees with his ears ringing and the nine-millimeter in his hands. He spun toward the stern, thinking that he was moving too slow— *Move fast and shoot straight,* Johansson had said— and by the time he turned, he saw Mathias closing on him with the revolver in his left hand, the muzzle rising.

Barrett pulled the trigger on the nine.

The gun fired with a sound that seemed soft after the shotgun blast, but Mathias Burke's body kicked sideways as a wave hit the boat and knocked him down on top of Barrett. Barrett rolled onto his left shoulder and brought the muzzle of the Taurus to Mathias's face, but he could already feel the warm rush of the other man's blood against his own belly, and Mathias dropped his gun and rolled onto his back, both hands going to his belly, trying to compress the wound, to hold himself together.

Barrett staggered up and kicked Mathias's revolver away. He nearly fell from the motion; the deck was already slick with blood. He got his balance back and turned to help Johansson.

Johansson was draped over the gunwale, nearly knocked off the boat by the shotgun blast. The shell's scatter pattern had left his torso crisscrossed with bloody gashes, like the laces on a baseball. His pants were hiked up on his left calf, showing the empty ankle holster he'd drawn his backup gun from. The gun was nowhere to be seen—probably on the ocean floor by now.

"Got 'em," Johansson said softly.

"Yeah."

"Thought Mathias had you. You shot fast, though."

He spat blood onto the deck and took a breath that made the chest wounds bubble. Barrett knew he should be trying to help, but he felt numb and unsteady, disembodied.

"Real firefight that time," Johansson murmured. "Right guys too."

"Yes," Barrett said.

Johansson nodded weakly and glanced down at his lacerated, bloody chest with near disinterest.

"Cleaner now," he said, and his words were slurred. "Clean as I can get."

When he heaved himself up, Barrett thought he was attempting to stand. "Stay there," he said, but then he realized that Johansson was trying to fight over the gunwale, into the water. He was too weak to make it all the way, and for an instant he was half in the boat and half off, but then the next wave hit and gravity claimed him.

He went over the side and into the sea, and the spray from the wave washed his blood down as if the ocean were determined to remove all traces of him as quickly as possible.

Barrett moved after him, looking for a line or a life ring or a boat hook, but he couldn't find anything. He was struggling to focus suddenly, and as he turned, the horizon rose and fell and took the vertical axis with it and then he was down on his knees without much idea how he'd gotten there.

It wasn't until he set the Taurus down and used his hands to help push strangely disobliging legs into action that he saw the hypodermic syringe buried just under his rib cage.

54

He pulled the syringe out with his right hand. The plunger was down, and the syringe was empty. The steel needle glinted and held his attention. He'd never seen a needle like this one before. It was captivating, gorgeous—

Deadly.

"Howard," Barrett called weakly. "Howard, help."

But Howard Pelletier couldn't answer, because there was duct tape over his mouth. Howard couldn't help him unless Barrett freed him. Even then, what was Howard going to do? The old fisherman could not help him with this. If Johansson were alive, maybe. Maybe he would know…

He did know.

Barrett fumbled in his jacket pocket for the naloxone. He'd been through a training seminar about this once. There was a process. What in the hell was the process?

Inhale it.

Yes, that was it! It was a nasal spray; you just

squirted it out and breathed it in and it bought you time, bought you life.

He was surprised to find another syringe in his hand. It did not look like a spray. Maybe it worked the same, though. Just depress that plunger and breathe?

His heavy, clumsy fingers managed to get the cap off. The world was peeling back in the bright fog, and the fog was gaining speed and color, and it wasn't so bad at all. It was compressing his lungs, and that scared him a little because each breath took more effort, but otherwise, the bright whirling fog was not so bad.

Just relax and let it take you, then. Ride the fog and chase the colors.

A wave threw spray over the boat and into his face, and he sputtered and choked and suddenly the syringe in his hand made sense once more. It was not a nasal spray. This was either an older-school approach or a stronger one. This was simple. Stick yourself and push that plunger down.

The bright fog rippled and danced and now it had a spinning motion in addition to its speed, and his breath was very short and the urge to just ride with it was overwhelming.

Hurry, a voice distant and dull said from somewhere behind that whirling fog. *You've got to hurry.*

And make it count. He had to find a vein. What

vein? He'd never injected anything. The wrist was good, wasn't it?

He tried for his wrist, but the boat was beam-to against the water now, and another wave knocked him sideways and he missed his wrist entirely in an awkward lunge. He fell and landed on his left elbow on the decking but managed to keep the syringe.

He struggled back up, hunting for a good vein. Why was this so hard? A million addicts succeeded at this task every day, but he couldn't? Good veins were easy, they were big and blue and led right to the heart…

That's it, he thought, and jabbed the needle at his heart. He missed again, his unsteady hand swinging high. The needle pierced the skin just over his collarbone, in the side of his neck. He felt the sharp pain and decided it was success, and then, just before the next wave hit the boat broadside, he remembered the plunger.

He depressed the plunger and felt a warming sensation in his throat as the wave hit and he stumbled and fell again.

Only after his legs cracked off the side of the boat and he went airborne did he realize what a mistake it had been to stand.

Then he was in the water, and sinking fast.

55

The stunning cold of the North Atlantic didn't bother him. Sinking deeper into it didn't bother him. All that bothered him was that the water seemed to be dimming the splendor of the fog.

He'd begun to enjoy that, and if he was going to drown, he wanted to drown in the fog, not the water.

He fought for the surface with little consideration of survival. He was merely chasing the bright, pleasant warmth and whirl of that fog, which seemed to have been left behind.

Then he broke the surface, choked on the water as a wave lifted him and deposited him into the shallow trough between swells, and he leaned back, trying to float. If he could float, that would be a good thing. He could lose himself within that bright swirling fog then.

So just float. The easiest thing in the world, a natural thing for the body, and yet he couldn't seem to achieve it. The waves drove him under each time, and each time he had more trouble getting his head above water again, and then he couldn't remember how he was supposed to position his body to float.

His breathing wasn't so tight anymore, though. He'd noticed an improvement there. The vise around his lungs had loosened, and if he could just keep them clear of water, he thought that he'd be able to keep breathing. The problem was the water, the damned chopping, slapping water. Too much weight; too little body control. It was better down below, he decided. Darker and colder, but better, because it was easier.

He was ready for something to be easy.

He took as deep a breath as he could and held it, and the next time a wave drove him under, he didn't resist. He let it hammer him down and was disappointed when it didn't drive him deeper, when he began to rise despite his best efforts. Something was raking over his face, a cruel hand determined to pull him back up and not let him have his peace down here.

He fought back, struggling to push the unseen enemy away from his face, and it snapped at him, trying to rip his hand right off his wrist, a savage pain that forced him to open his eyes.

His hand was caught, but it wasn't by anything with teeth. It was wrapped in a net. The braided mesh jerked again, sending a fresh bolt of pain from wrist to shoulder and on up to his brain, and for the first time a rational thought rose: *This is help. Take it, and hold on.*

He got his left hand up and wrapped that in the net as well, and now he needed to breathe but knew that he shouldn't, not just yet.

The mesh bit into his hands and tugged him upward, and he tried to kick to help it, but all of his motions were clumsy and weak. *Just hang on, then. Just hang on and see where this thing leads.*

It led up, up, up. The cold stayed with him but the shadows receded and he could see the daylight like something viewed through fractured glass. It was far away, but it was there.

He broke the water with what seemed an extra burst of speed. He gasped in a breath, and this time when the waves lifted him, they dropped his whole body into the net, and it was easier to stay afloat now. He wondered where the net had come from, and a sudden dark fear gripped him.

Mathias. He's caught you.

He tried to free himself, kick loose and let the water take him again, but he was too tangled and the net was pulling too fast. He slid over the surface of the water, and he turned to face the boat as he was dragged in, thinking that if he got in even one punch at Mathias, it would be better than nothing.

It wasn't Mathias on the other end of the net, though.

It was Liz.

She reached down for him and he tried to reach back but couldn't find her. He was out of strength, and breathing had become a challenge again, and he was trying to tell her that she was too late when he felt himself leave the water and strike something hard. It hurt his shoulders and sent pain rippling through his spine, but it was solid, and that was good. Then he was out of the water entirely and on solid ground.

No, not solid ground—on the boat. A different boat than the one he'd left. This boat had a mast and sails. All of that confused him. So did Liz's face, hovering above his, asking questions he did not understand and saying his name over and over. He couldn't follow the questions, but he figured she wanted to know how he'd come to be in the water, and that was complicated. Explaining that would require more energy than he had, and more memory, and so he told her the only thing he could think of: "Needles," he said. "I need more needles."

56

He got more needles.

The Maine Marine Patrol arrived first, and they administered a second dose of naloxone. They knew to do it because once they got the tape off Howard Pelletier's mouth, he was able to explain what was wrong with Rob Barrett a little better than Rob Barrett had managed to.

A Coast Guard cutter from Rockland arrived on scene next, and the medic on board took a look at Barrett and sent the marine patrol boat racing him back to shore to meet a helicopter. He was unconscious by then and had no memory of the medevac flight that followed.

He was at Pen Bay Medical Center before he was finally stable, let alone coherent.

The police got to him first, and so he learned why Liz had been there from them, not her. He'd asked her to keep an eye on Howard Pelletier, she said. When she saw two men on Howard's boat, she was curious, so she kept watching from her boat but kept her distance. She also put the sails up. People didn't think of threats coming from sailboats. She was just a fool out chasing wind, not worthy of a critical eye.

The police had a few other updates.

Ronnie Lord had been pronounced dead on arrival, but Mathias Burke was still alive. He'd been transported to Portland, where a trauma surgeon was working on him. His odds of surviving were low.

Howard Pelletier was bloodied and bruised but otherwise well, and he told the police that Mathias Burke and Ronnie Lord had been lying in wait for him on his boat. He'd gotten aboard that morning and walked right into the barrel of a shotgun. From there, he said, things had gotten messy.

Barrett couldn't dispute that.

He asked about Don Johansson and was told that Johansson's body hadn't yet been recovered. They were looking for him, but it was deep water out there.

Those were all the answers the police could provide. They went through them quickly, because what they wanted was to ask questions, not answer them. This time, Barrett didn't make any calls to a lawyer. This time, he just talked.

By the time he was done talking, George Kelly was in custody.

The first visitor without a badge was Liz.

She sat beside his bed and held his hand to her

cheek with her eyes closed, and she didn't say a word for a long time, and neither did he. Eventually, she kissed his hand and released it.

"Thank you for today," he said.

She choked out a laugh. "No problem."

"I never liked the way you kept those old rescue nets on board," he said. "I felt like they kept you in the past, thinking about your dad out there in the water. I have a different opinion of those nets now."

He was going for a laugh or a smile, but she leaned forward, eyes intense, her hair falling across her face, shirt pulling away from her collarbone just enough to show the top edge of the inked script about fair winds and following seas.

"Do you remember what you told me on the boat?" she asked. "When it was just the two of us, do you remember what you said?"

"I asked for needles, right?"

"Yes. But before the marine patrol got there, you were trying to explain something else. Do you remember that?"

He didn't.

"You wanted me to know that the sky looked friendly," she said. "I thought you were trying to convince me of that because of the story I'd told you about my dad. About his question of how it would look to you if you were drowning in open water.

Whether the sky held any hope. You don't remember telling me that?"

"I'm sorry," he said. "I don't."

She considered that and then said, "That's better, actually. I'm glad you don't."

"Why?"

"Because it's more likely that it was true."

He reached out and touched the side of her face and she took his hand again and kissed it gently.

"How much did you see of what happened on Howard's boat?" he asked.

"None of it. Once Howard got so far from his traps, I knew there was something wrong, so I followed him, and I saw he wasn't alone. I was keeping my distance and changing course, but then the fog came in and made it easier to stay out of sight. I couldn't see a damn thing, though, and I was terrified I'd run right up on them. When I heard the shotgun, I just figured it was time to take chances. I think his idea was to get isolated and get deep. It's about seven hundred feet deep off those rocks."

He thought about that and wondered how long it would have taken him to make the bottom.

"Don's still out there somewhere," he said.

"Yes." She studied his face. "I've heard that they're searching his house now. Treating it like a crime scene."

Barrett closed his eyes, thinking of Megan and David and the police who were surely arriving at their new Florida home. "It is a crime scene," he said. "But the man still saved me twice today."

She didn't answer. He said, "And then you did the same, of course."

"And then the marine patrol did. And then the Coast Guard. And then the doctors. It takes a village with you, Rob."

"How's Howard?"

"Better than he looked, I'm told."

"He won't be for long. If they haven't told him about George Kelly yet, they'll be telling him soon," Barrett said. "And when he learns the truth, it is going to be devastating."

They told Howard that night, and a few hours later, he came by to see Barrett.

His arm was in a sling, and he had stitches in his lip and a bandage on his forehead, but he moved all right. His first questions, predictably and excruciatingly, were all about Barrett—how was he feeling, was there any long-term damage, did he think the doctors here were good enough, because Howard had a cousin who had a friend who worked at a hospital in Boston that was supposed to be the best, and he could call...

"I'm fine, Howard. I'm just fine."

"Ayuh, good, I just...you know, want the best for you. If you need anything, you just say the word."

"What have you heard from the police?" Barrett asked.

Howard's eyes watered, and he blinked, looked away, and gathered himself. Then he spoke facing the wall.

"That Ian's father was holding a lot back all this time. Is that your understanding too?"

"Yes."

Howard nodded slowly, as if turning that thought over and giving it due consideration. He started to speak twice and had to stop each time. Then he finally got his voice back.

"I liked that kid," he said. "I really did. And Jackie? She loved him. Would've left the island for him."

"I know it."

Howard turned back to him, a slight tremor in his jaw, and said, "I'm real glad she didn't know that about his family. Or about him."

Barrett watched him and the memory of George Kelly saying *clean grief of tragedy* floated through his mind and he couldn't think of anything to say.

Howard broke the silence. "Mathias might make it, I hear."

"Really? They told me he was dying."

Howard shook his head. "Doctors down there got him stabilized, I guess. He's supposed to pull through."

"How you feel about that?" Barrett asked, though he wasn't sure himself.

"He'll go to prison if he lives," Howard said. "And he'll stay in. No question about that this time."

"No, there isn't."

"So it's fine, then. Maybe I'm even rooting for him to pull through, a little bit. Because maybe now he'll answer questions."

"Don't count on that," Barrett said.

"Ayuh, I guess I should know better than that by now. People who know things, they don't share them, do they?"

Barrett didn't respond. Howard looked at the floor.

"I liked that kid. He was good to her. I need to re-member that." He looked up at Barrett again, and his eyes were hard. "I'm going to need you to re-mind me of that, okay?"

"Okay. We'll both need help remembering that."

"You think Jackie knew about the drugs?" Howard asked. "About all the trouble that was around him?"

"Nothing I've heard suggests that she knew about that."

Howard adjusted his sling, shifting the weight of his wounded arm. When he finally spoke again, his voice was so soft that it was scarcely audible.

"I hope she didn't."

57

Mathias Burke would go from his hospital room to the courtroom, where he would be charged with two murders and two attempted murders, among other offenses.

According to Nick Vizquel of the DEA, the charge sheet was much too short.

The DEA had been investigating the link between deaths in six states from devil cat heroin laced with carfentanil. The strand had its epicenter in Virginia and traveled out in the summer in shock waves, carried by students returning home, vacationing, taking internships or jobs. Many of the dead were unusual by opioid demographic standards—educated, affluent, and absent criminal records. They were the types who made the hometown news when they died. They were not like Cass Odom or J. R. Millinock. Or like Kimberly Crepeaux, who'd made headlines when she'd died, but only because of her famous lie.

In most places where devil cat appeared, people either died from it or fled from it. Mathias Burke had collected it. The drill-bit case with the syringes had been recovered from Howard Pelletier's boat, and the remaining four needles provided matches of the carfentanil cocktail that Vizquel had chased around the country.

"They can charge him with Odom's murder if they can prove he got it to her," Vizquel told Barrett. "He's got knowledge and intent. I want to know when he learned about it, and how much there was, and where else it went. But he's a close-mouthed son of a bitch, even when he's facing life in prison."

Barrett asked Vizquel to accelerate toxicology tests on the drug that had killed Kimberly Crepeaux.

"I want her on his charge sheet," he said. "I want them to read her name in the courtroom with the others."

"I'll try, but it doesn't matter—he's already going down."

"I know that," Barrett said, "but it does matter. I want them to say her name."

Vizquel didn't seem to understand that. He left Maine after Mathias refused to answer any of his questions. The death toll from the drug known variously as devil cat, devil's cut, and devil's calling was now at 265 nationwide, and Vizquel had eight fresh cases to look at in Colorado. There was no time for him to slow down. Port Hope was an outlier for him, and probably an annoying one, because it had pulled him off course. The drug had taken lives in Port Hope, and then survivors had seen that more lives were taken, but those cases were only quicksand to Vizquel, who was tasked with the questions of origination and supply networks. The drug hadn't come from Maine or even been intended for it. It had just passed through, that was all.

It had just visited from away.

Four days after his life was saved by a trauma surgeon named Abeo, Mathias Burke was charged with two murders and two attempted murders, kidnapping and drug possession, and a litany of lesser crimes. Mathias entered a plea of not guilty on all counts.

He was held without bond.

George Kelly, who had also declined to speak to police, was charged with obstruction, collusion, failure to report evidence of a crime, and conspiracy to commit murder. After a lengthy bond hearing in which three attorneys presented the reasons that George was not a flight risk or a threat to the community, he was granted bond set at two million dollars.

He paid it that day and left Maine for Virginia, equipped with an ankle tracking bracelet. He instructed his wife, son, and daughter to stay away so they could avoid the media, and he assured them the truth would come out.

On his first day in Virginia, he summoned his assistant to his home office and asked her to notarize three documents for him. He was wearing a suit and tie, and they didn't speak of the charges against him or the crush of media outside. He was cordial and calm and he thanked her for her time and professionalism and gave her a check for her next month's salary and a bonus for what he called *all this unpleasantness*. When she left the house, he took the shotgun with the silver inlay off the wall of his office, removed the skeet-shooting ribbons, and fitted a double-aught shell into the breech. Then he moved away from the desk, put the muzzle in his mouth, and pulled the trigger.

When they found him, there was blood on the walls and ceiling, and most of his brainpan had been emptied onto the floor, but the notarized documents on his desk were clean. There was an updated will, a letter to his family, and an eleven-page confession.

The confession included a revised theory. In the moments before his suicide, apparently for the first time, George Kelly had finally been able to contemplate the possibility that his unknown adversary was in fact his trusted summer caretaker.

Even then, his notes were tinged with disbelief.

There had to be something bigger in play, he insisted. Someone more powerful. Someone more important.

These were the last thoughts he had before he put the muzzle of the shotgun in his mouth.

Police and prosecutors went to see Mathias Burke once more. Once more, he refused to answer all questions.

He held this stance for three weeks. Then, in the first week of July, he contacted the state police and said he was ready to talk, on one condition.

He would speak only to Rob Barrett.

Nobody liked it. The police and prosecutor wanted someone else in the room. Mathias refused. It was Barrett, and Barrett alone.

It was personal, Mathias said.

They met in a visitation room, separated by a wall of glass. Mathias sat down and studied Barrett for a long time without speaking, and Barrett began to wonder if this was the point, if Mathias had grown bored and wanted to taunt and torment in whatever limited fashion he could. Then he finally picked up the phone.

"Do you know," Mathias said, "just how pleased I was when you searched that pond?"

"No," Barrett said. "Why don't you explain it to me?"

"I will. You just listen, okay? Just sit there and listen. You know why I picked you to talk to?"

"I don't."

"Because you think you understand. You always did." He paused, smiled at Barrett through the glass, and added, "And I'd like to watch your face when you hear this."

"Okay," Barrett said. "Enjoy it, then. Tell me how it happened."

58

Kimmy told it right, mostly. Looking back, it's kind of impressive. I hadn't expected her to have that vivid of a memory, really, especially since she thought it was all unfolding right then. That it hadn't been in motion before.

In reality, I wasn't going for Ian. Didn't even think he'd be at the house that summer. I was going for George.

You should know that there are fifteen previous versions of George. I'd been doing the same thing for six years. It was something my dad taught me originally, though he never understood how to capitalize on it. He told me that if you just paid attention to who came and went from the summerhouses, you'd find that lots of people who bought a second place had a reason for it that didn't have shit to do with sitting on a deck by the ocean and eating lobster. You know the kind. An old guy shows up with some bitch who looks like she's just out of college. Next weekend, he comes back up with his wife. Women do the exact same thing, trust me.

All you have to do is pay attention. Those people look

right over a man like me, like my dad. They looked over me, past me, through me. But I was always watching.

Unlike him, I did something with it.

I made forty grand the first year, and that was just with threats. Some people didn't pay, but I'm not sure if they were more scared of me or of Bitcoin and Ether. Some of these guys, they'd rather watch their marriage implode than try to move currency that they don't understand. But digital currency is the best way. Trust me.

I got better cameras the next year, and then I made ninety thousand. That was just off two people. One guy, one woman. Funniest thing about that? It was the same house. The same couple, cheating on each other on different weekends. Then they both paid to save the marriage. I always wonder if they'll end up figuring that out. I'd love to see that moment.

By then I was charging people to set up cameras. Reduced the risk of having them noticed, for one thing, but I also figured if I didn't get anything useful, at least I wasn't wasting money on the cameras. Defray your costs whenever possible, you know? I put seven systems in that summer, and guess how many people changed their original password? One. I didn't even have to hack anything. Not because they trusted me, but because they overlooked me. I was just there to serve at their pleasure, right? Once I'd done my thing, I was out of sight, out of mind, until they needed something else fixed.

I was making more in one summer, Barrett, than

you'll make in the next five years. I checked what your salary would be once. Pretty easy to estimate with federal pay. You don't make shit unless you've got graft on the side.

Tell you something I really enjoyed—living the way I'd always been living, and watching the way people looked at me and treated me, and knowing the whole time that I had more money than they did. I had an idea that eventually I would buy one of those big homes where I worked. George's house, maybe. I like to imagine someone like George coming up at the end of June, once the days are warm and all the dumb little lobster shacks are open, and finding out he has a new neighbor. Who owns the big house on the hill? *he'd say.* Your caretaker does, do you remember his name? Didn't think so.

I really like that image.

Okay, so the year before his son died, George started bringing someone around who wasn't Amy, and I got interested. I didn't have any cameras in back then, so I just shot a little video, made sure to get some close-ups, and then George and I enjoyed a clean, professional transaction. He paid twenty-five thousand.

While that was going on, I sent him an invoice for the end-of-season cleaning and closing up, and I suggested he might consider upgrading his security. He was worried about his stalker by then, you know, so he thought that was a good idea. He could catch the son of a bitch.

I'm telling you, they never saw me. Never. They always imagined someone else in their lives, someone who mattered to them.

I changed to cameras with microphones that year. Cost came down on those, quality went up, and audio is a huge game changer—people don't like to see themselves, but when they can see and hear themselves? Man, they feel awfully vulnerable then.

So the cameras were waiting, but George didn't come back the next year. He went overseas and sent his kid up alone. I was disappointed about that, but then Ian started having those parties, inviting locals to the bonfires on his private beach. I heard from Mark Millinock that he was offering drugs to them. Ecstasy, mostly, but I also heard heroin. Now, I was surprised by that. He didn't look like the heroin type, right?

He didn't use the drugs, and he didn't sell them. What was the point? I think it was about feeling like a different kind of guy, trying on a different identity. He didn't like his dad much. Didn't like his place in the world, really. He was so damned desperate to get people to look at him in a different way. I think the drugs were one way of pushing back on his life, and that always pissed me off. You don't like your life? You kidding me, man? You don't like your rich-bitch life?

It was feeling like a lost summer to me. I'd been counting on George. I thought about trying to capture some video of Ian with the drugs, but it didn't seem valuable enough. Not initially. Then one morning I went there to give them an estimate on a stone fire pit down by that beach, his party spot, and found Molly Quickery's body in the sand.

It was nearly high tide, but the water still only came up to her ankles. She was dead, but she hadn't drowned. I looked around a little—there were beer cans and Solo cups, somebody had left a one-hitter, and there was an empty pony keg in the sand. Seemed like it had been a hell of a party, and I guess when Molly wandered away, nobody missed her, or they just thought she'd passed out.

I sat there and thought about things for a while, and then I walked up to the house. Ian was still asleep. I got him up and told him I had something to show him. He was cooperative. He was one of those types who wants to be really nice to the help. Man of the people.

We went down there, and he saw Molly, and he threw up in the sand. He was shaking. I sat down and put my arm around his shoulders and said, Tell me how this happened.

He told me about the drugs then. He didn't use them, but he'd brought them up from Virginia, curious, I guess, and then Ronnie Lord offered to buy the whole supply from him, and Ian told him to just take it. Just take them. That was Young Master Kelly, nothing if not generous.

But now there was a dead girl in the sand, and that was very bad for Young Master Kelly. He'd crossed state lines with those drugs. He'd distributed them, even if he hadn't sold them. She was on his property. It was all very bad.

I'd been recording everything he said. Then I stopped recording and said, What if she wasn't on the property?

I pointed out at the ocean, and he looked at it like he'd never seen it before.

Maybe she drowned, *I said.* Maybe it didn't have anything to do with you.

Give him credit—he thought about it longer than I'd have expected. Moral compass, right? But they all spin around. With the right pressure, Barrett, you can always make them spin.

The deal we made was that I'd make Molly disappear, and Ian would pay for the help. I knew nobody was going to be looking too hard for Molly Quickery. It was a one-off, right? He'd made a mess; I cleaned it up. What better caretaker than a guy who hides the bodies for you?

At the time, we were both thinking she had just overdosed. We weren't thinking that all of his supply was lethal.

But then...then people kept dying.

I was hearing different stories about the drugs, and I thought about Molly and realized how bad it could get if she was part of something bigger. If anyone traced those drugs back to Ian, I knew he'd break, and then he'd also tell them the story about Molly, and they'd come for me.

I went to see Ronnie Lord. He was scared shitless, because he'd been selling the dope that was killing people, and he knew he could be charged for a lot more than dealing. I told him to hang tight and let me work on this. Then I went back to Ian.

Ian started talking about going to the police right away. I talked him out of that. I got with Ronnie and we tracked down what was left, and what he couldn't buy back, I stole back. There were six, maybe seven, others dead by then. Names you still don't even know. Look around Augusta sometime, if you're interested. And Bangor. Bangor in July was a bad place to shoot up. You'd think people would have noticed by then, right? Not anymore. Not with opioids. The dead people were all addicts. There were no surprises in that bunch, so nobody was paying attention to what they took and where it came from. It was happening all over the country. But it wasn't happening around people like Ian Kelly.

I gathered up all the shit that was still out there and brought it to him to prove that I'd cleaned up his mess. He was scared to touch it. I'm not kidding. He made me pick it up, like it was a snake.

I worried that he'd break right away if anyone ever asked him about it. That he'd confess to the first cop who hit the door. Ian didn't grasp consequences. He figured his dad would make a few calls, and they'd cut him a deal. Five dead people equals fifty hours of road crew or something. Then the more I thought about it, the more I wondered if he wasn't right. And I was really deep into it then, from moving Molly's body, to collecting the drugs, to concealing my knowledge of all these deaths. If Ian broke, then Daddy would make his calls and take his meetings and his son would be doing road crew while I did twenty-five years in Warren.

Now, you know who wouldn't break? George. If he knew Golden Boy was at risk, he would shut the show down before cops were called, not after. So, I e-mailed George from an anonymous account. Videos and some articles about the OD deaths. He paid so damn fast—it was literally the same day, no hesitation, no who are you, how dare you, none of the stuff I usually got. He just paid. And I knew he'd shut Ian down too. I knew there weren't going to be any trips to the police once George saw his exposure.

George wasn't sure who he was paying, but he was working on that. He always thought it was somebody from outside, back in Virginia, maybe overseas. Anyone extorting him had to be a major player, he figured. This was beautiful—guess who he hired to take the cameras down? Yours truly. He told me that someone had hacked his cameras and they needed to come down. I said no problem, sir, and then I took most of them down and sent him a bill. I left a couple up, but those were just for me.

It all seemed pretty well in hand.

Then, at the end of August, I misunderstood some-thing that I saw. You've seen the clip I'm talking about. Ian and Jackie out on the deck. They were talking about going to family and getting out of trouble and I just kind of...I jumped too fast on that. I thought I knew exactly what they were talking about. They walked out of the frame too early. Jackie got cold, and they went inside, and I lost the audio. Nobody ever said pregnant.

I figured if anybody was going to push him to confess, it was Jackie Pelletier. She wasn't anything like George. Neither was Howard. I didn't know how to manage that family. It was going to get too big, too fast.

I had two weeks to think about how to handle it. I realized that I knew where they were going to be and when they'd be there. Out there in the cemetery, all alone.

I saw a different way to manage things then.

I'd never killed anyone before, but I'd thought about it plenty. I always wanted to. I'd figured I would have to at some point. I'd had the idea about the pond for...I don't even know how long. I can tell you this—I had the idea for the pond before I ever saw the pond. It was a matter of picking the right spot. Most areas like that, there are too many people around. But when I saw that place, I thought: This could be just right.

When you kill someone, you have two choices. The first one is to try to hide how you did it, which is what almost everyone does, and almost everyone gets caught. The second one is to show exactly *how you did it—and then prove it couldn't have happened that way.*

I needed to be ready for you to come at me hard. I needed to let police hear a story they believed but could not prove. I needed witnesses for the night. People who would talk eventually, but not immediately. They needed to have certain...credibility issues too. Kimmy was perfect. I didn't need both her and Cass. I needed one to talk, not two, and I needed the least reliable one. That was Kimmy, obviously. Cass was collateral damage.

Now, you've got to have a fall guy, of course, and Girard, he was perfect. He was a stone-cold idiot. I actually wish you'd gotten to talk to Girard. You remember that show where the kid confesses to killing the girl, and he wasn't even part of it? That was Girard. If the two of you had gotten together, you'd have had him doing life without parole and him agreeing the whole time.

The paint...that was more personal. I wanted Ian to see what was coming for him, that he'd brought it on himself. I wanted him to see me coming and just... understand.

In the end, I guess he did. The way he looked at me right before I clipped him? He saw the world differently then.

All night long I put on an act for the girls. I drank a

little, but I didn't actually use any drugs, and I kept up the act of being angry, fired up, out of control. It was supposed to be like a hit-and-run—Oh, shit, we were high and this happened and now you bitches have to help me dump these bodies! *That was going to be good because I'd never done any drugs, my blood was clean, and people wouldn't believe the picture the girls painted of me. Because it was not me.*

I went back to the pond at night. They came out easy. I had them in Girard's truck and gone in twenty minutes flat. Stripped them and shot them because I knew that wasn't the story that would be told. It's a magic trick, make them watch the right hand, then use your left. Whole thing was clockwork. Swiss-watch shit. I knew you'd show up at my door someday, but I also knew the evidence would never back up what you'd been told.

Your guys bought the e-mail tip about the bodies right away. Never really questioned it. You know why you didn't question it? Because of how you see me. Mathias knows leaf blowers, but computers? No chance! That e-mail trick is the simplest thing in the world. Dead man's switch coding. Your tech guys would've given it a look if the suspect was some kid in Boston with a basement full of computers, but Mathias, now, he might be able to winch a body out of a pond, but write a simple piece of computer code? Never.

I know you asked about the dead man's switch, but you don't deserve credit for that. You weren't looking at me any different; you were just desperate. Your ass was showing, and you wanted any way to cover it up. That was all it was. You were trying to send me up for murder and didn't even respect me enough to wonder how I did it.

George was the exact same way, looking everywhere but at me, because the whole deal was clearly too sophisticated for Mathias Burke.

By the time police got involved, George knew someone out there could expose his family for what it was—affairs and drugs, corpses and lies. Not a nice story. It was an interesting test—would he tell you guys about that right away? Later? Never?

Turned out to be never. Turned out he was willing to go pretty far.

I was always going to let Kimmy live. She had to live so she could tell the story, that was the whole point. But then she brought you back into it. I wasn't scared of that, but it was frustrating. It was clear that she thought you were in control, not me. So I sent Ronnie out with something special for her. She always trusted Ronnie. That's how you get to people—who do they trust, who do they love? If you want to own someone, you start there.

Now, you're looking at me and thinking this is a win. It's not. You should understand that by now. You never caught up. But I will not...I cannot tolerate sitting in the courtroom listening to a judge send me up with all of you smug assholes sitting out there thinking you got it right.

You were never close. Do you see how far out in front I was? Do you finally fucking fathom who was rigging the game, and how? Do you understand who was in control? It wasn't you, it wasn't any of your people, it wasn't George Kelly or his baby boy. It was always me. Every step. I made the rules. All of you played by them.

You better remember that, Barrett. From the first day to the last, I decided how it happened.

59

Howard Pelletier asked Barrett to come to the island to share the story. He would hear the second confession in the same place he'd heard the first.

Liz took Barrett out, and Howard's boat was already tied up at the wharf when they arrived.

"You want to go with me?" Barrett asked Liz. "Maybe it'll help him, having somebody else there when he hears it."

Her eyes were tender when she shook her head. "It'll help somebody," she said. "But not Howard."

He nodded and went up the hill alone.

Howard was waiting with a screw gun. When he saw Barrett, he went wordlessly to the studio door. The screw gun howled as he zipped twelve long wood screws out, and the stainless-steel hasps that held the padlocks fell free. Howard swept them aside with his foot, put the screw gun down, and unlocked the door.

"Go on up," he said.

Barrett crossed the threshold and faced the hand-laid, curving stairs. The ascending stairs. His throat felt tight and his mouth was dry as he went up. The building still smelled of sawdust and paint, somehow both fresh and stale, stillborn.

At the crest of the stairs, sunlight filled the room from panoramic windows. You could look out to sea, back toward the mainland, or north or south. You could watch the sun rise and watch it set, and you'd never miss a cloud or a storm or a curious shaft of light. You would see it all from up here.

There were two easels set up, empty, waiting for canvases. There was a daybed beneath one of the windows, positioned so the afternoon sun would fall on it.

Howard sat on the daybed. He took his weathered ball cap off and set it on the floor between his feet and then leaned forward and clasped his hands together. His head was bowed when he spoke for the first time.

"Okay," he said. "Tell me."

Twenty-three months after his daughter had vanished and sixteen months after he should have experienced the birth of his first grandchild, Barrett told Howard Pelletier how they'd been taken from him.

Howard didn't speak while Barrett told it. He made a few soft sounds, little grunts of pain, but he never spoke, and he never looked up.

"That's how he explained it to me," Barrett said, and then he took a breath before he broke the rest of the news. "But he recanted before I made it into the parking lot. Turned right around and told the next cop that it wasn't true. That he'd just wanted to jerk me around."

Howard looked up, his face stricken not by surprise or even pain but a simple and profound confusion. "What is the point of that?"

"To make us wonder. To leave some doubt. He knows he'll be convicted, but he wants us all to know that he is the smartest person in the room. He also hated to tell me. I think that decision was a tough one for him. He could not abide watching us believe we'd reached the truth, but he also hated to remove the questions."

"Well…*was* he lying about any of it?"

"Maybe."

"What? You're not sure?"

"There are holes," Barrett said. "There are some gaps. But memory is an inherently unreliable narrator, even for people with good intentions. Mathias is not a man with good intentions. He might have filled in some of the truth with a lie where it made him look smarter, and he might have forgotten some of the truth. But I believe I heard most of what happened, and how, and why."

Howard seemed unsatisfied. "You *believe* it was true. You don't know."

Barrett took a deep breath. Howard was asking

him the question he'd been asking himself for most of his life: *How can I be certain?*

"I think that's all we're promised here," Barrett said. "We gather as much evidence as we can, and then we choose what to believe. We can't always *know*. At some point, some of it is going to have to ride on faith."

"I think we got it right," Howard said.

"I do too."

Howard ran a hand over his face, shook his head, and then reached down and picked up his baseball cap and tugged it on.

"You stayin' on through trial?"

"I'm staying." That would require a resignation from the Bureau, most likely, but at this point Barrett didn't think he'd find much resistance there. He was neither sure of his next steps nor concerned about them. Until a verdict was issued, he had no thoughts of leaving.

"Good. I've been thinking about moving myself."

"Leaving Maine?" Barrett was shocked, but maybe he shouldn't have been. What was left for Howard in Maine but a lot of painful memories?

"No," Howard said. "Leaving my house. I've been thinking about coming out here. I'm not sure yet. It'd be hard. No question about that. But...she loved it for the right reasons. It's a special spot." Howard spread his hand to the expansive horizons in all directions. "Ain't another place in the world that gives you the same views as an island."

"That's the truth."

Howard got to his feet and then turned slowly, taking in the light-filled room with its freshly painted trim. He spoke with his eyes on one of the empty easels.

"I can't tell you how much I loved my daughter."

Barrett could only nod. He couldn't have spoken right then even if he'd had any idea what words to use.

Howard gazed back across the water toward the mainland. "She liked to be in a cemetery at sunrise. A lot of people thought that was strange. But I liked that she could look at the world a little differently than most. See a better version of it, maybe."

He gave a broken smile. "Wonder how much of her I got left in me." He looked around the studio, from mainland out to the endless sea, and when he said, "I'll try," Barrett knew that he wasn't the intended audience.

Howard took a deep breath that gusted at the end, like the sound of a lit match. Then he said, "We ought to get going. The sun goes down on you fast out here."

Barrett followed him down the stairs, descending out of the light and into the shadowed room below. When they were outside, Howard gathered the locks and hasps and carried them. He wasn't wrong about the sun—it was dropping quickly, the bay falling into shadows while the sky over the low mountains went crimson and tinted the clouds above with rose-colored wisps. It would be night before they reached the mainland, but Howard had navigated these waters at night before.

They walked down the hill together and on toward the darkening sea that lay between them and Port Hope.

ACKNOWLEDGMENTS

Richard Pine shepherded this one along from a conversation into a draft and then into a book. Joshua Kendall's exemplary, insightful, and patient editorial work made all the difference. And my wife, Christine, not only read more pages than anyone and made them all better but somehow dealt with me at the same time.

The always incredible Little, Brown and Company and Hachette team: Reagan Arthur, Michael Pietsch, Sabrina Callahan, Heather Fain, Terry Adams, Craig Young, Nicky Guerreiro, Alyssa Persons, Maggie (Southard) Gladstone, Ashley Marudas, Karen Torres, Karen Landry, Tracy Roe, Nick Sayers, and so many more. It's a pleasure and a privilege to work with so many great people.

Friends and first readers who endured either early drafts or me during the process, or, in some terrible cases, both: Bob Hammel, Pete Yonkman, Tom Bernardo, Laura Lane, Jayd Grossman, Stewart O'Nan, Ben Strawn, and my parents.

ACKNOWLEDGMENTS

Thanks to Ryan Easton and Seth Garrett and David Lambkin for technical expertise.

Lacy Nowling-Whitaker single-handedly allows me to preserve an illusion as a functional member of computer-based society. She only rarely throws chairs at me.

A special thanks to the great state of Maine, which dug deep into its bottomless wells of inspiration during the writing of this novel, providing record cold, record heat, record snows, record power outages, and even raccoons in chimneys. And to the people in Maine who went out of their way to be helpful and welcoming, particularly Bob and Cecile Caya, Brian Wickenden, Rob Dwelley, Adam Thomas, Robyn Tarantino, Israel and Kathryn Skelton, and Melinda Reingold.

ABOUT THE AUTHOR

Michael Koryta is the *New York Times* bestselling author of thirteen novels, most recently *Rise the Dark*. Several of his previous novels—among them *Last Words, Those Who Wish Me Dead,* and *So Cold the River*—were *New York Times* Notable Books and national bestsellers. His work has been translated into more than twenty languages and has won numerous awards. Koryta is a former private investigator and newspaper reporter. He lives in Bloomington, Indiana, and Camden, Maine.